CAMOUFLAGE

by Kyell Gold

Dallas, TX

Camouflage

Production copyright FurPlanet Productions © 2017

Copyright © Kyell Gold 2017

Artwork © Rukis 2017
https://www.furaffinity.net/user/rukis/

Published by FurPlanet Productions
Dallas, Texas
www.FurPlanet.com

ISBN 978-1-61450-400-9

Printed in the United States of America
First Edition Trade Paperback 2017

Typeset in Garamond Pro and Montserrat

Table of Contents

Chapter One   9

Chapter Two   25

Chapter Three   44

Chapter Four   65

Chapter Five   77

Chapter Six   96

Chapter Seven   110

Chapter Eight   132

Chapter Nine   141

Chapter Ten   152

Chapter Eleven   163

Chapter Twelve   175

Chapter Thirteen   194

Chapter Fourteen   205

Chapter Fifteen   213

Chapter Sixteen   221

Chapter Seventeen   234

Chapter Eighteen   245

Chapter Nineteen   253

Chapter Twenty   264

Chapter Twenty-One   269

Chapter Twenty-Two   274

Chapter Twenty-Three   280

Acknowledgments   290

About the Author   291

About the Artist   291

Other Books by Kyell Gold   292

For you who don't believe in yourselves.
You should.

Chapter One

The great bulk of the elk and black wolf crowded the other side of the table where Danilo had been trying to study, the elk's immense hand shaking the newspaper over Danilo's Intro Psychology text. The other students in the Student Center at the Université Catholique, bent silently over their books and computers, offered Danilo no more help than did the portraits of the twelve aspects of Christ on the walls, reproductions of a famous series by some Renaissance master. The one Danilo could see to Cobb's left, if he slid his eyes that way, was not the Lion Christ, which the tiger might have found somewhat comforting. No, beyond the elk's white shirt and tan fur beamed the Stag Christ, and even as Danilo's gaze flicked back to the glossy reproduction of the painting, the beatific smile and the haloed antlers, his line of sight was blocked again as Cobb shifted to command his attention, and the unreality of the scene asserted itself again.

The careful weeks of building his identity, of trying to fit in, they'd all been destroyed by the image on the paper and the words over it. A tiger, very like Danilo save for his orange fur where Danilo's was white, looked out with a smile beneath the headline that screamed "COMPLETELY TRUE" no matter how hard Danilo tried to believe that this was a trick. He wanted this to be a dream, for his cousin the anonymous U.S. football player to be a trick of his subconscious, his brain forcing him to live out the fear that Cobb would discover his secret through the symbolism of having it appear in a newspaper. But the silence, the smell of the newspaper and of Cobb's and Georg's scents, the way his throat closed up and his eyes began to tear, those were all too real no matter how hard he wished them away.

The rustles and murmurs of studying around him had faded to a blank tableau upon which Cobb's words clattered with his harsh

States accent. "That's your cousin, ain't it, Danny? The tough one, the football player. Turns out he's a fag."

Danilo's claws extended, retracted, extended again. He couldn't think of anything that would possibly make sense to say at this point.

"What'cha think, Gyorg?" Cobb pronounced the wolf's name oddly, perhaps so as not to have to say "Gay-org" at this particular moment. "Ya think it runs in the family? Ya think they were butt-buddies up there in Chelling-HAM?"

"He never came to visit us," Danilo said, fixating on the thing he could deny. He had only hazy memories of Devlin, from when his mother had taken them to the States and they'd played in a forest, shouting through piles of golden leaves. Devlin and his older brother...the name slid away now...they'd teased Danilo about his white fur, but Devlin, younger and possibly used to being picked on by his brother, later said he thought Danilo looked neat. Devlin and—Gregory, that was his name—had looked right at home among the leaves, while Danilo'd covered himself in them and still his white fur shone out. So together they'd rubbed dirt and leaves into it until he was as invisible as they were.

"Aw, so you came to my country to do it?" Cobb dropped the paper. "You know what God thinks about faggots, right?" He swept his arm around the room, indicating either the portraits of Jesus or the students, or maybe both. "He hates them. He definitely hates that mouse friend of yours. Maybe he hates you, too."

Now one of the students nearby stood up, a doe. She rattled off something in Gallic that Danilo didn't catch, and when Cobb looked equally confused, Georg said, "She says not to be speaking of hate."

"Hey," Cobb spread his arms out, dropping the paper and pointing to it. "It's all right there. See where the church told this guy to turn his life back to Christ? I'm just trying to save our buddy Danny here."

Danilo took the opportunity to grab his textbook and bag and stand up. He'd intended to make a graceful, quick exit, but the chair didn't quite get out of the way, and he knocked it over with a clatter. Not that Cobb wouldn't have noticed anyway, but now everyone was staring at him and he looked like an idiot.

"Gotta go," he mumbled, and turned away from the table without looking back. There, as he headed for the exit, there was the

Lion Christ. The tawny muzzle and sad, serious eyes looked down on Danilo as he hurried through the tables, past the other students in their white shirts and black robes, and the awareness of his own lilac shirt burned in his ears. Of course this would all happen on the day he wore the shirt Taye had picked out for him. "It's fashionable," the mouse had said. "You're not going to be a priest, you don't need to wear black and white."

It felt bright red as Danilo pushed his way to the door of the student center and out into the cloudy grey day. Sprinkles of rain fell on his head, nicely cool against the hot flush of his ears. He paused to catch his breath and let his racing heart slow, but a moment later, the door opened again behind him. "Hey, Danny," Cobb said. "Where you headed?"

His tongue felt huge in his muzzle. "Class," he said.

"Well, gosh," the big elk said, stepping closer, "it's only half past two. You've got half an hour 'til the three o'clock class, don't you? Maybe he doesn't like us, huh, Georg?"

The black wolf said, "Hah," or something like that and folded his arms. Danilo scanned the street frantically to either side, but on either side of the narrow alley outside the college's city campus rose apartment buildings, ruddy brick facing the ochre plaster of the college, and in mid-afternoon there were not many people walking there. Danilo retreated toward the intersection that led down to the river; along the quay there would be more cars, more people, more witnesses.

"Hey, now." Cobb walked closer. "Didn't mean to scare you back there. I mean, I'm not going to be a priest like Georg here." His lips pulled back, eyes fixed on Danilo with a grin. "You know, just 'cause you're a faggot doesn't mean we can't get along. I seen you staring at me. You want some of this, huh?"

The elk dropped his hand to his crotch and squeezed it there, a gesture Danilo had seen in movies and music videos and never in person. The tiger stepped back again and bumped into a post in the street. "Leave me alone," he tried to say, but it came out as a squeak.

"Or hey," Cobb went on. "If you don't want that, maybe you want to suck Gyorg's Siberian wolf dick, huh? What do you think, Gyorg?"

The black wolf had lost his smirk, but he kept serious green-yellow eyes on Danilo. "He can want but he cannot have," he growled.

"Aw." Cobb turned back to Danilo. "Looks like just me, then. What do you say? Tonight, my room?"

"No." Danilo recovered his balance. He could see down the street now, the brighter open space where the Saône ran, the maroon posts of the pedestrian bridge over it and the reddish-orange faces of the buildings rising on the hill beyond. With an effort, he stumbled backwards and then hurried down the street.

This street was just as deserted as the alley he'd left, and when he glanced behind him, he saw Cobb and Georg sauntering behind him. Georg was talking to Cobb in a low voice that Danilo couldn't make out, but when Cobb saw him look back, the elk raised his antlered head, ignoring the black wolf. "Hey," Cobb said, "Classes are the other direction, Danny."

Danilo ignored them, though his feet sped up. If he could get to the corner, he thought, they would surely leave him alone. It wasn't much, but it was all he could think of, and the end of the street was a close enough goal.

At the quay, he hurried across with the light and then realized his mistake. On the river side of the street, fewer people walked and he was more exposed. He would have run back, but the light was already changing and Cobb and Georg were coming along anyway. So he turned right and walked quickly along the river, staring at the crowds on the other side and looking back for the high crown of antlers coming after him.

At least his hurry didn't seem unusual, with the rain. Most of the residents walked as quickly as he did, tails curled up to keep them off the wet ground, and on the less crowded side it was easier to dodge the umbrellas which bloomed like great flowers all about him.

Cobb and Georg hadn't yet reached the corner, and there, up ahead—there was his salvation. Steps descended from the corner down to the river. After checking over his shoulder one more time, he ducked between a rabbit and a badger and hurried to the staircase—too quickly. His feet skidded on the slick stone, sending him past the first step and nearly tumbling down the entire stair, but he caught himself on the banister and hurried down, heart racing. At the bottom, he ran around behind the stair and looked up, searching again for those antlers against the backdrop of plaster and stone walls, windows reflecting the restless clouds, red-tiled roofs darker and glistening.

Tigue, like many Gallic cities, contained many identities within her borders. The main campus of the Université Catholique lay on the edge of one of the newer parts of the city, a small suburb that had been built up twenty years ago, stretching sleek glass and elegant steel skyward. Old photos of the Université's stately limestone buildings from before the expansion showed their red clay roofs over grey-white arches amidst of modest forests and fields. In the Presqu'Ile campus in the heart of old Tigue, ancient limestone and red clay dominated, broken up by cold grey churches, and through them, modern cars honked along the rain-slick street, though down on the riverbank, the babble of the crowd faded next to the light hiss of rain into the river.

He'd discovered this walk a month before, and marveled that with all the activity above, so few people cared to descend to the peace and quiet of the river. On a sunny day, the walk might be crowded with picnickers and strolling couples. In the misting rain, gulls and pigeons—and the occasional homeless person wrapped in blankets, today a ragged rat asleep under the bridge support—were Danilo's only company.

Minutes passed, and still no antlers appeared above him. Finally, the knot in his chest loosened. His tail unwound, heedless of the damp stone, and he massaged his neck as he breathed in the cool damp of the river. Beside him, the Saône flowed on serenely, and Danilo paced it, trying to clear his thoughts.

His phone buzzed, making him jump. But none of the friends who had his phone number had been in the student common, and if they had, they would have texted him right away. It wasn't even quarter to three yet, so Anita wouldn't be worrying about why he wasn't in his three o'clock class.

Maybe it was Taye messaging him. Danilo growled inwardly. Sometimes the mouse didn't know when to leave him alone, and now was definitely not the time to send him one of those texts he always did. But no, Taye was in classes now; some specialized branch of economics, Danilo thought.

So if it wasn't Taye, and it probably wasn't Anita or Fernand, who was texting him? His roommate Orwin to ask him to pick up more tissues, maybe. Yes, that was most likely. Nothing for him to be worried about. He sighed, reached into his pocket, and pulled out his phone as it vibrated again.

The name on the front of his phone wasn't that of any of his friends. He stared at it, wondering why Lena would be texting him, and then it hit him that of course his sister would have heard the news and would want to talk to him about it. He put the phone back in his pocket. As far as she knew, he was in class and couldn't talk—that's why she'd texted rather than calling. And he didn't want to talk about his cousin right now, because the only question he would have is "why now?" and he was at least aware that that was not really the right question to ask.

He could drop out of college altogether, he supposed. Cobb would certainly not leave him alone now. He could make up some excuse for his parents—the religious aspect of the school had gotten too much for him despite his assurances to them that the psychology program was worth it, the exotic foreign adventure wasn't exactly working out. Perhaps he could plead homesickness, although that would mean returning to Anglia for university, and Danilo hadn't really liked any of the universities at home.

No, that was just self-pitying whining, escape fantasies. He would have to stick it out here in Tigue, keep to his room (if only his room wasn't up near the suburban campus, a fifteen-minute bus ride away), not go to any of the public places anymore. Cobb and Georg would likely forget about him in a few weeks or a month.

Or maybe not. It wasn't as though the commonality of language was going to go away, and there were only a dozen or so English speakers in the intensive class to learn Gallic. Besides, they lived on the same floor. He wouldn't be able to avoid them. Would they force their way into his room? And what about his roommate? Orwin was a nice guy, but he was Catholic too, and who knew how he would react? He'd told Danilo that there was no need to bring up his tough States cousin unless he was hiding something, and Danilo should've listened to him.

Gah, this was going to drive Danilo crazy. All because some cousin he'd only met a couple times decided to make his sexual preference public. Who did that, anyway? There was a question he could ask: why would you do that, declare that you're gay in a big spectacle for everyone to see? Nobody needed to know. Maybe when you were a big football star, you lost sight of the fact that not everyone cares about your private life. Maybe you didn't stop to think about the other people who would be affected by your actions, like your cousin across the ocean who had used you as a shield because he couldn't play footer, and nobody in this country wanted to play cricket.

Not that Danilo particularly wanted to play cricket, but at least he was reasonably good at it. He liked the gentility of it, and the languid pace punctuated by bursts of activity. Here, all the sports played seemed frenetic to him. But he was a tiger, and despite his ten-stone scrawny frame, everyone expected tigers to be big, burly fellows who would bowl you over at rugby or shoulder-check you to get the football by you. And Danilo just wasn't interested in any of those games.

Of course, this whole mess was his own damn fault anyway, like Orwin said. He could've said he wasn't interested. It was because Danilo was a tiger, and perhaps because of his accent or his white fur, which made people think he was aristocratic and not very physical, that he'd felt compelled to tell Cobb that he'd played football with his cousin who was now a professional. And when the elk didn't believe him, he'd brought out the pictures, had shown off the newsletter from his aunt and uncle, had basked in the reflected prowess of his famous (or partly-famous; they had to go look him up on the Internet because Cobb had never heard of him) cousin. It had worked, too. Cobb had ignored him with some deference for the last couple months, saving only a couple barbs about tigers who wouldn't play sport.

And now all that fame had turned bitter, and Danilo was walking along the Saône instead of studying in the Union. He kicked at a stone. If only he'd been a white hare, or an orange tiger, or a tiger who was more interested in sport, or come to a place where language didn't isolate him to a small community of friends and enemies... studied in Cambridge, perhaps, like his mum had wanted him to. Or even gone to the States.

This stretch of the Saône curved around to the left ahead of him; bridge after bridge rose above it, old Mediterranean-style Gallic buildings clustered on either side of the river. This had all seemed like such a wonderful adventure a few months ago. New country, new language, modern town with a history, a place where he could go exploring. And then he'd found that all the Anglophones were housed on the same floors of the same dorm, to make their transition easier. He'd decided to make friends with them first, telling himself he'd make more friends when he'd improved his Gallic.

His phone vibrated again, and this time he hurried under the nearest bridge, an ancient stone structure, and picked it up. He would ask his sister why their cousin was making such a spectacle of himself.

But it wasn't Lena's name on the phone; it was Anita. He was already flipping the phone open as he noticed, and then he hesitated and withdrew his thumb, and it clicked shut, hanging up on her.

He cursed and opened it, found Recent Calls, and dialed Anita. The zorro picked up quickly. "Danilo?"

"Sorry about that," he said.

"You are not in class." Anita lived with the Iberian students, but she was actually a New World zorro, fluent in Iberian, English, and Gallic, and she knew Roman on top of that.

"I had a bad afternoon," he said. "Can you take notes for me?"

"Of course. Are you sick with what Orwin has? I will bring over some *sopa de pollo* after class for you. Have you the right drugs?"

"I'm fine, I'm just—I need to walk around for a bit." He paced under the shelter of the bridge. Across the river, amid long administrative buildings, rose a cathedral that he and Orwin had explored their first week, a grand austere old lady like Nôtre-Dame de Lutèce, but more crowded with neighborhoods and buildings around her. At his feet, an eddy of garbage swirled, suspended in the river's currents. Danilo looked between the cathedral and the detritus as he talked.

"Was it Cobb?"

He started and almost dropped the phone. By the time he managed to force a word through his throat, Anita was already talking again. "Czuxa said he was picking on someone in the Student Center, a white tiger. I did not think there was another one, but if there is, you should meet him."

"No," Danilo said, unable to laugh even though he knew she wanted him to, "no, it was me. It was nothing, just—"

Anita was quiet a moment and then said, "I will tell Taye."

"No!" Bloody hell, why had he ever introduced the two of them?

"I know you won't tell him," she said sharply, "and he will be upset, so he should know."

"Anita—"

"The professor is here," she said coolly. "I will take notes for you."

It was only 2:48 according to his phone, so it was unlikely that Father Lafontaine had arrived. But Anita probably wanted time to tell Taye before class. By the time Danilo had put that together, though, the vixen had hung up.

To forestall Taye calling, which he was sure the mouse would, he called his sister. "I was in a class," he said.

"Oh, Danilo." She was in her gushingly-excited mode. "You remember our cousin Devlin?"

"Of course." It would be easier to let her tell him the news, but then he would have to fake a reaction, and he wasn't up to that. "I saw—"

"He's the first professional athlete to come out. He's a homosexual. Isn't it wonderful?"

"So he's a—so he's gay. What's wonderful about that?"

"Danilo, really! He's famous! All the people in the office are talking about it and asking if I can get an autograph and I told them, I haven't even spoken to him in years, I'm not sure I have his number, but of course our family is *quite* brave and forthright and it doesn't surprise me at *all* that a Miski would be the noble paragon of—"

"It's all very selfish," Danilo interrupted. Into the shocked silence, he went on. "Really, Lena. He holds a press conference just to tell people he wants to sleep with males. What if I were to hold a press conference to tell people I like—I like hazelnut spread. How is that noble?"

"I'm sure I don't know." Her voice grew tart. "Might you be expelled from your sport club for liking hazelnut spread?"

"I just don't understand it. I mean, I don't understand why it's so much of a fuss."

"Don't be stupid, Danilo. I'm going to call Auntie Duscha and wish him congratulations. I'll convey yours as well. I know you're busy with classes. But maybe we can talk to Devlin in a few days."

"Why would I want to talk to him?" His heart sped up slightly. "I don't need to talk to him. He made this announcement without talking to me, he doesn't need to hear from me now. I doubt he even remembers me."

"How you do go on! Of course he remembers you, and I'm certain he'd appreciate a kind word from his relatives."

"Fine. You call them, just leave me out of it."

She said she would, but he knew Lena and knew that within a day she would have sent him his cousin's phone number anyway. And before he could hang up with her, his phone rang again, and this time it was Taye.

Danilo inhaled the mossy scent of the stone of the bridge abutment, felt the cool dampness working its way into his fur. His phone showed the call waiting number, bright in the shadowy darkness. "I have to go, Lena," he said. "I have another call."

"All right. Ta," she said, which was her sign-off when she was annoyed with him.

He closed his phone on both calls. Outside his shelter, the rain pattered down more loudly, a squall coming through. Good, he thought, an excuse to stay here. He leaned back against a lichen-covered stone post and closed his eyes. Under the bridge, in the rain, he was hidden from anyone walking above, and even someone on the river bank itself would have to look twice to see his pale fur in the shadows.

The sense of isolation calmed him, gave him a distanced perspective on his predicament. This wasn't going to kill him. He could survive. He would have to maybe stop seeing so much of Taye. Certainly he wasn't going to encourage the mouse any further. If he didn't do anything, then Cobb and Georg could never find anything out, and this whole business with Devlin would blow over.

His phone buzzed with a text message. Taye, and the first word was "Tiguey," which was the mouse's pet name for him. He'd only known Taye a month and already he had a pet name.

Danilo put the phone back in his pocket, but felt as though the message were pulsing against his hip. He sighed and took it out again, and read the whole thing.

Tiguey, I heard about stupid elk. Hugs. I am sorry but you cannot let him define your life.

What could he say to that? "Yeah, I'm sorry too." And hugs weren't going to make things any better. Anyway, it wasn't like he and Taye were even dating, and they certainly weren't boyfriends. Danilo had met Taye at a gay bar he hadn't even had the courage to walk into—a fox who'd approached him outside had gone to fetch Taye upon learning Danilo was a student at the Université Catholique. They'd gotten along, and Taye hadn't even pressed him about being gay, had just let their relationship grow in its own time. It was still at the 'friend' stage, but definitely 'friends with interest.' Taye had a way of making Danilo feel like he didn't have to worry about the world outside, like he could be brave and do things he'd dreamed of without worrying about what it would mean.

Danilo's crush on Anita, by contrast, was clearly going nowhere. The zorro's exotic beauty and colorful, quirky fashion sense put her in another league from him, and if they hadn't been assigned to be study partners in their Continental history class, Danilo doubted she would even have spoken to him. But she was smart as a whip, and kind to boot, and she reminded him of a fox from his prep school who had deserved far better than the louts she dated.

Taye had felt naturally close to Danilo in a way nobody else had, not in prep school, not at Université. Taye's family, a Romany clan, had lived in three different countries during his childhood; he had seen the toppling of one autocratic regime from his bedroom window and had fled one city, his family pursued as thieves. Danilo's quiet life in Chellingham felt as dull as the Saône's placid blue water compared to the quick, lively mouse's tales, but Taye kept asking him questions about boarding school, about cricket, about Anglic pop music and the wonders of Londinium, and it wasn't just that first night, when they'd talked in a small café until well past midnight. The comfort, the closeness had only grown stronger.

And now, thanks to a cousin he hadn't seen in years and an elk he wished he'd never see again, he was going to have to stop hanging out with Taye. He couldn't just be friends because, to be perfectly honest, Danilo was intensely curious about what would come next if he did decide to act on his urges. Partly, he rationalized, it was the comfortable feeling he had with Taye. Partly it was just that someone was interested in him that way for the first time in three years.

Partly, too, it was that Taye's warm, lively manner made Danilo want to be near him. No; he was happy when he was near Taye, or at least happier, and had spent so much time with him that Orwin had commented just two days ago that he felt like he had a single room. But that world with Taye, that was separate from his real life, and Cobb had just nastily reminded him of that.

Danilo looked down at his phone again and sighed. He texted back: *I'll be fine. Thanks.*

The phone was growing slick with the moisture in the air. He lowered his paw to his pocket, but before he could slide the damp phone into it, it buzzed in his paw.

Taye's name again, and the words "Come over after…"

The tiger sighed, his sense of peace fading. He extended a claw and read the whole message: *Come over after class, we'll talk about it.*

The words shone in the dim twilight under the bridge, with the rain dancing over stone and crackling into water, all around him. He stabbed at the button to reply and typed out: *I don't think I should see you for a while.*

They looked like words someone else had written. He paced forward to the edge of the shelter, back again, forward to where stray drops sprinkled his phone screen. His thumb hesitated over *Send,* and then stabbed down with grim resolve.

His paw slipped. He fumbled, clutched at the phone, but it shot out of his paw as though yanked by a wire. There was a sharp crack as it hit the stones, and that was bad enough, but it kept going, sliding toward the river.

"Oh, no." Danilo's feet felt rooted to the ground. He pulled them forward in slow motion as the phone slid ahead of him across slick grey slate. He leapt as it slowed, lunged with fingers outstretched…

His fingers closed over the phone. A brief flash of triumph warmed him, even as the warm metal and rain slid against his pads and the phone squirted free.

Lying prone on the bank, he watched it hop once, twice, and then vanish over the edge. He didn't even hear the splash as it was swallowed by the water.

His elbow and hip ached where he'd fallen on them, and he'd banged his jaw, too. But the shame and anger overwhelmed all of that. On top of everything else, he'd lost his mobile and he would have to get a new one. He might have enough money. Probably he would have to ask his parents for help.

Balefully, he stared at the river. If only it had been a little farther, or if he hadn't taken one more step. If only the surface of the water were rubber, so that the phone would bounce...

And then he noticed another raft of debris, two sticks and a sodden mass of paper floating just beyond the stone edge he could see. Heart beating, he crawled forward. The floating garbage island revealed itself to him: more paper, a cardboard box lid, three crushed cans. And as his head slid over the side, there, incredibly, rested his phone. Half-submerged, probably ruined, but—but no, it was still glowing.

Danilo stretched a paw out, but the phone was a good foot beyond where he could reach. He stared at it, willing it closer even as the slow swirl of the current carried it away, not closer. There was nothing he could reach to pull it to him, and he worried that it was so delicately balanced that if he disturbed the mass, his phone would sink into the Saône, gone forever as he'd feared just seconds before.

Without taking his eyes from the glow, he rose to his feet. No sticks or branches lay on the bank—curse Tigue's effective public cleanliness. He eyed the murky water again. Well, he was already somewhat damp. Getting a little more wet to get his phone back wouldn't be such a tragedy.

He dropped his book bag and stepped back to jump in, and then his eye caught the cuff of his lilac shirt. He wouldn't want to get that dirty in the water. And there was nobody watching, nobody above or below. Even in a teeming city like Tigue, the rain had driven everyone to shelter. So he stripped off the shirt, tried not to think about how his scrawny frame would look when wet, and then paused again. He took out his wallet and then thought about sprinting thieves, black-furred and hiding in the shadows, waiting for the moment he dove to snatch his valuables and run off. He growled and put his wallet back in his pocket. He could just take off his pants. He wore boxers that were close enough to swim trunks, and besides, he would be in and out of the water in a minute.

Taking one more long look to either side, he slid his pants down and bundled them with his shirt and bag in a pile at the base of the old stone pylon he'd been leaning against. They almost disappeared into the shadows themselves.

Danilo looked down at his white fur, black-striped, and the white boxers with the pink-stitched fox icon on them, now the only bit of color on his body. He brushed it and then glanced back at his clothes, and around the river bank again. A shadow flickered in his peripheral vision, but when he focused on that part of the bridge support, all remained still. He crossed his arms over his chest and walked to the edge, looking down at his phone. He would have to jump in beside it and grab it—no, maybe just diving in headfirst, paw outstretched, because if he dove beside it, the swell would take the phone elsewhere. But then what if he pushed the phone under the water? No, maybe he should lower himself into the water gently and then come up under the phone.

His clothes were still there. The shadow wasn't moving. The rain slackened, and the small island of debris rotated slowly before him. He took a breath and rubbed the fur along his arms, and then crouched down at the edge.

It would be easy, just like the swimming pool back at Chellingham Academy. He pressed his paws to the stone and was distracted for a moment by a worn groove in the large stone under his fingers: a number three. Beside it, three more numbers, so faint he could only see them from this angle and up close, the sheen of water accenting the lines of the numbers: 1503. A year? The stones could be that old, for sure.

He sighed. Stop procrastinating, he told himself. He lowered one foot to the water, lower and lower, waiting for the chill lap at his toes. It didn't come. He stretched his foot down farther and still didn't feel the water.

Maybe the air was chill enough that it was the same temperature. But he ought to have felt the water before now. He tried to turn his head to look while extending his leg to its full length.

The water rippled an inch below his toe. He slid his other foot off the stone, but one of his claws snagged on the edge of the stone. Muscles pulled against unexpected resistance, overcompensated, and Danilo scrabbled at the lichen-slick surface. His claws scored ridges in the grey and green patterns but found no purchase solid enough to stop his body toppling backwards. He twisted, trying to catch sight of his phone as he sucked in a quick, desperate breath. A flash of glowing blue, and then the water hit him, closed over him, and he shut his eyes and fell into cold darkness.

Chapter Two

His arms and legs thrashed, trying to bring himself back to balance, and for a moment he swam disoriented, unsure which way was up. Relax, he reminded himself. You know gravity and buoyancy.

After a moment of calming his limbs, he opened his eyes. The darkness to his right seemed deeper than to his left, so he rotated his body until the dark was down and the light was up, and indeed, when he let his body float, it moved toward the light. His breath was running out. Water rushed past him, pressure on his ears eased, and then he burst up into the air again.

His phone had been—over there? He turned around and around. The water looked different from this angle, the choppy rain churning its brown surface into foam. The little raft of debris was nowhere to be seen.

Brilliant. Just splendid. He'd no doubt sunk it when he fell gracelessly into the water, and the paper and sticks and cardboard and phone were all drifting to the bottom of the Saône. Danilo treaded water and stared through the murky brown. There was no glow of blue, no matter where he looked, and he couldn't see past his waist, much less track a small clump of garbage. The surface of the river hid currents he could not track, and though the phone had most likely gone directly to the bottom, it could have drifted in any direction. The battery had probably shorted out, and there was no way he would find it. He was lost. He was lost, and now he was soaked on top of it all.

The stone bank seemed higher than he remembered, but by bobbing in the water and wedging his fingers into cracks in the stone, he was able to throw a paw over the top. Then he had to pull himself up.

He had assumed that would be the easy part, but even with the water's buoyancy helping, he struggled to pull himself up. His paw slipped, and he stayed plastered to the wall, fur sticking to the stone, breathing hard and fast. This was going to be okay. He was not going to be stuck in the river. He could always float downstream; there were places where the river wall wasn't quite as high. But not being able to pull himself out felt like a justification of everything Cobb and Georg would tease him about: weakling, wimp.

(*homo*)

He growled inwardly, and lunged upward again, fingers clawing at the stone. And then he heard a voice, the first sound he'd heard over the rain (which had stopped, though the air still smelled of it) in a quarter of an hour.

"There's someone in the Saône!"

Footsteps, and then a face appeared over the edge, an otter's whiskered muzzle. He extended a thick paw down, fingers wiggling. "Can you take hold of my paw?"

Danilo nodded and grasped it gratefully, using the otter's strength and his other paw's grip on the stone to pull him up. He sat on the stone, wrapped his arms around himself, and shivered. His fur was not only soaked, it was filthy. Even in the half-light under the rainstorm, he could tell that the water had stained him a light brown.

Water pooled on the stone beneath him, running into the 1503 he remembered. The numbers were clearer now, much clearer. The light must have improved, or the angle.

"However did you manage to fall into the river?"

The otter crouched beside him, smiling. He wore a loose white shirt, fastened with a leather tie around the collar, and both the shirt and his slick brown fur were damp with rain. Just inside the collar of the shirt, he wore a tan scarf of some sort.

"I…jumped in." Danilo paused, not sure how to tell the rest of the story in a way that would not make him sound like an idiot.

"Luc," a high voice said from behind the otter, "we haven't time for this. He's out of the water; send him on his way."

The voice rang familiar in Danilo's ears. He looked up and saw a grey figure in a similar white shirt, with a similar touch of beige beneath the collar, but where the otter wore dirty grey pants with ragged cuffs, this figure's pants were the same color and oddly loose fit as his shirt. They looked like costumes from some medieval recreation society. He stepped forward, out of the deeper shadow, and Danilo gasped.

"Taye? What are you doing here?"

The otter's eyes widened. He jumped backwards and to his feet as the mouse brought up his arms. It was only as Danilo stood that he saw the thin silvery blade the mouse's paw was clasping. He took a step back and then felt the edge of the stone below his heel. "Whoa," he said. "Hold on. Let's not get crazy."

The otter remained guarded. "What is this?"

The mouse's eyes, too, were wide, his ears back. "Sir, how come you to know my name?"

Danilo stared. "Taye, it's me, Danilo. From the Université? You just sent me a message…"

Taye—if it was him—shook his head slowly. "You are mistaken."

"But—your name is Taye."

"Théodore, yes. But I do not know any 'Danilo.' Are you Etruscan?"

"No, I'm Anglic—look, I just talked to you…" Danilo trailed off, for the first time taking in the clothes they were wearing. "Are you doing some kind of costume thing?"

"An Anglic tiger?" Théodore laughed sharply. "I have seen tigers in Etrusca, yes, even in the south of our own country, but none from so far north as Anglia."

"You do not speak with the harshness of an Anglian." The otter's voice was gentler, but still wary.

"With the sound of—" Danilo shook his head. "What do you think we're speaking…now?"

Both otter and mouse stared at him, and he became aware that the words he was speaking were not English words. He understood them as though they were, but his mouth was forming other words and speaking them fluently.

"The water's addled his mind." Théodore waved a pink, hairless paw. Danilo remembered the touch of those fingers on his arm, his side. "We'd best leave him for the garde. Anyway, if he's from Etrusca, and alone, he's probably diseased."

"What the hell is going on?" Danilo demanded.

"He shows no signs of disease," Luc countered. "Look at him. He's frightened, he's cold; that is all. Would you want to be left to the garde?"

"That is a different matter," the mouse snapped. "And yet...he recognized me, somehow. Perhaps he's one of LeSevre's spies."

"He would hardly let your name slip so easily if that were the case. But it might be best to make sure."

"I don't know who LeSevre is." Danilo stepped forward. "I came down here to get away from Cobb. Taye, I just talked to you..." He still had no idea what was going on, how this language was spilling from his lips, and any thread of familiarity had to be seized as though he were still flailing in the water.

Again, otter and mouse turned to him with wide eyes. The mouse lowered his paw, and put his knife away. "Cobb? You mean Argile?" He turned to the otter. "I don't suppose one of LeSevre's would claim to be chased by *him*, personally."

"I'm not!" Danilo gestured down his body. "Just let me get my clothes, and I'll go. I won't bother you any longer."

"Where are your clothes, then?" Luc stepped back.

"They're right..." He walked between otter and mouse, to the stone pylon. It gleamed in the grey light, free of lichen, its edges sharp and fresh. Around its base, clean stone glistened, and nowhere did Danilo see a purple shirt and khaki pants. He rounded on the mouse and otter. "They were here. Did you take them?"

Théodore scoffed. "And put them where?" He showed both his empty paws. "We saw no clothes."

"Then why did you come down here?" The breeze was chilly. Danilo hugged himself, rubbing his arms again, and glared at the two.

They exchanged looks. "I tell you, we should leave him," the otter said.

"I don't think we should leave him." Théodore rubbed his whiskers. "Unless you mean 'in the Saône.'"

A chill breeze rose from the river, or perhaps the chill ran the other way, down Danilo's back. His tail curled around his legs, and the gulf of water behind him yawned like a bottomless pit. "Whatever you're playing," he began, and then stopped and looked, really looked, around him.

The stone pylon, free of lichen. The '1503' carved freshly in the stone on the river bank. The grey-white stone of the bridge that rose above him streaked with dark stains from water and moss but with no painted graffiti. No buildings scratched at the northern horizon, nothing but greenery and trees on the hill where the Université

(*should have been*)

was, and, as he turned slowly, only a row of brown-roofed buildings on the other side of the river surrounded the familiar cathedral where just a moment ago there had been big blocks of apartments and office buildings. And no more bridges lay between him and the curve of the Saône. Down the river, an unsteady-looking pile of wood extended half into the river: an otter community. They weren't allowed to build on the river like that, not in cities; it was unsanitary and blocked other people's access. Back in Chellingham, Danilo had learned about the dismantling of the great otter houses on the Thames, and that had been…well, after the Restoration, he thought. Sometime in the 1700s.

What's more, the air was different; he didn't have Anita's sense of smell, but there was a raw earthiness, damp from the rain, that permeated everything. No smell of automobile exhaust, no sewage—well, no processed sewage. He could smell some waste, but it was the smell of a backed-up toilet or a stable, not of a septic tank. A smoky tang hung in the air, too, like the trace of a fire that had been quenched by the rain.

The sensation he'd had in the river, of being trapped and never able to escape, returned with such force that he staggered back, his heel landing on the edge of the stone. "What's going on?" he whimpered. "Where am I?"

"Stay calm." Luc looked alarmed, and reached out to grasp Danilo's arm. "You're in Tigue."

"No," Danilo said. "This isn't Tigue—it's not the Tigue I know—it's—"

Pressure in his chest squeezed his heart like a vise. He sucked in a breath against it, and exhaled it in a loud sob. His legs buckled, but the otter caught him before he could fall. Don't cry, don't cry, he told himself, clamping his mouth shut and sealing his throat against the sobs that wanted to come out.

"City has changed." Luc sounded more patient now. "Maybe that's it, Théodore. He must have been here years ago. Maybe he knew you then."

The mouse hadn't sheathed his knife, but he didn't bring it back up either. "I'm not the same as I was years ago." He looked up and down the bank, away from Danilo.

Luc ignored that comment, and Danilo hung on his words. "If it's been ten years since you were here, well. This stonework all went in about five years ago, and the market's burned down and been rebuilt, too. I wouldn't recognize it."

"Five years ago?" Danilo looked down at the carved numbers in the stone. "What...what year is it?"

"'Tis the year of our lord fifteen hundred and eight," the otter responded promptly.

"Fifteen...oh eight?" Danilo shook his head. "Oh, then I'm dreaming. That's what's happening."

Luc's grasp on his arm loosened. "He is delirious."

Théodore still didn't look at Danilo, but now looked mostly to his left. "It's no use staying here now. We can meet again tomorrow."

"Aye, but what of..." The otter turned to Danilo again. "Danilo, was it?"

Danilo nodded. For a dream, his fur was very cold and his boxers very wet, and he was aware of a fetid smell that was coming from him—or, more accurately, from the water soaking him.

Théodore waved a paw. "What do I care? I—" He stopped, and then sheathed the knife with a curse. "Run!"

Luc released Danilo and hurried after the mouse without a question. Danilo stared stupidly after them, then looked at what they were running from.

Two pairs of feet—no, three now—descended the far staircase. They had grey pants, but before Danilo could see more, a paw grabbed his arm and yanked him away. He looked down at Luc's whiskered muzzle. "Come on," the otter said. "It's no good if you're caught here."

"But we weren't doing anything," Danilo protested, running along anyway.

Behind them, a cry echoed, "Stop!"

"Doesn't matter," Luc said. "It's a suspicious place to be. We can lose them up top."

Théodore had already almost reached the top of the dirt path in the embankment—no stairs here, just mud and scraggly grass. Luc sprinted up ahead of Danilo, and the tiger, leaping after him, slipped and fell flat on his face in the mud.

"Danilo!" Luc hissed, looking down from the top.

"You there!" came a voice behind him. Danilo turned despite himself and saw a fox, a ram, and a grey wolf just reaching the bridge.

What would they do if they caught him? Who even were they? The only two people he knew in this place—in this time—wherever he was—were up atop the bank, and if he didn't make it up there, they would be gone. He struggled to his feet and ran up the slope as best he could.

"Hoy! You!" The shouts came from much closer as he stretched out his arm and Luc grabbed his paw, pulling him up with surprising strength.

"Hurry," the otter said. Danilo followed him across the street, where there were no cars, no asphalt, only small clusters of people in earth-drab tunics and pants, and uneven stones that jabbed at the pads on his feet. Théodore had paused at the entrance to a narrow alley between two stone walls stained with rain. The alley smelled like a toilet, enough that Danilo almost gagged when he got between the walls, but the other two kept running ahead of him and so he followed. It was only when they turned onto a wide street that he realized that the streets were barren of lights, looking strangely naked without street signs, and that none of the shops or buildings bore any markings at all save for some carving in the stone and the occasional hand-lettered wooden sign. Shirts and pants, along other other, less recognizable pieces of cloth, hung from a few windows, dripping onto the stone below.

Théodore led them into the small alcove of a nondescript building, but did not open the thick dark wooden door there. "Right gents," he said, "here's where we part ways."

"Danilo," Luc said, "you have somewhere to go?"

Théodore rolled his eyes, but waited for Danilo's answer. The tiger swallowed and shook his head. "All right." The otter took his paw. "You will come with me."

"You cannot do that," Théodore said.

"Then where?" Luc turned on him. "He will stay with you?"

Théodore bit his lip, and his paw trailed to his belt, where the little knife hung in a sheath. "So. If you are determined, I will go with you."

"You've no need to. The garde is still out there, and if we are seen together…. Go, be sure of your own safety."

Théodore brushed aside Luc's words like gnats. "Quiet already. I'm coming along or else Bertrand will flay you. And then you will both be scraping at my door and what then? Return to Belle Soleil a week early? I have other business in Tigue. No, I will take care of this matter for you."

Danilo let the names and words wash over him without even trying to understand them, still getting used to Taye's voice coming from this familiar-and-yet-not snout. Then the mouse turned to him. "Hey, you. Tiger."

He jumped. "Yes?"

Théodore held up one skinny finger, the claw yellowed. "One night you stay with Luc, and tomorrow you find your own accommodation, yes? And you say nothing about me to anyone."

"You plan to walk with us into the Repos," Luc said quietly.

The mouse again waved Luc's objections aside. "I care nothing for Bertrand. He is a sniveler and a coward. But should LeSevre capture this one, as I think likely—just look at him!—I do not wish my name to be spoken." He turned his bright brown eyes on Danilo again. "You understand?"

"I don't know who LeSevre is." Danilo was trying to keep his voice even, but it kept sliding up into whiny frequencies.

Luc put a paw on his arm. "God willing, you will never need to find out."

"The guards chasing us, yes?" Théodore flicked his paw impatiently. "He is the wolf. They are his soldiers."

"So they are part of an army?" Danilo frowned; had there been an occupying force in Tigue in the early 1500s? Was this an alternate history? Maybe nothing he knew, or thought he knew, or could dredge up from his lessons, would even be useful here. "Are you…" He lowered his voice to a whisper. "Are you part of the rebellion?"

At that, Luc cracked a smile, while Théodore rolled his eyes and walked on down the street. "Of a sort," Luc said softly, "but hush. The less you know, the less you tell."

"I'm sorry." Danilo walked alongside the otter, several paces behind the mouse. "I'm just trying to understand…" What could he say next? Understand the world of fifteen-oh-eight? What did time travelers say in science fiction movies? Problem was, he'd never been all that into science fiction, so he'd only seen a few here and there, and in every case, the travelers had been better prepared for their journey, not arriving in the past (or future) nearly naked.

Fortunately, although most of the other people they passed wore tunics, Danilo's bare chest did not seem to draw much attention, though his water-soaked boxers did catch a couple female eyes. Perhaps more; preoccupied in the internal argument between "time travel" and "hallucination," the tiger only noticed he'd drawn attention when a female rat paused and then averted not only her eyes, but her whole head, so violently that she nearly smacked a wolf's arm with her cloth-wrapped bundle, which proceeded to squall loudly. Or when a female fox touched his arm and murmured, "I like what you've got on display," and then Luc pulled him forward before he could respond.

The strange thing was that despite the plain cloth tunics on the mostly Gallic species of people around him, despite the simple wood and limestone buildings, despite the hazy, musky air that every so often brought him the aromas of rotting food or an open sewer, every so often Danilo would round a corner expecting to see a Nike t-shirt, a metal-grated storefront, a neon sign, a car. When the next street proved the same as the last, his hope was merely postponed, not crushed.

And then Théodore led them to a noisy building on the corner of two broad streets, where the smell of smoke thickened and a wooden sign with a haloed otter swung in the light breeze. He held aside a stout wooden door for Luc and Danilo and let it swing shut, admitting them to a warm, smoky room. In the far corner burned a merry fire, and all around the room, badgers and wolves, foxes and rabbits, all dressed in loose ivory-white tunics and various colors of pants, sat and talked over tankards and plates. Danilo curled his tail up between his legs and dropped his paws to hide his crotch.

Luc led him onto the floor, but stopped when a stout badger wearing a filthy apron stormed up to them shaking a paw. "No no no," he said. "No more halfies in here. I've no more rooms."

"He will stay in my room," Luc said.

The badger put his paws on his hips and thrust his muzzle forward. "Never! I have a respectable establishment, and the church has already been here three times in the last month."

"It's just for a night," Théodore said with some irritation. "And if the Church has been here, it is because you offer the garde free wine so that they will not look too closely at its provenance."

"My *restaurant* has always been a model of respectability," the badger thundered, "except when my soft heart allows rabble like you into it."

"Your heart is as soft as a piece of coal." Théodore sneered. "They say, 'at Bertrand's, the plates are always full unless they are copper.'"

Danilo didn't understand that, but it infuriated the badger. "I'll tell you one more plate that will remain empty," he cried, and the paw that had been hidden from Danilo came into view, brandishing a butcher knife that gleamed in the firelight.

Strangely, only a few of the patrons were even paying attention to the confrontation. Most of the room remained cheerfully immersed in conversation, either oblivious or uncaring, even when Théodore brought the dagger out of his belt and said, "I've seen you butcher meat, grey-coat. I'm hardly in awe of you." His sarcastic wit reminded Danilo of Taye, only his Taye rarely made remarks without a gleam of humor, and certainly never with a blade half as long as his forearm that had a discoloration along its tip.

"You would draw a knife on me in my own house?" The badger shook his own knife.

"If you draw one on me, certainly."

Danilo mewed, having no idea if a fight were actually going to break out, if Théodore was going to be slashed or hurt someone else on his behalf. "I can go," he said quietly.

Luc was the only one who heard him. The otter patted his arm. "No, no, you'll stay," he said, and took a step forward.

"Bertrand," he said. "If you are so devoted to charity, then simply look on this poor soul. We fished him from the river, and he has no friends, no relations in Tigue to care for him. He's soaked to the bone and needs warmth inside and out."

"I—" Danilo began, but Luc waved him quiet.

"It will be for one night only. Then Théodore will take him to Bas-Colline and show him the road north."

Both Danilo and Théodore started at that, but Luc's eyes remained calmly on Bertrand. The badger didn't lower his knife. "Can he work in the kitchen?"

"Well—" Again, Danilo was cut off by the otter's paw.

"Of course," Luc said pleasantly.

The knife point dipped. The badger's expression had become greedy, calculating. "And you?"

"No," Théodore said sharply.

"It's all right," Luc said. "Yes, if you require it."

"Hmph." The knife flashed, then vanished. "He stays in your room."

"Of course."

"And starts work immediately you find him some clothes."

Luc smiled. "Surely we can feed him first?"

Bertrand made a rasping snort of disgust. "He can eat from the kitchen as he works. He's bound to do it anyway. I need him now. My kitchen boy hasn't come in."

"Church took him, did they?" That was Théodore, his voice sharp as the dagger he still held out.

The badger pointed at him. "You, out. Unless you want to pay your way like the others."

Théodore gave him a long look and then sheathed his dagger. "I'd pierce your heart with this, only I've no confidence even my paw could find a target so small." He turned to Luc. "Tomorrow, then?"

The otter nodded, with a smile. "Aye."

They held each other's eyes for a long moment, and then the mouse swept out of the room without another word.

Danilo reached out and grabbed the rough cotton of Luc's shirt. "Don't leave me," he said, with just enough self-control to keep his voice low. Most of the people who had paid any attention to the fight had turned back to their meals or conversations. Only a slender weasel continued to watch him, eyes glittering with reflected firelight.

Everyone here had knives and nobody had phones and Danilo didn't know anyone, even the people he thought he knew. Taye was Théodore and Cobb was someone here also, somehow, someone Taye—Théodore—didn't like either. And the year was 1508. It was four hundred and eighty-two years before Danilo had been born.

He followed Luc through the room and to a door at the back. The smell of piss and shit grew stronger as they walked through the door into a short hallway, and just as Luc took him to the left, up a stair, someone came in at the end of the hallway, and Danilo glimpsed a small wooden building outside. An outhouse, he told himself as he marched up the stairs, thick wooden boards that felt solid as stone under his paws. That was an outhouse.

"You can stay in my room tonight," Luc said, coming out into a long hallway with doors on the right and windows looking out over the outhouse and neighboring buildings on the left. "It's around the corner, third one on that side. Not too big, but cozy enough for two."

"You live here?" Danilo said. Some of the doors were open, but only shadows were visible within, so he kept his head turned to the right to look out the windows, where red clay roofs spread in a jagged checkerboard to the river and along the other side. From here he could see the Rhône as well, flowing down to meet the Saône at the heart of the city, both rivers looking freer than in his time, less encumbered with bridges and buildings.

"For now." They walked past four doors to the corner of the building. Luc caught Danilo's eye as he turned the corner, and flashed a whiskered smile. "Bernard lets me stay here until I can rebuild my father's shop."

"What happened to the shop?"

Luc glanced out the windows, which now looked out onto the immense bulk of the cathedral, upstream and across the river. "Here we are," he said, pushing open the third door. "Please, come inside."

Danilo took a moment to stare at the cathedral. In 2008, it had been impressive, but as a monument. Buildings surrounded it on all sides and a wide plaza had spread out in front of it, reminding Danilo of his great-grandfather, who had once been a captain in the Siberian army and who, before he died, had shrunk in stature and presence.

Here the cathedral rose in its prime. One square tower stood behind its twin, and to their right, the arched roof extended on and on, five times longer than the largest other building Danilo could see, all of it shining bright and new. No, wait; that part on the end was something older, where the stone did not gleam as brightly. But the cathedral itself still towered over the town, even across the river, and Danilo's paws trembled against the window. As far as he could tell, it looked the same as it had been in his time (*in the real world?*); he wondered whether that weird clock was there and if the other features he remembered would be the same.

"Do you know Saint-Jean le Baptiste?" Luc asked behind him.

Danilo swallowed. "It's…familiar."

"For those who have known Tigue," Luc said quietly, "it has always been there. My father helped lay the marble in the nave; my grandfather lay some of the stones in that tower—the far one, not the near one."

Danilo's eyes slid up to the hill overlooking the city for the first time since this adventure had started. He was used to seeing the gleaming white spires of the Basilica there, as it was often pictured with the cathedral from this angle, but the hill was bare save only for some grey stone shapes—the old Roman forum. For a moment, he felt a flash of excitement at being able to see the Roman ruins for himself—in his time only two amphitheaters remained, the rest cleared away to make way for the basilica—but then the magnitude of the five hundred years between now and then crashed back upon him. He returned his attention to the cathedral, and nodded. "It's magnificent," he said, and held his paws one in the other, trying to stop their shaking.

"It is indeed." Luc smiled. "Best not to stare at it too long." He took the tiger's arm and pulled him gently into the dark room.

He left the door open, allowing light to filter into the room, and after a moment, Danilo's eyes adjusted.

If he spread his arms from side to side, he would be able to nearly touch both walls. Luc, though shorter, also looked crowded into the small space. The straw cot that began near the door ended at the back wall, not quite long enough for Danilo to lie down in. There was little else in the room but for a large clay pot in the back, which looked like something a small ficus tree might have been planted in at one time.

"Excuse me," Luc said, stepping toward Danilo. He gestured toward the tiger's midsection. "I need to get in there."

The tiger stared down at his boxers, plastered tightly around his sheath and balls. He cleared his throat. "Ah, if I owe you for…um…"

"We can talk of debt later," the otter said. "But I think it would be best for you to remove those wet clothes, don't you agree?"

Danilo's heart pounded. This was a porn dream, that's what he'd gotten himself into. Caught in the rain, seeking shelter from a handsome guy (Luc was pretty good-looking apart from the ratty clothing), the stripping off of wet clothes and *wouldn't you like to get out of those wet things and into a warm otter?* He backed against the wall and gave a nervous giggle. "Ah ha, well, er…"

"They must be uncomfortable." The otter moved closer.

"They'll dry!" Danilo slid farther into the room, away from the door.

Luc reached up to scratch his whiskers. "I suppose," he said. "But still, would you not rather have a tunic to wear over them?"

And then Danilo saw what the otter was moving toward: a rectangular chest in the corner of the room behind the door, which he'd been blocking. "You—you mean to give me clothes." The flush of danger was replaced by one of shame at what he'd suspected the otter of.

Luc opened the chest and dug through it. "Of course. I fear everything I have will be short on you, but try this one."

He brought out a pile of the same raw cotton-colored cloth, picked one tunic from the pile, and held it out to Danilo. The tiger reached for it. "Thank you," he said.

"You'll need pants as well." Another bundle of cloth, another shy thanks from Danilo. "And I'm going to change my tunic."

The otter lowered the chest lid and swung the door partly closed, enough to block their view of the corridor outside while still letting some light into the windowless room. Without preamble, he pulled his wet tunic over his head and draped it over the chest. His torso, thick and powerful in the shadow, held Danilo's attention as the otter lifted the sopping beige scarf from around his neck. He let it drape over his paw for a moment and met Danilo's eyes, then turned away from the tiger and lay the cloth over the wet tunic.

Danilo kept watching as Luc pulled the dry tunic over his head, turned it to settle the collar in front, and smoothed his paws down the fabric with a smile. "That's better." He raised his eyebrows, seeing Danilo still holding the tunic and pants in his paws. "Are the clothes not to your liking? I suppose you may be used to finer things, coming from Etrusca. Especially if you're Firenzan or Venetian. We have had their merchants come through on occasion, and, well." He smoothed back his whiskers with a wider smile. "I confess, I purchased a shirt from them. I can show it to you if you like."

He moved toward the chest. The tiger shook his head. "Maybe later. Why aren't you wearing it?"

"Ah, it is for happier times, and shall be saved for them." The otter looked up and down Danilo's frame again. "I am sorry I have nothing finer to offer."

"No, no." Danilo sorted the tunic from the pants, and yanked it over his head. He'd been hoping for a towel, but was only just realizing that everything the otter owned was in this room right now. He wasn't in a guest house where towels and sheets (the sheets on the straw pallet looked rougher even than the tunic) were magically brought out of hidden closets, or even staying at a friend's house where they were happily provided. This was fifteen oh-eight, he reminded himself. Did they even have towels? Did they have baths?

Of course they had baths. The Romans had baths, and that had been over a thousand years ago. Surely bath…technology…wouldn't be lost so easily. He pulled the tunic down and tried to smooth it out, and Luc laughed, coming toward him.

"Oh, tiger…"

He looked down at himself. "What?"

"You've put it on backwards." Strong paws lifted the cloth of the tunic. Danilo lifted his arms, feeling about six years old. "Kneel down, I am too short to get it over your head."

He knelt obediently and let Luc lift the shirt off his head and then settle it down. "There, see? The fastener sits in front. You can pull the collar shut if you like, although you have a nice chest ruff. I would leave it open." The otter glanced down and then turned his back. "If you desire privacy…"

Danilo hesitated. His boxers were still soaked, but the pink-stitched fox and elastic waistband were the only assurance that he had really once lived in another time. Besides, he didn't know what Luc would make of them, given a chance to inspect them more closely. If this were just a dream, it wouldn't matter, but it felt real enough to Danilo that he did not want to take the chance. So he pulled the pants on over them, as uncomfortable as that was. You should be grateful to have clothes, he told himself sternly. "Thanks," he said.

Luc stepped back and opened the door to let more light in. "You look quite presentable now."

Danilo looked down at himself, at the pale white shirt that, as Luc had warned, ended at his waist, where the otter's tunic hung to mid-thigh. Below that, dark brown pants covered the tiger's legs to his knees, below which his dirty fur and black stripes were visible again. His feet were filthy, but not as bad as he'd feared, and though he could feel grit on the pads beneath, he wasn't sure if that was on his pads or the wooden floor. All the floors here were probably dirty. He tugged the tunic down farther. "I look like I'm wearing hand-me-downs," he said.

The otter frowned. "There are worse things than wearing church clothes."

Danilo began to object. "Church clothes? No, hand-me-downs are…" He stopped, confused. The two terms were different in his mind, but sounded the same when he spoke them. Luc still looked confused, and Danilo realized that he was wearing someone else's clothes and was complaining about how he looked. What must Luc think of him? Vain white tiger, consumed with appearances… "Thank you for the clothes," he said. "I very much appreciate it and I will pay you back."

Luc laughed. "You can begin by telling me your story. I admit that I have been consumed by curiosity, but courtesy forbad me questioning a bedraggled, barely-clothed tiger."

"Thank you," Danilo murmured again. His claws extended and retracted, tension spinning slowly in his stomach. He had no idea how he was going to answer all the questions Luc might ask him. To someone in 2008, he could say "I come from the future" and at least the person would have a context in which to understand that. But here, Luc had never seen "Back to the Future" or "Star Trek" and time travel was the domain of sorcery rather than science. And there would be fewer things more dangerous in 1508 than being regarded as a sorcerer, especially with the grand bulk of the cathedral looming over as a reminder of the power of the Church. If his history classes had taught him little else, he at least remembered that.

"How did you come to fall into the Saône?"

That was an easy one. Danilo exhaled. "I jumped in."

"Into the river?" Luc's brow creased. "Oh, Danilo, what could have driven you to that?"

"I—oh, no, I wasn't trying to kill myself. I…"

He trailed off. At those words, the otter's eyes had widened, and he brought a paw to his muzzle. "Do not speak so casually of ending your life," he said, his voice sharp and low. "Such thoughts are unworthy, even if…even if you think there may be no other alternative."

His expression relaxed as he spoke, and though his eyes didn't leave Danilo's, the tiger had the impression that Luc was looking past him, or through him, or at some memory. "No, no," he said hurriedly. "I said I wasn't. I jumped in because I lost my, uh." There wasn't even a word for "phone," he realized, because even though he'd stopped himself from trying to say it, his brain refused to process the image he could see in his mind into a word he could speak. Disoriented, he stammered, "Uh. Something valuable."

"What could be so valuable to risk your life?"

"The river isn't that dangerous. And there are always people…" In his day, there would always be people around, although there hadn't been any at the time. But even as he'd made sure nobody was watching him strip to his boxers, he'd felt in the back of his mind the assurance that if he needed help, it would be nearby. Nobody would drown in a river in the middle of a city of a couple million people.

Here—now—though, there were not a couple million. There were perhaps a couple hundred thousand, and who knew how many of them could swim, or would be inclined to risk their lives to save a stranger?

Luc's mind ran along similar paths. "You have greater faith in God and people than I would be inclined to," he said with a smile. "But what was so valuable? An heirloom?" When Danilo didn't answer, Luc tapped the side of his muzzle. "Your purse. Well, if it contained gold, it is likely lost in the mud."

"Yes," Danilo said quickly. "It was given me by…by my father. He was sending me to Tigue for…"

Desperate for an idea, he looked away from Luc, out the door and window. What did people send children away for in the fifteen hundreds? His medieval studies classes had focused on lords and countries and power structures, on the sweeping political and religious events that had shaped the countries from the nomadic tribes through the Roman Empire to the Renaissance and the present-day. He could tell Luc volumes about the principles that had founded the Holy Roman Empire some twelve hundred—er, seven hundred—years ago, and could tell him why Tigue and its surrounding kingdom no longer belonged to that Empire; he could not predict much more of the future, because the class had covered Tigue's history from A.D. 500 through about, well, now, and was about to move on to events in the surrounding countries. At the time, he had thought that his class would fit well with his psychology degree, because the study of history was, after all, the study of human behavior. But his classes had taught him nothing about the everyday life of the people who lived under those grand empires and kings and popes, the people whose lives passed from birth to death in shadow, who vanished from the world and left little trace behind.

Fortunately, the talkative otter interpreted his look for him. "To become reacquainted with the principles of the church?"

"Yes," Danilo said quickly, relieved.

Luc smiled wryly. "You're not the only one here, I may assure you of that. May I ask your age?"

"I'm nineteen."

"Nineteen!" The otter examined him. "Strewth. Have you had a marriage fail, then?"

"What? No, I was just…my father wanted me to get an education…" He trailed off again. There were universities in the Middle Ages, or Renaissance, weren't there? He was almost sure there were.

"A scholar by nature, unmarried, coming to Tigue to be reacquainted with the church." Luc relaxed, examined Danilo again, and chuckled. "You fell in with the right company, I'll say."

"See?" Danilo tried to relax and joke as well. "God looked after me."

It was, for some reason, the wrong thing to say. Luc's smile faltered, though it didn't die, and the otter nodded. "May He continue to do so."

Danilo curled his tail around his ankles. The light from the window seemed to be growing richer and brighter. He lowered his head and saw the glow of the sun, about to dip below the rainclouds. The cathedral had receded into ominous shadow, backlit by the coppery afternoon sky. "So I'm to work in the kitchen here?"

"For tonight." Luc followed his gaze again. "Tomorrow I can take you to the Church of Saint-Nizier in the morning, before my appointments."

"Not the Cathedral? The…Saint-Jean le Baptiste?"

Luc shook his head. "I have a friend at Saint-Nizier who may be able to help."

"I don't want to trouble you any further," Danilo said out of reflex, and then was seized with a moment of panic: what if Luc agreed? What if he were left to his own devices? He couldn't even hold a conversation without inadvertently saying the wrong thing. At least, he thought, he was limited to saying stupid things in a common language. He couldn't say "phone" or "airplane" or "Internet."

Fortunately, even as he started to panic again, Luc smiled and reached up to scratch behind an ear. "Théodore would say I have too soft a heart. No, you may stay here tonight, and tomorrow we will go to St. Nizier, and you may see about more appropriate lodgings. I do not know whether the church will provide a way for students to earn wages. My understanding is that the church expects payment for the privilege of an education. And your payment now lies at the bottom of the Saône."

Danilo stared down at the floor, caught between the small triumph of his cover story working (with a sizable amount of help from Luc to explain it) and the much larger fear of how the hell he was going to survive in this world.

Chapter Three

The first half hour in the kitchen was the worst. He entered a haze of acrid wood smoke through which he glimpsed a large black bear in a filthy apron, a cast iron stove, a wide uneven sideboard, and sacks of food just sitting about on the floor, the table, anywhere. He stumbled as his eyes teared up from the smoke and his hip smacked painfully into the sideboard.

"Get fowl from stove," the bear said with no preamble, no offer of an apron, nothing. Danilo swallowed and looked into the stove, where three pans cooked, each containing a crackling-skinned fowl. There were no potholders, and when he asked the cook if he had to handle the metal pans with his bare paws, the large black bear pointed at a long wooden stick leaning against the wall.

He tried to pull the pans by the corners and then balance them on the stick, but they threatened to fall, and in a rush, Danilo grabbed at the pan to steady it. His paw seared and he yelped, dropping the stick and pan with a clatter that spilt the fowl to the ground.

"Sorry," he said as the bear turned and picked up the stick. "Sorry."

"I will handle fowl. You peel roots," the bear rumbled. Danilo watched him insert the stick into the roasted fowl to lift it onto the counter, bits of dirt still clinging to the skin. "There," the cook grunted, and put the end of the stick back onto the filthy kitchen floor as he prepared to carve the fowl.

Danilo swallowed his disgust and addressed the mound of potatoes. This was another chore that was hardest the first four or five times, because he didn't have a rubber-grip vegetable peeler; he had a kitchen knife that was dull enough to require a good amount of force to go through a potato skin, but slid easily through tiger skin. Danilo stopped to suck his finger without realizing what he was doing until he tasted dirt and blood mingled on his tongue, and then

he withdrew his finger hastily. Probably the cook would not mind if he spat on the floor, but he couldn't quite bring himself to do that, so he collected the dirt and blood taste in a mouthful of saliva and wiped it off on the back of his forearm. He definitely would have to ask Luc about a bath, after this.

The otter did stick his head in the back door to see how Danilo was doing, but the bear growled and shook an immense paw at him, and Danilo only had time to make a quick thumbs-up. Luc's brow creased, as Danilo cursed himself for the anachronistic gesture, but then Luc smiled and gave him a thumbs-up back, and it was all right.

Even the stubbornly thick-skinned potatoes and carrots fell into line when he got the hang of scraping the knife across the peels. The cook came over, glared at his pile of peelings, and held up a thick one. "Peel skin, not potato," he said, and tossed the dirty peel into his mouth, crunching it.

Considering he'd only learned how to do this an hour ago, Danilo thought he was doing rather well. But he swallowed his response and just said, "Yes, sir." Then he tried to keep the peels thinner and that took more time, so that he ran out of potatoes when the cook wanted more and the bear yelled at him, and so in a panic he peeled as fast as he could, hacking off chunks of potato along with the skin.

When finally the potatoes and carrots were all done, the cook set him to watching the boiled vegetables. He'd boiled potatoes at home, so he felt somewhat comfortable, though he didn't know at first what to do when they were done; there was no gas to turn down, no colander to drain the pot into, and the pot was as large as his chest, so he couldn't have lifted it even if there had been a sink to pour the water out into. The cook had filled the pot from a pump out back, behind the kitchen, not too far from the outhouse. But then he spotted a wooden spoon with holes in it sitting beside the stove, and that proved adequate to remove the potatoes without burning his paws further.

He grew hungrier as the hours ticked by, and as he lifted potatoes gingerly out of the boiling water, the temptation to take a bite out of one grew. "Do I get dinner?" he asked the cook timidly as the hundredth bowl of potatoes and fowl disappeared out the doors into the restaurant.

"After," the bear said, lifting his head from the fowls he was chopping to pieces. Very deliberately, he lifted a drumstick and put the whole thing into his mouth, sucked the meat from it, and dropped the bone to the floor. "This is for the customers." He tore a piece off the end of one of the many baguettes that sat in a wooden crate and ate that as well.

Danilo licked his lips and swallowed. Just for tonight, he told himself. Tomorrow he would go and find a better job, and he wouldn't have to endure this again. He must have some skill that nobody in this time had. He knew algebra and geometry, and science. Well, geometry was from ancient times, right? Periclean era, Aristotle or Archimedes or some such, one of those old sun-bleached wolves and sheep who'd written plays and discovered math. But science, acids and bases, and physics, and astronomy…

Well, maybe not astronomy, as it was around this time that that one weasel who said the Earth revolved around the Sun had been executed or excommunicated or something. He would have to remember that. But physics and chemistry…

Of course, all he knew about physics and chemistry was equations on paper. He could calculate the volume of a solid object and he knew the Ideal Gas Law and he could quote the laws of thermodynamics. And all of that would do absolutely nothing to impress anyone who didn't already know enough to care. All of his knowledge of chemistry gave him exactly zero advantage in this kitchen over the cook who knew how all the tools and foods behaved from experience.

So what could he do? What use could he be in this age, other than quoting books that hadn't been written yet and describing events that would take place three to five hundred years in the future? Maybe he could deposit a penny in a bank and then claim the interest-fattened balance when he got back to 2008.

When? How about "if"?

Bertrand came in to discuss the number of fowl required with the cook. As the evening wore on, they began calculating how much fowl was required on each plate. "You can make these last," Bertrand said. "Put a little less on each." He ignored Danilo completely.

When he'd gone, the bear grumbled. "Less on each. He gives the order and the cook gets the blame." But Danilo saw him put one and a half pieces down from then on, rather than the two he had been portioning out previously. The potatoes would not run out, so he added more of those, and Bertrand did not complain further.

By the time the badger came in to say, "We're closed," Danilo was panting, his clothes almost as damp from the heat and exertion as if it had rained in the kitchen. The hunger in his stomach had become a consuming need, his restraint around the food in the kitchen taking its own physical toll on him. He had discovered that visiting the outhouse's foul stench, whether he needed to go or not, killed his hunger for a short time, but the bear snapped at him when he went for the fourth time, and after that, Danilo hadn't dared go at all. Fortunately, not having eaten or drunk anything, he didn't have to.

"Well," the bear said, removing his apron, "I suppose you were better than nobody at all."

Danilo swallowed and pressed a paw to his stomach. "Dinner?"

The cook pointed at the pile of carrot and potato peels. "Pick your dinner out of that," he said. "Throw the rest in the outhouse. Then clean pans."

"Wh—" Danilo stared at the—garbage, it was garbage, wasn't it? "I have to eat that?"

"In there." The large stewpot, now empty of potato and carrot save for the smell, still steamed on the stove. "Boil it with that." He extended a claw toward the cutting board where he'd been working to chop apart the fowls, where a pile of bone and fat stood heaped. "Share with the others. Take what bread is left." As he said that, he reached into the wooden crate and pulled out an entire baguette, as long as one of Danilo's legs.

"What others?" Danilo asked, but the cook was already out the back door, chewing on the end of his bread.

Alone in the kitchen, he swallowed and stared at the peels. Well, he'd eaten potato peels before. He would wash them, and boil them, and throw in the chicken fat. It wouldn't be too bad.

He put on the bear's apron and carried the peels in it, holding up the corners of it, just as he'd seen in some old movie, and knelt by the pump, too tired to care that his tail was lying in the mud. He reached up to pull the handle down, but after five or ten minutes, no water had come out. He was just looking up at the clouds wishing for the rain to come back when a presence came up behind him.

"You have not pumped water before?" a light, amused voice said.

He turned to see a rabbit, soft brown fur damp with exertion, in a plain dress with a blue apron over it. "Not—not in a long time," he said.

"How lucky for you. Here, you must pump it hard. See?" She walked around him. With a strength he would not have expected from her thin frame, she thrust down on the handle. A spray of water gushed from the pump, soaking his apron and the potato peels he carried in it.

"Thank you!" He scrambled to clean off the peels, aware that the dirt was being trapped in the apron but not caring. They were cleaner than they had been, and that was mostly what he cared about.

"Ah, you are not like Gauchon. You wash your dinner. Very good."

"Yes." He smiled back at her, and her manner and sympathy relaxed him. "I am new in Tigue. I wondered if perhaps it was the custom here to eat dirt."

She laughed and patted his shoulder. "Only if you are a bear from the Black Forest. No, we prefer our meals clean. But look, let us not spend the water. It is clean now."

He would happily have spent another five minutes rinsing the peels, but it was easier and more comfortable to agree with her, to let her guide him through custom. If this was clean enough for her, it would be clean enough for him. "My name's Danilo," he said.

"I am Seline," she said, and her ears kept their long, graceful curve as she bowed. "I clean the rooms and tend the tables. And I must say, it is unusual to see a tiger here, especially working as a kitchen-servant. Did you come from Turkiya just to peel potatoes?"

"No, from—not that far." He couldn't decide whether to say Anglia or Etrusca, and in the end said neither. "I'm—a scholar," he said. "But I have lost my money."

"Ah." Sympathy filled her eyes and muzzle. "Lost to a thieving merchant?"

"Er." He straightened, holding the apron full of potato peelings out. His tail flicked mud against his legs, and he felt foolish. "I dropped it in the Saône."

Sympathy met confusion, and then a tender smile spread her whiskers. "I will not ask how that came to pass."

"It's a terribly complicated story," he said.

"Come." She gestured him into the kitchen. "Maria and I are hungry, and you must be as well."

His stomach growled in answer, and she laughed.

There was a whole baguette and a half left over, and he, Seline, and Maria, a wolf who did not appear to want often for food, shared out the bread. Maria had brought in piles of used plates, and before Danilo could object, she took uneaten pieces of fowl and vegetable from them and threw them into the soup. He opened his mouth, and then he looked at the stick resting on the floor that had been used to pick up hot fowl, at the dirt clinging to the apron he'd just taken off, and he closed his mouth again. Nobody else was objecting, and while Danilo's twenty-first century knowledge of hygiene might be superior to that of this time, the only thing it was likely to gain him here was an empty stomach. Besides, he thought, these people did know enough not to eat dirt, and that diseases could be spread, and the leavings were going into boiling water.

The two female servants chatted merrily about the customers at dinner, the various merchants and church figures who'd been seen eating, while Danilo sniffed the pot in a daze, their words flowing over and around him.

"I think it is ready," Maria said. "The poor boy. No money, no breakfast?"

"No." Danilo shook his head. He had had lunch, but it was forever ago. He'd missed his afternoon snack, and was used to dining around seven or seven-thirty. "No food since…" He suppressed a hysterical giggle. No food since five hundred years from now. "Er, what time is it?"

"Oh, you should see the clock in the church." Seline smiled. "It tells so much! But here, it is past nine, I think?"

"I heard the clock strike nine." Maria nodded and ladled out a pile of potato peels and chicken parts onto a plate. She gave it to Danilo, who looked around for utensils while Maria gave a plate to Seline, taking more care with it. The rabbit picked up a piece of potato with her fingers and ate it.

"Oh." Danilo picked up a scrap of fowl and held it, looked at it, then put it on his tongue. It tasted—good. Hunger might be the best sauce, but this chicken was also spiced and tender. He picked up potato peels two, three at a time, and shoveled them into his mouth.

"Oh?" Seline gave him a teasing look as the plump wolf prepared her own plate.

"I was just wondering, uh…" He searched for something to ask about that wouldn't be as anachronistic as asking for a fork. His eyes lit on a large piece of fowl on his plate. "Uh, most rabbits I know don't like vegetables cooked with meat."

Seline's nose wrinkled. Her ears did droop, but she kept her smile. "It is bearable. Better than no food, and it is free."

"You, mister scholar," Maria said, picking up a large gobbet of flesh and fat, "you should know the value of free food."

"Oh, yes." Danilo talked with his mouth full, because they were too, and because his stomach kept demanding that he push more food down.

"What are you studying?"

Seline had asked the question casually, and Danilo, caught off guard, said, "Psychology" around a mouthful of potato peel.

The wolf and rabbit both looked curiously at him. "I did not quite understand," Seline said. "Repeat, please?"

Danilo froze, then chewed deliberately. He'd said the word, so it must have existed, must have some meaning. He swallowed. "Er. Behavior. Um. Why people act the way they do."

"Oh, a philosopher." Maria laughed heartily. "Well, I can tell you why men act as they do. To fill an urge, or because someone powerful compels them. That is all."

"Now, now," Seline said. "Let the scholar tell us what he has learned."

Danilo found a piece of carrot and ate it, savoring the sweetness while Maria went to the bread bin. "Ah, some bread remains!" She pulled out a small pile of bread scraps and gave a piece each to Maria and Danilo.

Seline still looked expectantly at him, so Danilo swallowed his mouthful. His stomach's demands were starting to lose their urgency. "Er," he said, trying to figure out how to distill Freud and Jung and Skinner into sixteenth-century talk. "People behave as they do because they have needs, but also we are brought up from children to believe that we should act a certain way, and a lot of our upbringing as children affects how we perceive the world as adults."

The rabbit's large eyes held his. "And where is God's hand in this?"

"Oh," he said, and the weight of the cathedral, even though he couldn't see it, bunched the muscles in his shoulders. "God has a plan for us, but we don't always know the plan…and so what I meant was that if we are raised in God's way from childhood, then we follow God's path as adults."

He was babbling, but it seemed to satisfy her. Maria, who had finished her plate and was fishing out more from the pot, scoffed. "God has a plan for some."

"He has a plan for you, too," Seline said, so amiably that Danilo could tell it was a familiar conversation, even with only the scant attention he was sparing from his own terror over saying the wrong thing.

"Oh, I know His plan." Maria devoured her meal with gusto. "It's to keep me flat on my back in Bertrand's bed until a handsome wolf rides through Tigue to carry me away."

"Your wolf will come one day." Seline licked her fingers and set her plate down.

"Yes, the wolf Michael, and he'll take me to God's kingdom, and that is the plan." Maria put a paw to her muzzle, and then set her plate down and leaned against the kitchen wall with a satisfied exhalation.

Danilo was pleased enough to be a spectator to the conversation. His stomach was settling nicely, and when he took a bite of the bread, his eyes widened. It was delicious, still warm, with a crackling crust and a fluffy interior that was as good as any he'd had in his own time. He set about devouring it, not even wanting to sop up the liquid on his plate as Seline and Maria had done because the bread tasted so good on its own.

Meanwhile, Seline shook her head and sighed, and collected the dirty plates. "I'll do those," Maria said. She pushed herself away from the wall, took one more plate, and collected what Danilo supposed was the last of the vegetables from the pot.

"You need to wash up for Bertrand."

"Not tonight."

The rabbit stopped. "Oh?"

Maria picked her teeth with a claw. "A rare night off. Perhaps he is feeling his age. But never mind. You do the dishes every night."

"I'm supposed to do the roasting pans." Danilo indicated them.

"Then it will be a small party," Maria said. "Come, Seline, take the dishes, and Danilo and I will carry the pot, yes? Big tiger, so strong."

Danilo had no doubt that Maria could flatten him if she wished, but he grasped one side of the pot and she took the other. It was still quite warm, but nothing to what his paws had been handling all night, and in ten seconds they had it out the door. Seline held the outhouse door open and in went the remains of their soup.

"It will at least improve the smell." Maria smiled as she guided Danilo to the pump. They filled the pot halfway to the top with water and then brought it back to the stove. As the water heated, Seline and Maria dipped the plates into it, rubbing them cursorily with a wet cloth and then handing them to Danilo to pass over with a dry cloth. Seline said she would sweep the floor, and Maria guided Danilo out the back.

The sun had set completely, but the clouds remained. Still, the blackness was so absolute that Danilo stopped, disoriented, even though firelight glowed faintly from the restaurant and surrounding buildings. Maria paused with him, her muzzle nearly six inches below his, but close. "So, scholar," she said softly, one strong paw on his arm. "Have you taken vows of chastity?"

"No," he said, startled away from his contemplation of the deep lightless night.

"We have a little space of time while Seline sweeps the floors before she comes back to our room. Unless you have a room to yourself."

"Oh, no," he said. "I don't, but..."

"Not married, are you? No wife would allow you to go out dressed like that. Did you steal those clothes? Oh, no, one moment." She pressed her nose to the side of his chest, right into the fabric. "Ah, those are Luc's clothes."

"Yes. He loaned them to me. Mine were—lost."

"Oh. Is that how it is?" Her voice lowered; her eyes studied his. "Luc should know better than to bring his boys here. Bertrand will—"

"No, no!" Panic flared again. He wasn't sure what it meant to be gay here, but he was pretty sure it would be worse than five hundred years from now. Was it that obvious? Was there a scent he exuded that told people he might be interested in males? His tail, upon which mud had dried and crusted, whipped tight around his bare calf.

"Settle down, boy. I'm not the Church. I just want to know if you know how to show a lady some pleasure."

"I, er..." He glanced back at the kitchen. "I thought you and Bertrand..."

"Yes, well." Her lip curled, and her ears flattened. "It's all very well for him."

"I don't know..." He licked his lips nervously.

Maria's hazel eyes gleamed in the darkness. "Can you follow orders?"

"Y-yes?"

Fangs showed in her smile. "Good. Come along, then."

Her paw tightened around his upper arm. He allowed himself to be pulled to the back entrance of the restaurant, but not up the stairs; a smaller door led behind it to a close, dark space that was nevertheless as clean as his room upstairs. It smelled strongly of rabbit and wolf—Seline and Maria, specifically—and of a smell that made him think of the ocean, until he realized it was simply salt.

When Maria closed the door behind them, she wasted no time pulling him down to one side, onto a straw pallet. His eyes still hadn't adjusted, and so he dropped hard to one knee and then half-fell onto his side next to her. He saw nothing, and then she moved her head and her eyes flashed at him.

"You stink." Her teeth shone white in the dark room, enough for him to make out her smile. "Mud and filth, not just the kitchen."

"I haven't had a chance to wash." He felt acutely conscious now of the grit in his fur, the smell that his poor nose had been subjected to for so many hours that it had simply ceased to acknowledge it. Maria's observation brought it back.

"You needn't worry," she said softly. "I'll hold my breath."

His whiskers tingled as she moved closer to him and put a paw on his shoulder. "Wait." This was not at all how he'd envisioned losing his virginity.

Her tone held tolerance, but a little disbelief as well. "If you want to go, you may go."

It occurred to him that if he were giving off some kind of signal that he might be gay, sleeping with a female would be one way to counter that. At least Maria would vouch for him then. And really, how had he imagined losing his virginity? A romantic night, a girl-friend (or boyfriend) of many weeks?

(Taye?)

He took a breath. "No. I just was thinking about…about what you said about people acting on urges."

She chuckled, deep and throaty, and reached out to take his paw. He let her guide it to what turned out to be her naked breast. "We can satisfy some urges together," she said, and leaned forward to lick his nose. "Welcome to Tigue."

Despite the awkwardness, it was probably the best half-hour Danilo had spent in 1508 thus far. Maria was not at all shy about telling him how to pinch her nipples. "Not so hard. Roll between your fingers. And keep those claws in!" He found that he enjoyed her exhalations and her arm around him. And when she said, "You can touch more" (which was more a command than permission), he did let his paws roam over the ample curves of her body, soft under the fur. The only objectionable part was the smell of her breath, which carried a faint perfume of decay with it, but if he kept his nose pointed to her fur, all he smelled was her musk and, faintly, a floral scent he couldn't identify.

He kept stroking along her stomach, over and over, until she breathed frustration onto his muzzle and grasped his paw, moving it between her legs. "It won't bite," she growled. "There, keep it there. And I'll attend to you in a…" He started rubbing at the folds of skin he felt through the fur there. "Ohh. In a moment."

Danilo didn't need much tending to. His erection strained at his boxers, and he was already rubbing it against her thigh. How had she gotten all her clothes off so quickly?

Maria asked the opposite question of him when her paw dropped to his chest. "You're still wearing your shirt."

"Um," he said softly, and lifted his paw from her, pausing. Her closeness overwhelmed his awareness of everything else, and in the dark, if it weren't for the thick musky dirty smells constantly assaulting his nose, he could imagine he was simply lying on a mattress in one of the dorms with a large wolf he'd met at one of Tigue's bars. If it weren't for the pain in his paws from the unforgiving knife, the fabric of his unfamiliar shirt and pants...if it weren't for his mind constantly replaying the events of the last half-day...

"All right, then, get it off." She waited while he struggled out of the shirt, and then she found the cloth strips that tied his pants shut and undid the knot. Her paws dove inside, following his fur from his stomach down inside his boxers, and closed around his aching shaft.

Danilo jumped and made a noise. Maria laughed softly, and slid her fingers up him. "Am I more forward than the girls back home?"

"Y-yes," he breathed. Nobody else had ever touched him there, and now here was this wolf, her fingers rubbing, and his tail lashed against the ground and his body felt consumed by sparks. He had gotten his shirt off by this time, the air cool on his fur, and so she placed his paw back between her legs again.

"It feels to me like you were wasted on them." She pushed his boxers down, exposing him to the air, and cupped his sac with her other paw.

"Nnn..." Danilo swallowed, his breath coming faster, aware that his body was overloading, lighting up all over, and he tried to scramble up to his knees.

"What is it—oh, take your time, youngster. You—"

But she kept rubbing, and then Danilo was far gone, his whole body shaking, and the tension and fear and anticipation burst in a throaty gasp from his throat as his hips flailed forward and he felt himself come all over her paw and arm. Maria made a surprised noise but kept rubbing, reaching up to steady him as he shook and moaned.

"Well," she said when he was done, "you should have told me it was your first time, dear."

The excitement of sex had left him, and all he felt was a crushing shame. He couldn't even have sex properly, and he was pretty sure that hadn't changed in five hundred years. There was no chance that spurting all over the paw of a female who wanted you inside her was somehow viewed as noble and good, not unless he was the kind of lover he dimly gathered Bertrand was. "I'm sorry," he moaned, and slumped down beside her, nose buried in the crook of his arm, where he was treated to the smell of river dirt.

With difficulty, she extricated her paw from beneath him. "The only reason you'll have to be sorry is if you stop now," she said in a voice that was both gentle and firm.

His eyes had adjusted well enough that when he turned, he could see her expression, a smile stretched over her long muzzle. "You're young, if not so young," she went on. "I won't ask how you got to this age without knowing a female touch. But I wager you'll be ready again in a short time, and until that time, you're going to make sure *I'm* good and ready for you when you are."

"What about Seline?" he whispered.

"Oh, if she comes in, she'll see us and go back out. Besides, she likely suspects where we've both disappeared to. Seline is quick."

He propped himself up on his elbows. The odor of sex assaulted his nose, and he thought about how much worse it would be for Maria, with her wolf's nose. "Sorry about the smell, too."

"Yes," she said. "You will help me clean it and then we will both wash off in the back."

So there was a bath. That small piece of news afforded him some relief; his sticky fur and the empty sensation in his groin lessened. "All right." His voice remained small. "Tell me what to do."

And she did, guiding his paw with experience and a drive that Bertrand's abuses must have stoked. With his own urgency faded, he could appreciate the noises she made, could work at following her instructions as best he could.

It was likely no more than ten minutes before her paw reached down between his legs and found him hard again, and when she said, "You're ready," it was not entirely (nor even mostly) a question.

So Danilo found himself atop a female wolf, thrusting into her as her paws held him and his tail lashed over his bare rear, his pants still around his ankles. Again, he felt his climax approaching, but slower; somehow this felt less exciting to him than her paw had. He inhaled her musk, felt the grip of her slick passage on him, and although it took him longer, he came while she was still gasping and arching below him.

"Don't you...stop," she ordered him, and so even though his climax had left him sensitive and a little sore, he kept thrusting until she squeezed a long, low moan out through clenched teeth, and her body shook below him.

Then her arms closed around his back and she buried her muzzle into his shoulder. "Ah," she breathed. "Ah. Ah. Yes."

"Did I do okay?" He rested his cheek against hers, their whiskers tickling each other.

"Yes." She breathed hard, and then rolled him gently over, sliding him out of her. "Quite 'okay.' It is easy for one to forget, lying under that badger, that God intended lovemaking to be pleasurable."

A profusion of scents assaulted his nose, but fatigue overwhelmed him, pulling his eyelids down. "I'm glad," he murmured.

Her paw slapped his stomach, jolting him awake. "You're not to sleep here! Come, we will take a quick wash."

He didn't want to pull his boxers up over his messy sheath and erection, but he didn't want to get Luc's clothes dirty and he didn't want to walk out the door with his bits hanging out, so reluctantly, he pulled his boxers up while Maria slid the robe over her head. "Your underthings," she said, "they feel unusual. And very fine. You must have lost a good deal of money."

His paw closed around the elastic waistband. "Er, it—they are made specially near where I live."

"I hope to see merchants here offering them soon." She smiled and helped him pull his pants up. "And I hope to have enough coin to buy some."

Her comment about the elastic had jolted him back to the realization that he was five hundred years before his time. It had been easy to submerge in the sex, to be nothing but a male with a female, losing himself in, as Maria had said, his urges. But now the elastic hugged his hips, reminding him that it did not belong here and neither did he, and his tail hung limp as he stood and reminded himself that he was likely not going to a hot bath in a gleaming porcelain bathroom with fluffy towels to dry off afterwards.

He pulled his pants on over the boxers and picked up his shirt from the floor, while Maria picked up a bucket that sat just inside the door and carried it with her. They met Seline in the back corridor, rubbing her paws on a small cloth that Danilo thought was a towel until he drew closer.

"Oh, you're finished?" The rabbit's tone held a little disdain, or maybe Danilo was imagining it. He couldn't see her expression clearly in the shadowy corridor.

"Just going to wash up," Maria said cheerfully. She walked on, and Danilo paused to glance at Seline, but the rabbit didn't look at him as she went back into the room she and Maria shared.

Had he done something wrong? His body still tingled with the physical memory of his first time (his first time! and his second!) and Maria's and his scents still mingled pleasantly enough in his nose that he found himself purring without realizing it. But Seline had not approved; perhaps Maria was a 'loose' type and she'd thought Danilo was better than that, or perhaps she'd hoped she could have the tiger for herself?

Danilo shook his head, following Maria's lazily wagging tail out into the back yard. He should just enjoy the moment and stop worrying about it so much.

"Is something wrong with Seline?" he asked Maria when the wolf set the bucket down next to the pump.

"Wrong with? No, she's lovely and healthy." Maria eyed him. "And she's quite proper, so even if you were an ordinary rabbit instead of an exotic tiger, she wouldn't have anything to do with you without a long period of courting and a blessing from the Church."

"There's nothing wrong with not being proper," Danilo said hurriedly, afraid now that he'd offended Maria by asking about another female so soon after they'd made love.

"I'm proper enough." Maria pumped ferociously. "I'll be asking the Lord's forgiveness for this come Sunday."

"Forgiveness?" Danilo faltered. "But…thank you, I mean, it was a really nice thing."

She stopped pumping, placed the bucket under the spout, and rested her paws on her wide hips, her tail still wagging. "Bless you, youngster, but is this the first time you've crept out from under your family's roof in your life?"

"No!" He lashed his tail. "I came to school on my own, and I've had plenty of experience…"

"In books," she murmured, and shoved the pump handle down again, filling the bucket with water.

Danilo looked up at the thick layer of clouds, faintly glowing with moonlight. The sky was still darker than any he'd remembered seeing in a city. But the air wasn't as clean as it had been out in the country when he'd seen a million stars; it smelled of people and brick and dirt and the outhouse standing ten feet away. He inhaled and then looked back at Maria, as the wolf stopped pumping. "It just seemed like Seline might have been upset," he said, more calmly.

The wolf lifted her shirt off, revealing the breasts Danilo had touched but never seen properly. Her nipples shone light grey and pink against the soft whiteness of her fur, and the rounded curves matched up well to the memory that made his fingers twitch. "She believes I should not be so free with my affections."

Danilo jerked around, staring back at the building, and then turned again to Maria. "You're..." He gestured to her naked breasts. "Anyone could—what if someone comes out?"

She reached into the bucket, picked up a dripping cloth, and worked it through her stomach fur. "Then they see the body God gave me."

"But isn't that—I mean, people don't walk around—" He stopped, confused. Maybe female breasts weren't as big a deal now as they were in his time? That seemed backwards somehow, but there was a lot he didn't know about life here, apparently.

"Dear," she said, "I've lived twenty-six years and learned that there are many more things to trouble your mind about than what people have seen of your fur." She dipped the cloth into the bucket again and rubbed it along the wrist he'd spurted across, then lowered her pants and rubbed the cloth between her legs, at which point Danilo looked away and then realized that the quick glance he'd seen had shown nothing but a thick brush of ivory-white fur. He looked back in time to see her pull her pants up. "And you'd best learn that lesson quickly, too."

She dipped the cloth back in the bucket, agitated it, and then threw it to him. "M-me?" he stammered, catching the cloth. Cold water splashed up his wrist, and his claws, involuntarily extended, snagged the fabric. "Oh, no, I can't—"

"You can wash off here," she said, tugging her shirt back over her head, "or you can go into the kitchen and do it. Or you could go to my room and wash off in front of Seline. Or your room, and wash in front of Luc. Although guests are discouraged from bringing water up into the rooms."

"Isn't there a—" He tried to say 'bathroom,' and it came out as "outhouse," so he tried again. "A room in which guests may bathe?"

She laughed. "In the palace of your tiger family, certainly. We had many public baths, my mother said, until the plague came back, but they've not been open in my lifetime. Here, you may use the back yard." When he still hesitated, she said, "Oh, come now. You haven't anything I haven't had my paw around, and certainly you boys have thick enough fur down there to keep modest when you're not in the presence of a lady."

"I am in the presence of a lady," Danilo pointed out.

"Seline would argue that point." Marie grinned a wide lupine grin, her fangs showing. "But regardless, the only 'lady' here is one who has already known you, so you have nothing to hide from her."

Danilo took a breath. He'd never actually been naked in front of anyone in recent memory, even his parents. But a tiger who was no longer a virgin didn't have to worry so much about being naked, especially in front of a wolf he'd slept with (*he had slept with her, he'd been inside her*).

Remembering the sex stirred his groin, and so before he got himself into a less presentable state, he turned toward the kitchen, shoved his pants down, and rubbed the washcloth through the fur around his sheath and balls until it dripped. For good measure, he reached around to wash his rear as well, and when he did, a paw took the washcloth from him.

"Oh, let me do that," Maria said, and rubbed vigorously under his tail and around his hips. Before he could stop her, she'd pushed his pants the rest of the way down.

"Hey," he said.

"I don't know what you've been in," she said, "but you want that out of your fur." And she proceeded to refresh the washcloth and rub it all up and down the fur of his legs, by which time he was very distinctly not modest any longer.

"You don't have to," he protested, but she scoffed.

"For certain I don't, but it is not every day I get to run my paws over a nice young body. If I'm to confess my sins this Sunday, I might as well have enough to confess to." She chuckled, and as she brought the washcloth up his inner thigh, her paw cupped his balls. He jumped, and then her paw was around his front and rubbing the washcloth over his shaft.

Danilo had to shift his feet, his tail finding her leg and curling against it. "I—uh—"

"Oh, don't worry," she said softly. "I can resist temptation as well." She moved the washcloth up to his stomach and then around to his back, then dropped it in the bucket with a soft splash. He felt her movement and then the tug of fabric along his wet legs as she pulled his boxers and pants up.

"This is interesting fabric," she murmured

Danilo panicked and grabbed the boxers away from her, yanking them up along his legs. "I can do the rest," he said, turning and bending to get the washcloth from the bucket.

Maria watched him clean his tail and chest, even though by this point the washcloth smelled dirtier than he did. When his fur was dripping and he was rubbing his shoulders, she peered close. "By the Lord," she said, ears back. "You're *white*."

He froze, washcloth dripping over his fingers. There really wasn't any denying it; even in the moonlight, his fur shone palely now that the Saône water and mud had been cleaned out of it. What puzzled him more was that she hadn't noticed until now. He'd been walking around in the daylight, in the kitchen…true, Maria hadn't seen him until it was dark. "Yes…" he said.

"You are meant for the church, then. Well…" She recovered her smile and her ears came back up. "It could be I will be your first and only, once the white robes go on. I hope you will remember this night kindly."

"I…of course." Danilo squeezed the cloth out onto the ground. "It was lovely."

"You were dirty," she went on, "and I thought you were just pale orange. I've only seen two or three tigers and that was from a distance. But they were all orange."

The way she said it, the way she looked at him, he got an inkling of why she had been so keen to bed him. In a way, it felt cheap. It hadn't been his personality or the way he acted or anything like that that had gotten the wolf excited. He was like a spot on a scavenger hunt, a rare type she could claim to have bedded. In another way, though, fuck it, he'd slept with her and had done okay enough that she was happy to help him wash up afterwards. So right now he'd take advantage of it.

"White tigers aren't common," he said, which was true, but also made him seem more exotic. He left out all the stuff about being a recessive gene paired with another recessive gene, and about the disease screenings his parents had had to do with him until he was fourteen to make sure he didn't have any other recessive-gene traits that were less innocuous than white fur. He'd never met another white tiger in person, but in Siberia, he knew, a lot of them had died early in life, before modern hospitals.

"No tigers are common here." Her muzzle curved into a smile. "Despite the name."

He tried to remember the name of the restaurant, and couldn't. "I don't know what this place is called."

She laughed. "Tigue? The city you're in?"

"Oh." He felt stupid, and folded his ears down. To cover his embarrassment, he picked up his shirt and slid it over his head. "Well, you know, 'Tigue' comes from the old Roman word for 'tail,' *tægl*, probably because the way the rivers meet makes the central part here look like a wolf's tail, with the pointed tip…or there's a legend that the Roman general Severus lost his tail in a battle here and buried it up on Fourvière Hill…" He stopped talking at her amused look. "What is it?"

"You're a scholar indeed," she said. "And I'm a cleaning-bitch who has not much time to sleep before the sun's up."

"Sorry," he said, ducking his head.

"Get on with you," Maria said, and reached up to pat his ear. "But let me give you a lesson as well."

He couldn't help grinning. "Another one?"

She laughed. "Less complicated. The lesson is—don't tie your fortunes to Luc."

Startled, he drew back and frowned. "He's really nice."

"He's got not very much money, doesn't have much in the way of prospects for more, and his friends are…" She wrinkled her nose.

"Let's say that if you're going to the Church, they aren't the sort you'd be running into."

He thought of Théodore, the violent mouse with the confident, smooth manner. "I suppose…"

"I thought you might be one of *them*, wearing his clothes and all. Also." She leaned close. "Bertrand tolerates him, but would be pleased to be rid of him."

"Why doesn't he just go somewhere else?"

"Oh." Maria waved a paw. "Some matter between them, that Bertrand allows him to stay for free. But he does not like Luc's friends and he does not like losing a room that might bring in money. I would advise that you find rooms at your school with all haste."

Danilo nodded, feeling he was closer to understanding Luc. Impulsively, he pushed further. "Maria?" She had bent to pick up her bucket, but paused to look up at him. "Who's LeSev?"

Her eyes narrowed. "You mean LeSevre? The wolf?" He nodded again, and she dropped her eyes. For a few seconds, she remained silent, and finally said, "He serves the Church. Best he comes to know you as a student of the Church and not as a friend of Luc's."

"But what's Luc done?" Danilo asked. "I'm sorry, but I'm a stranger to Tigue…"

"Tchah." Maria shook her head. "Let's say he has no use for my charms, and leave it at that."

"All right," Danilo said, beginning to understand. "Thank you."

Her ears perked up and her eyes brightened. "Thanking me! You do make a wench feel like a lady." She winked at him, and then dumped her bucket out and carried it back inside. He watched her tail swing behind her into the shadows, and she was gone.

Chapter Four

Danilo took one more look around, preparing to go inside, and then steps sounded in the kitchen. The tiger's reflexes took him down the muddy path to the door Maria had disappeared through before he'd consciously processed the movement. Curiosity caught him just inside the door, though, and he turned, hoping he was hidden enough in the shadows to see who it was.

The stocky badger, Bertrand, wandered out from the kitchen and applied his weight to the pump, grunting. Unlike Danilo, he had very little shame or modesty; he carried his pants loosely over one arm, and from the bottom of his tunic to the ground, nothing but his black and white fur covered him. Before Danilo could look away, Bertrand had dipped a paw into the water and lifted the bottom of his tunic with the arm holding his pants, giving Danilo an excellent moonlit view of the badger's half-erect penis.

He did look away then, ducking back into the hallway. The splash of water continued, along with some satisfied grunts, and Danilo left them behind, retracting his claws to pad up the stairs as silently as possible.

All the doors in the upstairs hallway were closed now, but he thought he remembered which one was Luc's, and a sniff of the door handle confirmed it. The otter's oily scent pervaded the room, but Luc himself was absent. He stripped off Luc's tunic and, after a moment's hesitation, Luc's pants, and lowered himself to the bed.

Perhaps it was odd that Luc wasn't in his room at this hour of night, but what did Danilo know about how Luc spent his time? Perhaps the otter had a night job, or liked to wander the streets. Maybe he went to church at night. There had been plenty of bells from all around, clear above the muted noise of a city without cars, with a tenth or a twentieth the number of people.

He lay on his back and stared up through the blackness at the ceiling. If this really was 1508—and the solidity of the world was wearing down his disbelief—then perhaps it wouldn't be so bad. He'd lasted a day, or at least part of a day, and he'd already had more sex in the sixteenth century than he'd had in the twenty-first. Sure, that wasn't the only measure of success in life, but he had more general knowledge of how the world worked than most people, enough to probably get a berth as a scholar. He might have to work more horrible nights in kitchens, and he probably would never feel completely clean again, but at least he wouldn't have to worry about Cobb and Georg.

His paw scratched at his side. The air around him was oppressively silent. Even Chellingham had had its share of urban noise, cars and people and trains, airplanes overhead. Here, of course, there were no cars, and there would be no trains for three hundred years, no cars for four hundred thirty, no planes for four hundred sixty or so. Four hundred years. He would be dead and no more than a skeleton by the time the first car rolled through Tigue.

The blackness of the ceiling felt as massive and heavy as a starless sky. Danilo closed his eyes, but could still feel the silence all around him, the smell of otter in the room and the smell of straw, which made him think of playing in the barn as a cub, throwing bales of hay back and forth with one of the neighbors. But outside that barn, there had been a car; he and the neighbor, a red deer who tried to get him to eat the straw, had been wearing jeans and t-shirts. That was what was missing, he realized: the faint, pervasive background odor of chemical dyes and fabrics, of laundry detergent and car exhaust and cigarette smoke and a thousand other small smells he had gotten so used to, he only noticed their absence, and that only when given time to think about it.

(Though it was true that he'd spent most of the evening in a smelly kitchen full of other odors.)

His side itched again, and he scratched it more firmly. He remembered his last conversation with Lena, now, there on the riverbank, the text message to Taye that he'd never sent. What would they think when he vanished? Probably that he'd fallen in the Saône and drowned. His clothes were right there, after all. They would think him dead, and they wouldn't be too far off. To them, he might as well be.

Perhaps this was all a dream. The weight of the blackness above him pressed down again, and wondered if he were drowning. Was this all a sort of Owl Creek Bridge hallucination? His paw scratched a little lower down on his hip. There was no way he would see any of his family or friends again, either way. One way he would be dead and floating in the Saône in 2008; the other way he would be dead and buried sometime in the early sixteenth century. If this were really happening, and he would never in a million years have believed it if it weren't so minutely real to him, then he had no idea how it had happened, no jump point to return to that would get him back to his time, no pylon nor TARDIS nor transporter beam. He could jump in the Saône again, but what if he surfaced in 1008 this time? Or, more likely, what if he just remained in 1508?

The itch came again at his side, and this time when he scratched, he felt something move against his paw. For a moment he lay there, and then he thought, *well, if this is a dream, it's a really shitty one, because I'm dreaming I have fleas.*

And that indignity brought the weight above him crashing down. His chest tightened and he could only breathe in hard, gulping sobs. He would never see a computer again, or a wristwatch, or eat a pizza or a hamburger. He would never see that new James Bond movie, nor the Shadow Knight one that had been getting such good reviews in the States. He would never talk to his friends or his family again. He wished he'd said something more to Lena, that he hadn't hung up on her in a huff.

The sobs came harder now, and he turned onto his stomach. There was no pillow, but he gathered up the discarded pants and tunic and pressed his muzzle to them, tears leaking out. He was lost, completely lost, in a strange world and time, and his chest felt as though he really were drowning, constricted on all sides, each breath coming at a cost. He drew his arms beneath him, starting to curl up, and moaned into the fabric. Once he started crying, it was difficult to stop; each pause brought another image, a word he regretted or a promise left undone. He'd said he would help Anita research monasteries, and that he would pick up cold medicine for Orwin, and that he would have dinner with Taye…

The click of the door latch registered, but though he tried to muffle his sobs, Luc came to his side immediately. "What is it?" he asked.

His concern, his paw light between Danilo's shoulders, set the tiger off again. This simple expression of caring from someone he barely knew touched him, and at the same time reminded him of how inadequate it was. His best friend in this world was someone he'd known for seven hours, unless he counted Maria, but he'd only known *her* for two hours.

"I, I, I want to go home," Danilo gulped out. He pulled his arms in toward his chest and pressed his nose into the clothes. He could feel and smell his own tears now, but he still could not stop.

Luc's paw continued to rub between his shaking shoulders. "Tigue is a long way for you, and you've lost your money. It's no wonder you're feeling nervous."

His voice was calm, but it reminded Danilo of all the things Luc didn't know, couldn't know. "What am I going to do?" he whimpered.

"Well…" Luc rubbed his shoulder and paused. "You could write your father. Tell him you lost your money. In two or three months, you might have more."

"I, I can't," Danilo wailed, and tightened his grip on his own chest at the thought of his father, the tall gruff tiger with the warm smile. His father had always been patient with him, had encouraged his studies and not worried about sport, and had told him that The Université Catholique would be a great adventure. He hadn't talked to his father in the last week while he had been worried about Taye and what to do about his feelings, but only because he'd wanted to sort things out for himself. He'd always thought he would be able to talk to his father when he needed to.

"All right," Luc said. "It's going to be fine. Did your family spend all their money to send you here? Is your father still alive?"

Still alive? He won't be born for… "No," Danilo said. "I…I can't go back to my family. I can't get any more money from them. I have to stay here. If I can't live here, I'll die here."

"You're not going to die," Luc said immediately, and his paw reached around Danilo's shoulders to pull the tiger toward him. Danilo resisted at first, but Luc insisted, and the tiger gave in and let the otter hold him. Luc's short, powerful arms couldn't reach all the way around even Danilo's skinny chest, but they reached far enough. "I pulled you out of the water," Luc said. "I'm responsible for you now. We'll go to the church school tomorrow. They should have your papers, and you can work for your lodging there. If you're a scholar, they will take care of you. God's charity extends at least that far."

Danilo didn't believe any of that, but his breathing eased anyway. He slipped down onto his side and squirmed one of his arms out to reach around the otter's chest and hug him back. "I don't belong here," he managed to murmur out against Luc's tunic.

"Shhh." Luc held him and drew claws through his fur down his back. "I am with you, and no-one shall attack or harm you." The otter settled down on his side facing Danilo, on the floor next to the small pallet. His breath ruffled the fur between the tiger's eyes, and his warmth pressed up against the tiger's trembling form, and slowly, Danilo's shaking slowed and eased.

Up close, Luc's scent filled Danilo's nostrils. Awkwardly, he found his body responding to the close embrace with arousal, even though Luc had his hips politely angled away from Danilo's. Maria's words came back to him, and for a moment he thought, *here in the room, would anyone know? If Luc is gay (too), we could just do it…*

But even had he not had sex twice in the last hour, this wasn't exactly a romantic mood. He angled his own hips down, his tail flicking away over his own legs. Luc didn't say anything, just kept holding him, and although the arousal didn't diminish, Danilo stopped worrying so much about it.

Luc murmured something more to him, something that sounded like a prayer. Danilo didn't focus on the words, but the low tone of the voice lulled him to sleep.

***

He woke in the dark, needing to use the bathroom. He stumbled off his futon, which was oddly low to the floor. For some reason, his room smelled like a barn. He found the door, much sooner than he expected, and swung it open.

In the hallway outside, there was a window where there should not be one. The clouds had cleared, and across the rooftops and the river, the immense cathedral glowed by the light of the moon.

Danilo stopped to stare at it. Right. Tigue, 1508, Luc. He had not magically awoken back in his room in his present time, which he now realized subconsciously he had been hoping would happen.

But no, the cathedral and the restaurant were as real as the pressure on his bladder. He hurried out and down the stairs to the outhouse, used it, and came slowly back up. He didn't look at the cathedral.

When he entered the room, Luc stirred. "There's a chamber pot," he said with some amusement.

"Oh." Danilo didn't know what to say. The thought of peeing in a pot in the dark and then lying there in the same room smelling it made him queasy. "Okay."

He lay down again on the straw bed, pulled the sheet over him, and stared at the ceiling.

"You may think," Luc said quietly, "that God has abandoned you. But if He had, would He have sent me to pull you from the river?"

No, Danilo thought, God wouldn't have sent me to your river in the first place. But the expectant silence weighed on him, and he said, "Thank you."

He might have dozed off after that. He remembered anxiety gnawing at him, trying to imagine how the next day might go, scratching at fleas and wondering if he could ask Luc how to get rid of them. The otter's breathing had settled into regularity and Danilo thought he might be asleep. So he just scratched and then recalled what Maria had said about the plague. That drove him into a panic during which he very nearly hyperventilated enough to pass out. He tried to convince himself that during a time of plague, no reputable establishment would allow fleas, and returned to imagining ever less plausible scenarios for the next day.

In the darkness, in the solitude, his mind ran along fatalistic lines. He tried to rein it in. If he were trapped here, then how could he make the best of it? That was what his father would say—had said, when Danilo had called him homesick from Tigue. "Make the best of it, otherwise it's a wasted experience." Well, all right; at least here was a chance for him to start over. His main worry as he'd plunged into the river had been being outed as gay, but here, nobody had heard of his cousin, and nobody would come after him if he just minded his business and stuck to willing females (his paw crept down to fondle himself as he thought this). He had a few friends, he had worked a night for his keep, and as unpleasant as the world was compared to what he was used to, well…he could survive. He clung to that thought.

Then Luc snored, and the tiger pulled his paw back to his side, worried Luc would think he was masturbating, which, yeah, he sort of had been. That was the other thing he would have to do: he would have to leave this place and not associate with Luc. Maria had as much as told him that Luc was gay and that that was a crime against the Church, which explained Bertrand's outburst, so the sooner Danilo was away from here, the better. Maybe when he got his own place here, Luc could stay with him—no, not if Danilo enrolled with a Church school. Luc the gay otter would hardly be welcome there. Danilo's stomach twisted, but he forced himself to breathe. Luc had a life here and he hardly wanted some foreign tiger messing around with it. He'd likely welcome Danilo's departure.

And eventually, time moved on, as it usually (usually) did, and grey dawn became visible through the cracks in the door.

Luc stirred. Danilo turned; the otter's one dark eye was open. "You are awake?" Luc asked.

Danilo nodded. "Having trouble sleeping."

"It is understandable. Yesterday, after all, was a very trying day for you."

Understatement of the century. He thought about that and had to suppress a semi-hysterical giggle as he stretched. "What time should we go over to the school?"

"The bells should be ringing the Lauds soon enough, and then we will make our way over."

"Will we have something to eat?" Danilo's stomach, used to an energy bar or bowl of cereal at this time of morning, growled.

Luc paused. "Until you resolve the question of your money, you should expect to eat once a day."

"Once a day? Nobody can live on that."

The slowly-brightening room fell silent. Danilo felt immediately stupid, even before Luc said, "I have, for many months now."

"I'm sorry," the tiger said immediately. "I'm used to—I didn't know—"

"I am sorry that you have to learn." Luc's voice held no rancor. "It is not easy, but at least I have a roof over my head, and that one meal, and good friends. Many lack all three of those."

"Are you going to live here for very much longer?"

"I hope not to." The otter breathed a sigh. "Bertrand honors the debt he owes my father, but I feel that he now views it as more than repaid. With just one more month...perhaps two...before the winter sets in, definitely..." His voice slipped away into his ruminations, as his mind built futures out of the darkness that Danilo could not see. And then he came back, sharply, as though scolding himself. "But that is none of your concern. We will get *you* out from Bertrand's roof today."

In the short time before the bells rang, Danilo asked Luc more about his shop and business. It turned out that otters and many others had actually built shops and homes on the bridge. Last year, though, when the Archbishop had returned from Lutèce, he had decreed that all the structures on the bridge that were not of the bridge should be demolished, and Luc had lost his shop and his home all in one go. Danilo struggled to find the words to ask about compensation; surely the authorities could not just demolish someone's livelihood? But Luc, clearly uninterested in discussing the matter further, asked Danilo similar questions about his home. He evaded them as best he could, retelling the story that his family had used all their money to send him here and that he had then lost it. Luc thought this odd, that a family would spend their last sous (his word, a new one Danilo filed away) for a scholar, but Danilo said that scholars were much respected in Etrusca, and Luc accepted that.

When the bells did come, they were not as loud as Danilo had thought. "They sound different from last night," he said.

"Compline," Luc said, getting up. "Vespers also rang while we were returning."

Danilo rose slowly. In the dim light, he saw Luc's tunic and pants, and also saw that the otter was lying on the floor. "Oh, no," he said. "I forgot there was only one bed. I'm so sorry."

"You needed it more." Luc smiled. "I'll have my bed back tomorrow, never fear."

They dressed, Danilo getting the tunic on properly by himself this time, and Luc dressing simply, without the beige scarf. Out in the hall, in the dim morning light, other residents were stirring as well, yawning and making their way to the outhouse, or already gone, their rooms empty. The rain had stopped, but smoke hung thickly in the air, and Danilo rubbed his nose. It was like standing in last night's kitchen again, only without the smells of food.

In the main body of the restaurant, Bertrand was serving bread from a large platter. At the sight of Luc, he slid the platter behind him and narrowed his eyes. "He's out today, you said."

"Good morning to you, too, Bertrand. Yes, yes, Danilo will find another bed tonight." Luc kept walking.

"He'd better! I've told you, I won't have this place become some halfie meeting house. I'll have the church here myself!" The badger called it loudly as they left, enough that the few patrons eating bread and honey (Danilo salivated at the look and smell) looked up.

Luc's little ears didn't go down the way an upset tiger's would, but he lowered his head and lost his cheerful manner. Danilo followed him out, wishing he knew what to say.

A few clouds still dotted the sky, but the sun shone brightly on the wood and brick of the town. The streets were already crowded, and down here, Danilo heard more of the bustle of Tigue. If he closed his eyes, it was not so different from that last busy afternoon in 2008: people spoke to each other rather than into phones, and they dressed in tunics rather than collared shirts, but the sense of purpose was the same, the press of the crowd and the smell of the people—well, all right, the smell was rank. But there were no more public baths, and they all bathed by washing off at pumps. Of course it wasn't going to be as clean as high pressure showers with shampoo.

But these were people, after all, and Danilo focused on the similarities of this world. The buildings were old, but still looked like houses and shops. Shopkeepers called out in front of their stores, their cries of "bread, fresh bread," and "cheese, well ripe," and "finest clothings," rising above the crowd to a rhythm that Danilo quickly grew accustomed to. As they passed the bakery, a small store with "Boulangerie" written in script over the door, the smell of freshly-baked bread overwhelmed him and actually slowed his steps.

Right. No money. He patted his unhappy stomach through the rough cotton tunic, and hurried to keep up with Luc.

One thing that was unusual here was the amount of attention Danilo drew. He was the tallest person in the streets, for one thing, and more importantly, he saw no other tigers. Foxes, badgers, deer, mice, rats, squirrels, and wolves passed him by and stared a moment longer than they stared at anyone else. Danilo avoided their glances as best he could, feeling in each one the reminder that he did not belong on this street.

Those glances he was growing more confident in handling. But when Luc turned at a corner with a smile, and said, "I am sorry for my silence—" and then stared at Danilo in the same way, the tiger felt his heart turn icy.

"What is it? Luc?" People pushed around them, and for a moment Danilo was sure he'd done something wrong, something terrible that even Luc's kind heart could not forgive.

"You are white." The otter reached out to touch his paw, then drew back. "I'm sorry, I did not realize."

"You didn't notice either?"

Luc shook his head. "The mud of the river water, the rain, the tunic over your fur…I am sorry. I had thought you a pale orange." He tilted his head. "'Either'? Who else said something to you?"

"Oh, uh." Danilo swallowed. "I had dinner with Maria and Seline last night, and Maria and I washed at the pump, uh, after."

Luc's eyebrows rose, but he only said, "Well, this is a good thing."

"A good thing?" Danilo walked quickly around to the otter's side. "Just because I'm white?" There was the chance that the otter understood what had happened between him and Maria and thought it was good that Danilo wasn't gay.

"Perhaps it is not the same in Etrusca. Your family, many of them may have been white?"

Danilo shook his head. "I'm the only one."

"Well, white fur in Tigue—in Gallia—is quite rare. White-furred people are said to be pure, to be touched by God. And so you will be more welcome in the church than…well, than if you were not white, we will leave it there." Luc lowered his voice.

"I thought the Church opened its doors to all." Danilo matched the otter's low tone.

"God opens his doors to all." Luc did not have to continue the comparison, and the way he closed his mouth after saying it told Danilo not to pursue the subject.

So the tiger kept quiet and followed the otter through narrow streets until they reached a small square. To their left stood a small church, five stories tall, above which a pair of spires rose. The left-hand one held a small clock whose hands seemed to indicate the time as a little before nine in the morning, but the hands were the same length and Danilo wasn't sure he was reading them properly. The two spires topped a façade dominated by an elaborate archway over which a carved Lion Christ hung from a cross, his eyes turned up to the heavens. It could have been the same Lion Christ that hung on any old church in his time, the mane shorn, the golden eyes beseeching the heavens; this one was gruesomely detailed, with blood dripping from the nails in the tawny paws and feet, blood from the ring of cuts left from the shearing of the mane, the wound in his side.

Only as he raised his own white paw did Danilo remember that in the story of Jesus rising from the grave, his fur was said to have turned completely white. In 2008, nobody thought that white fur made you particularly sainted; in fact, a common trope of zombie movies was to have the zombies' fur turn white. He wondered if Christians had objected to that at the time, and then those thoughts reminded him that that movie would not be made for hundreds of years, and he looked away from the crucifix and around the small plaza he'd followed Luc into.

Carts of fish and vegetables ringed the open area, and here the din of the merchants calling their wares was deafening. As they entered the square, Danilo and Luc were beseeched on all sides.

"Blessed white sir, come see my flowers—"

"Freshest of carrots—"

"Lettuce, fresh picked lettuce!"

"The square will be quieter once the harvest is past," Luc said, guiding Danilo through the carts. In the center of the square, a statue of a wolf in robes with her head bowed faced the church. All around the square, two-story row houses stood, with brick foundations and wooden walls, and people loitered around them talking. Many of them wore more ragged clothes than Luc and Danilo, and more than one leaned on a crutch, but they talked with a bright, animated spirit regardless.

Luc made directly for the church, where Danilo now saw a sign proclaiming it the "Eglise de Saint-Nizier de Tigue." He tried to repeat those words, but they came out as, "Saint Nizier's Church?"

"Aye." Luc turned. "The school is down the way a bit, but Sister Colquez will be here in the morning."

"Wait," Danilo said, following the otter in beneath the grand archway, through the front doors into a cool, airy space. Pillars rose in front of them; Luc hurried around one to the right side of the church as Danilo said, "Colquez?"

"She teaches young cubs," Luc said. "I was her student for many years."

"But—is she—"

Danilo barely saw the stained glass windows he was passing, or the small alcoves and their mysterious contents, caskets and statues, small bowls and layers of cloth. A figure at the back of the church, bent to extinguish a row of candles, held his eye. Even in the multi-colored reflections of the stained glass rosette, there was no mistaking her long, russet, white-tipped tail.

"Anita?" he blurted out.

Chapter Five

The vixen turned toward them, her muzzle set in a smile that turned to confusion. "Sir, you have the advantage of me." A moment later, she spotted Luc, and her expression relaxed. "Ah, you have learned my name from Monsieur Romain here. But he has not done me the courtesy of telling me yours."

"Danilo." He swallowed. It *was* Anita, the narrow muzzle with the large coal-dust patch, the spot of white amid the red fur over each eye, the darker reddish-brown between her ears, and the Iberian accent to her words. "I—"

He couldn't go on. Luc, who had been looking back and forth between them in confusion, cleared his throat. "Danilo is a young tiger come to us from Etrusca. He was to continue his education here, but he had the misfortune of losing his family's purse on the journey. Danilo, this is Sister Vasquez."

Anita looked at him as his Anita in her time never had, and yet still not the way he'd hoped, or had thought he'd hoped. Her interest was not sexual (that would've been a little weird in a church) but it was a deep fascination. "Tell me, blessed Danilo, what education you sought here in Tigue."

He tried to remember what Luc had said the previous day. "Psych—why people do the things they—Philosophy. That's what it was."

"We do have some of the foremost scholars on interpreting the mind of God." She turned her russet muzzle to catch the light. Danilo caught his breath and almost missed her next words. "But alas, the building of Saint-Jean has cost the Church dearly, and we have been instructed that we are no longer to offer charity. If you cannot pay the school, we cannot provide an education."

Luc stepped forward and rested his paw on Danilo's arm. His fingers brushed Danilo's white fur. "Even for one blessed by God?"

"I see that." Anita sighed. "If he were not a foreigner…"

"Is there nothing you can do?" Luc lowered his voice and entreated her. "For me?"

"You are not what I would call a great friend to the Church." She said it mildly, but firmly.

Luc lowered his head. "Then for my father?"

The vixen's ears lowered. She looked down at the candles and extinguished the last one with a small copper implement. At last, she said, "I will speak to the Bishop and see if there is something that may be done. If blessed Danilo is willing to work in the service of the Church."

"Yes, yes," Danilo said eagerly before he could think, spurred on by his desire to have a job and a place in this city and time. As he spoke, he was aware of the tension in his shoulders. What work would the Church would ask him to perform? Beyond that question lurked the problems of his own struggles with religion, especially around his sexuality. (But was he really attracted to Taye now that he'd slept with a female? Was he attracted to Luc? To Anita?) Beyond that lay Maria's words and Théodore's, all leading to the calculation of a transitive equation of friendship that would question whether Luc, no friend to the Church, would continue to be his friend if he worked for the Church. The hurt of that question gripped him even as he avoided actively considering it.

It was too late to back out anyway. Anita was asking where he was staying, and he didn't know what to say.

"At the Repos du Saint," Luc said.

Anita frowned. "I do not know this place."

Luc was quiet for a moment. His paw dropped from Danilo's arm, and he looked away. "It used to be the Trois Fleches Dorees."

She fixed Luc with a stern gaze. "Bertrand's place. You are still there?" When he nodded, she sighed. "You must leave."

"To go where? Live in the square with those people?" He waved a paw toward the door. "Bertrand is rough, yes, but he is not a brute."

"No? Well, perhaps miracles do arrive."

Danilo's thoughts, now worrying about Luc and Bertrand, skipped at that word and jumped to a completely different track. "Anita—Sister Vasquez—what do you know about miracles?"

She frowned, and her ears flicked to the sides in exactly the way his Anita's did when she was trying to solve a problem. "Our Lord performed miracles to inspire people's faith. He fed the poor, turned water to wine…"

"We could use some of those miracles these days." Luc looked past her to the stained glass, which sparkled in muted green and blue. Below it the Lion Christ gazed beseechingly out at the rest of the church.

"But I mean, were there signs when they happened? The people all knew that it was God performing a miracle, right? They weren't just drinking wine and all of a sudden it was—I mean, water, and it suddenly turned into—God told them while the miracle was happening, right?"

Anita's dark eyes studied him. "Do you believe you have experienced a miracle?"

"Maybe?" Danilo breathed in the stillness and felt the weight of stone and age upon him. To claim to be the subject of a miracle in this house of God now felt like the height of hubris to him. "I mean, something strange happened—when I lost my money—but nobody appeared and said 'this is a miracle.' Are miracles—do miracles always make something good happen?"

"You would want to ask the Bishop," she said. "He is far more learned in the gospels and histories of Our Lord than am I. He would be the authority on what constitutes a miracle."

"Not the Archbishop?" Luc's tone was sour. "He proclaimed the completion of Saint-Jean a miracle."

"Nobody sees the Archbishop. I mean, none of us do." Anita looked shocked that Luc would even suggest such a thing.

"I know some people who do." Luc muttered it very low.

Though Anita's ears perked, she appeared to understand that the words were not meant for her, and she did not respond to them. Instead she turned to Danilo. "Blessed Danilo, if you would return tomorrow at this time, I will hope to have good news for you."

"All right. I mean, thank you, Sister Vasquez." It was still unsettling for him to see Anita in a religious habit, speaking to him so formally, so he was not entirely unhappy to take his leave of her. Still, as he walked out of the church and back into the square, he had the sensation of leaving behind a link, however tenuous, to his own time.

He turned to look at her, but standing in the bright sunlight, Anita's form inside the darker church was no more than a shadow.

"She is lovely." Luc smiled up at him. "I know at least two young foxes who were sorely disappointed by her choice to serve the Church."

"Yeah," Danilo said, thinking of Anita helping him with his medieval studies homework. "She's—she's great."

The otter stopped at a stall, looked longingly at the food, and then walked on. "Well, you must stay with me for one more night. You may go back to Bertrand's if you like, but be cautious if you do and enter by the back. I will discuss your lodging with him when I return, but before then, I have an appointment to keep." He tilted his head upward, squinted at the sun. "I should leave shortly to arrive by Terce, I think."

"What's Terce?"

Bells had begun to ring from St. Nizier, echoed elsewhere around the city. Luc pointed a finger upward. "That is Prime. Terce is the next you will hear." His brow furrowed. "Are the bells so different in Etrusca?"

Danilo inspected the stone buildings, wooden signs, and everything he could see that did not require him to meet Luc's questioning look. "Do you think I could just walk around the city while you are away?"

"You needn't ask my permission." Luc smiled and swiveled his pointing finger toward the river. "I would stay on this side of the river, if I were you. LeSevre's men patrol more frequently around the river and over there."

"All right." And Danilo walked with Luc to the end of the street, where the otter said his appointment was the other way. He left Danilo with another admonition to see the cathedral and to stay out of trouble, and Danilo promised to do his best.

Walking past the shops and market stalls, the people hurrying along in their duties, all so sure of their place, all of them belonging here, his homesickness returned, as did the rumbling in his stomach. If he had money, at least he could go into a shop and buy a loaf of the incredible-smelling bread, or a lump of cheese or meat (he passed a store with hams hanging in the windows and stood staring at it for a moment). But there was nothing he could do save walk hungrily back along the street.

He did once see a small fox clutching a bread roll, running toward him as angry shouts followed. But the fox cub was gone before Danilo could move, and nobody else moved to intercept him (or her). The baker, when Danilo reached his store, was an older wolf who did not seem particularly upset, as though it was his job merely to yell and carry on when the cub stole a piece of his bread.

The rolls were just sitting by the door, and Danilo was tempted, but the wolf did stand right beside them. Danilo thought he could outrun the old baker, but how many white tigers were there in Tigue? He would be spotted blocks away, described to the garde (*and LeSevre*). So he pressed a paw over his stomach and walked on.

His feet crunched over stones and dust, fragments of wood and clods of dirt. Around him, the stone buildings with their red-tiled roofs were tantalizingly familiar, and even the lack of street signs might be explained away if Danilo imagined he had stumbled into a meticulously preserved Old Town of Tigue. The food sold in the markets, after all, was much the same. Though he tried to resist it, his mind told him again and again as it had the previous day that just around the next corner he would find street signs and metal grates in front of stores, pharmacies that sold sanitizer and antibiotics, an ATM and cars and electric lights, and he hurried up to the corner only to encounter the same dirty streets and people, the hazy, smelly air, the old stone and pitted wood.

All his false hope had fled by the time he came to the street he'd walked down behind Luc and Théodore a day ago. He tried to raise his spirits by remembering Maria. Perhaps she would be free, and perhaps she would want to take him back to her room again. That appetite, at least, he could sate for free, and would take a little time— more time than last time, he hoped.

His body appeared to approve of the idea, so he glanced at the cathedral, now gleaming in the noonday sun, and turned his back to it to hurry back to Bertrand's. The idea of sex with the plump wolf had become a full-blown fantasy by the time he arrived back at the restaurant, a daydream in which Maria swooned to see him, fell into his arms, and proceeded to yip and howl with pleasure as he made love to her like none other had ever done. The dream was so powerful that he even forgot his current troubles as he burst through the front door of the restaurant and looked around, expecting Maria to be there waiting.

Only a crowd of patrons turned to look as he stood there in the doorway. Many stared; others, who'd likely seen him the night before, turned back to their meals almost immediately. Bertrand himself looked up from a table where he'd deposited a tray of bread and cheese, and his thick black brow lowered over the white-striped muzzle. "No! No no no! Out, halfie! You are to be gone."

Now people were looking up again, and Danilo's awkwardness returned with the force of a spring thunderstorm. He curled his tail around his leg. "I'm just going to get my things," he said. "Where's Maria? I—I gave her something I need back."

"You can't put that back in, youngster," someone at a table called, and the room erupted in laughter. Bertrand did not join in, but looked positively murderous.

"Out with you!" he roared. "One brings in many, like fleas, they say, and how am I repaid for my kindness? With this infestation! First the other, then you—no, no, no! Out!"

"I have to get my clothes!" Danilo cried, and when Bertrand did not object immediately, Danilo, ears back, fled upstairs.

Few of the patrons were about, and none in the hallway as Danilo ran along it, frantic to get his things and get out, Maria forgotten. Only when he was standing in the room he'd shared with Luc did he realize that he didn't have any clothes to get, nor any other possessions. Everything he owned in this world was one pair of boxer shorts, which he was wearing.

Already his breath was coming back and his tail was uncurling. He didn't want to wait here in the inn, not with Bertrand downstairs. But he also didn't want to just wander around the city aimlessly, just waiting on Anita to secure a meeting with the Bishop that might or might not happen. If he could just find the Bishop himself, there had to be some way Danilo could impress him. He had five hundred years of extra knowledge. He knew about mobile phones and electricity and a little astronomy.

Of course, most science would be viewed as heresy in these times. Well, there was always history.

Not that the Bishop would be much interested in who the Kings of Anglia would be in three hundred years even if he were inclined to believe anything Danilo said. And knowing that the world was round—another heresy; the Spanish wolf Colombe was only just returning or maybe was already on his way back to the New World—would benefit him little.

But... He paused. He could read and write and he knew mathematics. Maybe he'd been aiming too high. What passed for a basic education in Anglia could be impressive here in the Dark Ages. Maybe all he would need to do would be to read a few words, write a few more, and he would be deemed worthy to work at the church. Yes, that seemed like the best and easiest plan.

So he would seek out the Bishop himself. Probably the best place to do that was at the recently finished cathedral; if he was anywhere, he would be there. Danilo only wished he had better clothes to wear.

Glancing down at the chest, he saw Luc's beige scarf resting there. He could wear it, if Luc was not; after all, everything else he wore belonged to the otter, and it might help him fit in better.

He picked up the cloth and draped it about his neck. There were no mirrors in the room, but he hoped it gave him a jaunty, confident look as it had Luc. And he would be back here tonight—he would sleep on the floor this time—and Luc would make it right with Bertrand somehow. Danilo just had to avoid the badger until then.

He slipped out the back, again hoping to see Maria, again disappointed. Seline was working in one of the rooms he passed, though. "Hello," he said.

The rabbit looked up. "Good day." He couldn't even tell whether she recognized him. She held a ragged broom, with which she swept around a floor that looked identical to the one in Luc's room: wooden boards littered with a straw bed, a chest, and a chamber pot.

Danilo cleared his throat. "Do you know where Maria is?"

Seline stopped sweeping and raised an eyebrow. "She works at the rag-merchant mending clothes in the mornings. Is there something you require?"

Require, no. Danilo swallowed, and Seline shook her head. "Do not grow attached to Maria. I can assure you that she has not grown attached to you."

"I didn't—I mean, I wasn't—"

"Hah." Seline did not smile as she thrust the broom at him. "Here. Hold this while I carry the chamber pot."

Only as they reached the base of the stairs did it occur to Danilo that the gallant thing would have been to carry the reeking pot for her. But Seline emptied it in the outhouse with professional efficiency, where Danilo was sure he would have spilled it all over his paws, which would be a disaster without any antibacterial soap. Seline rinsed out the pot under the pump and then took the broom back from him. "Did you wish to follow me in my work all afternoon?"

"Er...no, I guess..." He lowered his head.

"Whatever you do, work vigorously, as for the Lord. I wish you luck." She turned away.

"Seline?" He didn't know why he wanted to prolong the conversation, but her companionship had been comforting; maybe that was all. When she turned, her large ears facing him, he said, "How would I get to the cathedral?"

She raised her eyebrows higher, and her mouth parted to show her large front incisors before she spoke even a word. "You keep it always in your sight and you walk toward it. When you come to the river, go to the bridge."

"Okay. Thank you."

This seemed to disconcert her; she turned and walked inside without another word. Danilo scratched behind his ear, confused, and then took stock of the back. He had assumed that he would be able to slip out a back door in the fence (Luc had told him to go in through the back, he now remembered with a blush of shame), but as he scanned it, no gaps appeared to his eyes. There was nothing for it but to go back through the restaurant.

Some of the diners turned to look at him, but Bertrand, though he growled, did not say anything, probably because Danilo was moving quickly toward the exit. He got to the door and out into the street, where the cathedral rose up before him, far beyond the wooden houses and red clay roofs of the city around him. He took a breath and began walking toward it.

With the sun higher, the city streets warmed below his paws, and the smells of the city assaulted him with renewed vigor. Down one street, piles of refuse created a miasma that everyone avoided; down another, the smells of fresh cheese competed with the tinge of rancid milk. At least he did not feel self-conscious about the linger-ing remnants of river odor in his fur, walking through the crowds of musky, unbathed Tiguans. But he watched the clothing around him, listened to how people talked and what they talked about, and at least tried to apply what little he'd actually studied of psychology.

When people talked to each other, most often he heard about the weather, food, or health, and always God was a part of it. "God's sent us a fine day," a rabbit said to her companion. "God willing the wheat hasn't mouldered," a fox carrying a sack over his shoulder said to another fox he met in the street—a brother, perhaps. "God keep you," he heard upon many partings.

Danilo practiced some of the phrases to himself, repeating them over and over. He wasn't used to mentioning God at all, let alone every other sentence, and Luc and Théodore had used the Lord's name sparingly as well, but if he were to be working with the Church, this might be a useful habit to acquire. He murmured to himself, "God willing," and "God grant it," and "thanks to God," and looked up to find himself at the edge of a busy street, where horses pulled carts in both directions and people scampered between them. And on the other side of the street lay the Saône.

Danilo made his way over to the riverbank and looked down. In the daylight, the water still appeared a murky, ugly brown. As he watched, a weasel lugged a sack to the edge and emptied its contents into the river—garbage, not a body, Danilo was relieved to see. The weasel hurried back and out of sight, but his or her actions were being repeated at several points along the bank.

The only bridge visible spanned the river about a half kilometer to Danilo's left—quarter mile, he chided himself. They didn't have the metric system in 1508. Between here and there, stairs led down to the bank: the stairs he'd climbed with Luc and Théodore yester-day. (Was it only yesterday?) He walked slowly toward them, keeping an eye on the river, as if perhaps someone else from his time might emerge from it.

That, he thought, would be the second-best thing to actually going back to 2008. To have company, someone else as bewildered as he was to whom he could serve as guide, someone else who might have an idea of how to get back to the year they belonged in. But though he kept close watch, nobody else emerged gasping from the thick brown sludge of the river.

The stones of the bridge looked old, which Danilo accepted as natural until he remembered, again, that he was five hundred years in the past. How old must this bridge be? A hundred years? Two hundred? It must have been rebuilt many times, of course, and would be many times more; none of these actual stones would exist in his time. He walked across, wondering how skilled ancient bridge-builders were, but the bridge held. Partway across, he stopped and stared down. If he were to jump in, would he drown? Would he re-emerge in 2008?

He would have to try it. It was his only clue to how this had happened, and apart from asking the Bishop about miracles, he had no other ideas about how to get back. But he would not jump in broad daylight, and not from the height of a bridge. As if to underscore this decision, the cathedral bells tolled, drawing his attention back to the shining colossus. He left off looking down and made his way to the opposite bank.

Here, fewer buildings blocked the view of the cathedral, which in consequence looked even more magnificent as Danilo approached. It towered over the city, gleaming white in the sun with gold atop its decorative spires, the immense building almost large enough to stretch from the riverbank to the foot of Fourvière hill. When he rounded the corner and the front came into view, Danilo stopped to stare.

The two magnificent towers were integrated into one broad, solid face at the front of the building. Between the towers, a triangular section of the wall rose to a point topped by a cross, and below that, the rosette bloomed, a marvelous construction of narrow stone and colored glass. All of the reliefs strained upward, from the pointed arches over the wide front doors to the small point between the two towers, topped by a golden cross. Gargoyles and other decorations studded the corners and ledges, far more elaborate than at St. Nizier's. In fact, everything about the Cathedral Saint-Jean was at least twice as large, and St. Nizier's was not a small church.

Danilo had visited the cathedral in his century, or at least he had walked around it with Taye. Here (*now*), though he recognized the structure and reliefs, the surroundings transformed the Saint-Jean of

1508 into a much grander edifice. The neighboring buildings, smaller and plainer, contributed to this effect, but even more of Saint-Jean's grandeur came from the reverence people showed while passing. In his time, to gawk at the cathedral was the province of tourists, while locals and jaded college students admired it with a much more world-weary air: this is lovely, of course, but have you seen the cathedral at Cartes-Belles? And of course there is Notre-Dame de Lutèce, and then Beckett's and the Abbey in Anglia...

Here in 1508, probably none of the people here had seen another building this majestic in their lives. That was plain even when they weren't looking at it. People entering the plaza often crossed themselves, and walked more slowly than they did on the other streets of Tigue. Danilo, caught in the crowd, matched their pace, and much as forcing a smile can make one a little happier, slowing his pace instilled in him some of the awe the people around him felt.

Only the large front doors were open, and only a small amount. There might be services going on inside; Danilo couldn't tell, because the plaza outside the church was filled with buskers and beggars, calling out loudly and reaching out with grimy paws as he walked past them. Danilo edged away, copying the example of the other people who walked by without acknowledging them.

Not everyone did, though. Here and there, a rabbit in a clean white robe walked with a basket of bread giving pieces to the homeless, and not far behind her, a mouse in a similar robe carried a jug of water and a cup, which he filled and offered to each beggar in turn. Large, visible wood crosses hung around their necks. Was this the work he would be doing for the church? Ministering to the homeless and destitute?

The thought filled him with dread; here in the sixteenth century, the homeless were not merely unwashed and ill-clothed. Here a fox stared up out of a single milky-white eye, a gruesome scar where the other had been, his fur greying, one ear little more than a nubbly mass of scar tissue; there a deer sat reaching out with his one arm, one leg curled under him, dirty cloths wrapped around the stumps of the other arm and leg and a crutch beside him; farther along, a pair of weasels sat on a filthy cloth, their fur falling out in patches, dried blood showing on the white throats and chest of both.

Danilo dithered, fascinated by the horrible sights and unsure whether he could simply walk into the great cathedral; nobody else was, though a few appeared to be waiting. After a few moments, the doors opened and a small group of people—two wolves, a sheep, a mouse, and a weasel—walked out, talking quietly among themselves. The wolves crossed themselves as they left.

More people began to stream out, and those Danilo were with began to drift toward the doors. A plainly-dressed rat walked boldly in past the exiting crowd, and Danilo followed his lead. He slid through the doors, stepped forward, and looked up.

Gothic arches rose impossibly high above him, continuing down the nave to the crossing and the transept. Near midday, the sun lit both east and west faces, so the apse and small rosette Danilo faced, far at the eastern end, shone almost as brightly as the rosette over his head. Stained-glass saints looked down on him, tiger and fox, wolf and deer, sheep and otter. On the lower story of the cathedral, the stained glass sparkled in kaleidoscope patterns.

Before him, rows of polished oak pews stretched, many still occupied with kneeling figures. Around them, people gathered in small groups, conversing. As Danilo stood, blinking his eyes in the surprisingly bright cathedral, the people nearest him fell silent. They watched him walk around to one side of the church, and then their conversation resumed in his wake. He was certain they were talking about him, that somehow he had made a mistake that showed he didn't belong here.

Yesterday that would have sent him into a crippling spiral of anxiety. Today there was so much else occupying his mind that he told himself it was merely that he was an unusual color and species, and lost himself in the grandeur of the cathedral. Coming from the simple buildings outside, Danilo couldn't stop himself from touching the marble and marveling at its smoothness. Because the cathedral looked almost the same as it had in 2008 (only much newer), if Danilo looked only at the walls, the glass, the reliefs, he could imagine that he was back in his own time, strolling through the cathedral, that the people around him held cameras instead of rosaries, that the smoky smell in the air was from the candles lit all around rather than nearby fires, that the strong smells of the people around him were simply tourists who hadn't bathed. He barely noticed the roughness

of the tunic on his fur now; it might be a cheap shirt he'd bought on sale.

The one place where the knot of people did not disperse drew him halfway down the church, because towering over the people at a height of maybe ten meters was the clock.

Above the crowd of people, the clock faces showed ten minutes to noon. Elaborate sculptures rose above the clock, figures standing around and below a carved archway on each side of the column. High above, as though it were a real tower made for two-foot-high people, a bronze cupola rose, and atop that, a smaller cupola.

He took a step toward it and then movement drew his attention to the front of the church, twenty meters away. There the priest stood, a slow-moving fox in black robes with a stole around his neck. He was speaking to two people and then gestured behind him, where a figure in white robes emerged from the shadows to stand in the light of the rosette.

Danilo's breath caught in his chest. The figure towered over the fox, and the white of the robe caught the light, so the black-furred muzzle was difficult to distinguish. But his black tail was a wolf's tail, and then a cloud went over the sun and the light on his robe dimmed just as he turned and his bright yellow-green eyes met Danilo's across the church.

The wolf looked down again almost immediately. His paw landed on the priest's shoulder, and he laughed, as demurely as befitted a member of the clergy. Danilo stared at him a moment longer and then stepped backwards, or tried to; the crowd around the clock had thickened as people moved toward it. He struggled and managed to move around behind the clock, telling himself he was being stupid. It wasn't Georg. There must be a hundred black wolves; he'd seen one on the way here, he remembered, and that one hadn't been Georg. This one was far away; that was all.

But perhaps seeing a maybe-familiar muzzle in a church brought back his worries from the morning and his conversation with Anita. He tried to push his way backwards, and a rabbit elbowed him. "Leaving before noon? Come, stay, it's a marvel."

Of course the clock would do something special at noon. Danilo vaguely recalled it from his tour of the city, one of those "we'll have to come back at the right time later" kind of things. But here it would be something truly special—perhaps miraculous.

Five minutes to go. While waiting, he studied the sculptures. An angel, a fox or wolf with wings and a kindly expression, held an hourglass. A rabbit and a deer, above that angel, stood near bells, and a third angel around the front held a small wand. High above, in the cupola, Danilo thought there might be other figures, but the shadows hid them from his gaze.

Around him, people talked amongst themselves, and sometimes his ears caught words like "white tiger," but the conversations ebbed and flowed, and when someone said, "a disgrace," he didn't know if it was about him any more than the person who said, "a wonder," or "inspired by God." Though that person was most likely talking about the clock.

Danilo wished he had someone to talk to. Taye, or Orwin, or his sister...but that road threatened to remind him of his past—his future—and undermine his calm. So he looked around, smiled politely at the people who met his eye, and then stared ahead with everyone else as the clock whirred and the cathedral fell silent.

The angel holding the hourglass moved, turned the glass over in its paws. The angel around the front, a badger, waved its wand, and the rabbit and deer angels began to strike the bells. A carol, not one Danilo recognized, but he was entranced by the display. After just a day cut off from modern technologies, the whirring figures on the clock felt marvelous to him. He knew about clockwork, of course, but automated machinery felt as though it should be still three centuries away, at least.

A panel opened, and another angel emerged, waving to the crowd. Someone next to Danilo pointed up, and he lifted his head to the cupolas. From the topmost, a dove descended along a track, and the fact that he could see the track didn't make it any less magical. Gasps and prayers filled the air around him, growing when the cupola below the dove opened to reveal a bed of clouds and a leonine figure in white robes blessing the people below Him.

The opening was toward the front of the clock, around the side from where Danilo was. Craning his neck to see it, along with those around him, he noticed the white-robed black wolf, watching the clock as intently as everyone else. The tiger ducked back, watching the automatons move and then fall still as the carol ended and the twelve chimes of noon began.

They came from the clock, echoed by the cathedral bells above. A fox next to Danilo flattened her ears; her cub put paws over his. The sound of each toll reverberated through his bones, and he could think of nothing but counting to make sure there were twelve of them. His tail curled and uncurled and he lifted his head to the clock, which had stopped moving. God remained with his paws out-stretched, the dove remained below, and the crowd held its breath through the twelve strokes. Here was a moment that Danilo felt was frozen in time, and stronger than ever was the feeling that if he shut his eyes, let the bells fill him, he might open his eyes again and find himself surrounded by cameras, designer clothes, electronic wiring.

But when he opened his eyes, no guardrail kept the crowd away from the clock, and the people around him smelled just as bad pressed together, and the marble and limestone in the church still gleamed brightly. The clouds had moved away from the sun, so both rosettes glowed, filling the church with light.

Many people around him were crossing themselves, so Danilo did the same and shuffled out with them, keeping an eye over his shoulder for the wolf. The last he saw, the white-robed figure was on his way back to the altar, black tail held still and arched behind him.

Outside in the plaza, the beggars and buskers and low stone buildings surrounded him again, and before him rose Fourvière Hill, looking bare without the Basilica and the Metal Tower. Only low grey stone topped the hill, but it looked close and there were now two paths he could see to the top. Better yet, there were no people up there. Maybe this would be a good time to go up and investigate the ruins, get away from the tantalizing smells of the food he couldn't have, away from the people who reminded him of his peculiar situation, and just look around. Maybe, he thought as he set out, he could find some old Roman coins and trade for a loaf of bread to bring back to Luc. That would make him feel useful. That would be something he could—

An arm seized his. He turned and saw a weasel, a foot shorter than him, staring up with sharp eyes and teeth bared. "You think I didn't see you leaving the church?" he said.

Danilo tried to pull away, but the other held fast. "What?"

"You came out of Saint-Jean." The weasel pushed him back toward one of the wooden buildings. The smell of lye tickled Danilo's nose. "Don't try to deny it."

"I'm not. I was looking at the clock. I was—" He lifted his head to the passing crowd, trying to meet someone's eyes. Nobody came to his aid. The people who did raise their heads looked away again quickly.

"Aye." The weasel's paw shot toward Danilo's neck. The tiger flinched, but the paw grabbed only Luc's scarf. "That's why you wear this." The weasel pulled it free and brandished it, snarling to show off a row of yellowed, blackened, and missing teeth. His sour breath assaulted Danilo's nose.

Danilo gaped. "That?"

"Not yours, is it? Where did you get it? From Coumier?" The weasel brought the scarf to his nose and his eyes narrowed. "Otter. Who is it, church bastard?"

"Luc?" A pressure at Danilo's stomach; he looked down to see a short blade in the weasel's other paw, its point snagging his tunic. His voice rose an octave. "Luc's a mate, a friend of mine, he, he gave it to me."

Now the point pressed in farther, against his skin. He retreated and found himself against a house, the smell of lye growing stronger. His eyes traveled up past the weasel to the cathedral. Was it possible that people were killed here in the shadow of God's miracle?

"'Gave it,' hah." The weasel stepped forward again. "Just get yourself back in that alley and we'll have the truth of it. You've taken this 'Luc,' have you?"

"Taken? I don't know—" Danilo stepped backwards under the force of the weasel's blade and then realized that if he stepped out of public view, that would be the end of things pretty quickly.

The end of things. He would *die*. If this were a hallucination, that might mean he could wake up in his own time. But…if he weren't hallucinating or dreaming, or even if he were, he might really die. The blade, the weasel's presence and his foul breath, all this felt very real. He wasn't willing to wager his life on a maybe, and he certainly wasn't giving up enough to let himself die.

Along with this realization came the dawning understanding that he outweighed the weasel by at least fifty pounds, and even if he weren't the most athletic of tigers—of any kind of people—he could probably shove a weasel down and run away.

The knife point tore through the tunic, poked into his flesh with a sharp, galvanizing pain. "Go on," the weasel hissed.

Danilo took one more desperate look around. Nobody was paying him any attention. He had nowhere to turn for help but inside.

Instead of stepping backwards, he lurched forward, trying to go around the knife. Pressure stopped him, as though he'd snagged his tunic; a moment later he felt a sear of pain. Still, the weasel was taken by surprise and staggered back, and Danilo helped him all the way to the ground with a shove to his shoulder. A moment later, he was sprinting across the plaza, heart pounding, fists clenched, his side burning.

Go and explore the city, indeed! What had he been thinking? He shouldn't have taken Luc's scarf, but how was he to know it was something special? And what was that weasel going on about, with the church and everything? It was all too confusing, and as he ran, now people took notice of him, with calls of "Ho, slow down there," and "what's on your tail, son?"

He slowed but didn't stop, not all the way back to the bridge, where he hurried to the middle and stayed there, watching the end. He could see the weasel coming from here, and he would know if he were being chased any farther.

Of course, he remembered as he saw his paws on the railing, there weren't many white tigers in Tigue. The weasel was going to find him again whether he waited here on the bridge or walked up to the ruins or went back to the Repos. Hell, he stood half a foot taller than most people here anyway—stupid twenty-first century food and medicine.

As the minutes passed and no weasel appeared at the end of the bridge (at least, none brandishing a beige scarf), Danilo's breathing evened. He spared glances again for the Saône below him and the cathedral's majestic walls, stained glass, and towers. How could it proclaim God's mercy when he could be nearly killed just outside it, when he felt safer here on the bridge than right next to God's house? He put a paw to the sore spot on his stomach where the knife had stuck him out of reflex, but that proved to be a mistake. At the slippery touch of blood on his fingertips, his head spun and his paws shook and he had to grip the railing.

Only hunger, he told himself, only hunger, because if he had a panic attack here in the middle of Tigue, he wasn't sure he would be able to recover from it. He needed to get food, somehow. He could work in another kitchen to pay for a meal; did someone just walk in and offer to work for food? He hadn't heard bells ring again, so it wasn't Terce yet, unless Terce meant noon? Would Luc be back? He didn't know where to find Théodore, or anyone else who might do him a kindness...

Wait. There was someone in this city who was well-disposed toward him, and he knew where she was.

Chapter Six

St. Nizier's remained as he had left it, quiet and sedate. Anita—Sister Colquez—was not in evidence when Danilo arrived, but he poked his head around and soon found her in the back of the church. "Hello," she said. "The Etruscan student. I'm sorry, your name escapes me."

"Danilo." He smiled. His Anita had taken a week to remember his name, too.

She inclined her head. "I have not had an audience with the Bishop yet. I expect to see him this evening."

"No, I know." His stomach rumbled, and he placed a paw across it. "It's only that—well, you know Luc. He doesn't have a lot of money, and I don't have any, and I'm—we're both very hungry. Only he won't ask for money..." Why would people not ask for money? Maybe Luc had a prior relationship with Anita? How well did she know him? He started to tell her Luc was too proud, and then realized that she probably knew the otter better than he did. "Well, you know him," he finished lamely.

"I do." She did not smile. "I have tried to help him in the past, but he refuses any assistance."

"I was hoping to help him myself." Danilo didn't want to ask her directly, and honestly he had been thinking to ask if she knew of a place where he could earn some money quickly.

Anita forestalled him, beckoning for him to follow her. "That is very generous of you. I admit that it pains my soul to see him suffer so. Anything I may do to help, I will, but he makes things for himself very difficult."

He padded behind her along the back of the church to a small office marked "Sacristy." Anita withdrew a heavy key and unlocked the wooden door, bidding him wait outside while she entered, still talking. "I know that he took his father's death badly, but—well, how well do you know Luc?"

"Not very." Danilo looked politely aside at the stained glass windows, which here looked like children had designed them after the grand, rich windows of Saint-Jean. "I only met him when I came to town yesterday."

"You had not corresponded with him before your arrival?" Her narrow muzzle poked back into view, ears half down. "I had supposed…"

"No. He rescued me when I fell into the Saône." Danilo ducked his head. Falling into a river, in any century, was the move of an idiot.

Anita, as gracious in this century as in his, said nothing about that part of it. "Luc is a very generous fellow, but he has little to be generous with, these days."

"Taye—Théodore didn't want to rescue me. Luc and he argued about it."

He dropped Taye's name intentionally. Taye and Anita knew each other only through him in 2008; he wondered if they knew each other here.

"Luc has been told by many of his friends that he should keep some of his generosity for himself." She reappeared and closed the door behind her. "Here. Take this and buy food, bring it to him."

He held out his paw; she dropped three coins into it. Danilo turned over the two copper and one silver pieces, both worn, but saw no numbers on them. "Er…I'm sorry, but how much should these buy? I don't know the money here."

"Of course." She smiled. "One loaf of bread, a brick of cheese. That should feed the two of you for a day."

"Thank you so much." The still atmosphere reminded Danilo of everyone's mentions of God. "God bless you," he added.

"God keep you," she replied. "I hope that we will be seeing more of each other."

"Me too." He closed his fist around the coins, preparing to leave, but another thought struck him. "Sister? If you wouldn't mind, can you tell me something of why Luc is in such trouble?"

Her ears flattened, and her eyes lowered. "It is not my place to say." She began to walk away, her tail down.

"I only want to know if I can help." Danilo hurried after her.

She shook her head. "Pray for him. 'Confess your sins to each other and pray for each other so that you may be healed. The prayer of a righteous soul is powerful and effective.'" She smiled.

It sounded like a Bible verse, but Danilo did not know which one. He nodded. "Right. Like it says in Scripture."

Her ears remained flat, and he felt she expected more of him, but she said only, "Your friendship is important. If you can guide him along the proper path…at least if he does not repeat his sin against the Church…"

"What sin?" Danilo said, and then regretted it, because Anita turned away and shook her head, and he thought he knew what the sin was anyway. He swallowed his question and bowed. "I will buy him lunch and I—I will pray for his soul."

Money in paw, he hurried from the church and to the first boulangerie he found. There he bought a long baguette loaf, which cost him one copper coin, and asked for directions to a cheese shop. In the cheese shop, he traded his silver coin for a block of deliciously fragrant cheese that made his mouth water. He had nowhere to put the remaining copper coin, so he held it with the baguette as he walked back to the Repos.

The smell was too much for his stomach. Before he got five steps, he was already tearing a piece from the end of the loaf. The bread was delicious, better even than the bread he'd had the previous night: crunchy and warm, soft inside and warmer still. At the first bite, his stomach erupted in a riotous chorus of rumbling, as though it had forgotten what food was like until this moment and demanded more of it. Danilo took two more bites of the bread before arriving back at the Repos.

Across the street from the familiar doors, he stopped. He couldn't go back in, not until he was sure Luc would be there to smooth things over with Bertrand. But he couldn't just sit down in the street and wait for Luc, and anyway, what if Bertrand came out front and saw him? He scanned the area and saw, halfway down one of the streets from the intersection, a small grassy area with stone slabs upon which some people sat. He hurried down that way and found an empty spot.

He'd been intending to wait for Luc before eating, but the smell of the cheese proved too much for him. He broke it in half and

devoured half of it with the rest of his half of the baguette; the meager meal was gone within minutes.

His stomach clamored for more, but not so strongly that he
couldn't ignore it. The other half of this was meant for Luc, and he
would resist his baser urges to make sure the otter got it. Otherwise
he would be a terrible friend, and he would have taken money under
false pretenses from a nun, which he was pretty sure was some kind
of terrible sin against God, and not the right move for someone who
wanted to become a student in the church. Or even someone who
was going to become a student in the church, whether he wanted to
or not.

A person plopped down beside him, and reached for the
baguette. "Give us a bite, I'm starving."

He pulled the baguette away, and then recognized Taye—
Théodore. The mouse held his paw out patiently. "We did pull you
from the Saône yesterday, did we not?"

He had the same ingratiating smile that Taye put on when he
tried to get Danilo to do something for him. It was weird; the confrontation with Bertrand yesterday had almost erased Danilo's connection between Taye and Théodore. The mouse had been nothing
like Taye when he'd sat down, and then one turn, one expression, and
there was Danilo's friend again. "Luc did," Danilo said, but held the
baguette out to the mouse. "I got this for him, so don't eat all of it."

"No, no." Théodore took the baguette and ripped off a good
quarter of what was left. "Is that cheese I smell?"

Luc was smaller than he was, Danilo reasoned, so if he'd had half
the bread and cheese, and Théodore had a third of what was left, then
Luc would still have enough for a meal, and anyway it would be better than nothing. "Have you seen Luc?" he asked as Théodore sliced
the cheese with his knife.

"Just left him an hour ago." The mouse's lips stretched into a
smile. Taye's smile had been less tense, but just as bright. "He's off to
visit a friend and then said he'd come back. Asked me to come look
after you. Said you'd be staying in Tigue, not heading up north."

"That was nice of him. I'm doing all right, though." Danilo
recounted their meeting with Sister Colquez in the morning. "I hope
tomorrow I will have work in the Church so I may continue my
studies."

"Better you than I," Théodore muttered, so low Danilo could barely hear it.

"Why?" the tiger asked, his tail curling around behind him.

Théodore shook his head. "What did you see in Tigue after you left Luc?"

"I went to the Cathedral Saint-Jean and saw the clock."

"Ah, indeed. A marvel, is it not?"

Danilo nodded. "It's…miraculous," he said, searching for words. "Truly inspired by God."

Théodore did not seem as enthusiastic about that attribution as the visitors in the cathedral had been. He broke the baguette open and arranged the slices of cheese inside. "God's inspiration is…" he trailed off and then took a bite of his sandwich and chewed noisily.

"Something odd happened, though." The mouse had been wearing a beige scarf yesterday, too, though today he was not. Danilo told him about the weasel outside the church, and as soon as he mentioned the scarf, Théodore's head snapped around and his eyes locked on the tiger's.

"You wore the scarf into Saint-Jean? Who told you to do that?"

"N-nobody." Danilo cringed back. The mouse's demeanor had changed in an instant; the sandwich was held lazily in one paw as a slice of cheese protruded from the bread, the mouse's full attention on Danilo.

"Did Luc tell you to take the scarf?"

"No! I just saw it there, I thought it looked nice. I thought it was fashionable."

Théodore searched his eyes and then relaxed back on the bench. The slice of cheese fell to the ground, but the mouse didn't notice. "Fashionable! By Saint Pothinus, you've a guardian angel looking after you, that's for certain. So what happened with this weasel?"

Danilo told him, and the mouse chuckled. "Ah, that's Armand. Quicker with a knife than his wits, that one." He moved Danilo's arm aside. "Let's have a look at that side. Does it hurt still?"

"You know him?" Danilo's voice rose, and he almost squeaked.

"Only in passing. We met a time or two last year. It's healthy to be vigilant, but that one sleeps with both eyes open." Théodore lifted the edge of Danilo's tunic and probed with fingers at the wound.

"Ow! Are you a—" He tried to say 'doctor,' but the word came out as "surgeon."

"Ha." The mouse's fingers brushed the edge of the wound, and now pain danced in their wake. "I've bound my share of wounds, though. No, this one doesn't appear to be deep. I fought with worse than that."

"You fought?"

"Aye, at Cerignola and Garigiano. But if you are from Etrusca, you must know of those."

"Oh, er. Of course." Danilo waved a paw. "I had heard of them, but my family is from a—a different part."

"Which part?"

The mouse spoke casually as he picked his cheese up off the ground and brushed it off before replacing it in his bread, but the question tensed Danilo's fists again. His claws extended and he flicked his tail to the side away from the mouse. "Oh—Firenza," he said.

"Mmm." Théodore nodded. "We were south of Firenza, but passed through there on our retreat. Well, I suppose it's as well you have not heard much of those battles. Our armies did not shine so well in them. Truth be told, there was more retreating than fighting done at Garigiano anyway."

"I'm sorry," Danilo said, though he didn't know why.

"Bah. Betimes it is the wisest course. Stay and fight and be destroyed, or retreat and lick your wounds, live another day?" The mouse finished his small sandwich and turned to grin at Danilo. "You should have that wound washed, but you'll live, I would say. It may not even scar."

"Thanks." The tiger relaxed, and impressed on his memory that he was from Firenza. He'd visited there with his father and seen the Duomo and Michaelangelo's David, though…that would not have been made yet, would it? He was fairly sure Michaelangelo was in the 1600s sometime.

Théodore inclined his head. "I will remonstrate with Armand when next I see him. I am certain he was assured of doing the proper thing."

The "proper thing" was threatening to kill someone? "What does the scarf mean, if I may ask?"

The mouse considered, and then shook his head. "Better that you do not know."

Great. Well, maybe Luc would tell him. In the meantime, Danilo asked what kind of work he might expect to do in the church, and though Théodore clearly thought it an odd question, he talked amiably enough about cleaning of the windows, sweeping the floors, preparing the church for the congregation, and so on. "It will be easier for you because you are white," he concluded. "They may trust you in time with the ritual trappings."

Luc still had not appeared, so Danilo asked, "What do you do in Tigue?"

"Ah." The mouse smiled. "I own property. South of here." He gestured toward the Repos. "A farm; my wife manages it and pays the workers, while I spend much of my time here in the city to arrange for the sale of our grain and viands. In this season, the only thing we produce is honey from two hives on our property, so I sometimes take it to the markets to sell, now that the King has seen fit to reinstate them. This morning, Phillippe at the Deux Frères purchased all that remained in my stock. So I have some time before I must return."

"Don't you want to get back to your wife?"

The mouse exhaled and then looked around. "Tigue is such a beautiful city," he said. "I spend as much time here as I may."

"You seem much happier today than yesterday."

There again, the echo of Taye in the mouse's smile, this one more comradely. "Your appearance was ill-timed yesterday. We did not know you and feared what your arrival might mean."

"Oh, right." Danilo remembered another question he wanted to ask. "Who's Cobb?"

Théodore sprang to his feet and had a paw across Danilo's mouth before the tiger could react. He brought his muzzle very close to Danilo's ear. "Do not mention that name in public," he said, so very softly that the hairs in Danilo's ear barely twitched with the breath that accompanied the words.

Slowly, Danilo nodded, and the mouse released his mouth. He looked nothing like Taye now; he looked like a mouse who'd fought in two battles, serious and hard. "I'm sorry," Danilo whispered. "Is that something I'm better off not knowing?"

"It's something you will know, soon enough, but not something to be discussed in public." Théodore lifted a paw. "Leave it there."

He'd had almost nothing but frustrating conversations since arriving here, Danilo thought, but perhaps that is what happens when you're dumped into a time period where you don't belong. Or encountered a set of shifty-acting people with beige scarves.

He asked Théodore about the battles, and the mouse told him some amusing stories: one friend of his had drunk too much wine and kept complaining of headaches all during the retreat; another, a marmot, had bedded a willing Etruscan demoiselle and claimed he was going to marry her, only to appear in Tigue the following year with fantastical stories of what her family was like.

It was in the midst of one of these bawdy stories that Luc reappeared, and Théodore said, "I'll tell you the rest later, if you like."

"Yes," Danilo said. "I am curious to find out what he did with his wife's aunt."

"Whose wife's aunt?" Luc's whiskers were down and he kept rubbing his cheek.

"An army friend of mine. You don't know him." Théodore rose and gestured to Danilo as though presenting him to Luc. "Here is your tiger, safe and as purely white as I found him."

"Quite a shock, eh?" The ghost of a smile danced around Luc's muzzle. "The Saône masks many things."

"Aye." Théodore turned to the otter. "How did it go?"

The ghost vanished. "It went as it must. As yours did."

They stood together looking down at the street, until Luc sighed and said, "There but for the grace of God."

"God's grace," Théodore said in a low, hard voice, "has naught to do with it."

He walked off without another word, leaving Luc and Danilo. The otter simply stood, lost in thought, until Danilo held up the bread. "I got you some food," he said.

"Oh, sweetheart." Luc lifted his head, his reverie dispelled, and now turned his full smile on Danilo. "You eat it. You're much larger than I, and I'm used to waiting for my food."

"I already had some. I'm not hungry now," Danilo lied. He held the baguette out. "Take it. I got it for you."

"I don't need it." But Luc sat next to him and allowed Danilo to place the baguette in his lap, following it with the cheese and the small coin. "Where did all this come from?"

Luc wouldn't take it if he knew it were charity. Well, Danilo could be as frustrating as any of them. "It's better you not know," he said, grinning inwardly.

But the otter's eyes widened in alarm, and he rose slightly from the bench. "You didn't steal it? Oh, Danilo, say you did not!"

"I didn't!" He put a large paw over the baguette, keeping it steady in Luc's lap. "I bought them. I—I earned some money and I bought food, that's all. I did a little bit of work in the morning."

Luc settled back and looked doubtful, but lowered his head to the bread. "It does smell good."

"It is. Taye—Théodore had some too."

"All right." Luc lifted the bread and nibbled at the end, then ate some cheese. Very soon, both were gone.

***

On Luc's advice, they waited a little longer before attempting to re-enter the Repos du Saint. "In mid-afternoon, Bertrand is often in back," Luc said, "and we may slip through the dining-room unobserved."

They peered in the windows at the almost-empty dining room when Luc judged it time, and the otter opened the door to check. He gestured quickly for Danilo to follow him, and the tiger hurried inside.

The stocky badger was nowhere in evidence, but Maria was cleaning tankards behind the bar. She looked up at Danilo's entrance and called out, "Good afternoon, tiger!"

Luc froze, then hurried more quickly across the room. Danilo raised a paw to Maria and smiled, his groin tingling at the sight of her, and then he heard movement behind her and ran to follow Luc, heart pounding.

"What is this?" Bertrand's voice shouted.

The otter stopped dead, and Danilo, unprepared, piled into him, knocking them both into a chair and to the floor. Heavy footsteps approached as they struggled to get up. "I told you," Bertrand said, waving a shaking finger at them, breathing hard, "*no.*"

"It is…" Luc struggled to his knees and remained there. "One more night. I promise. Then he will be gone."

"No more nights, no more lies!" The black-and-white muzzle twisted over them.

Danilo struggled to his feet. "Honestly," he said. "I'm getting another lodging tomorrow. I promise. I'll, I'll work in the kitchen again tonight."

His words sped past the badger with no effect. "I have warned you again and again and again, and this is too much. I will lose patronage! No, you have—"

Luc made some kind of motion that stopped the badger's words, and Danilo didn't see what it was because he'd been staring over the otter's head trying to attract Bertrand's attention. He felt the motion of Luc's tail, and saw Bertrand stop, untwist. "No," the badger said, more calmly. "Not even…"

"It is for one night," Luc said. "Show mercy."

"Mercy!" The badger rubbed his whiskers and looked around at Maria, at the two foxes sitting at a table who were staring. "Very well! Though you deserve no mercy, you will have it. But you will leave tomorrow as well. My mercy can only extend so far!"

He gestured with his arms and spoke loudly enough to make Danilo's whiskers pull back, his ears flatten. But Luc rose and bowed, and then took Danilo's paw and hurried for the stairs. Behind them, Bertrand shouted, "Kitchen work begins in one hour!"

They hurried up to Luc's room, where Luc closed the door and Danilo sat on one side of the bed, drawing his knees up to his chin. "I can't believe he's such an—" Asshole, he tried to say, but the word came out as "son of a filthy mother," and he felt instantly ashamed of saying it even before Luc turned with a reproving look.

"Bertrand is…well, he runs his business." Luc reached up to scratch his ears. "I have been imposing on his generosity for far too long."

"He owes your father a debt."

"Owed." Luc ran fingers across the chest. "Have you seen my beige scarf?"

Heat flushed Danilo's ears and tail. "I, uh."

The otter turned. Danilo met his eyes and looked down. "I lost it."

He told the story, adding that Théodore knew the weasel and hoped to get the scarf back. Luc listened patiently and then laughed softly at that part. "The scarf matters little. But I should have cautioned you against wearing it."

"I'm sorry I lost it," Danilo said. "And sorry I got you kicked out of the room here. It's a nice room."

Luc sat next to the tiger on the bed. "It is an adequate room. And I will find a place to live, I am certain. I still have some friends."

"Maybe Théodore could let you stay with him."

"It is a possibility." Luc folded his paws in his lap. His thick tail squirmed around as he settled it, brushing against Danilo's.

The tiger moved his tail courteously aside. "Or if I get a room with the church, you could stay with me."

At this, Luc's whiskers flared up in a smile, and he turned. "That is truly sweet. But most student rooms are not private. You will likely be sleeping on a mat in a semi-public space with other students or church workers. And besides," he raised a paw as Danilo started to argue, "no church would grant space to me."

"Why not?" Here was his chance to let Luc tell him what he already knew.

"Oh," Luc said. "You know already, do you not? Last night, I tried not to allow my nature to show through when I was comforting you, but you must have sensed it." Danilo gave a half-nod, unsure how to respond. Taye had met him outside a gay club, so their confessions had been implicit in the first moment their eyes met. He had no practice reassuring gay friends that he was understanding.

Luc went on. "You understand what it means when Bertrand calls me 'halfie'?"

"He calls me that, too." Danilo shook his head. "In Firenza, we don't have that term."

The otter bit his lip. "I can trust you? I sensed some of it in your nature last night as well, so you must at least understand what it is like to live this way, even if you are able to enjoy the company of Maria."

Danilo's ears flattened. "You know about that?"

"My boy, there is only one good reason for you to wash so thoroughly without a single objectionable stain remaining on your dry clothes. And the clothes, too, smelled of wolf."

"Sorry I got your clothes dirty." He curled his tail tightly in on itself.

Luc laughed again and put a paw on Danilo's knee. "My boy," he said, "if I could lose myself in a female's charms, do you not think I would do so as well? Maria may be…experienced, shall we say, but she is at least clean and friendly, which is more than I would say for many of the females in this city whose dubious charms you might have sought out. No, you've nothing to be ashamed of. Did she remind you of someone at home? Is this why you became so distraught last night?"

"No. No, Maria was wonderful." And then he felt guilty, because Luc had all but confessed his attraction. "I mean, you're really nice too, and I felt a lot better when you—when you held me."

His words hung in the silent room. Luc wasn't looking directly at him, but the otter's paw on his knee remained there, warm and comforting, and Danilo put his paw atop it. "Is that why the church wouldn't welcome you?"

Slowly, the otter nodded.

Danilo took a breath and then squeezed Luc's paw. "I. I think that's ridiculous. It's—it's like that in Firenza too, and it's—it's just wrong."

"It is heartening to hear you say so," Luc murmured, "though you should speak in whispers when you do."

"It doesn't have to rule your life, though." Danilo squeezed the otter's paw. "I mean, you can just work on your business and getting back on your feet, and…you can still have a life, can't you?"

Luc did turn his head then and looked steadily at Danilo. "Tell me," he said, "in Firenza, if you are caught…with another male, what is the penalty?"

Cobb's large hand mashing his paw into the table. Cobb and Georg chasing him down the street. Danilo swallowed. "Well, uh. I guess you don't get to do some things—some people might not want to do business with you, or spend time with you…"

The otter withdrew his paw slowly. "Here," he said, "the first time you are caught, the Church removes a testicle. The second time, you are castrated. Fully."

The words took a moment to register. At first, Danilo thought they might be mistranslated somehow, that whatever was altering the language he was speaking was getting the words wrong, that he was misunderstanding. "They can't do that," he said. "That's—mutilation, that's a violation of your rights."

"Do you not wonder why Bertrand calls us 'halfie'?" Luc's eyes slid away from Danilo's, out to the floor.

"Well, that's just a name, right? I mean, they haven't caught you yet, so…uh."

Danilo's words trailed off as Luc rose to his knees. The otter loosened his pants and pushed them down his hips before Danilo could protest. "There," he said, one brown paw cradling his sac. "They have caught me once."

His sheath was intact, though Danilo was trying very hard not to look at it. The sac held between his fingers bore an angry scar, bare of fur, and half of it looked deflated, like a three-day-old balloon. Danilo's own balls tried to climb up into his body, and he wanted to look away, but he couldn't. "I'm sorry," he choked out.

"It was my own fault." Mercifully, Luc pulled his pants up and sat next to Danilo again. "There are certain discreet locations we use, and I had been warned that one was compromised. My companion and I were caught and seized and…" His paw rested in his lap. "Punished."

"What happened to him?" The words choked in Danilo's throat.

"Oh, it was his first time as well. I believe he has married. The Church leaves us half our masculinity that we might yet amend our ways and start a family. But I suppose I am stubborn."

"Why?" Danilo kept his voice low, but his tail uncurled and lashed against the wall. "Next time they'll take—I mean, by God, how could you go on after that?"

"Some do." Luc looked again at the floor. "For some, the need for companionship is greater than their concern for personal safety. My embrace last night; would you have gone without it?"

"No," Danilo shook his head. "But…"

"And it is not so common to be caught more than once." Luc managed a smile. "I can perform quite adequately still, I have discovered. There are many discreet places in which we may still share affection, the kind of closeness that for my kind does not ring true with a female, the kind of closeness that comes from two like souls sharing

body and heart for a time. Tell me, Danilo, would you choose abstinence, if told it would prolong your life five years?"

Some people choose abstinence, some have abstinence thrust
upon them. He fought the urge to laugh at the phrase he'd muttered
to himself on many a lonely night where his paw was his release.
"Five years isn't so long. I mean…" He rubbed his whiskers. "It's a
false choice. You can't guarantee that."

"For us, it is not a false choice. Abstinence or the chance of a
terrible death."

"Death?"

"Oh, aye." Luc turned to him. "Have I not mentioned the penalty for a third offense? Burned at the stake as though you were a
witch."

Chapter Seven

*B*urned?"

Luc nodded. Danilo just kept staring at him. "Come on, I know this is—I know this is—" He couldn't think of a way to say "The Dark Ages" without having to add a whole lot of explanation he wasn't ready for, so he finished, "the site of the cathedral, but aren't we civilized? Burn people?"

"For witches, it's the only way, and they regard us as witches of a sort. If we cannot control our urges, they say it is a demon possessing us." Luc spread his fingers. "I do not feel in possession of a demon; or if I am, it is a rather benevolent one."

"Except for getting one of your balls cut off." Danilo was vaguely aware that even though he meant to use the cruder term, he said the same word Luc had used for "testicles." He forged on. "But witches—do you believe in witches, Luc?"

"Aye," the otter said promptly. "Théodore told me the Iberians used one in the war to move about unseen by our sentries. My grandfather told me that when they first built our houses on the river, it rained every day and the foundations washed away. When they caught the witch who'd been displaced and killed her, the sun came out." He paused. "It was long before his time, but the story has been told faithfully."

"That's…" Danilo paused. As ridiculous as someone traveling here from the twenty-first century? He'd be regarded as a witch if he told the truth about himself. "In Firenza," he said, "we don't burn witches. It's barbaric."

Luc blinked slowly. "Barbaric it might be, but for witches, we are assured it is the only means to cleanse their souls. Now, for such as me…" He rubbed the side of his muzzle.

"You're not going to be burned." Danilo caught Luc's paw.

"No…" The otter squared his shoulders and looked Danilo in the eye. "I have just come from visiting a friend of mine who is."

In Luc's eyes were the hurt, the sadness, the truth of what he was saying: he had just come from seeing a friend for the last time, a friend who was about to suffer a horrible death. Danilo bit his lip. "He was…a third time?" Luc nodded. "How—"

The otter spread his paws. "He trusted the wrong friend. He was betrayed by someone who pretended to care for him. But he will not tell us whom it was. His kindness forbids it. 'He was only protecting his family,' he says." He closed one paw into a fist.

Danilo had been about to ask how or why someone would go on trying to have sex of any kind after being "fully" castrated (which he assumed meant just removing everything in the groin area, and even that fleeting thought turned his own sheath and balls ice-cold), but he did not feel this was the appropriate time to ask that question, and he was not at all sure he wanted to hear the answer anyway. "That's terrible," he said. "I'm really sorry."

"It is a reminder of what may happen if we are careless," Luc said. "The best we can do is live more cautiously, and well, in his memory."

"I don't understand why you would take those risks at all. If it could cost you your life…"

"Life," Luc said, "is more than the beating of your heart. Life is your heart's connection to the people around you. If your soul is shut off, isolated, alone, is that living? Would you survive to the age of fifty without speaking to another?"

"I get it," Danilo said. "It's the same thing you asked before."

"Do you understand truly?" Luc's eyes remained focused on his. "Have you been alone all your life, and this is why you do not fear it?"

"No, I—I've had my family, and my friends." He couldn't look away from the otter's gaze.

"Someone you could trust your heart to? Someone you could turn to at the worst times in your life?"

"Yes." Danilo had always been able to pick up his phone and call family if he needed to. He probably wouldn't have told them about Cobb, about the bullying, but he was handling that on his own. He would've laid low, waited for it to blow over, and everything would be fine. The only reason he was alone here was because he had no phone, no way to get in touch with the people he depended on, who were all four-hundred-odd years from being born anyway. Well, the other reason he was alone here was that if he told anyone that he was from the future, they would think he was crazy. They didn't even have science fiction to tell him where he'd gotten his crazy idea from.

"You are lucky, then. I have been fortunate enough to have a few friends I could trust, in whose arms I could experience truly the joy that God made for me. Those bonds, that joy, is worth the risk." His tail moved slightly; the tip curled up. "I would rather go to an early grave having lived a full life than carry the weight of empty years."

"I would rather live." Danilo paused. "I'd rather have my friends stay alive, too. I mean, won't you miss your—" He gulped, but was already most of the way through the sentence, and there wasn't any other way for him to end it. He hoped Luc wouldn't think him callous. "Friend?"

"Of course. But all friendships come to an end." Luc smiled, but sadly, and his whiskers did not rise with his smile. "After tonight, most likely you and I will not see each other again, and I feel you are as close a friend as he was to me. We've talked more, for certain." He rubbed his eyes. "Coumier was not given to conversation."

"You've been a great friend to me." Danilo eagerly left the subject of soon-to-be-dead Coumier. "You pulled me out of the river and helped me get on my feet. Tomorrow I'm going to the church and I might have a place to stay and something to do, and I never would have had that if not for you." He put a paw on Luc's shoulder. "And you made me feel better last night when I thought I was going to lose it. I don't want to stop seeing you after tonight."

"It is much better for you if you do not," Luc said, but he leaned into Danilo's embrace and put his paw back on the tiger's knee.

"I trust you," Danilo said. "And you can trust me."

"I probably should not." But Luc didn't move, and his thick tail pressed against Danilo's back.

After several quiet minutes, the tension in the otter relaxed, and he squeezed Danilo's knee. "You'd best go down to the kitchen," he said, "lest they suspect some demon-inspired activity here."

"They wouldn't ever know." Despite all that Luc had said and even shown Danilo, the intermediate step of the church officials still felt unreal to him. What, did people barge into houses like the comedy skit Spanish Inquisition and grab people while they were in the middle of…his imagination raced with scenes. No; nobody would come barging into the Repos. Bertrand already hated them *because* he was worried about a church raid, and anyway, if he wanted to accuse Danilo and Luc, he would have sent the church people upstairs within the first half hour after they went up together.

Not that they had time to do anything right now anyway, although as Danilo held Luc close, he thought he might want to get closer to the otter, in time. The room here was safe; the door was closed, and if they were quiet, how would anyone know what had gone on? The chamberpot would surely mask any smells, and it would take all of—well, if Maria was any indication, about five minutes. The chances were that nothing would happen.

Wait, why was he trying to talk himself into sex with Luc when the otter hadn't made a single move toward him? Other than showing off his sheath—but Maria, too, had been very open with her body. Maybe it was just custom. Then there was the way his tail was pressed against Danilo's back—unavoidable in the small room, perhaps. Or the paw on the knee that was now no longer all the way down at the knee, but had crept up the thigh. Or the fact that he had specifically mentioned his "nature" to Danilo.

Was Luc hitting on him? Danilo cursed himself for his uncertainty, but he really had no idea what flirting felt like. Right now, being close to Luc felt good, and the chance to make the otter feel better, after so much Luc had done for him, appealed to Danilo. But he didn't want to be too forward, and anyway, he would have to get down to the kitchen fairly soon. So he just kept his arm around the otter.

Luc's fingers rested warmly on his leg, definitely on his thigh now. Maybe Danilo just wanted to think they were moving up toward his groin. His sheath already felt warm and full from the closeness, and the anticipation of the touch of the otter's fingers got him harder still. Luc could tell, couldn't he? Or could he?

Danilo's inexperience kept him from going any farther, which was probably a good thing, before Luc breathed a sigh and straightened. "Thank you for the comfort, Danilo," he said. "It really is time for you to start in the kitchen. I'm sorry you must work again tonight."

"I don't mind," Danilo said, which was only a partial lie; he minded being dragged away from a peaceful moment with Luc, and he wasn't looking forward to another three or four hours by the hot stove alongside the sullen bear. But now he knew a little better how the kitchen worked, and he would be much more confident. Hopefully he would not lacerate his paws any worse than they were.

That reminded him of the cut in his side, which hurt when he touched it. "I want to go wash up before," he said.

Luc shifted his tail and got to his feet as Danilo pushed up from the bed and did the same. The otter smiled and then gripped Danilo's wrist in what felt like an approximation of a handshake. Danilo gripped Luc's wrist in return and returned the smile. "Thank you for that," Luc said. "It has been a trying day, and it is pleasant to feel that I still have a friend."

"Of course you have a friend." Danilo was rather aware that his sheath was brushing against his pants, and wondered if the bulge were visible. He looked down at Luc's pants and saw what might have been an answering bulge there, or might simply have been a fold in the fabric. He closed his eyes and just squeezed the otter's wrist.

Luc squeezed back and then released it. "I have to put my things in order," he said, although Danilo did not see much for him to be arranging. Most of his clothes were already in the chest.

The tiger rubbed a paw down the tunic. His claw snagged on the tear the weasel's knife had made. "I'll return your clothes when I get new ones. I promise."

"They are merely clothes," Luc said. "For as long as they are of use, you may keep them."

But he would return them, Danilo vowed as he hurried down the stairs to the back yard and the pump. He stripped the tunic off and examined the rent as he pumped. This time, he was pleased to bring water up almost as quickly as Seline had. He cupped his paw under it and washed the pleasantly cool water over the cut in his side. Without soap or antiseptic, there wasn't a lot he could do, but he was sure he would rather have it clean than not.

It stung as he rubbed it, and a little blood came away on his fingers. He wet his fur thoroughly and then slid the tunic back on. His fingers found the cut again, a hole where the threads had been severed as neatly as his skin had. He shuddered again, thinking of the weasel and the knife. How close had he come to actually dying, there? Best not to think of it. He looked down at the tunic, keeping his mind on the injury to the cloth.

The tunic wasn't as badly ripped as he'd thought: a cut perhaps an inch long. It could easily be mended by someone handy with a needle and thread. Which was not Danilo. He began to brood about how few actual skills he held, but was mercifully interrupted by a growl from the general direction of the kitchen. "You workin'?"

He hurried in under the bear's watchful eye, paused to gasp in the smothering heat. The previous night, the oven had been going but winding down and the day had been cooler. After a day of bright sun, the kitchen had likely already been hot before the cook had lit the stove. Now Danilo breathed in hot, smoky air, and coughed, and coughed again, only managing to stop under the withering glare from the large bear.

A stack of potatoes and carrots waited for him, and without being instructed he attended to them with the same knife he'd used before. When the bear called him, he helped remove the fowl from the oven, and otherwise he applied himself to the vegetables. Kitchen work remained very low on Danilo's list of preferred activities, but as a way to get a meal, it was bearable. His paws hurt by the end of the first hour, his left from being cut (he slipped twice with the knife), and both cramping from holding the small vegetables and knife. Danilo imagined that they were saying, *We did this ALL LAST NIGHT and okay, we put up with it then, but now we are over it.*

Just a few more hours, he told them, and tried to stretch in between peelings, flexing his fingers. The bear growled at him twice for cutting too much flesh from the potatoes, but Danilo ignored him and continued without further consequences. He was even daring enough, when the bear wasn't looking, to chop a piece from a raw carrot and pop it into his mouth, crunching as quietly as he could, and whether it was covered by the noise of the restaurant or the bear simply didn't care, Danilo was not scolded for that either.

The cool of the evening relieved his breathing, and he fell again into the rhythm of peeling. The last fowl came out of the oven, the stewpot bubbled, and Seline came in to take plates out to the dining room. Danilo faced the back door while peeling and only saw Seline the one time he was helping with the fowl. She didn't acknowledge him with anything more than a quick nod.

Toward the end of the evening, Luc looked in the back door with a smile for Danilo. Danilo returned it, hoping he looked more encouraging than he had the previous night. The otter waved and hurried off just before the big bear turned and would have seen him. The cook squinted at Danilo, who was trying to hide a smile, then the bear scooped peeled vegetables from the table to the pot. He leaned against the wall and ripped a large chunk of bread from a baguette while Danilo continued to work.

In an hour or two, when Danilo was done, he could go back up to the room and wait for Luc. He would insist that the otter take the bed this time, but would offer him some affection. Just a hug, maybe lying together...or more, if Luc wanted it. In Danilo's head, of course, the otter did want it, and he imagined Luc's paws pushing his boxers down, the fingers that had lain warmly on his thigh exploring higher, his own fingers exploring in return.

That brought back images of the scarred sac, the single testicle. Not very sexy. Danilo frowned. There were no church people here, nobody to betray a trust except himself and Luc. He trusted the otter, and the otter had said he trusted Danilo in return. The more he thought about it, the more he felt he had a duty to help Luc out with some kind of physical affection. In a world where every encounter was unsure and could lead to torture, wasn't there an implicit obligation to take advantage of the safe times when they arose? Besides, it seemed fitting to Danilo that just as he'd had his first sexual experience in this inn, he could have his first gay experience here too.

In the midst of these thoughts, his erection alternately growing and flagging as he imagined first the details of the encounter, then the possible consequences, he paid less attention to his peeling, and the knife slipped again, this time scoring painfully beneath one of his claws.

He swore under his breath, but didn't drop the knife. The bear laughed, deeply. "Knife bites you, eh?"

"I'm fine." The pain, as it often did with this sort of injury, dropped off quickly from the sharp impact and then returned, getting worse as he curled his cramped fingers around each potato. They were the worst; with the carrots, he could at least peel with the same stroke all the way around the root, though these carrots were not all the straight, even carrots he was used to. They twisted, with bumps and scars, and the ones that were straight were small and needed more care. But the potatoes varied in size, and had to be turned around and around before they could be completely peeled, and every time he had to turn one, his finger flexed and his claw hurt.

Finally, Bertrand came in to tell the bear that dinner was done. The cook grabbed the remaining half-baguette and turned to Danilo with his mouth full, chewing. "Stew," he said thickly, pointing to the pot. "Share." And then he was gone.

As he had the previous night, Danilo washed the thicker peelings and shared his stew with Seline and Maria. Maria spoke as jovially as she had the previous night, and apart from the occasional sly glance at Danilo and a pinch of his tail, he would not have known that they'd slept together the night before.

Seline obviously knew, and kept her conversation to a minimum, but Maria was talkative enough that the rabbit's silence made little difference. When Danilo joined in to talk about his visit to the cathedral (minus the encounter with the weasel), Seline joined in because she too had loved the cathedral, but when she asked about features aside from the rosettes and the clock: the relics, the shrine to the Virgin, Danilo had to confess that he had not noticed any of them. "Reason for me to go back, I suppose."

The rabbit sniffed, and Maria laughed. "She believes the Cathedral is a miracle. It would be impossible for you to appreciate it enough."

"I really felt the presence of God there," Danilo said, because he wanted to make Seline happy, and because it was partially true. It felt right for the time.

"I know somewhere else you felt His presence," Maria said, and pinched his tail again.

Seline looked away. Danilo shifted and smiled at Maria, wondering inside whether Luc would pinch his tail. Probably not in public like this. He changed the subject back to the clock in the cathedral.

When the dinner ended, Seline offered to clean up again. Maria simply walked back to the inn, without saying more than "good night" to Danilo. She did pause at the hallway, but he didn't register that until he was already on the stairs heading back up to his room. He didn't hesitate; he could always come back tomorrow night or the night after, if he wanted to see her again.

Luc wasn't in the room when Danilo entered. His tail drooped, but he turned immediately to close the door, and a smile grew on his muzzle. He stretched out next to the bed, head facing away from the door, and imagined what Luc might do when the otter walked in.

His paw strayed inside his pants, and encountered the elastic waistband of his boxers. Maria had known right away that this was foreign. If Luc got that far...there would be questions. And Danilo didn't want to have that conversation, not if Luc was reaching into his boxers.

With an eye on the door, he slipped Luc's pants off, and then the boxers. He stashed them behind Luc's chest, stuffing them between the thick wood and the wall, and tweaked the cut under his claw again as he did. He cursed softly and stood, massaging the finger, his tail swinging freely over his bare rear.

The finger felt better soon, or at least the pain receded to a familiarly manageable level. The tiger extended his claws, which brought another flare of pain. He retracted them again and reached down to his waist.

The small tunic hung barely halfway down his sheath, leaving his sac exposed to the air. He slipped his paw under it, fondling himself and his two, count 'em, two balls. Poor Luc. If things went that far, Danilo would have to remember to be sensitive. Luc might not want that area touched. As a matter of fact, Danilo wasn't sure what the otter would want. His paw trailed back up to his sheath. He knew what he liked, but that wasn't necessarily what someone else liked. Taye had told him that he already had a leg up whenever he was ready to play with another guy, because he'd had years practicing with the same equipment, and certainly, Danilo felt more confident about playing with Luc than he had about sleeping with Maria. But maybe different guys liked different things.

His sheath was getting harder under his paw. He realized how that would look to a tired Luc, returning maybe only wanting to hold someone against him. He hurried over to the pants he'd dropped and pulled them up over his legs and hips, fastening them around his growing erection with some difficulty. The good news was that the erection was fading with his embarrassment, and by the time he sat down again, he was presentable.

But still Luc did not arrive. Danilo lay back, alternately imagining the otter caressing him, groping, stroking, and then forcing himself to stop imagining that. He must have drifted off, because he became convinced that his trip back in time had all been an elaborate joke. Taye had conspired with Cobb and Georg somehow, and they had constructed an immense set, a fake Tigue, and if only Danilo could get to the edge of it, he would find his way out into 2008. They had even stocked their set with fleas—he scratched at his side. The urge to call out to them bubbled up in his chest, torpid, slow. You guys win, he wanted to yell. Come out now.

The door opened, and he blinked at the silhouetted otter. So Orwin was in on it too. He opened his mouth, and then the door closed and so did his mouth. Struggling back to wakefulness, he recognized the movements and then the scent of Luc.

"Hi," he said.

Luc stopped, and then white showed as he smiled. "Good evening, Danilo. You may have the bed again."

"No." The tiger pulled his knees up and remained on the floor. "You've done so much...you have the bed."

"I am accustomed to meager accommodations. You are accustomed to wealth."

Danilo swallowed. His tail tip flicked. Luc's whiskers glimmered in the darkness. "We could...share."

The teeth showed again, and slowly, the whiskers lifted. "I am not sure that would be advisable."

"No, it's...it's okay." He swallowed against his dry throat.

The otter lowered himself to the ground and sat next to Danilo. "I am tired," he said. "I do not know what your intentions are...or expectations..."

The tiger leaned against Luc. Images whirled through his head. "No expectations," he said. "You talked about closeness being important to life, and you've done so much. I wanted to give you something back."

119

"You owe me nothing," Luc started to say, and Danilo cut him off.

"I owe you my life."

Luc hesitated, and Danilo summoned all the courage he had. He put one long arm around the otter's shoulders.

Tension stiffened the muscular shoulders, but Danilo kept his arm there, and a moment later the otter relaxed, and slumped against Danilo. "I really am tired."

The tiger pushed down the disappointment. Luc was enjoying the hug, and had not said no to curling up in the bed together. They would see what the morning would bring, after they'd both had a rest.

In the still air of the bedroom, a faintly sour smell came to Danilo's nose, but he had gotten used to ignoring hygiene issues, and he just held the otter close. "Danilo," Luc said patiently. "I am very tired."

The third time, it sunk in. "Oh." Danilo felt a little foolish. He sat back and let Luc lie down on the bed. The otter lay on his back facing the wall, and curled his tail between his legs, leaving room for Danilo.

The tiger hesitated a moment, and then crawled up behind Luc. He had to press his body close to the otter's to get himself all the way on the bedding, which was designed for only one person, and a sixteenth-century person, at that. Luc shifted as Danilo squirmed to get comfortable, pressing his chest to the otter's back and finding that that placed his sheath right against the arch of the thick tail. Not wanting to be that forward, Danilo squirmed a little more, trying to find a less intimate way to sleep in the same bed. He draped one arm over Luc's while he adjusted his hips one way, then another. No position was entirely chaste; both his awareness and the resultant rubbing of his sheath against Luc's tail aroused him, and the more he moved, the more his erection grew, and the more it rubbed against the tail.

His ears flushed. "I'm sorry," he mumbled.

Luc chuckled softly. He took the tiger's paw and brought it to the front of his own pants so Danilo could feel the bulge of an erection there. "Don't be," the otter whispered as he moved the paw back to his chest.

Danilo's heart thumped and he pressed his nose against Luc's ear, inhaling the otter's scent. He closed his eyes with a smile. Luc murmured something that Danilo perked his ears to catch. "…in this world you will have trouble. But take heart. For I have…" The rest was too soft to hear.

Was he meant to reply to that? He couldn't think of anything to say, and the way Luc had said it, it might have been a prayer. The otter didn't speak again, so Danilo exhaled against Luc's fur and didn't worry about it.

He thought he would never get to sleep. Usually when he was this aroused, he would take care of himself and go to bed, but that wasn't an option. Still, he didn't mind so much. Lying next to Luc like this felt close and warm, and he thought he understood what the otter had meant when he said it gave purpose to his life.

Besides, he wasn't the only one who couldn't sleep. Footsteps broke the silence, faint in the hall outside. Someone going to the outhouse, undoubtedly. *Don't they know about chamber pots?* Danilo thought with the smugness of the newly educated.

Then he was pushed violently off the bed, rolling to the floor and reflexively slapping a paw to the ground to stop his rolling. Unfortunately, it was his left paw, and his cut flared with pain. He gasped and brought it to his muzzle, which stopped him asking why Luc had pushed him out of bed, if it was just a dream or—

The door burst open.

Danilo scrambled back against the light of lanterns, which swung around to pierce his eyes. A gruff voice barked, "On your feet!"

Three figures crowded into the small room, and with the oil lantern's flame casting the rest of the room into shadow, Danilo couldn't make out any of them. He smelled burning oil more than anything else.

Beside him, Luc stood. "I'm the one you want," he said quietly.

"We want both of you," the voice growled. It wasn't the one holding the lantern—either lantern, for another one shone full in Luc's face, illuminating the whiskers, the steady, calm expression. Danilo tried to mimic it, but his legs trembled and almost gave way. He thought he saw the shadow of antlers on the wall behind the lantern, but then the leadmost shadow moved again and the antlers disappeared.

The room was barely big enough for five people to stand, but one of the lantern-holders kicked the door shut. "Now," the shadow in front said, stepping forward so that his nose was less than a foot from Danilo and Luc, "you are under arrest by order of the Church and the Archbishop of Tigue for crimes against the Holy Order and violations of God's commands."

With the lanterns behind him, the foremost intruder's small triangular ears and thick canine muzzle came into focus. His nose glistened in the light, nostrils widening, and his voice was the low rasp of immense stone blocks sliding across one another. "It reeks of blasphemy in here." He turned in Luc's direction. "And it is a familiar scent."

"We haven't done anything!" Danilo felt safe in protesting this; any evidence of his arousal was long gone.

The wolf half-turned, and in profile, Danilo could see his markings more clearly. He had no idea what LeSevre looked like, but there was little doubt in his mind of the wolf's identity. "Perchet. Inspect them."

The lantern in Danilo's eyes dropped to the floor, where it rested. In its diffuse light, the figures in the room resolved slowly.

All three wore dark brown tunics with a white cross stretching from neck to stomach, the crossbar defining each broad chest. Smaller white crosses adorned the sleeves, and a row of small white marks ran across the shoulder of the wolf in front of him, who was nearly his height.

The figure who'd put down the lantern, a shorter fox, crossed the room to kneel beside Luc. Danilo couldn't look away as the fox brought his nose up to the front of Luc's pants, then the back, and finally, standing, the otter's mouth. "Aye," he said. "Stinks all over, this one."

"Hah." The wolf's teeth shone in the lantern light.

"But—" Danilo said.

"Quiet," Luc rasped.

The lantern's light turned on Danilo. He still had not seen the third figure, and now he was blinded again. But his whiskers felt the fox's movement, and the large, grotesque shadows cast by the lanterns twisted about the room as the church official knelt beside him, poked his nose into the tiger's groin, moved to sniff below his tail, and finally stood.

"Lower your head," the wolf commanded, and Danilo obligingly bent to bring his muzzle close to the fox's nose.

This time, the fox hesitated. His eyes flashed as he looked toward the lantern and then away.

The wolf gestured, a 'come on' motion with his paw. "Well?"

"Sir, he is white."

"I can see that. Does he smell of sin?"

The large black ears flattened. "I do not think so."

"Think so?" The wolf leaned forward.

"I—I could be mistaken. The scent on the other is thick. But—no."

The wolf stared with eyes that glowed fire-bright in the lantern light, his muzzle in shadow save for the glistening on several teeth. When he spoke, his voice lowered, the growl in it closer to the surface. "Be very certain, Perchet. Our mission is to save our people from demons."

In the silence of the room, Danilo heard Perchet swallow. "He is no demon."

Demon? Danilo held his breath. The wolf turned those eyes on Danilo, the long muzzle an inch from the tiger's chin. "You had best hope not," he growled, and the sweet smell of meat washed over Danilo. "I know you now, tiger. I have marked you. And should you give harbor to demons, the punishment of the Church will be swift and sure."

No coherent thoughts formed in Danilo's head, save that he was being spared. His mouth felt dry as the straw he slept on, and even the bite of a flea on his leg couldn't spur him to move. The wolf's eyes burned into his, and for a moment he thought, *What if there's a demon in* him?

"Well?" The wolf snapped out the word, and Danilo flinched.

"Thank you," he croaked. And then, remembering his walk and the conversations he'd heard, he added, "God bless you."

Another tense moment followed. Had he spoken improperly? But then the wolf lunged at him with a loud, "Hah!" and Danilo, terrified, jumped back, tripped over the fox's tail, and fell hard on the wood floor.

Both the wolf and ram laughed. "Look at him quail!" the ram said.

The wolf said nothing, only turned with a swagger and walked to the door. "Dumond, the door. Perchet, bring the prisoner."

Perchet had straightened and was holding his tail. "Yes, sir," he said, and reached out to take Luc's arm.

Danilo began to scramble to his feet, but Luc turned. "Stay where you are," he commanded. "You may at least stay here for the night, as I promised."

"But—"

"Quiet!" This time it was Perchet who spoke, hushed. "You can do nothing for him, but you may yet save yourself. Would you suffer the same fate?"

Danilo's paw went to cup his groin, reflexively, and Perchet nodded grimly. "I see you understand. Best that LeSevre not see that. Follow God's path and you need never worry about the Church's punishment."

So the tiger sat on the floor and watched the fox guide Luc out the door, the otter walking with a stiff gait that Danilo had never in their brief acquaintance seen him use.

And then they were gone. He listened to them march down the hall and out of his hearing, and with their disappearance, shame flooded him. How could he just have stood and watched them take Luc? He had to at least vouch for his friend. Maybe if he told them how kind Luc had been, how he had taken pity on a stranger who had lost everything, who would soon be working for the Church—

Of course! He struggled to his feet and ran to the door. He would tell LeSevre that he was working for the Church, and then—well, then he would figure out what to do.

He hurried down the hall and to the stairs. Outside, LeSevre was saying something to Luc. Danilo paused, uncertain again. One foot down, then the next. He swallowed and forced his feet to obey him.

A shadow appeared at the base of the stairs, long-eared and small. "Go back!" it hissed.

He recognized Seline's voice and hurried down. "I have to help Luc," he said. "They're going to—"

"And what do you think you may do for him?" She pushed him. "Go. If they see you have come after him…"

"I'll tell them I'm a student of the Church…"

"If you go out," she hissed. "They will take you as well. LeSevre is—" She stopped and then grabbed his arm. "This way. Now!"

She pulled him off the stair and back into the little room where he'd lost his virginity. Maria sat on the bed, her ears up.

"What—" Danilo only got the one word out before Seline's paw sealed his muzzle.

He waited, and the familiar tromp of footsteps sounded outside. Dumond's voice called back, "Nothing here. Must have been the servants."

Danilo's heart pounded. He was certain now that the ram would come look in the servants' room, that he would find Danilo and that LeSevre would be happy to add one more prisoner to his night's haul. The wound in his side throbbed, and he imagined that pain between his legs. A whimper escaped him.

Seline's paw tightened over his muzzle. She glared up at him and shook her head silently.

After several seconds, during which Danilo became aware of every itch and flea bite on his body, footsteps finally sounded outside again, walking away, toward the back. The rabbit's paw remained across his mouth even when everything was silent outside. Finally, she released him and held up a warning paw as she slipped outside.

In the tense seconds before she returned, Maria got to her feet. Danilo tried to meet her eyes, but she would not look at him, keeping her gaze on the doorway. When Seline reappeared, Maria stepped forward, ears perked.

Seline nodded. "They are gone," she said.

"So." Now Maria turned on Danilo. "I warned you not to be involved with him!" The wolf looked nearly as fearsome as LeSevre, breasts bouncing as she stormed at him in the tiny room. She shoved Danilo in the chest. "You bring the church into this place, who knows what they may do!"

"You and he are lucky indeed that the church does not arrest fornicators," Seline said. "Other than that, he has done nothing wrong. Have you?"

She turned her gaze on Danilo, who backed into the corner of the room beneath the intensity of the two female stares. "N-no. I haven't, I didn't do anything with Luc."

"Good." Seline relaxed, and turned to her bed. "I will only have a small penance to say this Sunday."

"You can't stay here," Maria said to Danilo.

"I wasn't going to." His stomach felt ready to vomit up his stew. He kept seeing Luc's rigid gait, picturing the otter's genitals removed, cut out. Danilo felt as though he'd just emerged from the river again, the world around him unfamiliar and hostile. "I am to go to St. Nizier in the morning," he said. "They may have work for me there."

"So you said." She sat down on her bed.

"If Théodore comes looking for me, please tell him to go there?"

Seline grunted assent. Danilo sat quietly for another minute, letting the night's events recede into memory. But he kept seeing the fox bend to Luc's groin, rise and say, "Yes." He could perhaps discuss it with Théodore, but he didn't know if he would ever see the mouse again. And Seline and Maria would know what went on behind the closed doors of the Repos. "Luc hadn't been doing anything…recently," he said. "He had a meeting this morning, and maybe then …but after that, I don't think—could they smell it from hours before?"

"Ha," Maria barked. "Stupid boy."

"I don't have a fox's nose," he protested. "Or a wolf's. I don't know."

"You don't need a nose. You need eyes and a mind."

He shook his head. "He was meeting someone here? But who?"

Maria laughed, bitter. "Tell him, Seline." She turned back to the wall.

Danilo turned to Seline. The rabbit had tilted her head toward him. "He did not tell you?"

"Who?"

Seline sighed. "It is usually Maria's job to sate Bertrand's baser appetites of an evening. But when you arrived, in order to pay for your room…" She coughed, and looked down at her knees, then at the wall, then at her paws. Her voice lowered to a near-whisper. "Luc took over those duties."

For a moment, Danilo just sat. More pieces of the puzzle of this world fell into place for him, and he could not believe he'd missed them. "Luc…with Bertrand…for me? But I worked in the kitchen!"

"To pay for your meal. Luc paid for your lodging."

"Oh, my God." Danilo sunk his muzzle into his paws.

Seline coughed again. "Please do not take the Lord's name in vain in my presence."

"I'm sorry. I'm so sorry." So the fox had smelled Bertrand, because Luc had just come from doing God-knows-what—no, who-knows-what—no, *God*-knows-what; Seline couldn't hear him think. And that was why Luc was tired, why he still hadn't wanted to do anything.

"Bertrand is a filthy beast," Maria said without moving.

That was why Maria had been available to sleep with him: because Luc was occupying Bertrand, and she was desperate to have the company of someone who wasn't the crude badger. And Luc, poor Luc, think of what he must have gone through.

"He pulled me out of the river," Danilo croaked. "He gave me a place to sleep. And in return I let him be molested by Bertrand, and then taken away by the Church to be…" He couldn't say it. "But who called them?"

"Who? Who do you think?" Maria's voice echoed sharply in the small room. "Bertrand himself. He told you you would be gone tomorrow."

Danilo gaped. "Bertrand? That foul, filthy—" The language he was speaking did not adequately convey any of the curses he wanted to say.

"Filthy beast," Seline said in a low voice. "He will pay for his sins in the next world."

"He'll pay for them in this one," Danilo growled.

The rabbit put a paw on his knee. "You should not seek retaliation. 'Vengeance is mine, saith the Lord.'"

"In addition to which you would never triumph over him," Maria said. "The only thing to do with creatures like Bertrand is to take whatever they can give you, give as little of yourself as you can, and escape when you are afforded the chance."

"And you should take that chance now." Seline lifted her paw from his knee. "It has been enough time; the street will be clear."

"Wait one more moment," Maria said. "And silence yourself."

"For what?" Danilo asked, but neither of the ladies made answer.

They sat in silence for two minutes that stretched into five, and then a single set of heavy footsteps sounded on the floor, then the stairs outside.

"Now," Maria said. "While Bertrand is cleaning out your room."

Cleaning out...? Danilo struggled to his feet. "He can't take Luc's things!"

"Hush." Seline, too, stood. "This is your chance to leave. Take it."

"No. I'm not going to let him—"

"Listen to me," Seline said. "If you go up those stairs, you may not end up at the mercy of the church. You might even win a fight with Bertrand. But you will lose the battle. Leave his fate to the Lord, and take charge of your own."

"I..." He stared at the door. Beyond it, Bertrand was even now entering their room, where only half an hour, forty-five minutes before, he'd lain down close to Luc. The badger's paws would be rifling through Luc's clothes, would find—shit, his boxers. Luc's pants rubbed directly on his sheath. "I can't. I can't let him do that."

"For the love of all that is good." Maria sat up in her bed. "Have you not listened to what she is telling you? What I am telling you? Seline and I, we do not agree very often, so when we do, you would do well to listen."

His heart beat one-two, one-two, one-two. The room, completely still, waited for his decision.

Seline put a paw on his shoulder. "Luc would want you to remain safe," she said softly.

***

Danilo stumbled out the front door of the Repos and into a silent street. He ran first for the bench where he'd sat with Théodore, but that whole area was empty save for several prone forms, one snoring. The bench, the figures, the houses glowed in silver light so stark that they almost appeared to be statues, the moon a silver rosette surrounded by stars.

The rosette reminded him of St. Nizier. That was the only place Danilo could think to go. The Repos was closed to him, and he didn't know where to find Théodore. The cathedral was a destination, not a home. St. Nizier held Anita, the only other person in the city he might be able to call a friend.

He hurried toward the Repos, and then caught himself and made a wide berth around it. This took him out of the path Luc had taken him on that morning, and in an effort to work himself back around to where he thought the church was, he found himself on a narrow street.

Here, there was movement: shadows before him that flicked to life and then stilled as he approached. Danilo kept to the middle of the street and glanced nervously to either side.

Despite these cautions, he was caught unawares when a shape appeared behind him, and for the second time that day, a knife point tickled Danilo's tunic. "Just be still while I take your purse, good sir," a voice said.

"I haven't anything." Danilo kept his voice low and barely controlled. This indignity, on top of everything else that had happened…

Paws—or hands, perhaps—groped his waist. "Where do you keep it, then?" The fingers probed more private sections, and Danilo lost control.

"Leave me alone!" he shouted, and swung his elbow backwards. It connected, but even as his assailant uttered a muffled curse, he was springing forward, running down the street.

Around the corner he sprinted, turned again at the first corner, and stopped two more blocks down, panting. The streets around him echoed only with his harsh breathing. No shadows fluttered around the edges of the buildings.

Slowly, Danilo straightened. He placed one foot forward, then another, and continued on his way through the city.

It took him the better part of an hour to find the grand steeple of St. Nizier again, by which time the adrenaline of the raid and his encounter in the dark street had worn off, leaving his toes dragging on the stones of the street. But there was the small plaza and the church, and there were people sleeping around the edges of the open space.

He made his way to the doorstep of the church, but it was locked. The moon still shone down from high in the sky. Danilo sighed and walked over to the nearest sleeping figure, sat down next to it with his back to a wall, and closed his eyes. Luc's face swam before him with the memory of the otter's body against his. The night air chilled his clothes, and no matter how he hugged himself, he could not seem to get warm.

Chapter Eight

Danilo thought he would never sleep, but when he opened his eyes, he could make out more details of the square. The clock in the left-hand tower of the front of the church glimmered, gold hands catching the moon, but he could not make out the time from their position. He rubbed his eyes and looked up, where fewer stars were visible in the sky. He stood and stretched, and saw the sky behind him soft with dawn's light.

People around him stirred; the streets clattered with early travelers. The archway of the church still hid the door in shadow, so Danilo walked over to it, stretching his legs as he did. Still locked. He turned and saw a raggedly-dressed rabbit eyeing him from the corner of the church. "Opens for Lauds," he said in a rough voice, and then coughed, a hacking cough that animated his whole body.

Danilo didn't want to start a conversation, so he walked back to where he'd been sleeping and sat back down again. But sleep was gone from him, and all he could do was sit with his knees up and his chin on them, breathe in the lingering scent of otter on his clothes, and replay the previous day's events in his head.

Until tonight, the world had seemed to him very much like his own: people were people, after all. But here, people could be arrested, castrated, burned. People walking down the street could be assaulted in broad daylight or dead of night. People gathered around churches and threw garbage in rivers and betrayed each other.

Much as he'd betrayed Luc.

He shook his head. There wasn't anything else he could have done for Luc, and the otter himself had said as much. Danilo repeated that to himself several times, until he gave up on quelling the burning shame in his chest.

And then there was Bertrand. Danilo's claws extended whenever he thought about the badger taking advantage of Luc, then calling the church on him, those fat, dirty paws going through Luc's things. If only there were something he could do about Bertrand. Leave his punishment to the Lord, indeed. That was another difference between this time and his own. In his own, people took things into their own paws, they didn't trust to the Lord or magical powers or anything…

Magical powers, like the ones that had brought him here in the first place.

When he looked up, a small crowd of ten had gathered in front of St. Nizier's. More people were walking up to join, so Danilo struggled back to his feet and joined them. At least while standing, he could rub his arms to get some warmth into them; he could look at the people around him and try to forget what had happened.

The bells rang a short time later, but not at St. Nizier's. Ears around him lifted, muzzles followed, and noses sniffed the air. Danilo, a head above most of them, thought they were looking at him until he saw the unfocused stares, the wide nostrils flared as though the far-off tones of the cathedral bells could be seen or smelled. So he, too, lifted his head and let the sounds wash over him.

Above him, the Lion Christ looked down on the crowd, his suffering detailed in every drop of paint and carved line. Danilo tried to focus on the expression of the carving, the sad spiritual resignation of the feline face, but always had to look away, to the brightening sky, the fading stars, the rooftops around him; the haze of smoke growing thicker as people awoke and lit fires; the smell of unwashed fur as more people joined them.

Scarcely had the last peal died away when a clack sounded from the doors and they swung open. The crowd of people had grown to over twenty, and they filed in with Danilo among them. He followed numbly to a pew, where he knelt between a goat in a stained tunic who smelled of disease and a squirrel missing an ear and several teeth.

Now the bells of St. Nizier rang out. The goat and squirrel bowed their heads and Danilo followed suit. When they too had finished and he raised his head, a slender rabbit stood at the altar. Latin words washed over Danilo like music, melodious and incomprehensible, and he did his best to follow his companions through the service, moving his lips when they spoke, bowing when they bowed.

The service calmed him, short though it was. At the front of the church, a crucifix hung with the Lion Jesus on it, as detailed as the one in front of the church. This time, when Danilo's eyes came to rest on the carved suffering figure, they did not slide away.

Christ understood suffering. He had been betrayed as well, and worse, and yet he looked out on the congregation and His disciples preached forgiveness.

They had also taken Luc away.

Danilo squeezed his eyes shut and pressed his paws together. He hadn't prayed since he was…five? Six? At whatever age his parents had told him he didn't have to, when he'd prayed to be better at football (and that hadn't worked out at all). Not even when he'd been struggling with his sexuality had he thought to turn to the Almighty, but here in the church, with Latin droning around him, he felt the urge, and so he addressed the figure on the crucifix and the Presence everyone else was kneeling to. *God, if you're listening, help me. If You did this to me, then help me get back somehow. And take care of Luc. And punish Bertrand.*

The service went on around him. He glanced to his left and right, and tried to emulate his companions' devotional poses. He was not at all sure that anyone had heard him.

When the service ended, his companions rose and filed out, but Danilo remained kneeling. He had it half in his mind to wait for Anita, but mostly he remained kneeling because he did not know where else he could go.

As the congregation exited, he said his prayer again. As he reached the end of it, his whiskers registered movement toward him. He didn't look up, but the scent of vixen reached him, and a moment later a paw landed on his shoulder.

"*Bonjour*, Danilo. I am sorry to interrupt your prayer."

He turned his head. The sight of her familiar muzzle, even in this unfamiliar setting, even knowing that she did not know him, made it easier to smile. "I was done," he said.

He made the sign of the cross, and Anita's eyes relaxed. "I have some good news for you." She gave him that smile he recognized from when she'd found the perfect book for an essay in their class. "The Bishop is very pleased to welcome a white tiger to our seminary. He says that if you know how to write, you may copy manuscripts

and it will help you learn. If you do not, you may work in the kitchens until you learn. Can you write?" He nodded, and she beamed.
"Excellent. And perhaps we will find you some better-fitting clothes,
as well."

She led him out of the church and down a short two blocks to
a large wooden building. With her by his side and the sun warming
the air, Danilo strode more confidently along the streets. Anita did
not speak, so as they left the plaza in front of the church, Danilo said,
"Luc was taken by the church."

Her ears flattened. She paused but did not stop. "I am sorry to
hear it."

"I was praying for him," he said. "Even though the church are
the ones who took him."

"That is kind of you."

"Well, I don't…" He sighed. "I don't understand it, really. I'm
praying to God to help him…but the church are the ones who took
him."

"When you pray," she said softly, "you are not praying for God
to intercede in the mortal world. You are praying for God to give you
the strength to cope with the mortal world. In this case, I presume
God would answer your prayer by guiding Luc to bear his punishment and continue his life according to His word."

Bear his punishment. Danilo's mind kept skirting around what
was actually going to happen to Luc. "What if someone's done
wrong? What if I prayed for their punishment?"

"Oh." Anita's ears remained down. "You should leave punishment to the Lord. It is not our place to exact punishment in this
world."

"If that's the case, then…then why is the church punishing Luc
for his behavior?"

Here, Anita did stop. She lifted her eyes to the second story of
the building they stood in front of. A simple cross looked down over
the main door, and above the top row of small windows, a sign read,
"St. Épipode's Seminary of Tigue." For a moment, Anita did not
move, her long russet tail curling behind her. Then her ears came up
and she said, "The seminary is new. It opened five years ago at the
command of the Archbishop. Previously, our students had to travel
to the monastery for their education. This allows the officials of the

church to participate in training. You will have the great privilege of receiving some lessons from the Bishop, and perhaps even the Archbishop. They are already building similar seminaries in Lutèce and Orléans, but this is the first of its kind."

It looked a far cry from the grand brick buildings of the Université. Danilo tried to view it as one of the foremost educational institutions of its time, and that made him feel a little better about perhaps beginning to live his life—his 1508 life—within its walls. And then he would become, what? A priest? Not such a bad option. Anita looked better fed than most of the other people on the street, her fur clean and well-groomed.

"It's lovely," he murmured.

She began walking again, to the front door. "What happens to Luc," she said, low and very soft, "is not punishment but correction. He is in the grip of demons and they must be exorcised."

The tiger chewed over that as Anita opened a plain wooden door in the base of the seminary and ushered him through. Something Luc had said when Danilo had first emerged from the river came back to him. "Will I be working for Cobb?"

When she didn't say anything, he looked at her in time to see puzzlement turn to shock. Her ears snapped back and her voice was hushed, scandalized. "You mean Archbishop Argile?"

He heard the name first and relaxed, and then whatever facility was allowing him to speak the language translated 'argile' into 'clay.' Danilo's tail curled again. Cobb's last name was Clay. "I'm sorry. I'd only heard him referred to by one name. Is he—is he an—" The word "elk" had no word for him to say, so he tried to describe the species. "Antlered person?"

"A stag, yes. You have seen him?" Her surprise animated her eyes. "He has not given a service since the Feast of Michael. Where have you seen him?"

Danilo shook his head, the fatigue of the night catching up to him. Of course if Taye and Anita were here in this dream, Cobb would be here too; he'd forgotten about Luc and Théodore discussing his guard at the river's edge. "I have only heard of him," he said. "His reputation is…great."

"He has done much for the Church, and for the city of Tigue. He collected funds to finish the cathedral, he has built this seminary, he has brought fine priests to this town…"

"And the guard who arrested Luc? Those were his? That wolf LeSevre reports to him?"

"There are many sinners in Tigue. He has brought us the means to rid our city of those demons." She said it tranquilly, as though she did not know Luc at all.

Anita in his time also had that ability to turn off her emotions, especially when she was focused on schoolwork. Danilo gritted his teeth. "Do you know the guards well?"

"No." They had entered a plain wooden room with a portrait of the Stag Jesus. This room, alone of any place Danilo had explored in this time, was furnished with a carpet over the hard wood floor. His paws relaxed onto it; he curled his toes against the short pile. One didn't realize how luxurious carpet was until it was taken away.

Anita now gestured to two doors at the back. "Your living quarters will be in a small room on the second floor. On the ground floor are the instruction and meditation rooms. You will join a group of students that meets daily with an instructor, and you will have a primary instructor who is responsible for your spiritual education. Mme. LeChamp will assign you a room and furnish the schedule, and your application will be presented to the priests so that one may choose you as a student."

"LeSevre," Danilo said. "Do you know who his superior is?"

The vixen turned and met his eyes with her dark brown ones, the slit pupils wide in the dimly-lit room. "You can do nothing for Luc," she said, keeping her voice low. "You should help yourself."

"I'm trying to." Danilo exhaled and rubbed behind his ears. "I'm sorry. I won't ask again."

She studied him a little more and then nodded. "Very well. Now, you had wished to speak to the Bishop about a miracle?"

Given what had happened the previous night, and all Luc's talk about witches, Danilo was no longer sure that he wanted to confess to someone in the church that he had been sent to this world from another time. But an audience with the Bishop…maybe here was someone who could help him see Luc. If the Bishop were really a holy person, perhaps he would be sympathetic, could see that Luc's case would be different, especially if Danilo told him Luc had been coerced into his actions by Bertrand. Of course, the Bishop could be as bad as LeSevre; Danilo knew perfectly well that there was unlikely to exist any sympathy between the viciousness of LeSevre and the intensely focused homophobia of Cobb (assuming that Cobb was as he'd known him, and thinking of the elk with the power of the church and the righteousness of God did not do much to improve Danilo's image of him). But he had no other choice. Nobody else in the city of Tigue had the authority to help him.

What was more, even if he couldn't explain his own particular miracle to the Bishop, at least he could ask about miracles that had happened previously in this city. Perhaps other things would give him a clue as to how he could reverse whatever it was that had brought him here.

Anita watched him patiently. "Of course," he said.

She smiled. "You have luck today. He would like to meet you."

***

The Bishop of Tigue held his offices in a building adjacent to the Cathédrale itself, off the plaza and around the side. Anita gave Danilo directions, although had she simply told him that the Bishop's offices were near the Cathédrale, he still would have found them easily. The white marble building had clearly been built concurrently with the cathedral, overshadowing the wooden buildings around it much as the cathedral dominated the town. Fancy gold lettering on the façade, much nicer than anything Danilo had yet seen in 1508, proclaimed it the "Official Ecclesiastical Offices of the Bishopric of Tigue," with a bishop's mitre on the sign on either side, and the ebony door bore a gold cross. No crucifix with Lion or any other kind of Jesus appeared on the front of the building, though.

Danilo entered cautiously, stepping onto another carpeted floor in a room that smelled gloriously clean compared to the smoky, unwashed body air he'd grown used to. Incense burned in one corner, and something like sandalwood was all he could smell once he passed the doorway.

A young sheep greeted him and brought him upstairs to another plush room where he was told the Bishop would send for him in a moment. He sat down in a chair with a cushion—another first in

1508—and curled his tail properly around his hips and placed his paws in his lap. This room also bore a painting of Stag Jesus, the same one he'd seen at St. Nizier, and two more paintings, one of which he recognized from his studies in 2008: Lion Jesus on the cross. The second one, closer to him, showed a young, attractive deer, so delicate in his features that Danilo thought at first he was Joan of Arc, Sainte Jeanne, before remembering that Sainte Jeanne had been a weasel.

The deer smiled out, standing alone, his right hand pointing up. The texture of his fur made Danilo want to reach out and touch it, and the dark featureless background made it seem that the deer was emerging from nothing, pointing the way to the light that shone on him. Pointing to heaven. Was there a texture of water in the background? He peered closer.

"You like this one, yes?"

Danilo's fur prickled at the deep, smooth voice and the confident strike of the words. Though he didn't want to now, he turned. Standing in a doorway, smiling a friendly smile, the black wolf he'd seen in the cathedral the previous day was holding out one paw toward the painting.

He was again dressed in white robes, although at this close distance, Danilo could see their gold trim. The wolf stood every inch as tall as Danilo himself, black ears perked and lips pulled slightly back in a smile that showed his long canine teeth. Green-yellow eyes measured Danilo.

"It arrived here only a month ago, from Etrusca, the master da Vinci. You are from Etrusca, yes? You have seen his work?"

Danilo's throat was dry. He nodded.

The Bishop inclined his head. "I am pleased to see that your education has included the arts. I am Bishop Lukin."

There was no need for him to make that introduction. Danilo knew Georg's last name as well as he knew his voice, with or without the Siberian accent.

Chapter Nine

I'm Danilo." The tiger stood.

The wolf waited. Danilo swallowed. "From Firenza."

"You have family? Sister Colquez did not inform me of their names."

He should have guessed. How could he have been so stupid? With part of his mind repeating those two phrases over and over, it was difficult to marshal his remaining mind to answer the bishop's question. "Er, yes. We are the Mitin—Mitini family."

The wolf's ears flicked back and then up again. "I have traveled often to Etrusca and I have never encountered this family."

"We are a small family." The advantage he had was that he knew Georg, but Georg did not know him yet. If he professed to be loyal to the church, then he could perhaps get Georg to be on his side. "I was fortunate enough to study in the Vatican for a year."

This brought widened eyes. "You studied with His Holiness?"

"Not directly, of course." Deception was difficult. Keep it simple. "And only for a year. My family made a donation to the church, but we fell on hard times. They sent me here to finish my education, but I lost the money that had been entrusted to me."

The wolf studied him. "And, it seems, the clothes from your back. So. Come in and we will discuss your future."

He showed Danilo into a plush office, to a wide, cushioned chair before an ornate wooden desk. The bishop walked back to sit behind the desk, trailing incense and perfume in his wake, and then placed his elbows on it and bestowed a warm smile on the tiger. "It is a rare thing, a white tiger, especially one who has studied at the Vatican. I wonder that I was not informed in advance of your arrival."

Crap. Yes, that was a thing that would probably have happened. "You see," Danilo said, "my family…" Wait, it was the 1500s, right? No computers, no cell phones. Messages were sent via horse, or maybe bird in extreme cases. They took weeks and were unreliable. He coughed. "My family employed an unreliable messenger. I am not surprised that he did not arrive."

The bishop's eyes narrowed, but his expression showed no surprise, nor suspicion. "I see. It is unusual that you would be dispatched before a response was received from our seminary, of course, but we can certainly accommodate you."

Again he stopped, and Danilo felt the pressure of an explanation required. "It was my eagerness to come here before the winter. My father...my father told me that if nothing were available, I could find some other work easily."

"Such as kitchen work?" The wolf's smile stretched wider. "Yes, I can smell the oven and potatoes on you. We do appreciate resourceful students here. What was the name of your priest at the Vatican, again?"

"Father Green." Danilo blurted out the name of the pastor of his village, the only name he could think of on the spur of the moment, aware that hesitation would be more suspicious. He heard the word as "vair," when he said "Green," and added an "ee" to make it seem more Etruscan.

"Verdi?" Bishop Lukin cocked his head to the side.

Danilo made himself nod with as nonchalant an air as he could. "Verdi," he said. "He was—is—a tiger as well. So we worked together."

The wolf's tail made a soft sound as it brushed the floor. He clasped his paws together in front of him. "I see. I will send word to Father Verdi to ask about your previous instruction, so that we may have his assessment of your skills. Of course, such an unusual tiger, with fur of your color, is clearly favored of Our Lord. I expect only the best response."

Well, he had to have expected that. Now he had a time limit. How long would it take to send a messenger to Vatican City and back? Driving by car it was possible to get there in a day, about ten hours going at 90 kilometers per hour. How fast did horses go? A third of that, a quarter? So he had a week. He cleared his throat and nodded. "Thank you, sir."

"Now," the bishop said, leaning forward with his ears cupped toward Danilo, "Sister Colquez said you wished to talk to me about a miracle."

"Yes." He couldn't lie. His mind raced. "Can you tell me what constitutes a miracle?"

The wolf smiled, eyes narrowing. "Surely you must have studied miracles at the Vatican."

"I studied Christ's miracles. The miracle of multiple species, the miracle of fishes, turning water to wine…but I did not study general miracles."

Danilo flushed as he said the words, pulling out all the miracles he could remember Christ having performed. Too late, he remembered that some saints had performed miracles as well. Indeed, Bishop Lukin reminded him first of that, and then went on, "We think of three classes of miracles: things that cannot happen; things that should not happen; things that do not happen. More generally, if the moon were to disappear from one place and move to another place in the blink of an eye, that would be a miracle of the first order."

"Or if a new star appears."

"Just so." The wolf seemed pleased. "If an animal rises and walks after having died, then that is a miracle of the second order. Animals may rise and walk, but they should not do so after death. If a person manifests boils of the plague, or scars of leprosy, and is later cured, then that is a miracle of the third class—it may happen, but does not. And if rain comes at an unusual time or frequency, or at a time requested in prayers, then that may also be a miracle, but that is subject to closer inspection." He smiled. "Some might say that a white tiger is a miracle as well."

Danilo had been called a lot of things in his childhood, but not a miracle, and the appellation discomfited him more than he'd expected. He cleared his throat and said, "I see," pushing that aside to focus on his original question. If he were classifying things, then his trip back in time was definitely a first-order miracle. He didn't quite have the guts to ask the difference between a miracle and witchcraft, not now, not of the bishop, and especially not of Georg. "What miracles have taken place in Tigue?"

"Oh…" The wolf leaned back in his chair. "Saint Épipode, who is buried beneath the altar of the cathedral, is said to have worked many miracles after his death. The harvest was saved, people were cured of the plague...what miracle did you witness?"

"Me?"

Bishop Lukin inclined his muzzle, his ears perked forward. "You question with the air of someone who has witnessed a miracle and yet hesitates to call it such."

"Oh, I—" He swallowed. "I thought I saw a manifestation of Christ's face—Lion Christ—on the surface of the river. That's why I jumped in."

Stupid, stupid, he thought. Why not just tell him you saw Jesus on a tortilla? But strangely, this story put the bishop at ease. He relaxed and nodded slowly. "Our Lord and Savior is often associated with water. And here you are near the very cathedral consecrated to Saint Jean-Baptiste, who is also associated with water, for obvious reasons."

Obvious maybe to you, Danilo thought, until he listened to the translation in his head. Saint John the Baptist. Baptism.

His claws snagged the wood of the chair arms. It all made sense now: the saint of baptisms had called him back to this world through the water.

Sure, he told himself. Because that happens all the time. Did the saint of languages magically make you understand and speak 16th century Gallic as well? And yet, still, the idea that this bizarre experience might have a purpose or an explanation stuck with him.

"I see your excitement," the bishop said. "It may well be that you witnessed a miracle. Perhaps Christ wished you to lose your worldly possessions. Have you been covetous, my son?"

"I—I didn't think so." The accusation drained his excitement. What if this experience did have a purpose, and it was a punishment? Danilo lowered his head, and then remembered the gulf between reality and the face he was presenting to the bishop. Humility would be a good virtue to show. "Perhaps."

"And have you been less covetous? Have you appreciated the gifts you had been given?"

"Yes, sir—" He said it automatically, knowing that was the response that was expected, but he stopped partway through. Had he been appreciative? He certainly had learned to appreciate food, like the bread and cheese he'd had. He'd appreciated the value of friendship, someone who would reach out to take care of him out of charity. And yet, hearing the sanctimonious homilies in Georg's voice kept him cautious in his responses. "I have been trying," he said, more truthfully.

"Making the effort is all God requires of us." Georg's yellow-green eyes stared back at him.

"I look forward to making an effort here in the seminary," he said.

Bishop Lukin's smile remained fixed. "I will have my secretary show you the work you will be doing. We can advance you a small sum, enough for a little food and clothing."

"Thank you, sir."

The wolf smiled beatifically. "And then I would be most pleased if you would accompany me on my noontime walk. I always visit the cathedral to see the clock strike noon. Though it is the same each time, every day presents a new audience, a new lighting."

Danilo thought of the weasel who'd attacked him and hesitated. If he were seen in the company of the bishop, it would not look any better than whatever it meant for him to be walking out of the church. But he did not have the scarf, and in the company of the bishop, at least he would have less to fear from strangers who happened to take a dislike to his clothing.

"Yes, sir," he said. "I would like that."

"Be downstairs at fifteen minutes to the hour, then." The wolf brushed a paw toward him in an obvious dismissal.

Danilo stood. "Thank you, sir," he said again, and walked for the door.

"One more thing," the wolf said, his voice still casual. Danilo turned in the doorway, his tail twitching once before he stilled it. "You should address me as 'Your Excellency,' you know."

"Er." Danilo swallowed, his stomach fluttering. The yellow-green stare and slightly exposed fangs faced him directly. "I'm sorry, Your Excellency."

"Forgiven." The wolf smiled, though his eyes remained deadly serious.

***

The secretary was the young sheep, and he took Danilo to a room on the first floor, windowless and stuffy, that contained a pile of printed copies of the Bible. The sheep opened the thick books to show Danilo the hand-crafted words and intricate illuminations inside, page after page, and Danilo thought to himself that he would never be able to finish a single volume, even given his whole lifetime in which to do it. "There's that printing shop," the sheep said, "makes Bibles for the poor, but for Church copies, they must still be written out by hand or paw."

"Do I have to copy them exactly?" Danilo asked, tracing a finger over a letter D with branches and leaves wound around it, the ink bright against his white fur.

The sheep shook his head. "We are aware that you may have been taught with a different style. As long as the copy reflects well on the Church, you may copy them in your own manner."

His own manner was likely to be far less elaborate, Danilo thought, staring down at the bright colors, the gold leaf, the crisp, precise lettering. Then again, he only had a week before Bishop Lukin's messenger exposed him as a fraud anyway. He wouldn't have time to ruin more than one page. Even those gloomy thoughts could not dim his appreciation for the craft in the books, and he turned page after page, marveling. The vellum pages, soft and bright, did not resemble anything he'd seen five hundred years in the future, although they definitely aged better than paper.

He would get his money that night, he was told. Until then, the sheep gave him the schedule for the seminary. "You have luck," he said with a small trace of envy. "The Bishop has elected to supervise your education personally."

That did not make Danilo feel any better, but he smiled anyway. It would be much harder for him to focus on rescuing Luc if he were to be constantly supervised by suspicious, smooth Georg. But perhaps he could use the Bishop to bring justice to Bertrand, anyway. Leave his punishment to the Lord, yes; but perhaps the Bishop could help the Lord along. Danilo would have to be very careful; thinking back on the number of times he'd almost been trapped in their one conversation gave him great respect for the wolf's intelligence (and that made him wonder about Georg himself, back in 2008— had he simply attached himself to Cobb for convenience, or was

1508-Georg really smarter than 2008-Georg?). But he could lay the groundwork, perhaps—starting with the noon visit to the cathedral.

While waiting in the lobby with the sheep, Danilo tried to plan for what he would do. He had to get back to St. Nizier's at some point; Théodore would be waiting for him there or would have sent word to someone there, if the mouse cared at all about him. He thought Théodore would come at least for Luc, if not Danilo. So after noon, he could hopefully get away and back to the church, and then he could tell Théodore about Luc, and then about his own situation, and then…

And then what? Théodore would almost certainly recommend he flee the city, just leave and go somewhere else. Maybe stay on his farm for a little while, although how they would hide a white tiger in 1508 was anyone's guess. It would be safer than staying in Tigue, at least marginally, and definitely once the messenger returned from the Vatican. The way the bishop had been talking, Danilo was sure the messenger had already been dispatched.

Danilo didn't want to leave Tigue, though. The strongest reason was that he still held out hope that he could help or save Luc. He'd tried leading the conversation with the sheep around to where the prison was, without success. The secretary did tell him that since Bishop Lukin had taken office in Tigue, demons and miscreants had been enthusiastically prosecuted, and that in the Archbishop, the Bishop had found a willing ally in the enforcement of God's laws. This raised Danilo's hopes of revenge on Bertrand. Whatever Lukin thought of Danilo, he seemed the sort who might happily punish another transgressor.

And he smiled at Danilo when he entered the lobby, a genial smile, and Danilo remembered to call him "Your Excellency." They felt like a close group of friends, all three of them, as they walked over to the church behind a large boar in uniform, who swiveled his head from side to side as the bishop walked the short distance in the open. Any people who glanced their way drew back at the sight of the broad, muscled soldier's fearsome tusks and ready sword.

He stood discreetly behind the bishop when they entered the cathedral through a small back door, and remained in the shadows as Bishop Lukin greeted the priest again. He introduced Danilo to the old fox, and the three of them plus the secretary stood and watched the marvelous clock as it whirred and struck noon. The same display took place, but Danilo noticed things about it that he had not before, and he understood what the bishop meant when he'd said that each time was different. The light was softer today; clouds muted the sun and the church was suffused with warm colors rather than sharp light beams. One of the people began to sing along with the hymn the clock played this time, and others joined in.

"So uplifting, the sight of people filled with the spirit of the Lord," the black wolf murmured. "But I suppose these crowds must be meager indeed compared with what you have seen at the Vatican."

The first sentence might have been to himself; the second was definitely directed at Danilo. The white tiger had been trying not to look back at the people who were staring at him, and only half-heard what Bishop Lukin said. "Ah, Your Excellency," he said, while forcing his brain to replay the words so he could process them, "it's not the size of the crowd in the house of God, but the size of the house of God in the hearts of the crowd." He winced as he said it; it was a tired old twentieth-century saying repurposed badly. "That matters, I mean. It's not—"

But the bishop was already laughing and turning to the sheep. "You see, Culliver, we have a scholar in our midst. He has great facility with words. One can see that his year studying with His Holiness was not wasted."

"Indeed." In the company of the Bishop, the sheep's previously friendly manner evaporated. He didn't look at Danilo at all, as if they hadn't just spent over an hour talking together.

"I can see I will not regret taking a personal interest in your education." The wolf's smile turned back on Danilo, though his eyes, greener here in the shadows of the church, remained devoid of mirth. "Truly you have a great deal of potential."

"Thank you, Your Excellency." Danilo waited, but the bishop returned his attention to the clock, and so the tiger did, too. But his tail twitched whenever he was not immediately focused on it, and he kept glancing sidelong at the black wolf. His unease might be simply from standing next to Georg, especially if the Siberian wolf were pretending to be friendly. But Danilo didn't think that was all it was.

When the last peal from the cathedral's bells had died away and the crowd had begun to disperse from around the clock, Danilo composed in his head the way he would ask the bishop for the after-noon off. Before he could say anything, the wolf's muzzle swung his way. "I wonder if you might accompany me for a short time. I have one more duty to see to. It is somewhat unpleasant, but you know, this life is not all clocks and adoring masses." One black paw swung out over the crowd.

"I—of course," Danilo said.

"After that, you will be free to go. I suggest you spend the after-noon purchasing new clothes. A scholar of the church does have a certain appearance to maintain."

"Yes, Your Excellency."

Danilo followed the boar and wolf out the back of the church, with Culliver the sheep by his side. Even though clouds crowded the sky, the air they moved through was warm and stagnant, filled with not only the sweet perfume the bishop wore, but also the thick smells of the people who had recently moved through that space.

"Tell me, Danilo," the bishop said as they walked, "what you think of our city. How does it compare to the grandeur of Firenza, of the Vatican?"

"Oh, well," the tiger said, "Your Excellency, it is a splendid city. I like it quite a bit. I think if I had not fallen in the river when I first arrived—"

"But you did so in the course of experiencing a miracle."

"Yes, that is true. I—I may not have appreciated it as a miracle at the time. But the cathedral is one of the most marvelous things I have ever seen. Including the Duomo."

"And Saint Peter's?"

"Yes, of course." Danilo had no idea what that was, but the best course was to agree.

The wolf smiled, showing his fangs. "I suspect His Holiness would not agree, but then, no-one need tell him, eh?"

"No, Your Excellency."

"Danilo, it was a joke." The bishop shook his head. "We bish-ops may be justly proud of the monuments we raise to God, and I will be first to admit to some friendly competition between us. But His Holiness is above all that. He is concerned only with the spiri-tual duty he bears to administer to his flock, and his chief concern about the building in which he performs his duties is that it be large enough to house all who wish to come before him."

From what little Danilo remembered of some of the popes—and he wished he could remember which one was reigning in 1508—this was not strictly true, nor even a little bit true in some cases. But the way it was phrased made him think it was also a lesson for him, and so he bowed his head. "The Cathédrale Saint-Jean seems quite spacious enough for the citizens of Tigue."

"Indeed. But tell me more of your arrival. You fell in the Saône yesterday?" They walked away from the river on a road angled up toward the Roman ruins atop the hill. Houses grew sparser as they got farther from the cathedral, but unlike in 2008, no trees filled the empty spaces; here there were merely bushes and small patches of ground that in spring might be gardens.

"The day before." The truth came out before he could stop it.

"Why did you not come immediately to the church?"

That was a great question. "I—I was ashamed. I hoped that I might earn some money to replace at least my clothes."

"And you found some Good Samaritans."

Though the road they walked on skirted the edge of the city, the street was as crowded as any in central Tigue. The upward slope became more pronounced, so that even the Bishop was panting. Danilo glanced around and behind from his small isolated island. Behind him, he thought he saw the weasel who'd attacked him, the yellowed teeth and needle-sharp stare, but then a panther walked in front of him and he was lost. "I, er. Some people loaned me clothes, yes."

"What kind of people?"

Caught in the flow of conversation, Danilo replied without thinking. "A mouse and otter," and then said, "Your Excellency" to cover his inward cursing at himself. "But they did not even tell me their names."

Great. That sounded even worse. The bishop did not question it, though, just nodded his long black muzzle and said, "You were fortunate to encounter good people. Though we strive against evil and demons, Tigue is rife with both."

They turned a corner and emerged at the side of a small amphitheater, standing on the edge of a stage half-ringed by ten rows of wooden benches. The people walking with them moved to sit on the benches, but the bishop's small party kept walking along the stage—all except for Danilo, who had stopped the moment he saw what occupied the center of the stage.

Two church officials, a badger and a ram, stood on either side of a three-meter pole, at the base of which a small pile of kindling had been laid. A strong tarry smell came to Danilo on the breeze, along with the smell of fresh-cut wood, but he barely registered them.

Tied to the three-meter pole, paws bound behind his back, an otter stood, his head bowed.

Chapter Ten

Danilo's heart thudded in his chest like the tolling of the cathedral bell. Bishop Lukin spoke, but his words were difficult to make out. "One of those regrettable but necessary actions...the demons are least powerful during the noon hour...this one caused its host to engage in the sins of Sodom against the strict dictates of the church...given many chances, but the demon is inextricably bound to his soul...to prevent it from infecting others, we must destroy it."

The bishop and his bodyguard and secretary stepped down from the stage, to the front row of the amphitheater. "Danilo," the sheep said in a low tone.

Danilo hurried to follow, but could not take his eyes from the bound otter, and nearly fell down the stairs, though they were only inches high. He caught himself, ears burning, and then he did look up at the bishop. The wolf's attention and tight smile were fixed on him.

This was not happening. This was a nightmare. He was going to wake up floating in the Saône in 2008. Or he was going to wake up drowned and dead. Any of those would be preferable to this, to the hot stone under his feet as he hurried to the bishop's side, to the fierce stares of the people behind him, everyone watching the tall, gawky white tiger who had a front-row seat to a public burning.

He'd never even seen anyone die, and now he was going to have to watch his best friend in this world twist and scream, smell his flesh...Danilo's stomach churned and he was glad he hadn't eaten yet today.

"It would please me," Bishop Lukin said with a low growl under his words, "if you would sit by my side."

The huge boar shifted to make room. Danilo took his place and made as if to sit, but the bodyguard gripped his arm and pulled him up. What had he done wrong? He started to ask, but then the bishop sat, sweeping his black tail behind him, and the boar released Danilo's arm. On the other side of the bishop, the sheep took his seat. Danilo sat quickly, so quickly that his tail got kinked under him and he had to get up to resituate it. He stared down at the dusty ground, not willing to look up.

The bishop raised a black paw to the officials on the stage. The badger stepped forward.

"Coumier de Marche, having been convicted of your third violation of church law, and thereby being found guilty of the additional crime of willful compliance with a demon of satanic and most unnatural character…"

Danilo's head snapped up at the name. He had been avoiding staring head-on at the otter, but now he took a good look. This otter was broader, thicker than Luc and better-fed. His eyes were closer-set and appeared to be swollen shut, and his neck was wider. Black streaks broke the matted yellowish-white fur down his front. All of that Danilo took in in a moment's glance before his eyes were pulled downward, horrified but unable to look away.

Between the otter's legs, there was nothing but an angry red scar. The wound had blackened in parts, remained dark red in others, and Danilo could not stop staring at it, as though he could heal it if only he would stare hard enough. His own groin tingled in sympathy, but he did not move to cross his legs, afraid of showing weakness or attachment. The bishop might be watching the stage, but his right ear remained cupped toward Danilo and those yellow-green eyes could turn in a moment.

As the official on the stage concluded the charge and looked up, the bishop raised a paw and nodded his head. The badger continued on. "Therefore it is the judgment of the church that in order to rid the world of the demon which possesses you, we shall cleanse your mortal body with fire and commend your soul to God."

The ram stepped down behind the stage and returned with a torch. Danilo's attention jerked to the flame, the hot brilliance that warped the air around and above it. This was all a play, it was an act, and as soon as he said the right thing, apologized for sleeping with Luc, renounced his attraction to males, the players would step off the stage, the otter would remove the elaborate codpiece concealing his unharmed groin, and the bishop would shake his paw, the malice dropped from his manner.

But even as he struggled for words, the ram lowered the torch. Fire licked at the woodpile, and only now did the otter shift and seem to take note of his surroundings. He looked blearily out at the crowd and croaked a word.

Danilo leaned forward. Beside him, the bishop rested a paw on his arm. "It is best not to listen to the rantings of demons," he said in a low, even tone. "At the end, even given a soporific to dull their thoughts, they will say anything and everything."

The tiger leaned back, but kept his head up. Behind him, the crowd began to cheer, with cries of "Burn, demon!" They stirred and stomped their feet, and some of them chanted words in Latin.

The otter's lips moved again. Now, even through the noise, Danilo caught the words, "Thierry, my love." Then Coumier's eyes closed and his mouth stilled.

The fire caught quickly, leaping from log to log and surrounding the otter. He shifted on his pole, and lifted first one foot, then the other, a pathetic gesture. Bound at the legs, he could barely move them at all.

Danilo closed his eyes. A moment later, his whiskers twitched at the warmth of the bishop's muzzle and breath. "It is important," the wolf said in a low growl, "to bear witness to the punishment of devils. Understand that there is no way to hide from God's authority. All those who do not acknowledge it meet this end."

The tiger took a breath and opened his eyes. He had to shut them again immediately, take another breath, and force himself to watch. It's just a horror movie, he told himself lamely. The black pitch burning as it melted into the otter's fur, the smoke curling up oily and black from the pyre, all that was special effects. The otter, an excellent actor, writhed and now screamed as the flames reached his head. But the acrid smell of cooking flesh filled Danilo's nose and heat licked across his nose and whiskers. Next to him, the bishop's muzzle wrinkled, the yellow eyes fixed on the person burning before him. The slightest tip of his canine tooth appeared between those black-furred lips.

The crowd chanted their Latin and their curses more loudly now, but not enough to drown out the terrible screams. The otter struggled in earnest as the fire ate through his fur, yanking at his bindings. His legs came free, and he kicked one burning log away from him. It skittered to the edge of the stage and lay there, smoking.

Danilo jumped when the log came toward him, but the bishop barely moved. The otter's screams were interrupted by wracking coughs now. He kicked out one more time through the thickening smoke, but more weakly, doing nothing but shifting the pile. Flames rose from him as though he were nothing but wood himself, a fuel quickly consumed and even now nearly spent.

Another agonizing scream, a twist, and the otter's arms came free. But he fell forward, onto the pile of burning logs, and though the officials snapped to attention, he did not move any farther. He struggled to lift his head, and when Danilo saw the otter's eyes through the bright glowing flames, they were rubbery-white and cooked.

Bile rose in his throat. The noise behind him deafened him; the smell of seared flesh overwhelmed all else. He doubled over and retched, dry-heaving onto the dusty ground. Once he'd started, his stomach convulsed again and again, trying to turn itself inside out, and the pain in his gut, the scraping in his throat, the horrible taste in his mouth, the ache of the stab wound in his side, all these distracted him momentarily from the atrocity on the stage. For the moment he had looked into the otter's face, he had seen Luc's face there, the eyes boiled and dead, the fur glowing and charring away from the muzzle, the lips parting to whisper, *your fault.* He hacked and spit, eyes shut, until the vision left him.

When finally he dared to sit upright again, the otter's body lay still and silent, mercifully hidden by the flames. A few cheers came from the crowd, but many were already filing out of the auditorium. Over the cracks and pops of the fire, he heard murmured blessings as they passed the bishop's entourage.

"This one went quickly," the bishop said conversationally, raising a paw to the passers-by, "because of the pitch. Some loved one of the condemned took pity on his mortal form and wished to shorten his suffering. We do not condone attachment to demons, but the donation to the Church can provide for good souls in need, and there is little harm in it at this point. In this case, the guards apply some pitch to hasten the burning. Otherwise it might have taken twice the time for the mortal form to die and the demon to be returned to Hell."

Danilo did not trust himself to speak, but he did turn to meet the bishop's gaze. He had thought that anything would be better than staring at the pyre, but the hard emotionless eyes nearly made him sick again. The wolf's black nostrils flared as if relishing the smoke, but as the bishop spoke, he licked his lips and grimaced. "Likewise," he said, "temptation burns hot and fast in we mortals. But we must bind ourselves with faith, for God's word will hold us fast. Some of us may fall..." His eyes flicked to the stage, where the body on the logs was blackening, the fur mostly gone, skin charring. "But for those of us who remain upright, the kingdom of Heaven is our reward."

The thing on the logs was barely recognizable as an otter. It was easier to look at when Danilo could forget it had been a person. Now the smell of a wood fire dominated the other smells, and Danilo's eyes were watering, perhaps from the smoke. Perhaps.

The bishop's eyes were clear and dry. "This is your first lesson," the wolf said, and rose.

The sheep rose after him, and when Danilo remained still, the boar grabbed his arm and yanked him to his feet, wrenching his shoulder. "The rest of the day is yours," Bishop Lukin said. "You will attend Lauds tomorrow morning at the seminary, where your education will continue." He gestured to the sheep as he walked away. "Culliver?"

Without a glance at Danilo, the sheep pulled several coins from his purse and held them out to Danilo. The tiger stretched out his paw and felt their weight drop against his pads. Had these coins paid for the pitch that had licked through the otter's fur, searing his flesh, bringing horrible mercy to him? He closed his fingers reflexively and dropped the arm to his side, holding the coins there as the boar, the wolf, and the sheep walked across the front of the amphitheater to the street outside.

As he watched, they stopped to talk to a wolf, a grey one shorter than the Bishop. It wasn't until the grey wolf turned and stared across the crowd at him that Danilo recognized LeSevre. The wolf's lips stretched into a feral, humorless smile, and then he fell into step with the bishop as they vanished from sight.

156

The fire began to die down. The ram prodded at the blackened body on stage. Danilo hurried away from the front of the stage to join the last few stragglers. A female goat, who had evidently been watching him, said, "Good job, sir."

"What?" He tried to focus on her.

"Capturing these demons. Tigue is a more wholesome place today."

Danilo had never in his life wanted more to disagree with someone. He could barely think straight, but he knew he had to find Luc somehow, see the otter again and make sure he was okay. And that meant he had to find Théodore somehow.

He turned away from the goat and scanned the crowd behind him, and one figure caught his eye: a weasel stumbling down the steps along the outside of the amphitheater, staring at the ground as though it had mortally offended him, muttering to himself. His bared teeth flashed at Danilo in a familiar black-and-yellow pattern.

As he turned and passed Danilo, he spit at the tiger's feet. Danilo stepped back, ready to hurry away, but the weasel did not come after him nor even say anything. And then, as the weasel turned and made for the exit, Danilo saw a beige cloth hanging out of the waist of his pants beside his tail.

If he thought about it—if he thought about it, he would not jump forward. If he thought about it, he would stay and wait until everyone had left, would go with them out into the street, would go to St. Nizier and hope that Théodore had received his message or could figure out where to go. If he thought about it, he would sit and think about it forever and he would wait for things to happen to him and they might never happen, Théodore would never come and one day the bishop would bring him back here where there would be another otter tied to the stage, gruesomely castrated, covered in flammable pitch if his friends could afford it, and Danilo could not bear that.

So he pushed his way forward and grabbed the weasel by the shoulder at the bend where the amphitheater spilled out into the street. When the weasel saw who it was, he struggled and tried to escape. "You have no reason to accost me!" he screeched. "I have done nothing! Let me go!"

"I need to ask you something," Danilo said. "I'll pay you."

He held out the coins the sheep had given him. But the weasel smacked his paw, sending the coins clattering against the wall and onto the ground. "I don't want your filthy church money!"

A fox passing by glared at him and murmured something. Danilo cringed, until he noticed that the fox was glaring at the weasel. A mouse behind the fox murmured the same words and crossed himself.

"Shut up," Danilo hissed at the weasel. He leaned close, trying to lean imposingly on the smaller person the way Georg had leaned on him. "Don't take my money if you don't want, but I need you to get a message to Théodore."

The weasel spat again, into Danilo's face this time. Moisture and foul breath spattered the tiger's nose and whiskers. He closed his eyes, desperation mounting into fury. "Fine," he said. "Fine." He reached around behind the weasel and grabbed the beige scarf, yanking it free.

"Thief!" the weasel shrieked. Danilo glanced around them, but the crowd had thinned and only the occasional passerby kept them company. So he held his paw up as the weasel hopped at Danilo, swiping for the scarf. When he couldn't get it, his paw went to his side.

"Keep your knife where it is." Danilo glared down. "You stole this from me yesterday, and I'm taking it back. But if you want it again, I'll be happy to give it to Théodore to give back to you. If it means so much."

The knife came out despite Danilo's words, and glittered between them. "You'll give it to me now."

But whereas yesterday the weasel had seemed fierce and threatening, here with the smoke still in his nostrils, Danilo knew there were far worse things in this world. He pushed the weasel back as he'd done before, but this time did not run away. He stood and glared down at the smaller person, and thought about wresting the knife from him, in revenge for the day before. The wound in his side barely hurt anymore, certainly not in comparison to what was paining his mind. The weasel's defiance buckled in the face of Danilo's stony intimidation, and Danilo felt a stab of triumph with absolutely no joy. "Tell Théodore to meet me where we met yesterday," he said. "I will be there until sunset."

The hardest part of all of it was to turn his back, with the weasel still standing there, the knife out and shining. But he collected the coins that had scattered, as many as he could see (some of the people passing by had taken the ones that had rolled out into the street), and then walked away, down the slanted road, with Luc's scarf trailing from one paw.

No noise came from behind him, no hurried footsteps. Perhaps the weasel could see his ears turned back or perhaps he didn't care. There was a small part of Danilo that thought that if the weasel did run after him, did stab him in the back to take the scarf, that at least this nightmare would be over and the smell of smoke would be gone from his nose. He did not know if air would ever smell clean to him again. When he did glance back, he saw a thin column of smoke still rising from the top of the hill, and he had to look away as his gorge rose.

Hold it together, he told himself, rubbing his nose hard with the back of his paw. The images were coming back to him, the liquid fire running down the blackening fur, the charred body, the dead eyes. Don't, he told himself. He was coming out into the plaza in front of the Cathedral Saint-Jean, and he looked up expecting relief in the beauty of the immense monument. Instead, he saw marble white as bone, crosses black as char, and stained glass windows like skeletal mosaics pressed into the wall. For a moment, he imagined people— otters, mice, tigers—pressed into the wall while alive and left there to die, the sun streaming through their bodies as their weakening flesh stretched thinner and thinner. Then the vision passed and the windows were only windows again.

He brought Luc's scarf—a sniff confirmed that it was Luc's scarf—to his nose. But smelling Luc through the smoky residue of the dead otter only led him to worse panic, and so he tucked the scarf into his pants and hurried on his way.

Only once more did he hesitate, at the center of the bridge. Here, too, was another way for his adventure to end. The water had brought him here, and one way or another, the water could take him away. But though he could see himself standing on the stone railing, leaping, diving, plunging into the murky Saône, he did not get up to do it. Not yet. He raised his eyes to the cathedral. *St. John, if you brought me here, tell me how to get back.*

He received exactly as much answer as he was expecting, and with a sigh, walked on. He bought himself bread and cheese and went to sit on the bench in the little park.

To keep himself from seeing those horrendous images in his mind again, he tried to take stock of his situation. It didn't work, but it was better than nothing. Bishop Lukin clearly knew about Danilo's association with Luc. LeSevre would have told him, and there was no hiding or claiming it was another white tiger who'd been with Luc when he was arrested. But Bishop Lukin didn't want to arrest Danilo; at least, not yet. He had gone to great lengths to impress upon him that if he continued along the path he was on, he would end up

(dripping with flames, screaming as his fur blackened and smoke filled his lungs)

dead. If he'd wanted to arrest Danilo, he could easily have done it already. Therefore, he wanted something from him.

It was possible that the bishop thought he was merely a student who had been seduced by undesirable elements in the city. If that were the case, then he had certainly dispatched a messenger to probe Danilo's background.

It was also possible that the bishop realized that Danilo's story was completely made up. In which case he was hoping to, what, redeem him? Weren't church people all about redemption?

Or it was possible that the bishop thought him unusual but wasn't sure what his situation was yet. Which was fair; Danilo didn't know what his situation was, either. All he knew was that he had to rescue Luc somehow before he was castrated, if that hadn't already happened.

The best way to find out where Luc was being kept, of course, would have been to ask Bishop Lukin. He could have had that conversation if watching a person burn to death hadn't bothered him at all, could have asked, "so, any other horrible mutilations or executions planned in the next week or so?" He could have told him that he had a friend who'd been captured and wrongly accused, and the bishop might have appreciated his forthrightness. He might have taken him to Luc right away and Danilo wouldn't have to be here.

But no, the bishop was Georg, and Georg, though not as scheming in Danilo's time, was not trustworthy at all. Or was he? He hadn't really done much but follow Cobb around and join in the teasing, both light and harsh. Other than that, Danilo didn't know him very well.

There was the Archbishop, whom Danilo assumed outranked the Bishop, but he was a stag named Cobb. Who knew what he would be like? Best to avoid him.

That left only LeSevre as an authority figure to appeal to, and Danilo liked him less than Bishop Lukin. At least the bishop had appeared to believe Danilo, and he might enjoy watching people burn, but maybe it was out of an honest, twisted interest in their souls. Maybe he believed in demons.

Danilo sighed and rested his head in his paws. The only other option he saw was a movie-style jailbreak. And this was a sixteenth-century jail, so it was probably pretty solid, not one where you could bust up a computer panel or fake your entry and then knock out the guard and take the key. It was all as ludicrous as pretending that the immolation he'd just seen was only a special effect. He had to wait for Théodore to tell him what to do.

The smell of smoke remained in his nose as the sun descended in the sky. The emptiness in his stomach impinged only slightly on his awareness; he did not think he could manage any food right now. His mouth was dry and tasted of bile, and he would have liked some water, but he didn't want to leave the park for fear that Théodore would appear while he was gone.

The waiting and the stress and the lack of sleep the night before all pushed his eyelids down. He closed his paw around his coins, folded his arms across his chest, and hunched forward. He didn't want to sleep, but his eyes refused to remain open. He dozed; the smoky smell in his nostrils waxed and waned, and he imagined that some of the people who walked past him on the street were burning, the smoke from their fur drifting to him. In his dream, an otter turned to him with glowing embers for eyes and held out smoking arms, and Danilo knew he had to bring the otter to the water, to put out the fire, but the Saône had gone dry and he didn't know where he could find any water. "Water," he moaned, and jerked awake to the sound of the word on his tongue.

No otter sat near him, nor any mouse. A wave of loneliness crashed over him, and he gulped back sobs, and then his paws opened and he buried his muzzle in them. Coins pattered to the ground as his body shook, tears running against his fingers and through his fur.

Someone crouched in front of him, reaching for the coins. Danilo couldn't even rouse himself to object to his coins being stolen. He didn't care; they didn't make any difference to him in the end.

The coins dropped into his lap. "You'll need this," Théodore's voice said, roughly.

Chapter Eleven

D anilo rubbed his eyes and stared up. The mouse had his paw out, his eyes cold and hard. "I wouldn't have come at all. Armand thought I shouldn't. But he wanted Coumier's scarf."

The tiger wiped the back of his paw across his nose. The scent of smoke lingered there. "It's not Coumier's scarf," he said. "Taye—Théodore—I'm so glad to see you."

"Just give me the scarf." The mouse's voice remained as dead and neutral as his eyes.

"It's Luc's scarf," Danilo said. "They took him." The memory of that night crushed his chest inward, atop the burning he'd just witnessed, and he struggled to draw in a breath for a moment.

Théodore's eyes flickered, and when he spoke, his voice wavered. "How do I know this is truth? Armand saw you sitting with the Bishop."

Of course Théodore didn't trust him anymore. Danilo had spent the morning with his bitter enemy, apparently friendly. The tiger licked his dry lips and pushed his sleep-deprived brain to come up with words. His only ally—well, the only one who would help him rescue Luc—was about to walk away from him, and with good reason. If Danilo had met a new student and then seen him eating lunch with Georg and Cobb, he wouldn't have trusted him, not one bit.

He croaked, "I want to save Luc."

The mouse's ears lay back, and his eyes narrowed. He did not withdraw his paw, but the fingertips with their blunt claws curled upward. "I'll not be trapped by a Church traitor. Give me the scarf," he ordered.

"Please." When the mouse's expression did not waver, Danilo reached behind him and freed the scarf. He laid it across Théodore's fingers.

The mouse stuffed it into a small purse. "God have mercy on you," he said, and turned on his heel.

Danilo sat on the bench and watched the thin tail flick as Théodore walked away from him. *Get up, go after him!* his mind cried, but he could not force his legs to move. Finally he struggled to his feet and lurched into the crowd, his eye fixed on the mouse tail. People crowded around him, moving with him, blocking his way. He hurried past them, around a corner, and caught up to Théodore.

The mouse appeared not to notice him. Danilo laid a paw on his shoulder, and the mouse turned.

It wasn't Théodore. This mouse was the same height, but had a large boil just beneath her eye. She cringed back from him and said, "Don't harm me, sir."

"God keep you," Danilo said. He released her and looked around the crowd, but there were no other mice in view. He'd lost Théodore, probably forever.

***

The sun had sunk nearer the horizon, casting a golden glow on the hills, by the time his slow steps brought him back to the seminary. He had stopped in at St. Nizier's to find a service in progress and had not seen Anita there anywhere, so he'd decided to go ahead and settle into his room. At least then he would have a place to stay and to leave his things. If he ever acquired any things.

He still carried the coins clenched in his paw. Bread and cheese rested uneasily in his stomach and he did not feel up to the task of finding someone to sell him clothes. Mme. LeChamp, an elderly sheep with a black-furred face, showed him to a cramped room on the second floor of the seminary, a room barely larger than the straw pallet on its floor with a window that looked out onto the adjacent building and a door that did not lock. Despite Luc's prediction, it did not appear that he was to share with any other students, unless they were prepared to sleep as closely as he and Luc had. The memory almost pained him; he pushed his coins under the straw pallet and sat cross-legged looking up and out the window, trying to think about anything else. From the floor, he could see the sky, the clouds underlit by the sun, and he thought idly that sunsets were just as beautiful in 1508 as in 2008.

He could continue numbly on with this life. Forget about Luc, forget about Théodore, make up some excuse for his lie when the Bishop's messenger returned from the Vatican. But Luc's plight nagged at him, not only his own actions that had led to it, but the otter's suffering. He had to see him, had to tell him he was sorry, and if he could come up with some way to help, he had to do it. He'd let other people solve his problems and guide his life for years; he'd gone to Tigue for University on his father's recommendation; he'd majored in Philosophy because his mother said he had a knack for it. He'd gone to the gay club to meet someone, but hadn't had the courage to go in, even after Taye offered to go with him. He'd even fled college and ended up in this dream-slash-adventure-slash-nightmare not of his own accord, but because his cousin had come out in a public forum, because Cobb and Georg had bullied him and he hadn't stood up to them.

Now Luc was sitting in a cell, perhaps looking out at the same sky, and Danilo was sitting in this tiny room. The Bishop had warned him not to associate with Luc, and Théodore had refused to help him; and the easy thing to do would be nothing at all.

He found that he did not want to do the easy thing.

Anita had told him to forget about Luc, but he could not do that, not when his last memory of the otter was his stiff back as he told LeSevre to leave Danilo alone. Not when he could still see the raw wound where Coumier's genitals had been. Not when the smoke still—still!—tickled his nostrils.

He pushed himself to his feet, pushed the door open, and walked out into the late afternoon.

He strode through the crowds, sighting along the single tall steeple to guide his path, and though people still stared curiously at the tall white tiger, Danilo ignored their looks. At St. Nizier's, he walked past rows of supplicants praying in the pews and knocked on the sacristy door.

Anita opened the door and smiled when she saw him, but her smile faltered at his expression. "Danilo, did it not go well with the Bishop?"

"It went fine," he said. "Sister, please tell me where I might find the prisoners guilty of crimes against the church."

Her ears swept back and she looked down at the polished wood where her paw rested. Her claws scraped back and forth. "You should forget—"

"He saved my life!" Danilo's voice echoed in the church.

Several people turned to look at him. He ignored them, but Anita smiled around at them. "He means he was saved by the Christ," she said, and the confusion cleared from their muzzles.

"I need to see him." He lowered his voice. "Please, Sister. Christ would have mercy, would he not?"

She looked steadily at him, and then followed his gaze over her shoulder at the Christ hung over the altar. Her ears lowered and she spoke in a whisper. "The prison is on the Rue St. Bartholème, on the right bank of the Saône. Cross the bridge, go to your left, right below the second archway, and left when that street ends in a wall. You will see it, a grey stone tower, and you will smell it as well, no doubt. That is where the prisoners await their judgment. But there is nothing you can do for them."

What did Danilo think he was going to do for Luc? Stand outside and remind him that he was in jail and Danilo was free? Make empty promises to save him? His shoulders slumped. Then he remembered the coins under his mattress. "Is there a way to get food to them?"

She hesitated. He placed a paw on the pew and leaned in closer. The smell of the wood and the paper, the ancient stone of the church, died away before her musky scent. "There is, isn't there?"

"No." Her eyes remained cast down. Her next words were spoken in a whisper so soft that it died in the stone of the floor, the statues of the Virgin and the saints around them. "I have heard that there may be a way, but it requires bribing the guards with gold."

None of the coins he had with him were gold. "Thank you," he said. He turned and then a painting caught his eye, hung on the wall of the confessional near the back of the church. It was Jesus as a Fox, administering to the poor. The halo around the Fox's head did not strike Danilo so much as the beatific air about Him, the kindness as He extended His paw.

Danilo turned back to the vixen. "What about simple charity?" he said. "Company, reminding him that he's not alone?"

She lifted her head to frown. "Pardon me?"

"That is what I can do for him, if nothing else. I can tell him that his friends haven't abandoned him."

In her eyes, he saw glimmers of color from the stained glass shimmering and playing. She blinked, and then her lips curved into a smile. "Yes. I think that is very noble of you. You have a good heart."

He smiled back, tightly. In his heart, he warred with himself. Because while he had been able to say what he thought would be the right thing, and he had been able to come up with something tangible he could bring to Luc, what good was comfort? What good was a meal of bread and cheese when the otter was about to be mutilated? No, Danilo was afraid that what he was doing was simply to comfort himself, a selfish act at Luc's expense, that he was going to make the trip up to the prison simply to try to get Luc to tell him that he wasn't to blame.

Even if he were doing that, though, was it so bad if he did offer company to Luc? If he brought food, if he stayed and offered comfort, then at least it was an even exchange. And if he could figure out a way to help Luc, then it would be much more than even.

He told himself this all the way back to his room at the seminary, all the way down to the boulangerie, and across the bridge. Maybe he could get Luc out of the jail, and then Luc would know where he could go after that. Conveniently he did not remind himself that Luc had been free just a day ago and had had nowhere to go; things were different, more desperate now, and when they were more desperate, there would always be a solution. There would be an answer, there would be an answer.

Twilight stole over the rooftops, turning red clay to maroon and brown as the sun settled over the hills. The ruins atop the hills stood silhouetted against the clear mauve of the sky, and somewhere up there, the smoke from the day's burning had stopped coiling upward into the air. Danilo paused below the second archway and lifted his eyes over the shadowed houses. There were always older buildings, with newer ones built around them, wherever people settled. The buildings he'd touched with wonder in his own time, thinking about the ancient people who'd lived in them, were new here. But there were still ancient buildings here, where the wolves who'd ruled Rome had left their mark, where battles had been fought three times longer ago than he'd been thrown back. And when the Romans had come, there had been stone huts, old caves, and riverbank dens where the ancient tribes of otters and foxes, hares and wolves had gathered and made their homes.

Had those people worried about whom they loved? Or had they loved without abandon? He was fairly sure he'd heard that homosexual relationships used to be tolerated, but he couldn't remember why things had changed, or when. Clearly it was before 1500, if nothing else.

He shook his head. Luc needed him, and philosophizing about the people who'd lived here fourteen, fifteen hundred years ago wouldn't help at all.

The road rose up through houses, spaced more widely than around St. Nizier's and the Repos, whose fires lent a now-familiar harshness to the air. He hadn't realized that it was the same road that led up to the amphitheaters atop the hill, and the haze of smoke took on a more gruesome cast to him, making him gag. But halfway up, where the Bishop had marched him upward, Anita's directions guided him to the left, along the wall, where he paused gratefully. Below him, between the Saône and Rhône, red-roofed houses huddled together on the precarious bit of land called Presqu'ile. In the midst of them rose the churches, the stately St. Nizier's across the river, and at the foot of the hill, the glorious and terrifying St. Jean-Baptiste.

The sun's light had almost entirely faded, and the clouds, though scattered, did hide the moon. There were no street lights, of course, but Danilo found he could actually see well enough without them. And he wouldn't have had to see to find the prison.

Anita had been right. The smell came to him within five yards of turning left along the wall. He breathed in and then gagged, assaulted by not only filth and urine, but a sickly-sweet smell he didn't know immediately, that filled him with an instinctive dread, quickened his steps as he approached the great stone tower.

It stretched halfway from one street to the next, and as far back. Its squat shape rose three stories, and bars in the windows caught and reflected the meager light. Danilo stopped amid the scant crowds in the street and then edged into a space between a house and the prison. He stood with his back to a wall, so nobody could sneak up on him, and stared at the ragged stone building, the thick metal bars.

How would he even figure out which window was Luc's, let alone get to it?

Traffic on the street outside decreased as the minutes dragged on. Danilo glanced out at the darkening evening and then cupped his paws around his muzzle. "Luc," he called toward the prison.

No response. He called a little more loudly. "Luc!"

A pale goat's snout appeared between the bars of the window nearest him. "Quit yer noise," it said. "Leave us in peace."

"Do you know where Luc is?" Danilo stepped forward eagerly. "He's an otter."

The prisoner eyed the baguette in the tiger's paws. "Give me an end of that bread and I will tell you what I know."

Danilo tore off six inches of the baguette and stepped forward to hold it up to the window. The goat's filthy hand reached out, fingers scrabbling to grasp the bread, and as Danilo released it to him, he noticed that one of the fingers was missing. Thick blunt nails dug into the tender crust and the bread disappeared into the prison. The sickly-sweet smell drifted down to him with the sounds of desperate chewing and gulping, and at this close distance, Danilo recognized it as the smell of disease. Which one he couldn't tell, but he held the rest of the baguette to him, thankful he hadn't touched the goat's fingers at all.

A contented exhalation came from the other side of the window. "Where's Luc?" Danilo called up.

"How should I know?" The goat's voice drifted out to him.

"You said you'd tell me!"

"I said I would tell you all I know. I know nothing. I have never heard of your 'Luc' nor of any otter. There. So I have upheld my bargain." He laughed harshly. "Thank you for the bread. Come back anytime."

"You…" Danilo clenched his fist around the bread, and shouted the word. "Thief!"

"Report me to the Church, then." The goat laughed harshly.

Danilo stalked around the corner. Here no house bounded the prison, but a low stone wall surrounding a park of some sort. He stood with his back to it, and stared up. This prison wall looked identical to the other. "Luc!" he called, and here, away from the street, he dared to call more loudly. "Luc!"

A shape appeared at one of the second floor windows, a small round head without large ears. "Who's there?" Eyeshine gleamed down at Danilo.

"It's me! Danilo!"

"Danilo?" The head leaned out farther, and Danilo now recognized Luc's head. "What are you doing here? Go away!"

"I'm sorry!" He held up the baguette. "I brought you some bread."

At the word "bread," heads appeared at two of the other windows. "Who's brought bread?" "Is it fresh?"

"You need to leave," Luc said. "They will follow you. They knew about me because...because I came to see my friend."

"Bertrand betrayed you!" Danilo cried, and then his voice faltered, because what he was thinking was, *and so did I,* but he could not bring himself to say it.

After a moment, Luc said, "I have been imposing on Bertrand's kindness, but no. The guards told me I was...known to them."

It didn't make sense to Danilo. Who then had let the Church into the inn? Who had known exactly when Luc had returned to the room and had given him a small amount of time to perhaps end up in a compromising position with Danilo? But he didn't want to press, not here. "Was your friend Coumier?"

He'd thought he could say the name without thinking about it, but he was wrong. He closed his eyes and slumped against the park wall, because now Luc's face was superimposed on his memory of the burning otter. When Luc didn't say anything, Danilo said, "I saw him die. I'm sorry."

"You saw him? Why?"

"The Bishop took me. He wanted to warn me. He—he knows—"

"Quiet!" Luc's voice rang out sharply.

Danilo stared up at the two shining eyes. Of course he shouldn't confess to being gay right here beside the prison. Who knew what ears were perked nearby? He cleared his throat. "Did they hurt you at all?"

Luc laughed, but his laugh was short and had an edge to it, not like the laugh Danilo remembered. "My shoulder hurts," he said. "My stomach. But no, they have not exacted their punishment yet. Tomorrow, they say. Today they were otherwise occupied."

"Then there's still time."

"No," Luc said. "There's no time."

There's always time, Danilo told himself. But he would have to figure something out without Luc's help. He sighed. "Can I come in to give you the bread?"

"No. The guards—you can't visit me. It isn't safe."

"I'll throw it to you."

"Danilo—"

He ripped off another chunk of the bread. "Hush," he said. "Get ready to catch."

But his planned toss and catch went very badly. To start with, Luc was only able to reach about half a foot outside the bars of his cell. If Danilo had been able to throw accurately, it would have been hard enough. He'd never been a bowler at cricket, and what's more, the throwing motion stretched the wound in his side. The piece of bread sailed wide of the window, smacked into the wall, and fell to the ground before Danilo could catch it. He tore off another, which flew into the air, and at least that one he caught and threw again.

Five minutes later, he held the last bit of baguette, and three chunks lay on the ground. "I'm sorry!" he called up to Luc.

"It was well meant," the otter called down. "Do you have a place to sleep?"

"Yes, they let me in at the seminary. I'm studying there."

"Good. Go back there and sleep, and forget about me. When they release me tomorrow, I'll leave Tigue."

Danilo swallowed and lifted his head. "I won't forget you."

"Pray for me, then." Below the eyeshine, for the first time, he saw the pale white of a smile. "God keep you, Danilo."

His throat tightened so much that it was hard to get the words out. "God keep you, Luc. I'll find a way to help you."

The silhouette above him disappeared. The night sky, thick with clouds, shone faintly beyond the prison roof. Danilo's eyes lingered on the clouds, and then the smell of disease reminded him that he shouldn't linger here. He bent to collect the bread that had fallen on the ground.

"Ho." A weak voice called from the first floor window nearest him.

Danilo straightened and met the gleaming green eyes of a fox, framed between the metal bars of the nearest window. "Give me that bread," the fox said, "and I'll tell you how you can get in to see your otter."

The tiger stared and clutched the bread to his chest. "No. There's no way, is there? You just want bread. Forget it."

A dry laugh, and the fox tilted his head. "There's a way."

"So tell me. Then I'll give you the bread."

"You'll walk away."

"I won't." He held up the bread. "If there's really a way—I'm honest. I can't say the same for you."

"I swear by the Lord that I will tell you."

"Well, I swear that I will give you the bread." He glared stubbornly into the cell.

The fox exhaled and rested a paw between the bars. "Give me a small piece."

Danilo set his jaw, but then looked down at the pieces of bread pressed to his chest. All the prisoner wanted was something to eat. He was probably starving. Danilo himself hadn't eaten at all, and finally the ache in his stomach was not accompanied by nausea.

He took one of the pieces of the bread and laid it in the fox's paw. "Take it," he said.

"Thank you." The fox's paw withdrew, but his eyes remained fixed on Danilo's. "Sometimes when the moon is high and those blessed by God can sleep, a priest comes to hear the confessions of the prisoners. He sends the guards away, for the confessional is inviolate. We prisoners can hear murmurs and cries of repentance, but nothing more. Perchance you might slip in at that time."

"And the prison is empty then?"

"Not every night." The fox leaned closer to the window. His breath, sour and stale, at least did not carry the taint of disease. "But if your friend is to be executed tomorrow, he will certainly come tonight. He comes always to hear the confessions of the condemned. He came last night."

"Luc isn't to be executed!"

The prisoner stared out and then said, "I thought from what you said…I only heard your words…well, then, perhaps he will not come tonight. I am sorry." He lowered his eyes, and then, slowly, the bread appeared between the bars. "If my words have not been useful…"

"Keep it." Danilo waved a paw at him and then impulsively pushed another piece of the bread through the bars. "God keep you."

"God bless you," came the throaty response.

Only a flicker of hope, and one he hoped never to have to use. But…he turned back to the window. "One more thing," he said.

"Certainly." The triangular outline of the fox's ear flicked.

"Do you know where they carry out the punishments?"

The air remained still and mostly silent. Up the hill, a night bird cried. "Aye," the fox said, slowly. "Aye, I know. I had my lashes right here."

"But for…for…" Danilo swallowed. "For halfies," he whispered, "that is here as well?"

"Halfies?" The fox drew back, the glare of his eyes brighter. "Your friend is a halfie?"

"Y-yes, he—"

"Pfah! You should be in here with him. Truly there is no justice in the world." The eyes disappeared. A soft thump came through the bars: the fox sitting down. A moment later, the sounds of chewing.

"I gave you bread!" Danilo called in, but not too loudly. He sighed and returned to the wall over the park, trying to put the fox's words out of his mind. Was it worth waiting to see if the priest would come tonight?

He settled down by the wall to wait, but his eyes drifted shut almost immediately. He tried to force himself awake, but soon realized that if he were not walking or talking, he would sleep. So he pushed himself to his feet, and only then did he look over the wall and see what the park really was.

Granite markers and large stones lay about the field as though cast in a game of dice, most of them quite plain. He'd been leaning against a cemetery wall. No wonder this part of town was so quiet: a prison and a cemetery at night? He wasn't superstitious, but as he stared at the empty field full of graves, a shiver passed through him, so he hurried back to the Rue St. Barthólème. Among the few nocturnals who scurried about the streets, he felt more at ease, all the way across the glimmering river and back to the seminary.

He ate the last remnants of bread on the way back, and by the time he'd crossed the river, he had decided that he needed another plan. When he entered the seminary at the street level, no lamps were lit in the room, but soft light from the window fell on the picture of Jesus Stag. Danilo stared at the antlers, the gold of the halo reflected in their curves and points, the threat implicit in them negated by the softness of the brown eyes and beatific smile.

Slowly he mounted the stairs to his room. He had to try to save Luc, and if his ill-conceived prison break wouldn't work, then he had no choice but to appeal to the Bishop. Perhaps the information about Bertrand would be a coin he could barter; perhaps he could simply beg for mercy. But if he simply sat in his class while Luc was subjected to the Church's mutilation, he would never forgive himself.

Chapter Twelve

D anilo slept through Lauds, he was told when a grumpy rabbit shook him awake. He did not feel rested, echoes of fire-
filled dreams crackling behind his eyes as he rubbed them.
"I'm sorry," he told the rabbit, and pulled Luc's tunic over his head.

All the way down, he prepared the case he would make to the
Bishop, expecting to find him in the lecture room. His memory of
the wolf's fanged smile warred with some little hubris he felt; he
had escaped LeSevre twice, and his twenty-first century knowledge
would give him an advantage (ignoring that it had not done so to
date). One moment he pictured himself making his case eloquently
to the Bishop, and the black wolf setting a paw on his shoulder, con-
gratulating him on his devotion to his friend and his service to the
Church. The next moment he remembered the reflection of flames
licking at yellow-green eyes and he imagined the Bishop denying his
request only for the pleasure of taking a knife to Luc's genitals, the
wolf wielding a blade in his own paw and forcing Danilo to watch
the operation. This drawback to his noble plan had not occurred to
him the previous night. Coumier's mutilated groin resurfaced in his
imagination and would not depart, no matter what Danilo offered.

When he entered the small room on the first floor of the seminary, three seated students turned their heads, including the rabbit
who'd woken him, and a standing slender black-robed wolf—a grey
wolf, light of fur with black tips to his ears—looked up from the
book in his paws. "Danilo," he said. "My students are expected to
attend Lauds every morning."

"Yes, sir. I'm sorry, I didn't sleep the night before..." He scanned
the room, expecting the Bishop to be sitting in a corner, perhaps, but
the small room held only bookshelves and two desks with inkwells.

"You may address me as 'Father.'" The wolf gestured to one of
the several empty chairs in the room. "Be seated."

Curling his tail around the back of the chair, Danilo sat down and tried his best to pay attention. But the stuffy room set his thoughts to wandering. There was only one place where he was certain of finding Bishop Lukin, and one time. Danilo had longed for twenty-first century technology before, but now he felt he would give his—well, not an arm, but maybe a finger, or—or a claw—honestly, it was harder to think about dismemberment so cavalierly here in 1508, where he confronted people with missing appendages every day, but he would give *something* valuable just to have a clock in the room. Church bells rang outside, but not always with the familiar hourly carillon. When he did catch a carillon, he counted eleven peals.

After that, he had to trust his own sense of time. He was aware that the opportunity he had, to listen to a real sixteenth century lesson, was one he should be paying attention to, but he could barely keep his tail from lashing back and forth, much less keep his attention on what the wolf was reading from his book. It was something about the saints of Tigue, and he focused enough to hear the names: Pothinus, Epipodius, Alexander, Viator, Sacerdos, Lupicinus. At least two of those names rang familiarly to Danilo's ears. He drifted off again until the wolf read stories of the tortures the first three had endured at the paws of the Romans, and then Danilo had to hide his squirming, his tail curled tightly around the leg of the chair. He imagined Luc similarly strapped to a rack, pulled until his joints popped free of their sockets, battered under a barrage of stones, mauled by wild animals in an arena, strapped to an iron chair that was heated by fire.

He rested one paw in his lap as the wolf went on to talk about what the saints meant to Tigue, spending quite a bit of time on Epipodius, for whom the seminary was named and to whose remains, in the old days (old days! Danilo stifled a laugh), many miracles had been attributed. And Epipodius had been tortured for the crime of being Christian, while those who now revered him were torturing others in turn.

When the tiger couldn't stand the waiting any longer, he took advantage of a pause in the wolf's reading to stand up. "Excuse me, Father," he said. "I have an appointment at noon. With the bishop. Bishop Lukin."

The other students all turned to stare. The wolf's eyes widened and his ears stood up. "I had been informed that the bishop was taking personal charge of your education, but I thought that would be in addition to the regular lessons."

Danilo shook his head. "I don't know what he plans," he said. "He told me to meet him at noon at the Cathèdrale."

"Very well, then, you are dismissed. Go with God."

He hurried out into another cloudy day, the streets crowded with people, and by now he knew the way across the bridge to the cathedral so well that he navigated it by instinct. Again, he stopped on the bridge and looked down at the river, but this time the urge to jump in did not even present itself.

The cathedral's bells began to toll noon as he approached the plaza. He hurried around the back, walking beneath the flying buttresses and below the stained glass window. Faintly from inside he could hear the clock chiming its carol.

At the back door, he pushed his way through a small crowd gathered to watch for the bishop, and up to the ram guarding the door. "I was here with the bishop yesterday," he said. "He asked me to return."

"I was not informed of this." The ram gazed back at him with impassive, blank eyes.

"Well, then…" Defiant answers from action movies sprung to his head. Danilo subdued them and stepped back. "I'll just wait here."

In the shadow of the cathedral, his plan seemed foolish. All he was doing was putting himself in more danger. It would be easy now, to slip back into the crowd, to go back to the seminary. Luc would be punished and leave, and he had absolved Danilo of blame. The tiger looked down at his wrist and paw, the white fur dirty again but still unmistakable. If his fur marked him as blessed, then what did the Bishop's black fur say about him?

He took a step back, convinced now that Bishop Lukin would deny his request, force him to watch his friend's castration. Get a grip, he scolded himself. Do you really think your white fur is special? You think it means you're blessed by God or something? Didn't Mom and Dad tell you over and over that it's not the fur, it's what's inside that counts?

Remembering his parents wasn't the best thing for his emotional stability, but at least it reminded him that they too would have done whatever they could for their friends, and that stilled his feet. He put a paw to the cold stone of the church and waited.

When the bishop's little retinue emerged, Lukin's eyes found Danilo as quickly as though he'd known the tiger would be there. He affected surprise. "Why, Danilo. You've missed the clock."

"I understand you're carrying out another punishment." Danilo took a breath, inhaled the thick dirty street air, the hundreds of people's scents around him, the steadying old stone of the church. "I want to come along."

"Thinking of taking up a position in my guard? You've the size for it." The wolf smiled and crooked a finger. "Come, come."

On the way up to the prison, the bishop asked what he'd learned that morning. Danilo recited what little he could remember, mostly the names of the saints. "Ah, yes. Old Pothinus has developed quite the reputation—not here, but he has shrines farther south. People attribute potency to him."

"Potency?" Danilo was having trouble keeping up with this conversation, so focused was he on their destination.

The bishop, by contrast, walked as casually as if they were strolling through a garden. "In case of a childless or...un-consummated marriage."

"Oh, that kind of potency." In a land without Viagra, people substituted prayer to certain saints. It made as much sense as anything else, Danilo supposed. "Does that count as a miracle?"

The bishop laughed. "You wish to make a study of miracles. I will remember that. It may count as a miracle, aye."

Scraping his memory, Danilo said, "And Saint Epipodius had miracles attributed to him."

"Oh, indeed." They turned below the archway and walked up the narrow street, more crowded in the daylight. "You have stood upon his remains, you know."

Danilo looked down at the dirt and stones below his feet, startled. Lukin saw his movement and laughed softly. "Not here. He is interred below the altar in Saint-Jean. In fact, the ruined church next to it, outside my offices, was said by some to be dedicated to him. Of course, Saint Jean brought the word of baptism to the masses, and we celebrate his presence now. But Épipode the martyr is not forgotten by any means, especially by those who know the history of Tigue."

The history lesson helped distract Danilo as the large, squat block of the prison came into view, and so of course that was the moment the Bishop turned the conversation back. "What did you learn from yesterday's punishment, Danilo?"

"Learn?" He wrenched his gaze from the prison walls, unable to see around the corner to Luc's window. Between the shuttered house and the prison, a goat stood murmuring through the bars to the goat who had taken Danilo's bread.

"I hope you did not enjoy the suffering of another soul?"

The wolf's yellow-green eyes bored into his, the faint smile he'd worn while talking about history replaced by intent scrutiny. Danilo, unsettled by the expression, could not marshal his thoughts. "I—I learned that—it was a horrible thing to see."

"Demons are horrible creatures. And when they infest a person's soul, the results can be equally horrible. The process of destroying them appears terrible, but in reality the demon has already destroyed the person." The boar, walking alongside, struck a rabbit who was gawking at the bishop. The rabbit, no more than a teenager, fell to the ground. Bishop Lukin walked on without taking any notice. "So the lesson you should learn is that you must fight the demons should you feel them possess you. You will encounter many virtuous people in Tigue, but demons are sly and may hide their presence."

Danilo still could not work out in his head whether the Bishop really believed in supernatural demonic creatures who could possess humans, or whether it was a hyperextended metaphor for homosexuality and other bad behavior. "I will remember that, Your Excellency."

The guard at the prison door stepped aside. The boar grasped the door handle in one massive fist and pulled the door open.

Inside, Danilo breathed that sickly-sweet disease smell, urine, and the thick musk of people confined for weeks without running water. This stone-walled room appeared to be the guard post; a desk and large wardrobe occupied one wall, spiral stairs in the corner led up, and scraps of bread and cheese lay among crumbs on a small table, though how anyone could eat amid this smell, Danilo couldn't fathom. The chairs around the table had been pushed back and sat empty, while three guards in uniforms familiar from LeSevre's crew stood stiffly as the Bishop entered. A fox stepped forward at full attention, ears up, tail curled appropriately down. "All is in readiness, Your Excellency," he said.

"Thank you, Perchet." The wolf's muzzle inclined ever so slightly downward. "Is he...?"

"Yes, Your Excellency."

At the name "Perchet," Danilo gave a start. But the fox's eyes traveled impassively over his. It was rather impossible that Perchet did not recognize him, but he gave no sign. Danilo was thankful, and wanted to tell the fox so, and that it was not necessary for him to dissemble. He settled for nodding as he passed the fox, head down, following the Bishop. They passed several cells, one of which held a fox asleep on a board in the corner—perhaps the one that had taken Danilo's bread and cursed him. Just after the fox's cell, the Bishop turned onto a stone landing from which stairs led up and down. He descended, and Danilo followed. Culliver came behind the tiger, while the boar remained on the first floor.

One floor down, a door of thick oak beams stood closed, but the Bishop did not hesitate nor wait for the boar; he pushed it open himself. It opened on well-oiled hinges that only hissed softly as the black wolf walked through. Danilo stepped in after him and clapped a paw to his nose.

There was no question of the use of this room. A long table of wood stood at the center, near a side table that glittered with silver blades and a brazier that lent a smoky haze to the air nearby. The sight of the stains on the table and the stench of old blood made Danilo gag.

To the right, a polecat in a bloodstained tunic walked out from behind a long brown curtain rubbing his paws together. He reminded Danilo of Armand, but taller, and when he spoke, he revealed far less damage to his teeth. "All is ready, Your Excellency," he said, and then caught sight of Danilo. "What's this? New guard in training?"

The Bishop smiled, fangs showing. "Danilo is a new student of mine. I am supervising his education personally."

The polecat appraised him. "Truly the color God gave his fur is reflected in his good fortune. Welcome to Tigue, blessed Danilo."

"Thank you," Danilo croaked. The sight of the grisly table and the affable polecat in bloody clothes had sapped his resolve. He did not want to see Luc lie on that table, he did not want that pole-cat to come near him. He turned to the Bishop, preparing to argue Luc's case, but at that moment his whiskers twitched and footsteps sounded behind him.

He turned to see LeSevre pushing Luc into the room. The otter's paws were bound behind his back and he wore nothing but a tunic that fell to mid-thigh. As the wolf surveyed the room, his eyes rested on Danilo's, and his features brightened in a savage smile.

Luc's eyes lit on Danilo a moment later, and his dull resignation turned to wide-eyed shock. He controlled himself and looked away immediately, staring resolutely down at the wooden floor as he was marched over to the table.

"Danilo," the bishop said, his voice honey-smooth, "you will help LeSevre lift the prisoner onto the table, will you not?"

Another guard had come up behind LeSevre, a lanky rat with a patch over one eye, and he had been moving forward with Luc. Now he stepped back and waited at the door, attentive. The Bishop and LeSevre both watched Danilo, the first with a neutral set to his lips and eyes that hid his worst intentions, the second with feral glee that hid nothing.

Danilo licked his lips. In a way, he was glad the Bishop had forced him to action here, because if he were simply allowed to stand and watch, he did not know if he would have been able to act. "I want to say something first," he said, and hurriedly added, "Your Excellency."

The Bishop nodded as though he had known all along. "Proceed. But I pray you will not have the discourtesy to draw out the waiting period for our prisoner."

"I suppose you know that I know him," Danilo said. "LeSev here will have told you." He deliberately mispronounced the wolf's name and was rewarded with a flicker of annoyance.

Luc snapped his head up and stared at Danilo. The tiger couldn't meet his eyes, but he saw the quick shake of the otter's head. He ignored it.

Slowly, the Bishop nodded. "I am pleased that you have chosen honesty," he said. "Is that what you wished to say? To confess what you had been hiding from me?"

"No, Your Excellency. I mean, yes, but more than that. The—the prisoner took me in when I was lost and homeless and didn't know what to do. He is a good person, and what happened with Bertrand—I'm pretty sure Bertrand reported him—anyway, Bertrand is the innkeeper and he *asked* for whatever it was they did."

"Danilo, you don't have to—"

"Quiet!" LeSevre smacked Luc hard in the muzzle. "Prisoners speak only when ordered."

The bishop turned toward Luc. "Do you deny what Danilo says? Do you claim he lies?"

Luc lowered his head. LeSevre's paw came up under the jaw and snapped it up with a crack that made Danilo wince. "You'll look at the Bishop when he addresses you," the wolf snarled.

"No, Your Excellency," Luc said. "I do not contest what he says." He turned his head to one side and spit a dark mass to the floor.

"Filthy swine!" LeSevre lifted his arm and hit the otter on the side of the head again, so hard that Luc staggered into the edge of the table.

"LeSevre," the Bishop said calmly, "perhaps you will go and pay the innkeeper a visit tonight. He must learn that the Church is not his personal instrument of revenge."

The wolf's eyes gleamed. "With pleasure, Your Excellency."

"Now, Danilo," the bishop said. "If you have finished your confession, then perhaps you will help LeSevre...?"

"But—but he was forced to do it!" Danilo gestured. "Bertrand—he made him, because I was staying there."

"You have said that Bertrand *asked* for it. In any case, the prisoner could have sought lodging elsewhere. Were he truly devoted to the church, he would have refused to commune with demons in this way, no matter the price." The bishop's jaw tightened, flaring his whiskers out. "And it is his second offense. Therefore—"

"Please don't castrate him. It was my fault, and he shouldn't suffer—" Danilo stopped dead. The reality of the silver knives, of the reek of blood, pounded on his senses, undeniable. He should be the one to suffer, not Luc. If it were only his first offense, perhaps they would only take one testicle. His balls tightened against his abdomen, and he stared at the polecat's bloody smock. The image of one of the knives piercing him *down there* squeezed his throat closed.

And yet, what was at stake for him was less than for Luc, who now had blood running down his lower lip, who had risked his own well-being to save Danilo. Could Danilo do any less for him? He turned desperately around the room, waiting for a last-minute movie rescue, but only the silence, the polecat, the wolves, the otter, the rat returned his gaze.

"Yes?" the bishop prompted.

"If I—"

"No!" Luc shouted, and kicked back at LeSevre, then turned and spit blood at him. "Don't let him! Take me, the crime is mine! He is innocent!"

"Restrain the prisoner," the bishop said, unnecessarily, as LeSevre had already driven a fist into Luc's stomach and sent the short otter to the floor, doubled over and wheezing for breath.

"Luc, stop it. This is my choice." Danilo took a breath. "If I take a punishment for a first offense..." He had to add that part, to make sure he wasn't agreeing to being fully castrated himself. "Will you suspend his punishment for this one? Will you leave him whole?"

"He's not whole now!" LeSevre barked a harsh laugh.

"What would be the use in that?" The bishop smiled, ignoring the other wolf's words. "It is a noble impulse, but it leaves a demon unpunished and levies a harsh toll on an...innocent."

The pause before "innocent" was not lost on Danilo, but he ignored it. "Can't I take his sin onto myself? Like..." He remembered the picture of the Stag Jesus, his welcoming smile and golden halo. "Like Jesus did?"

For the first time, he saw the bishop's eyes widen and his composure slip. Then the wolf threw his muzzle back and laughed. "Oh, the blessed tiger compares himself to our Savior! Danilo, truly I have not regretted taking charge of you for a moment."

"Is it so funny, to model myself after Jesus? He, uh," he scraped for his knowledge of Christ, "died for our sins, and I'm just offering to take one sin. I mean..." He trailed off.

The bishop's laughter died, and his eyes resumed their calculating stare. "Forgive me. You are correct, of course, we should strive to emulate our Lord and Savior in all things. You took me by surprise, and for that I must applaud you. But I am afraid I cannot permit—"

"Lukin."

The voice came from behind the curtain, deep and resonant, the kind of voice born in a large sounding-board of a chest and forced up through a long, wide throat, a voice that made Danilo curl his paws and tail in against his body and look for somewhere to run. The curtain rippled, and then a white hand drew it aside, and a figure stepped gracefully around it.

His antlers preceded him, magnificently curved to gleaming points, and though he was not an elk, he was the largest deer Danilo had ever seen. He wore a white robe with gold trim and an elaborate miter between his antlers, and he stood taller than anyone in the room, even Danilo. His eyes, so dark they appeared in the shadowy room to be black, came to rest on the tiger. It was Cobb, all right, down to the swagger of the shoulders and the condescension in his eyes, but where Cobb's fur was a rich reddish tan, his 1508 analog's pelt was as white and pure as the fabric of his robes.

Everyone in the room was bowing already. Danilo caught himself staring and then hurried to bow along with them. As they rose, Lukin said, "Yes, Your Grace?"

The Archbishop surveyed Danilo up and down. "I will allow his petition. Our Savior took the sins of others onto Himself, and perhaps it will do our new student good to share that experience. As for the demon…" He waved a hand at Luc without taking his eyes from the tiger. "The demon will understand that any further offense against the Church will be treated as a third offense, that the punishment for his second has been commuted onto this willing subject."

Bishop Lukin bowed again, but despite the flare of victory, Danilo could not look away from the Archbishop. The white stag met his eyes with a smile that communicated some shared secret between them. His fur rose on his arms and his tail tingled; he felt that somehow, the Archbishop knew him.

And then the polecat turned to Danilo and said, "Remove your trousers, please," and the creepy feeling and fleeting triumph both evaporated.

The tiger turned to Luc, but the otter's bloody mouth remained closed. His eyes said what he was not allowed to speak: sympathy and shared pain. Then his lips moved, and Danilo thought he might be praying.

Not a bad idea. He tried to recall any prayers he knew, and could only muster up a brief prayer to Saint John the Baptist again. *If you brought me here, protect me now.*

The polecat was still waiting. The Bishop said, "Danilo."

Or…give me the strength to get through this. He lowered his eyes so he didn't have to see everyone watch him undress. His balls felt hard and tight against his groin as he hooked his thumbs into the waist of his trousers and pushed them down. At least his boxers were gone. That could have raised some awkward questions—or bought him extra time. But no, when his trousers fell down around his ankles, the short hem of Luc's tunic meant that most of his sheath and balls were visible to the room, amid the white fur of his groin. His tail curled around his leg, across the black stripes of his fur.

The surgeon nodded his head toward the table. "Lie there. Paws behind your back."

His breath came more quickly. He could not make his feet move him toward the table.

The Archbishop, in his deep, soft voice, said, "LeSevre will be happy to assist you should you require it."

Danilo jerked his head up to the stag's eyes. They were locked on his midsection, avid and eager. The tiger swallowed and shook his head as a heavy paw pushed him in the shoulder. "I'll do it." He shook LeSevre off.

"We have other duties today," the bishop said, a hint of a growl in his voice.

His heart raced; his head swam. He worried he might pass out. Actually, that would probably be best, if he lost consciousness. But he would have to get onto the table. And then, scanning the room, he caught sight of Luc again. The otter's bloody muzzle gave him the strength he needed.

The table smelled like an abandoned slaughterhouse. Danilo winced as he lay down on it, pinning his paws behind his back. He stared at the rough wooden ceiling and thought about the last time he'd been in a hospital, and realized that here there was no chemical smell, no sterilization, no antiseptic. There was the smell of burning from the small brazier, stronger here; that was all.

The part of him that did not really believe anything would happen to him was shrinking, walling itself away from the reality bombarding it, even as the polecat came around to his side. "Bite down on this," he offered, and with his left paw held out a piece of wood. Danilo took it in his teeth, which sank into the soft surface farther than he was expecting.

That was it. That was his anaesthetic, a piece of wood to bite down on. How many other people had sunk their fangs into this wood? Did they get a new piece of wood every time? His mind raced to avoid thinking about—

The instruments clattered as the polecat picked one up. "Wait." Danilo tried to say the word, but the wood muffled it.

"Did you wish to say something?" The bishop's voice was low, and he enunciated each word carefully.

If he backed out, he would have to watch Luc be castrated. Danilo swallowed and shook his head from side to side.

Nobody spoke, but the silence of the room gave way to soft movements. Danilo's whiskers felt the surgeon move to his side, and then a paw lifted the hem of his tunic up, folding it carefully back over his stomach, exposing the entirety of his groin to the room. He stared at the ceiling until he felt movement behind him.

Paws threw a rope over his thighs, securing them to the table. A moment later, the smell of LeSevre flooded his nose; the wolf leaned over his face, his tunic falling against Danilo's nose as he draped a length of rope over the tiger's chest. With deft, quick moves, he caught it below the table and wound it around again, pulling it tight.

The only thing Danilo could move was his head. He felt the imminence of the knife even before he heard the small scrapes of the surgeon laying two of his blades in the brazier, and turned his head from one side to the other. Unexpectedly, his eyes met Luc's.

The otter stood a foot from the table, and as LeSevre finished knotting the rope to secure Danilo's chest, Luc's eyes flicked to the big wolf. But LeSevre simply stepped back and allowed Luc to remain close. "It will be over soon," Luc whispered, quickly, and LeSevre's paw caught him in the ear, though not as hard as before, not hard enough to knock him over.

Though it was the Bishop who had orchestrated this, and the Archbishop who had given it his blessing, Danilo felt a flare of hatred in that moment that overwhelmed his fear. The Bishop and Archbishop felt to him like instruments of a cruel church, but

LeSevre was reveling in suffering, causing it by his own paw, and yes, it was irrational, but Danilo hated him more than anyone else in the room, or indeed, anyone else he had met in Tigue, past or present. People could draw knives and kill in this time, and if anyone deserved to be killed, it was this hateful wolf.

Blood dripped from Luc's muzzle. The otter, with his bound paws, could not stop it. Danilo opened his mouth to answer, but all he said was "Stay quiet" before he felt the surgeon's paw press down on his sheath and the touch of a blade on his sac.

He jumped, all six feet of him, and heard laughter around the room, soft chuckles. LeSevre, the Bishop, the Archbishop, perhaps even Culliver and the other guard. Not the surgeon, though. "Easy," the polecat muttered as the blade slid down, trimming the fur away in a small line down the center of Danilo's sac, which was doing its best to retreat from the touch.

"Least you know the bindings are tight." LeSevre laughed. "Stronger than he looks, though. Need another one across the midsection?"

He was tossing rope over Danilo's stomach before the polecat lifted his blade and paw and said, "That might be best." In a moment, the queasiness below Danilo's white stomach fur intensified, compressed by the binding of a rope. He fixed his eyes on Luc, who remained steady and calm.

Another clatter. The surgeon picked up his blades from the brazier.

Danilo shut his eyes and clamped his jaw shut on the piece of wood. The polecat's paw returned to his sheath, pressing harder on it. And then—

A stab of pain. That wasn't so bad. He could—

A searing line of fire on his balls. He cried out around the piece of wood, biting down hard, his body struggling but unable to move. The touch of claws on his sac dimly registered through the pounding waves of pain, fingers separating the skin and pushing inside. A burst of nausea in his stomach as the fingers pulled on a testicle, and he *felt* it, he felt it pull out of his sac.

Tears leaked from his eyes, running along his muzzle and down to the table. "Oh God," he moaned around the wood. It was really happening, this horrific torture, and nobody was going to save him, nobody stepped forward to help him, nobody—

Another shock of pain, a lightness, an absence. The nausea persisted, but disconnected now.

Danilo thought he might throw up, and then he would choke on his vomit because his teeth were firmly embedded in the wood. The fingers were prodding at his sac again, and then little starbursts of pain joined the deafening chorus, a point here, a point there, moving up from his fundament to where the paw still pressed on his sheath.

He opened his eyes. Through the blur of tears, Luc's brown eyes still watched his steadily, tears running down the brown muzzle as freely as Danilo's were running down his own. He squeezed his eyes shut and opened them again, and tried to smile, to reassure Luc, but oh God, the pain was terrible, and every beat of his heart made it throb that much worse.

The surgeon's paw lifted from his sheath. A moment later, the ropes around his thighs and stomach loosened. Something cool and damp pressed against his wound, secured there by a cloth circling his hips. "Keep this on for the rest of the day," the surgeon said. "In a few days you can pull the stitches out." He pulled the hem of the shirt down to partly hide Danilo's sheath, a gesture that only reminded Danilo how naked he'd been.

The words seemed to come from a distance, as humiliation joined the pain. Beyond Luc, Danilo saw the white cross on LeSevre's uniform, and farther back in the room, the white figure of the Archbishop, watching with his hands clasped together and the tip of his tongue showing. They had all watched as the polecat had taken half his masculinity and cut it out with a single slice. Images rushed into his head, amalgams of horror movies and surgery videos he'd seen. The wound between his legs pulsed, and his stomach roiled. He turned his head and made an urgent noise.

"Help him," Luc said, but before anyone could move, Danilo freed his trapped paws and turned, his guts heaving, body convulsing. The movement brought fresh pain, and thankfully that quelled his nausea. Fortunately, he'd eaten nothing that day, and so the vomiting brought up only spatters of bile. He reached up to pull the wood off his teeth, which took a good amount of leverage, and he smelled the bile on it as he dropped it to the floor.

He closed his eyes again. The Bishop said, "Take the prisoner upstairs and release him," and Danilo exhaled, not wanting to remain lying on the horrible table, unable to muster the strength to get up.

"Wait."

The Archbishop's voice cut across the room, stilling all movement. He spoke again when nobody responded. "Lukin, will you please review the charges under which the prisoner was brought here?"

Bishop Lukin did not respond immediately. Danilo struggled to his elbows and opened his eyes, his stomach beginning to churn again. The black wolf had his paws clasped before him, his ears flat out to his sides, and his expression was not one of pleasure. "LeSevre?"

The grey wolf barked immediately, "Prisoner was accused of unnatural acts perpetrated upon the person of Bertrand the owner of Repos du Saint."

"Acts, plural?" The Archbishop's deep voice remained smooth as silk.

"Yes, Your Grace," the wolf said. "Over two nights."

"Two nights." The Archbishop steepled his fingers together, and the corners of his lips curved slowly upwards. "Two separate instances. It would seem to me that young blessed Danilo has taken upon himself the punishment for the first of those in his friend's place."

"What?" Danilo finally put together what the Archbishop meant.

The Archbishop's eyes met his. "Which leaves the punishment for the third offense."

"No!" It burst out of him. "You can't! It isn't fair!"

LeSevre moved threateningly toward him. "You address the Archbishop with respect."

"It is God's judgment," the large stag said, "and God's judgment is supremely fair." He leaned forward, his eyes fixed on Danilo. "Unless you would like to take that punishment, too, upon yourself."

"No!" Luc cried. "I will not permit it."

"LeSevre," the Bishop said, holding up a paw, for the grey wolf had made ready to strike the otter again. "The prisoner has just heard himself condemned to death. I think an outburst may go unpunished."

"You can't burn him!" Danilo said. "He won't—you can't—"

"Do not despair," the stag said. "Your sacrifice has not been in vain. He will go to the pyre whole, which is more than most can say. At least—as whole as you are." His brown eyes glittered, and he waved his hand. "Lukin, see to it."

"Yes, Your Grace." The Bishop bowed.

"The day after tomorrow, I think." The stag watched Danilo with a smile. "I want to be sure that that one is well enough to attend."

Danilo bent his head to Luc as the Archbishop disappeared behind the curtain again. The otter's eyes were bright and sharp on his. "I'm sorry," Danilo said softly. "I didn't know…"

And then LeSevre pulled Luc away, marched him toward the stairs. The other guard accompanied them, and the polecat, who had watched the scene impassively, wiped his blades on a piece of cloth. He turned to the bishop and said, "Will you still be coming this afternoon, Your Excellency?"

The black wolf's muzzle remained down and he did not answer, appearing lost in thought. Danilo, too, was trying to sort out the thoughts tumbling through his head, which oscillated between the twin poles of *they cut out one of my balls* and *they're going to burn Luc alive*. The first paled beside the second, until his body reminded him with a throb of pain how immediately and intimately the first had changed him.

"Sir?" The polecat touched Danilo's shoulder, and he turned toward the masked muzzle. "If you'd care to trim the fur around your stomach and at the end of your tail, I'll not charge you for the service." He held up a small scissors. When Danilo stared, unable to process what was being asked, the polecat coughed politely. "It is looking a little ragged; that is all."

"No," Danilo forced out. Let this creature touch him with a knife again?

The polecat nodded and put the scissors down. He leaned forward and whispered in Danilo's ear, "It was brave, what you did."

"Yes," Bishop Lukin said in the surgeon's direction. "I will visit your business presently. Now, please leave me with Danilo. I would have a word with him."

The polecat bowed and hurried behind the curtain. A moment later, the black wolf strode to the curtain and pushed his muzzle behind it, then returned to Danilo. "You are excused from lessons for the afternoon," he said roughly. "Tomorrow morning you will resume them at the seminary."

"Do I have to come to the execution?" Danilo said in a low voice, and then added, "Your Excellency."

The wolf paused, and then looked directly at him. "Yes." When Danilo scowled and looked down, the bishop said, "Do you think you have been ill-used? You offered yourself for sacrifice."

"Nobody cut off one of Jesus's testicles," Danilo muttered.

"No." The Bishop strode toward him and lifted his muzzle with a paw so that he had no choice but to meet those yellow-green eyes. "No, they did not. They drove spikes through His paws and ankles and left Him in the burning sun to die over the course of days. They pressed a crown of thorns upon His head so the blood ran down His muzzle and they displayed him like a criminal. And He bore it all without complaint."

"Did they make Him watch His friends die?" Danilo asked, belligerently.

"Yes. That as well." The Bishop released him. "Perhaps your education in the Vatican should have prepared you better for the act you foolishly took."

Danilo remained silent. The black wolf stared down and then paced back and forth. "I will expect you when the clock tolls noon."

Yet still, he did not leave. Danilo said, "Yes, Your Excellency," because he thought that perhaps that was what the Bishop was waiting for, but still the wolf remained near him. Finally he looked up and saw the Bishop extending a paw.

The gesture disgusted him. He swung himself off the table and stood, though he could not help wincing at the flare of pain that stabbed upwards from his groin. He put a paw across his stomach to settle it, and reached for his—Luc's—pants.

"Buy yourself better clothes." The Bishop produced a silver coin from a pocket of his robe and held it out.

"I don't need your money," Danilo said, and again waited before adding, "Your Excellency."

The wolf turned the coin over and then replaced it in his pocket. "Very well." He watched Danilo pull the pants carefully up over the binding, remaining impassive even when the tiger let out a hiss of pain. When Danilo looked up, the yellow-green eyes were watching his, and the wolf spoke again.

"Your body is a temple of the Holy Spirit, who is in you, whom you have received from God. You are not your own." He paused. "Meditate on that while you are in pain."

Danilo did not think that would help very much. The pain continued to radiate from his groin, dominating his thoughts. He stared at the ground until the bishop said, "Come with me."

Every step up the stairs sent fresh spikes through the tops of his legs. He gritted his teeth, not wanting to give the wolf in front of him the satisfaction of hearing him cry out. The smells of the prison did not overpower the smells of wood and bile and blood that filled his head. He followed the waving black tail up the tight spiral stair, focusing most of his attention on keeping his paws away from his groin. The coolness of the damp poultice had faded already, and a trickle of moisture ran down one leg, which Danilo knew was water but which he kept picturing as blood.

At the stone landing, the wolf turned before stepping out into the room. His long black muzzle looked down at Danilo. "You have not disappointed me," he said.

Was that supposed to make him feel better? Danilo mumbled something and tacked "Your Excellency" onto the end of it.

The Bishop measured him with his eyes once more and then turned. He told Culliver and the boar to come with him, and when they had left, silence descended over the prison.

Chapter Thirteen

Footsteps sounded above Danilo. He flicked his ears in that direction, but with the smells of his ordeal still strong in his muzzle, the still air of the prison brought him no scent. He knew who it was, though, even before the grey wolf spoke. "Move yourself, halfie," LeSevre said.

The tiger extended his claws. "Come make me," he growled.

LeSevre paused, his short ears sweeping back, eyes narrowing. Then he aimed a swift kick at Danilo's groin.

Danilo jerked himself to the side, catching the kick on the side of his thigh. He slammed against the wall at the base of the stairs heading up, twisting to strike it with his shoulders rather than his hips. The impact stabbed upwards at his groin, and he slumped against the wall, protecting his crotch with a paw, and gritted his teeth.

LeSevre strutted past him, laughing. Danilo actually lifted his other paw, claws out, and then dropped it to his side. Not here, not now.

He waited until he heard the door close, and then a few moments longer until his stomach and groin settled. His legs, though wobbly, supported him, and he made his way out into the main guard room.

None of the guards paid him any attention or offered him any help. He pushed the heavy door open by himself, unable to restrain a moan, and stumbled out into the street.

The walk back to the seminary was torture. Where it had taken him perhaps twenty minutes to walk to the prison the previous night, this afternoon he scraped his way along the rough streets, and in twenty minutes had barely gotten to the turn off of Rue St. Bartholème. Every rounded cobblestone that turned his ankle was another flare of pain, spreading from his groin up to his abdomen; every time he had to step up onto a curb or stone, he had to suck in his breath against the fiery fists that twisted his insides.

He made his way across the bridge by holding on to the railing, and this time the water below brought back only the memory of how cool and refreshing it had been to swim in it. He stopped for five or ten or twenty minutes, watching the water flow by beneath him. Now more than ever, the temptation to jump in presented itself, to end this horrible adventure one way or another. But if it were real, then he would be abandoning Luc to the pyre; if it were not real, then—

The pain stabbing through him would not permit that belief. No, to throw himself from the bridge now would be an act of cowardice, and as much as he longed for any relief, an aspirin or even just a few ice cubes, he would not give in to the Archbishop. He gritted his teeth and pushed himself along the bridge.

Now the stares from people who passed him took on a different tone, a penetrating curiosity. They could see that he was a halfie, certainly, could smell the blood and see the dampness at his groin. They were used to mutilated people stumbling down the street, people like Luc had been some months ago, like Coumier must have walked around after his castration, and they pitied and hated him. The faces leered up at him, accusing eyes and bared teeth, flattened ears and flared nostrils. He shied away from them, his own ears lying flat, paws moving from the front of his hips to the sides, and then moving back to the front when pain surged there again. If his body was a temple of the Holy Spirit, as the Bishop had said, then his was a decaying, crumbling structure that any sensible worshipper would flee before the whole thing came down around their ears.

By the time he reached the seminary, the sun was halfway down the sky and Danilo was panting, sweating so much that his paws left wet smears on everything they touched. He stumbled in the front door (another step up, another extra flare of pain) and heard the wolf still lecturing in the first floor room. Then he rounded the corner and came face to face with the stairs up to the second floor. They rose above his head, so many steps. He would never reach the top.

He trudged into the lecture room and collapsed into an empty seat at the back as carefully as he could. The wolf lowered his arm with a susurration of his priest's robes and paused in mid-sentence, his ears flicking. His tone chilled. "Will you be leaving our lessons at noon to meet with the Bishop every day?"

The other students turned to look at him. Danilo's relief at being able to sit, at the strain in his abdomen lightening, weakened him so that he couldn't answer for a moment, and then he whispered, "At least the day after tomorrow."

The students made rustling noises, not talking but exchanging looks. The priest frowned, and then walked to the back of the room, nostrils flaring. "Are you well—merciful Savior!" He stopped two steps away. "What has been done to you?"

"I just…want to sit…" Danilo waved a paw, intending to tell the priest to go on with his lecture. "Until you're done."

"You smell of blood. Were you attacked on the way back?"

"No," Danilo murmured. "The Archbishop…"

The room went still. He barely noticed. "…punished…Bishop… sent me back."

The priest stood and stared down at him. His nostrils flared again, and then his whiskers twitched. "Laurent, Halbert," he said sharply. "Help Danilo to his room. Guillaume, bring water."

The students leapt to action. The lynx and fox hurried to Danilo's side and lifted him gently upright. His wound protested, but with their support, he managed the stairs and the hallway to his room, where they lowered him to the bed. He sank gratefully to the straw pallet, and then the priest's arm was behind his shoulders, holding him gently upright, and someone else was tipping a wooden mug to his lips. "Drink," the wolf said, and Danilo, grateful to be in the charge of someone who cared, obeyed.

Water flooded his muzzle, lukewarm and musty, but he gulped it down until the cup was empty. "More," the priest commanded, "and the rest of you, leave the room."

The room emptied, and the wolf bent to Danilo's ear. "Whatever punishment was levied against you, I will not enquire. Your crime has been expiated and is between you and God."

Danilo nodded, leaning into the wolf to communicate his gratitude. A moment later, there was more water, and then there was solitude and stillness, and then sleep.

***

He woke needing to pee. Holding it in was painful, the clenching of those muscles, so he fumbled at his pants as he crawled out of bed.

The clean chamberpot rattled as he bumped into it; he positioned himself on all fours over it and pushed the bandages down enough to let his sheath hang free. Still, it took him a moment to mentally relax enough to pee into a pot on the floor. When he did, his body sagged in relief.

It sounded as though he'd gotten it all into the pot, at least. Well, he thought, urgent necessity was one way to get used to using a chamberpot. He reseated the bandages and then, in the dim light, saw a cup of water that had been left by his bed. He drank it down almost to the bottom, then remembered that the surgeon-barber polecat had moistened the poultice he'd applied to Danilo's wound. With care and not a little wincing, Danilo shifted the bandages around to pour the remaining water onto the now-dry cloth.

The pain eased with the cool touch of water. He was able to run a finger over the bandages and feel only lingering soreness from the skin. The internal pain still hurt, and now his mind wondered if the priest could tell he was a halfie, if the speech had been made out of pity rather than honesty. Could all the students see that he'd been half-castrated? He put a paw on his stomach, fearing he might vomit up the water. If he did ever get back to his own time—a possibility that now seemed as remote as getting his stolen testicle back—how would he ever be intimate with anyone? For that matter, how would he ever be intimate here? He remembered Luc's half-full sac; if Maria had seen that, she would have laughed at him and pushed him out of her bed.

If celibacy were to be his future, then the seminary might be the best place. He did not want to stay here, to learn to be part of the Church that had done this to him, but his only other choice was to starve on the street or drown himself in the Saône.

A sharp tapping intruded on his melancholy. He craned his neck to the window and saw a rodent's muzzle silhouetted against the dim night sky. A finger pointed downward.

Danilo frowned. The finger paused, waiting for him to react, and when he did not, it pointed down again.

He rolled carefully out of bed and crawled to the window. Did the mouse want him to open it? He pushed his claws around the edge, but could not find a way to open the window.

The muzzle moved closer to the glass. "Meet me in the street." The words came faintly through the glass, but Danilo nodded to show he'd understood. The silhouette disappeared.

It occurred to him, as he winced his way down the stairs at a snail's pace, that it might not be advisable to go meet a random person in the street, here in this city and time in which he remained a stranger. But by the time he'd completed this thought, Danilo was already two thirds of the way down the stairs, and to reverse his decision would mean going back up. No doubt if he did that, the rodent would climb back and wake him up in about half an hour to demand he come downstairs again. And whatever he faced in the street—rescue, prison, death—it would at least be different from a lifetime in the church.

No torches burned in the silent lobby. Danilo had extended his claws to help his purchase on the wooden stairs; now he retracted them to pad across the stone floor. The large door through which he'd first come only that morning now stood closed and barred with a heavy wooden timber. He lifted the timber, bracing himself against the wall and lifting with his arms, and the timber slid through the metal supports. It wobbled for a moment and then fell to the floor with a thud that echoed through the silent room.

Danilo stood and stared at it, and while he was trying to work out what to do, the door opened and a narrow mouse's nose poked in. "Are you well?"

He stared. "No," he said finally.

"No, I suppose not." The mouse craned his neck to look behind Danilo. "Are you well enough to walk?"

He was tired, but the scent finally filtered through to his nose, the earthy farm smell and the cheese on the mouse's breath. "Taye?"

Théodore nodded once. "Aye. Can you come with me?"

"I thought..."

The mouse hissed. "I have spoken to—a friend who knows the sacrifice you made. I—I am sorry for how I acted earlier, but believe me when I say it was justified. I did not know—but now I wish to help you, to make amends." When Danilo still did not move, Théodore clacked his tongue impatiently. "Danilo."

The tiger blinked and focused on the mouse. "I'm sorry. It hurts, and I'm so tired."

"I can help. Come with me, and I will explain. If at the end of the explanation, you do not wish my help, then I will lead you back here. I promise."

Part of him thought it was not a good idea to go off in the middle of the night with a mouse who climbed walls and had pushed him away just that afternoon. But another part of him... "You know what they did to me?" The mouse's eyes narrowed, and he nodded. "What they intend to do to Luc?" Another nod. "And you're going to help us?"

Théodore's eyebrows creased. "Us? I will help you."

"Luc?"

The mouse shook his head slowly. Danilo nodded and took a step back. "Come now," Théodore said. "There's naught to be done for him. What would you do, break into St. Bartholème's prison? You'll end up there yourself."

"If you will not help Luc," Danilo said, "then what I did was for nothing."

Théodore's dark eyes, so like Taye's and yet hardened by a lifetime of scars, searched his. "Very well," he said. "Very well. Come along, we will see what may be done."

***

The walk through the streets was not as painful. Théodore insisted he drink from a bottle that proved to contain wine, and the sharp sting of alcohol and the subsequent warmth it brought dulled the edge of the pain. But already Danilo was growing used to it; or else it was indeed lessening. With the mouse's help, he walked more quickly than before, away from the Saône and toward the Rhône, into a crowded part of town he was not familiar with.

The mouse stopped in front of a narrow building crammed between several other identical buildings. Even outside, Danilo could smell the thick scent of rodents, and when Théodore opened the door and ushered him in, the scent drowned out even the wine. He hurried past a doorway through which he saw a wide-open space filled with sleeping mice, straw visible between them. And then he was on stairs, hissing with pain, and Théodore was hissing back an apology.

"Guests who are not mice are only allowed on the upper floors and then only during daylight hours." He helped Danilo up to the second floor and then out into a hallway that crooked and jagged like a maze, passing door after unmarked door until he pushed one open and pulled Danilo inside.

Chamber-pot smell and Théodore himself dominated the room, about twice as large as Danilo's at the seminary. The mouse guided him to a low bed and had him sit, and then picked up a pewter cup from a small side table. "Drink water," he said. "How is the pain?"

"Worst on the stairs. It's just an ache now."

Théodore nodded as Danilo took a drink. "Good. You are not as young as Luc was, but you heal quickly."

The cool night and water had awoken Danilo, but he was still tired. "Surgery takes days to recover from," he said. "But they're going to kill Luc the day after tomorrow."

"Yes." The mouse dropped to the floor, and his shoulders slumped.

"So what can we do to help him?"

In the dim room, the mouse's muzzle drooped into shadow. He rested his arms on his knees and swept his thin tail back and forth across the floor. "Let us worry about helping you, first."

"The water helped." Danilo took another drink, emptying the cup. "I'm better."

Théodore's eyes glinted as he turned his muzzle. "I'll fetch a lantern and then we will make sure. Remain here."

"Wait." Danilo held up a paw as the mouse stood. Théodore looked down at him, small ears flicking. The tiger took a breath. "Excuse me, but I really don't want to be left alone." Yes, it was Taye, but Taye would never have walked away from him the previous afternoon.

The mouse's eyebrows rose. "You are safe here. It is not advisable for you to be out in the corridors."

"You said the second floor was okay."

"During daylight hours."

Danilo rested his paws on his thighs. His tail flicked against the bed. "Please," he said.

Théodore sighed, and then stepped toward the door and gestured for Danilo to follow.

He padded as quietly as he could down the hallway after Théodore, watched while the mouse hurried down a stairwell to a fire and picked up a lantern, and then padded back. The house was full of the rasp of low breathing and the smell of a crowd of sleeping mice. Danilo had never been in a small space filled with so many people, and even though none of them were in the second floor hallway, the proximity made him nervous, his tail flicking back and forth all the way back to Théodore's room.

The mouse set the lantern on the table. "Please lower your trousers."

"Er." Danilo stood next to the bed. "I just had—"

"I know," Théodore said. "I want to make sure it is healing properly."

"Oh." Danilo's paws hesitated and then fumbled at his pants. "You know," he said, "Four days ago, I hadn't taken my pants off in front of anyone I wasn't related to."

The mouse raised an eyebrow as the cloth fell to the floor. "You have indeed lived a virtuous life."

"Not by choice." Danilo's modesty was preserved by the bandages, barely, but Théodore's manner was so clinical that he felt no arousal, and very little embarrassment, even when the mouse's paws pushed him gently to the bed. He winced and sat, and spread his legs.

Gentle fingers plucked at the bandages, lifting them away from the poultice. Danilo leaned back and closed his eyes, trying to remain calm as the mouse's fingers brushed the fur of his inner thigh, and then removed the poultice. A glow behind his eyelids showed him when Théodore brought the lantern closer.

The cool air felt good on his balls, and when the mouse's finger traced delicately down his sac, too lightly to cause pain, he shivered and did feel the first stirring of arousal. He tried to think of other things, but when he did, his mind went to the last time someone had touched his balls, and then he had to restrain himself from squeezing his legs shut.

"Relax yourself," Théodore told him, and he thought it would be a miracle if he could relax, and that made him think of saints and miracles. Épipode, interred beneath the altar of a church now named for another saint. What miracles had he performed? Danilo would have to ask the wolf lecturing them.

The mouse's paws cupped his sac, hefting it. The strange lightness made him queasy. What was the other saint? Pothinus. Pothinus was Saint Viagra. Now that was a miracle. That would be a miracle for him now. After that surgery, he would need some kind of divine intervention to have sex again at all. Even the concept was—well, not repulsive—actually, it was somewhat appealing, but then, he was still a teenager, and he supposed it would take a lot to remove his interest in sex.

Théodore's paw remained around his sac, his thumb and finger rubbing above it. The tiger stirred. "Are you still…?"

"Shh," the mouse said. "This is necessary."

"But I'm…" He didn't need to say it. The mouse could see or feel his arousal as well as Danilo could feel the air of the room on his now-exposed flesh.

"Shh," Théodore said again. Now his fingers were definitely moving up, squeezing, pressing gently. "Tell me if this hurts."

It did, a little, but mostly it was the tugging on the sutures, and Théodore's paw very skillfully stroked him, which did not pull on the incision much at all. There was another ache, one down in his balls, but he could ignore it, just as he'd ignored the patch he'd rubbed raw jerking off that year he was in Lower Sixth. After, it had hurt like bloody hell, nearly literally, and he'd sworn off masturbation for the rest of the year (actually, it had ended up being four days).

This didn't hurt nearly that badly, but it was a deeper pain inside, the kind he didn't have any experience with. It was almost like a muscle pull or a deep bruise, but at a small point. And that point receded, overwhelmed by the growing arousal that pumped around and over it.

"Taye," he gasped, and despite the close quarters, the smell of the chamber pot, and the soreness in his groin, he thought for a moment that he was in Taye's small room at the Université. If he closed his eyes, he could even picture that polo shirt the mouse wore, the one with the blue and yellow stripes.

Danilo clenched his teeth and gripped the bed. His body shuddered and jumped and sparked, hips bucking, and then the orgasm drained away. He slumped back onto the bed, panting. And then pain clenched him like a fist around his midsection puncturing it with extended claws. "Ah God!" he hissed, drawing his knees up and doubling over.

Théodore pulled his paw away. "It will pass in a few moments. Do you need to vomit?"

Danilo clenched his jaw shut as the mouse moved toward the lantern and held his paw to it. "Nnn," the tiger forced out through his teeth. The fist's claws had withdrawn. Slowly, the throbbing flames in his gut were diminishing. "No. Why?" Talking made his stomach unstable, stirred up the searing again, so he stopped.

"It will hurt for a few days." Théodore peered down at his paw. "There is no blood. Good. I thought not, but it is best to be sure."

"Blood?" Danilo turned his head to stare blearily at the silhouetted mouse. He had the urge to reach out and either hit him or hug him, but he was standing too far, and he dared not move lest the pain surge again.

"Aye, betimes the operation leaves one with bloody humors." Théodore wiped his paw clean on a scrap of cloth, then patted Danilo on the knee. "Well, you're in good health."

"Once I can breathe." Words were easier now, the fire faded to a dull ache. The mouse's words sounded so clinical that Danilo was almost embarrassed to have just come in his paw. But Taye was his friend, and Théodore appeared to be as well. He reached out and set a paw on the slender shoulder. "So you'll take me back now?"

"Back?" The mouse shook his head. "My God, no. You'll stay here tonight, and at dawn we will take the cart south to my farm. You have done kitchen work, you can do farm work. It will be safe and peaceful."

Danilo lowered his legs and took a breath. "I'm not going south. I don't care about the danger."

"You think LeSevre will be happy to leave you with one testicle? That that will be sufficient punishment in his eyes?"

"He tried to kick me right after they took it." Danilo cupped his paw protectively over his sac.

Théodore nodded. "It does not surprise me. That one is evil to his core. If any are possessed by demons…" He patted Danilo's knee again. "There is nothing you can do. If you stay, you will be marked, and they will come for you again. Perhaps you have simply had an ale with a friend. Perhaps someone has a grudge against you and wishes you punished. It takes very little to fall afoul of Cobb's guard."

"What about Lukin?"

"The bishop?" Théodore tilted his head. "What about him? He goes along with it all."

"Yes." Danilo put the poultice back in place, because his balls ached again. "But they aren't his men, even though LeSevre must be below him in rank."

The mouse stared at Danilo. "You are exhausted and you have had a traumatic day. Perhaps we can reserve the analysis for a lazy evening on the farm." The paw on Danilo's knee rubbed. "There will be pleasant evenings. Winter nights when the fire is warm."

"What about Luc?"

Théodore dipped his head. "I have not forgotten my promise. If you leave at dawn, I will help him."

"And then he can come south to the farm as well?"

The fingers on Danilo's thigh stopped their rubbing and gripped his knee. "Danilo," Théodore said gently, "I can help him escape the pyre, but not the prison."

"I don't understand." He was tired, and sore, and more peevish than he wanted to be. After all, Théodore had just given him a clean bill of health, even if it had hurt like hell, and was going to help him get away from the city.

The mouse sighed and patted his waist. Danilo craned his neck and saw that the mouse's paw rested on the hilt of his knife. "I can ambush them as they bring him from the prison to the amphitheater. I am quick; he will die in minutes."

Chapter Fourteen

Danilo sat up abruptly enough to send a pulse of pain through his midsection again. "You're going to *kill* him?"

"It is all I can do!" Théodore sheathed the knife and stood, walking away from Danilo. "Do you not think I have wanted to free all those they have taken? The guards would be upon us in moments. But I can throw a knife from a concealed location, or I can run up, stab, and vanish. Luc will be bound; he has no way to run or escape. I can spare him a painful death, but not death itself."

"You can't—there has to be some way—"

"There is none." Théodore's eyes gleamed black in the lantern light. Danilo could almost see his face in them. "Believe me."

"Wait. The fox said...he said a priest comes to administer to the condemned the night before their execution. And he said most of the guards leave during that time. We could go then and rescue him. That's tomorrow night!"

Théodore shook his head again. "I have never heard of that happening. Anyway, even if it did, the door will still be guarded; no priest would be left alone with the prisoners. And if you did break in, what would you do? Kill a priest? They will not allow you to escape that crime. You will be hunted even if you return to Firenza."

"Of course not. But you could sneak in, hide, wait until the priest leaves..."

"And then? Walk out the front door with prisoner in tow?"

Of course not. Théodore could not do that. But Danilo, now, maybe Danilo could. "I have been there in association with the Bishop and Archbishop. I could perhaps take Luc out."

"Very unlikely. Even then you would need some token of authority. A signed order, something of that nature."

Danilo pulled his pants up. "I have a day," he said. "I will see what may be done."

The mouse got to his feet and looked down as Danilo fastened the tie at the front of his pants, gingerly. "Every day you remain in the city, you put yourself at risk. If you attempt to help Luc, you will only succeed in damning yourself to the same fate."

"I have to try." Danilo strained to keep his eyes open. "Please take me back to the seminary. I promise, if I cannot figure out a way to help Luc by tomorrow morning, I will come with you."

"You're a fool." But Théodore spoke gently, and he turned to sit on the bed next to Danilo. "You have known Luc less than a week. What do you owe him?"

"It's because of me he was captured. What he did with Bertrand—"

"Luc is indiscreet and a fool," the mouse said. "Do not blame yourself for his plight. If it had not been with Bertrand himself, it would have been with someone else. Why do you think Bertrand behaved so badly? Luc brought other friends back to the Repos, even after his first capture, until Bertrand made him stop."

"Still—"

"If you save him, he will only be captured again. Tigue is a busy city in which Luc could easily hide himself if he had the inclination to do so. So far, he has not."

"He saved my life." Danilo exhaled. "I've never had someone put himself in harm's way for me. It wasn't just pulling me from the river. He gave me a place to live, brought me to St. Nizier's...I might have starved."

"You would not have starved." The mouse folded his paws in his lap. "You were sent here to see someone in the church. You would have found him regardless of what we did."

The tiger turned his head to breathe in Théodore's scent, to see the glint of the mouse's eyes on him. In the dark, silent room, he felt again that he could easily have been sitting with Taye at the Université. "I might not have," he said. "I was not really sent here to study with the church. I am a student, but...I came here by accident."

Théodore nodded, slowly. "You seemed unusually lost. I thought you might be disoriented from falling in the river. Then where were you bound?"

Danilo clasped his paws together. The temptation to tell him, to transfer the trust he had in Taye to this sixteenth century mouse, pulled at him. But Théodore's talk of witches made him hesitate. "I was…I believe I may have been under a witch's curse."

"Oh?" Now the mouse straightened. "How have you run afoul of a witch?"

Here Danilo again felt lost. Witches, how did one make a witch angry? "I don't know," he said honestly.

The mouse rubbed his whiskers. "And why should I help you, if I might by doing so also place myself in harm's way?"

"Whatever witch did this," Danilo said hurriedly, unwilling to lose his only remaining friend and ally, "is far, far from here."

Théodore's laugh, loud and unexpected in the quiet dark room, made Danilo jump. "I see," he said. "Witches are fickle, it is true. Even so, why should I guide you back? Why do you think you can succeed at a task that not even those who know Tigue well would attempt, you who have already been cursed once?"

The tiger smiled and held up his arm, letting the sleeve of Luc's tunic fall back. In the night, his white fur shone. "Because here, I am not cursed. I am blessed," he said.

***

Théodore walked him back and agreed to meet him again the following morning, at St. Nizier's before Lauds. Danilo's groin ached all the way back, but when Guillaume rapped on his door to wake him for Lauds, much of the pain had faded. He kept the poultice on anyway, though he suspected a simple cloth would work as well at this point.

He had asked Théodore for advice, and the mouse had told him only that the surest way to release Luc was to have a letter signed and sealed by Archbishop Argile. Danilo had a better rapport with the bishop, but Théodore said the bishop wasn't in charge of the prisoners. "Even with the letter, I do not like your chances," he said, "but without it you have none."

So Danilo would have to explore the Archbishop's quarters somehow, would have to find the Archbishop's seal and forge his signature, and would have to present them at a time that would not arouse suspicion. This was not as difficult as it might have been for most of Tigue's people; for one thing, Danilo could read and write. For another, he had seen multiple spy movies, which was probably not as useful as he'd hoped it would be, but at least gave him some confidence. And for a third, he did not hold the Church and its personages in the high esteem that most others did.

After Lauds at St. Nizier, where he looked for but did not see Anita, he expected another lecture in the morning. His fellow students, who had treated him with great care and a little bit of wonder, told him that today was a work day. The priest directed him to a small copying room where they sat for hours, through the strike of noon and a simple lunch of bread and cheese that was becoming depressingly familiar to Danilo. He asked questions about the Archbishop's quarters as innocently as he could, but gained no information other than the location, a street between the Cathédrale and the amphitheater. Wonderful, Danilo thought, and I have to go from there to the prison. All of his least favorite locations in 1508 Tigue were on the west side of the Saône.

The instruction in calligraphy and illumination, with the accompanying manuscripts, would itself have been interesting if he had not had so much else on his mind. Several times the priest had to explain a point of calligraphy to him, or ask him to repeat an exercise, while Danilo thought of excuses to enter the Archbishop's house or ways to explain his presence there if he were discovered.

"Well," the priest said with a weary smile, keeping his ears up, "that was a good first day. I understood you had been trained in churches?"

"Yes." Danilo was getting better at thinking on his feet in this world. "My father paid my way elsewhere, but he is gone—my money is gone—so I have not worked before."

"Ah." The wolf patted his arm. "You show promise. Come, dine with me and your fellow students. We are a small island of education in this world and we should all know each other."

"I, er—"

"I will not accept a refusal." The priest smiled at him. "You have been part of our seminary for two days and your fellow students know you only as the blessed tiger who speaks with the Bishop and…" His eyes flicked down to Danilo's lap and his voice faltered. "And was…was wounded?"

Danilo's ears flushed and lay flat to his head. "I don't want to—I mean, I don't feel able to talk about it right now," he said.

The wolf nodded. "It would do your fellow students good to see that you are a person just as they are, no matter how you were wounded or with whom you hold conversations. You should talk to them about your home, about your love of God, how you first came to the Church, and other matters you might have in common."

"I have an errand…"

The wolf closed his paw around Danilo's wrist. "You still must eat, must you not? Come, show your fellow students who you are and begin to build bonds with them."

Danilo wanted to ask when the Archbishop was accustomed to eat, but the closest he could come was a halting, "Does the Archbishop ever eat with us?" to which the wolf laughed and told him that a dinner with the Archbishop was a rare prize bestowed only on those who had given great service to the Church, which did not really answer his question.

At dinner, the students welcomed him with small talk until one of them asked what had happened to him. Danilo, who had been thinking about how to cover this since he could not stop fidgeting as he sat, showed them the rip in his tunic and told them he'd been accosted by a thief and stabbed. "It heals," he said. "I feel much better today." And he did, although he had been sitting all day. Inactivity and rest had been good for his injuries, if not for the tension that kept his chest tight whenever he thought about what might happen to Luc if he could not succeed in his mission.

By the time the students had finished the meal and the post-meal conversation, the sun had set. However, as it was the first real meal he'd sat and eaten with people in days, Danilo did not mind overmuch. The other students were earnest, pleasant company, and he left the meal thinking that it had reminded him of meals at the Université—with slightly less religion, actually, than the students in 2008. Here, it permeated life and came up naturally in conversation. Five hundred years from now, people felt compelled to call attention to their religion so that it would show against the secular world that had encroached so heavily upon it.

Besides, he thought as he walked up to his room, his groin paining him more with every step, the later it was, the more chance the Archbishop would be asleep and his study empty. He lay down on his bed, intending to rest only for a few minutes, as long as it would take the watchmen below to seal the doors, but the long day and the food in his belly had worn him out, and when he woke with a start from his bed, the moon shone through a black night sky outside his window.

He might have slept all the way through to morning, and then he would have to meet Théodore and Luc would die at the mouse's blade. How much of the night was left? Cursing, Danilo scrambled from his bed and then cursed again as pain stabbed up through his abdomen. Théodore might have proven that he had no lasting damage, but he would've given anything short of his last testicle for a bottle of Advil right about now. At least when he stepped to the window, he saw no glimmer of dawn in the air.

His chest loosened, and he left his room to hobble his way down the stairs. As he descended, either the pain grew less or he grew used to it. Either way, he was able to un-bar the door and slip outside into the street. He couldn't figure out how to bar the door from the outside, but he expected to be back within the hour.

From the seminary to the archbishop's quarters, the streets were somewhat busy with nocturnals, if less crowded than during the day, and the farther he got from the center of town, the sparser the crowds. He stayed out of narrow alleys, out of shadows, and anytime a shadow near him moved, he hurried along, wincing. Many people glanced at his tall, white figure, but none stopped him. The moon cast enough light for him to see easily, so even in his injured state, it took him little time to find the street upon which the Archbishop resided.

Humbler than the Bishop's offices, it must have been, for the street consisted of a row of a dozen well-kept houses, none more exceptional than the last. Danilo frowned. He'd expected the Archbishop's residence to be as ostentatious as the Bishop's. Now he would have to inspect each one.

The moon hadn't moved much, and still no light showed in the east. Danilo walked slowly down the street, nodded to a mouse as she hurried past him. The first house on the left, an elegant two-story wooden structure with the ubiquitous red clay roof and a small porch, bore no religious symbology, nor did the first on his right. The second on the left had a black door upon which a white cross hung, making Danilo pause, but then he noticed a cross over the door of the house just beside it, and the from the eaves hung small decorations that glittered in the moonlight. Either of them might be the Archbishop's, or neither. He turned to his right; one of the houses had crosses on either side of its door, while the other had a wreath on the door and a cross in the upstairs window.

He bit his lip, continuing to walk when a small ground squirrel looked curiously at him. He would have to sneak around behind the houses and peer in at the windows. How would he tell the Archbishop's study from anyone else's? The stag probably didn't leave his mitre and vestments lying about, but currently that was Danilo's only chance.

The street was deserted now. He looked behind him and then ducked between the two houses on his left, bracing himself against the wall as the quick movement speared him with pain again. He crept to the nearest window and peered inside.

The backs of the houses proved easy to navigate, but none showed anything that resembled an Archbishop's study. Danilo did see a church guard uniform draped over a chair in one study and wondered if that might be LeSevre's house, and if so, how flammable it was. He dismissed that notion and had just moved on to the next house when the noise of a door opening stopped him. He peeked cautiously around the corner of the house.

Out of one of the houses on the opposite side of the street, a tall, broad goat strode in priest's vestments. And behind him, in a plain brown robe—

It was Argile—the Archbishop. It had to be. He wore a hood and had wrapped his antlers, but Danilo knew Cobb, knew how he strutted and how he carried himself, and there was no doubt in his mind.

His breathing hissed through the night air as the pale goat and the dark hooded Archbishop descended from their porch and walked toward him. For the first time, he wished he'd actually used some of the money he'd been offered to buy new clothes, something dark like the Archbishop's robe. The tiger's white fur caught the moon's light and broadcast his location to anyone who would turn his way. He shrank back into the shadows, heart pounding, expecting one of them to call out, for footsteps to approach him.

But the footsteps went on down the street, and when he peeked out again, he saw the backs of their heads. They must be going to the prison, he realized. That goat must be the priest who heard last confessions. This would be the ideal time for him to enter the house, enter the study, and find a letter. He moved cautiously out from between the houses and watched the Archbishop round the corner

Why would the stag would go about concealed? Was he ministering to the poor anonymously, something he could not do officially in his station? That would explain why all the guards would have to be evacuated from the prison; the Archbishop would not want anyone to know he was there. Then the goat, the other priest, must be the one to provide an excuse for the guards while the Archbishop snuck in somehow.

Curiosity gnawed at Danilo. He could go, see whether there was a secret way into the prison, and then hurry back here with plenty of time to find a letter. And the longer he hesitated…

Besides, he did not think Cobb—Argile—was the sort to sneak out at night for any benevolent cause. The Archbishop moved like someone with a nasty secret, and it was not likely a coincidence that he had emerged when his street was deserted. Danilo rose from a crouch and pressed a paw to his sore groin. Argile had left that mark on him, and if the stag had a secret Danilo could use against him, the tiger wanted to discover it.

Chapter Fifteen

For the four blocks Danilo followed the Archbishop to the prison, neither the stag nor goat looked even to either side, much less behind them, and the few other people on the deserted streets they walked paid them just as little mind. Danilo could have walked boldly ten feet behind, claws sheathed so his footfalls would not sound on the cobblestoned streets, and they would have been none the wiser. But he lurked a good way farther behind, waiting until they'd turned or moved on ahead and then hurrying to catch up. Once he caught his foot on an uneven stone in the street, jarring his whole body, and he had to clamp a paw over his mouth to muffle his curse.

The looming prison at the top of the uphill road came into view before the smell hit him again. Now he had been inside the smell, and he could pick out disease and blood and the musk of the prisoners from the wave of stench as he drew closer. This street was completely deserted; he supposed that few people had business near the prison at this time of night, and none wanted to be close to the smell of misery and desperation.

Argile and his priest stopped at the small, dark house just before the prison. They half-turned, and Danilo shrank back, aware of how much more noticeable he was in the empty street. When he looked out again, only the goat was visible.

Where had Argile gone?

The goat walked into the prison, leaving the street empty. Danilo hurried up to the house and sniffed at the door. There was the scent of stag—although there was no trace of the smell of fine cloth, of oils and incense, the smells Danilo had caught on Argile when he'd seen him the previous day. If he did not know the Archbishop, he would have thought there was nothing remarkable about that scent. But he knew that smell, remembered it from the elk leaning over him in the study room days and a lifetime ago, and his claws extended into the wood of the door frame.

The door of the prison opened again, and guards stepped out into the street. In a panic, Danilo pushed on the door, and despite the metal-plated lock, it opened easily. Danilo slipped inside and closed it softly, shutting out the murmur of conversation from the guards outside. No windows opened out toward the prison, only the street, and those shutters were tightly closed.

Footsteps approached from the direction of the prison. Danilo's eyes hadn't quite adjusted to the darkness, but he hurried farther into the house as fast as he felt comfortable. It appeared to be deserted, any furniture long since scavenged, and many of the floorboards had been pulled up, leaving patches of bare dirt that were cool under his paws. He was standing beside the rotted wood stairs that had once led to the upper story when the front door creaked open.

From where he was, he couldn't see who had entered the house. The door closed again and the person shuffled about. He grunted, and then Danilo caught the sound of water spilling onto the ground—nope, no, not water; the guy was pissing on the wall.

He stayed still until the guy opened the door and left, then crept slowly along the floor, thankful for the dirt patches he could now see that were guaranteed to be quieter. In the last room, he found a staircase that led down into blackness. There was no scent of stag on them that he could detect, apart from the scent that hung throughout the house, but there was nowhere else for the Archbishop to have gone. Danilo listened to the silent house, and then carefully descended the stairs.

Smells of damp earth and mildew came to him a moment before he stepped off a rotting wooden landing and onto dirt. And still, compared to the streets above, this tunnel smelled surprisingly clean. He navigated the darkness by his whiskers, feeling the walls close on either side of him. The house was close to the prison, yes, with its terrible smells, and yet it stood empty while many Tiguans slept in the streets. Nobody had taken up residence here.

Every few moments, he stopped to listen. The tunnel remained silent, and he took a few more steps forward through it. He must be out from under the house now, and unless his sense of direction was off, he was somewhere under the prison. And it was the next time he stopped that he heard faint whispering ahead of him.

He crept forward and found himself at the base of a narrow spiral stair. The whispering came from above, but it was remote, and as he listened, it stopped. Here on the stair, he caught Argile/Cobb's scent, lightly. Slowly, he made his way up the tight stone spiral.

At the top of the stair, he pushed up on a light wooden trap door. The air in the dark space beyond held a whiff of blood that set his heart to racing. As he emerged into an open space, he didn't need to see the curtain to know where he was.

Keeping his eyes in front of him, he stepped around the curtain and deliberately did not look at the bloodstained table where he'd lain just the day before, where the smell of his own blood no doubt still lingered. Despite his attempts to ignore it, it intruded on his awareness, until he felt it was creeping closer to him as he padded across the floor of the empty room.

Abandoning caution, he hurried to the door and through it, heart beating. At the stone landing on the first floor, he stopped to listen to the silence of the prison, the guard room now empty, even the prisoners barely muttering—only the prison was not silent. From above, from the second floor, noises came, the Archbishop's voice. So it wasn't the goat priest; it was the Archbishop himself who heard confession, Danilo thought, but only for a split second. The tone of the stag's voice did not resemble the soothing tone of a confessional priest; it was more like Cobb's mocking growl. *You want some of this, huh?*

And then a moan, and Danilo hurried six steps up before stopping himself, his heart pounding faster than before, because the voice had been Luc's. His groin ached, but he barely felt it. What if the Archbishop were carrying out the second punishment himself? No, that was ridiculous. In the dead of night? And yet—had he counted the knives on the table? Was he sure that none of them were missing?

The tiger forced himself to pad slowly and silently up the stairs, though his claws threatened to extend and click on the harsh stone. The sounds grew louder and more textured. Luc did not moan again, but Danilo thought he recognized the otter's voice in harsh breaths that echoed down the hallway. Flickering light cast grotesque shadows on the wall as he neared it, creeping past cells where prisoners

CAMOUFLAGE

huddled, sleeping or ignoring what was going on. One cell's occupant sat upright, listening, but either he was turned away from Danilo or the tiger was invisible in the shadowy corridor.

The Archbishop spoke smoothly as Danilo drew closer, but with strain behind each word. "Do you accept the word of the Lord?"

And now there was no denying the sounds Danilo was hearing, wet sliding sounds and grunts of discomfort from Luc, grunts of pleasure from the stag. The shadows on the wall moved with a rhythm deeper and more primal than the ephemeral flickers of the light casting them.

The tiger crept to the edge of the cell, trying to keep to the shadow, and peered around the edge. There he saw Argile's gleaming white body, naked, the stag's muzzle twisted into a smile of savage ecstasy, one hand firmly between Luc's shoulder blades holding the otter to the floor, the other holding his tail aside as those thick, muscled hips thrust beneath it.

Danilo shrank back, paws covering his muzzle. Now the shadows, which previously had seemed arcane and obscure, revealed to him every movement. The Archbishop said, "Then...the Word... shall be...*given you.*"

The last words were spoken in a throaty, orgasmic rush. "Foul demon!" he cried. "Ah! I have heard your cries...and I will...ensure that your captive soul rises to Heaven even as we send you back to Hell."

The shadows stopped their movement. Silence beat on Danilo's ears. "Bless you, my son," the stag said, and the grotesque double shadow split and wavered. Cloth rustled; he was getting dressed. "Remember that your salvation will be revoked should you commit the sin of violating this confessional."

If Danilo were to get Luc out, he would have to hide while the Archbishop left, hope the guards had left keys in the main guard room, then get Luc out before the guards resumed their posts. He could do this. He just had to try to do it without seeing again the image that replayed over and over in his head: the sleek, muscled stag raping the smaller otter.

***

216

The first floor was as quiet as the second; quieter, as there were no priests performing unholy rituals. Danilo waited around a corner across from the sleeping fox prisoner until he heard the Archbishop descend the stairs, then headed for the guard room while his mind raced. How could the Archbishop do something like that? What if Luc told one of the guards tomorrow? What if he spilled the secret?

Bishop Lukin's voice teased at his memory. Even when drugged, he'd said about the prisoners, or something like. So they were sedated to stop them from escaping the pyre, which meant that anything they said would be put down to drugged hallucinations, even if anyone would believe a condemned prisoner, even if the prisoner could bring himself to disobey the Archbishop…

Danilo shook his head and tried to stop his paws from shaking. Focus on the secret passage, he told himself. That passage, Danilo realized, could get Luc out, if only they didn't lock the door—

"Halfie!"

The deep voice rang out in the stone corridor. Danilo spun to his left and came face to face with a black-and-white striped muzzle. "Filthy foreigner," it spat. "You wish to spread your misfortune?"

In this unfamiliar context, Danilo did not immediately recognize the badger. The pain between his legs seared at the insult, and then he remembered. "Bertrand?" he whispered.

"They will never dare touch me. They mean only to frighten me. They will not make me one of you." The badger's eyes burned.

"Shh!" Danilo waved the badger quiet. He was tempted to linger and take in the sight of the foul innkeeper behind bars, but he needed to hurry. And he was not prepared for the realization that he had done this, that because of him, tomorrow Bertrand might be lying on the same table with the same knife making the same incision in his scrotum…because of Danilo.

His wound throbbed. He hurried away without saying anything, but Bertrand raised his voice. "Hey! Halfie! Hey!"

The badger's cursed voice echoed through the prison. Ahead of Danilo, in the guard room, footsteps and voices sounded, approaching the same corner Danilo was hurrying toward.

He skidded and reversed direction, ran the other way for the staircase as silently as he could. When he passed Bertrand again, the badger said, "You're not allowed to be here, are you?" but Danilo passed him without even attempting to make a reply. Behind him, the badger yelled, "He went that way! Guards! Guards!"

Dammit. Danilo's only chance was to get back to the secret tunnel now. He made it to the stairs, the guards within earshot but not sight of him, thankfully. Heavy feet clomped on the stone behind him; he could feel their tread in the stone as his own light feet hurried from step to step. He reached the basement, and though he could not avoid looking at the table and its dark stains, he quelled his nausea and hurried behind the curtain.

There he stared at the shadows on the floor, trying to remember where the trapdoor had been. In the darkness, he couldn't see the lines. But he'd come up through this corner—or was it that one? Desperate, he knelt and scrabbled at the boards.

None of them moved. The sound of the guards had receded, but for how long? He moved to another part of the floor behind the curtain, and here the boards felt hollow under his feet.

"Check the basement," floated down the stair to him.

He pried at the boards, and wrenched the claw he'd twisted back in Bertrand's kitchen, an injury that he'd completely forgotten about until pain flared again, but the board came up. He traced the edge of it, found the front, and lifted. The smell of dirt and mold had never been so welcome.

On the way back through the tunnel, he slowed. He didn't know how long it would take the Archbishop to dress and prepare to leave, and with the commotion in the prison, he might stay in the empty house for a few minutes longer. Danilo couldn't risk alerting him, so maybe it was best he take his time getting back to the house. Although, he reminded himself, when the guards failed to find anyone, Cobb/Argile would suspect that that someone had followed his tunnel.

Or perhaps not. The Archbishop was bold or stupid enough to take this risk frequently, to come rape prisoners who were due to be executed. He might not conceive that anyone could find his secret tunnel, and he might not know what the guards were agitated about. If Danilo could only find a place to hide until the Archbishop left, then he might, he might survive.

And now that he knew about the tunnel...his mind raced. He could sneak back into the prison, avoid the guards, find the key, bring Luc through the tunnel, and make good his escape. They could go to Théodore's farm, live there happily.

He reached the stairs and turned to put his foot on the first, and then paused. Light from a lantern flickered above him.

Danilo stepped back down and waited, holding his breath. The front door opened, but the light did not disappear, even when it closed again. "Well?" Argile's voice came low, but clear in the silence of the house. "Was I spotted?"

The tiger didn't hear any response, but Argile went on. "Then it was someone else? Did they find him?"

Again, nothing but silence. "You'd best search the tunnel to be sure. Go only as far as the prison; do not enter it. You understand?"

A moment later, soft footsteps coming through the house, toward the stairs.

Danilo shrank back, took a step toward the prison—maybe he could outrun whoever it was—then stared at the blackness below the staircase. If there were room there, then the darkness would hide him best next to the light, and hopefully the dank smell would cover his own.

There was room, although he had to crawl over a support and wedge himself back into the corner. What little light there was came from above, and the stairs shielded him from it, enough, he hoped. The downside was that anyone coming along the tunnel from the prison would be staring directly at his hiding place. But the stairs were lit, though faintly, and Danilo couldn't think of any better place to conceal himself.

If it weren't for Berrrand, he wouldn't have to hide at all. That damned badger and all he'd done—but, Danilo realized, Bertrand was in prison here because Danilo himself had told the church about him, had insisted they go arrest him. If he had done as Anita'd advised and left punishment to the Lord, he could possibly be hiding in the prison with a key, rather than desperately crouching here to avoid detection. *Even when I try to do the right thing, I fuck it up,* he thought miserably.

Hard-nailed feet clopped down the stairs. Danilo closed his eyes, feeling the motion around him, seeing flashes of light through his eyelids. The person—the goat priest, probably—stood at the bottom of the stairs, then walked slowly down the tunnel.

Danilo cracked an eye open. It was indeed the goat, some fifteen feet away from him now, shining his lantern down the dark passage. So Danilo would have to be gone before he came back; the lantern light would show his white fur beneath the stairs like a beacon. The tiger squeezed his paws together and held his breath. In another twenty or thirty seconds, the goat would be far enough for Danilo to creep out and make his way silently up the stairs. The stag might still be in the house, but probably not in the room directly above, and if he was, he would be expecting his priest, so Danilo might have the advantage of surprise if he had to fight.

He also had the disadvantage that a blow to his groin might kill him. So there was that. But chances were the Archbishop wasn't waiting at the head of the stairs. Cobb would certainly not have the patience for that. Once Danilo heard silence, he could creep up, hide in one of the back rooms, then come back for Luc…

Footsteps sounded, hard toenails on the wood floor. "Dornier!" Argile's voice called down. "It smells like an outhouse here. I shall wait outside."

The goat turned, and the light of his lantern dazzled Danilo's eyes.

Chapter Sixteen

He shut them and hunched inward for a moment, praying the goat wasn't looking down. When hurried steps came toward him, he struggled to get out from under the staircase.

"Uhhh! Uhhh!" The goat's bleats echoed in the small tunnel. Danilo caught his foot on a beam and fell, bracing himself with his paws, and then a hand closed around his arm.

"What is it, Dornier? Did you find him?" Argile's voice came closer still.

"Uhh!"

The noise the goat made set Danilo's hackles rising. Briefly, he considered fighting. But metal gleamed in the goat's other hand, and adding that to Danilo's other disadvantages made fighting a suicidal risk. "All right," he said, trying to keep calm. "I'm coming."

Dornier stepped back and allowed Danilo to clamber out, but held a blade at the ready. He might be an idiot, or a mute, or something, but he understood words and appeared to be a good fighter from the way he held the sword (was Danilo already noticing things like this? and what kind of priest could wield a sword better than he could speak?). The goat prodded Danilo with the point of the blade as the tiger walked up the stairs.

"I'm going, I'm going," Danilo said, wondering if he could turn and knock the sword away before the goat could stab him, or knock the goat off the stairs. Probably not. Given his lack of any kind of training, if he were going to fight a soldier in 1508, his best bet would be to stab him in the back.

Right. Just like that. He sighed. As steeped in the violence of this world as he had become, he didn't know if he could actually inflict an injury on someone else.

Of course you can, his mind said. *Look what you did to Bertrand.*

And then he reached the top of the stairs and came face to face with a stark white face surrounded by the simple brown cloak below and gleaming antlers above. "Ah," Argile's deep voice said. "Below the stairs, was he?"

"Aaah."

"Excellent. Thank you, Dornier. You may have wine tonight."

"Aaahh."

"Danilo, was it not?" The stag fixed his eyes on the tiger's. Danilo nodded once. "I hope you will understand why I must insist you accompany me back to my house."

"I…" The blade poked him in the back again.

"If that is too much trouble," Argile said, "I am certain we can arrange for you to return to the prison. Or Dornier would happily leave you right here."

"Uhhh."

"I'll come," Danilo said in a low voice. After all, he reasoned as the Archbishop showed him out the door, he'd wanted to get into that house anyway. Granted, he hadn't wanted Argile to know that he'd been there, but at least he would get inside. Perhaps he could get the key that the Archbishop used to lock the door of the empty house; the stag had returned it to a small pocket in his cloak. Danilo could rescue Luc, or he could go back to his original plan of forging a letter. Now, of course, he had to rescue himself first.

"What—" he began, but the stag cut him off with a shushing sound before he could get another word out.

They walked back to the Archbishop's house in silence. Danilo scanned the streets for anyone who might be able to help him, but the goat turned a menacing glare on anyone who so much as approached them. It became more and more clear that the only thing priestly about him were the robes.

Inside the house, the Archbishop locked the door. "Dornier," he said, shrugging off the brown cloak to reveal a linen tunic, "the paws." He met Danilo's eyes as the goat seized the tiger's left paw. "Please allow Dornier to bind your paws. He does worry after my well-being, and it is the only way he will allow me to speak to you in private."

"What if I don't want to talk to you in private?" Danilo kept his right paw in front of him, but the left was a lost cause, already bound with a leather strap and secured to something in the wall. Perhaps the door handle or a candle sconce; there were several candles mounted on the wall by bronze sconces in the shapes of angels.

"Ah, well." The stag's smile didn't waver. He reached for a gold-trimmed white robe and pulled it on over his tunic. "It is a little late to return to the prison. Burglars have been known to force their way into this house in search of sacred relics, however. Dornier has had to dispatch them when they would not submit peacefully. It would be a shame if a blessed white tiger were to be overcome with greed in such a manner, but I am certain the few people who know him would understand that he was hoping to steal a valuable item with which to ransom his friend, and would mourn him appropriately."

Danilo glared as the goat gripped his right paw and forced it behind him. It was bound to the left one, and then they were released from the wall. He staggered forward.

"Thank you, Dornier," Argile said evenly. "One more thing. Please, before you go, do Danilo the honor of saying 'good-bye.'"

The tiger turned, bemused, in time to see the goat open his mouth and get hit with a blast of foul breath. "Aaah. Uhhhh."

Here in the candle-light, Danilo could see past the black gums, past the brown-and-yellow square teeth, into the goat's mouth where an ugly, ragged lump marked the base of where his tongue had been. He recoiled, and at that, the goat shut his mouth and regarded him with a nasty smile. "Huhhh," Dornier said, and took up a post at the door, behind Danilo.

"Now," Archbishop Argile said pleasantly, as though he were asking Danilo to admire the painting of the Stag Jesus that hung on the left-hand wall, "perhaps you will follow me to my study."

There seemed little to do but trot behind him, much as Danilo bridled at behaving like an obedient servant or slave. In any event, it was preferable to remaining in the room with the mutilated goat guard. "In the normal course of things," the stag said, "I would not hesitate to have you burned for heresy, or simply disposed of in a way that need not involve so much..." He waved one hand at his desk, and his antlers tipped toward it. "Ceremony."

The desk held stacks of papers and drew Danilo's attention, if only because there he might find paper, ink, and the all-important Archbishop's seal. "However," the stag went on, "you are not an

ordinary foreigner. There is something about you, something…"
He stroked the tuft of fur at the end of his chin in a gesture more
contemplative than Danilo had ever seen Cobb make. "Your fur, of
course, sets you apart; you have been noticed here, and your departure would be remarked upon. And yet I cannot simply set you free."

"We," Danilo began, and then had to clear his throat, which was
dry. His tongue seemed to be twice its normal size. "We can make a
bargain."

"A bargain?" The stag laughed, not kindly, and his antler points
wobbled threateningly forward. "A bargain is conducted between
two people in equal positions who each have something to offer.
It strikes me that I have everything to offer and you have nothing.
What bargain would you make, in such a position?"

"I won't tell anyone. I'll swear on the Bible, on the cross, by
whatever you wish. I won't tell anyone what I saw tonight."

Argile's white-furred face remained amused. "We will come to
what you think you saw momentarily."

"It must be something pretty bad," Danilo said, "or you wouldn't
be threatening to kill me."

Now the Archbishop's eyes narrowed. "What would you have
me promise in exchange for what you should give freely? Your life?"

"Luc's life."

"Still fancy yourself his savior? Would you take this bargain,
though it leaves your life in my hands, to do with as I will?"

Danilo swallowed. "I would prefer you let me go as well," he
said. "But I'm not going to be burned tomorrow."

"Do not be so certain." The Archbishop swept around in his
robe, the gold trim catching the candlelight and flashing. "The path
of one called to God's work is not easy, and I have grown accustomed
to the unpleasant duties it sometimes entails."

"Like raping prisoners?" Danilo said. "I imagine that wouldn't
go over so well. How would you like to lose a testicle? Not to mention that fancy robe."

The stag shook his head ponderously. "The world of Firenza
must be different indeed, if an itinerant traveler whose closest friends
are Sodomites may threaten a respected member of the church with
nothing but unfounded accusations."

"The other prisoners will vouch for me. They know."

"Oh, I see. I had not realized that you would have the support of cutpurses and heretics as well as Sodomites. No." Argile turned away. "I tire of this conversation. You have failed to demonstrate any compelling reason to take your words into account in my judgment, and therefore I will retire to meditate upon it myself. I will show you to the wine cellar. You may sleep there, or perform your own meditation."

Think! Danilo wracked his brain. What did Argile want? He wanted to rape condemned prisoners, so much that he was willing to take a risk fairly often to get that. Danilo couldn't give him that. He tried to imagine what it would be like to have such a drive to be gay and not only be unable to act on it, to have twisted it in such a way that he'd created—or at least stepped up enforcement of—a law that ensured the mutilation and death of the very people he wanted to join. It reminded Danilo of any number of movies in which a jealous lover opted to kill the object of his lust rather than let her choose another. He'd never understood that, but now he had to.

"Wait." An idea was forming.

Argile, waiting at the door at the far end of the study, turned. "Please," he said, "no more 'bargaining.'"

"I can give you something you want," Danilo said.

"I told you, I am tired of this game."

The tiger took a breath. "Myself."

Argile stared at him and then laughed, shortly. "Again you offer me what I already possess. Come, the wine cellar is this way."

"I mean..." Danilo walked across the study slowly. "I'm like you."

The stag stopped. He fingered the gold trim on his robe. "Apart from the color of our fur," he said, "I fail to see the similarities."

"I like sex with males," Danilo said.

The Archbishop stiffened and then stepped forward, lowering his head so that his antlers raked Danilo across the muzzle. The tiger staggered under flashes of pain from his ears to his cheek—not, thank God, his eyes—but remained upright. "How dare you?" Argile hissed.

"I—I just watched you." Danilo kept his eyes on those antlers, as blood dripped down his ear. He hadn't expected that, but he wouldn't be taken by surprise again. "What if you didn't have to go sneak around to prisons? What if you had—what if you had a secretary, and you could—you could do whatever you wanted with him, and he was bound not to tell anyone?"

"How would he be so bound?" Argile did not look any less furious, but at least he was looking Danilo in the eye and that meant his antlers were back, out of harm's way.

"Because—because the Church would employ Luc. At the cathedral or the seminary, or something. Some way that he would be alive and here, so if I ever did anything, you could put him back in prison, and I knew that." Danilo had resigned himself to living out the rest of his life in this world, but if he could at least spare Luc the fate that had befallen Coumier, he would have done something good in 1508.

"A willing partner." The Archbishop's thoughtful expression became a sneer. "Silly boy. What makes you think I want that?" He leaned close to Danilo. "I have been called. I am God's instrument to eradicate these demons from His world. He has tested me and made me strong."

"So why don't you rape them up on stage then?" He was aware, vaguely, that the word 'rape' had become something like 'fornicate,' but he was already pushing on recklessly, the memory of what he'd seen fresh in his head. "Why not let everyone see? What are you ashamed of?"

"There are many things the laity are not privy to. I would not expect you to understand any better."

"I think I understand it well enough," Danilo said roughly. "You want to be gay," and that word came out as "Sodomite," but he didn't stop. "But you can't. So you wrap yourself up in holy robes and you persecute the people who live the life you want," and all this was from Taye, from evenings talking about what drove homophobes, "and you go and fornicate in old smelly prisons with people who will never be believed, who will be dead before the next night so they can never tell anyone about you." Even those words failed to wipe the smug satisfaction off the stag's face. "You're pathetic."

"Pathetic." The stag swung his head from side to side. "You and your friends are pathetic. You allow these demons to rule you, you give in to them without a struggle, you corrupt others with them. I have turned my demons to the service of God, to subjugate other demons, to show the afflicted souls the true nature of their corruption." He stopped, breathing hard, and placed a hand upon his chest. His eyes lost some of their manic intensity, and his muzzle curled into a smile. "And I do owe you thanks for sparing the otter the disfiguration most of his brethren suffered. It was a more pleasurable duty with a whole subject." On those last words, his eyes traveled down Danilo's front.

"You're grotesque," Danilo said. "You're worse than any demon you pretend to hate."

"I believe God has made my path clear. But since you do not understand, it is my duty to force understanding upon you."

Malevolence and desire shone through his eyes with a cruel smile, and the tip of his tongue flicked out as though eager to taste Danilo. Hatred and revulsion seized Danilo; without thinking, he slammed his head forward, smashing his forehead into the stag's nose.

Argile staggered backwards into the door frame, both hands clutching his nose. "Filth!" he spat, and lowered his head. An array of antler points faced the tiger.

Danilo backed up two steps. He didn't regret his actions, only the situation. But he could also analyze it, and as Argile's antler points gleamed toward him again, he braced himself and hoped the stag was as bad at fighting as he was.

And then Argile lifted his head, blood dripping from his nose, and shouted, "Dornier!"

Danilo backed up again and spotted the window to his left. He had the wild idea that he could escape, and indeed, Argile did not stop him as he slammed his shoulder into the shutters, then bit at the fractured catch and threw them open. But at the same time, the door clattered behind him, and even as he tried to get a foot up onto the sill, strong arms gripped his and pulled him back. "Help! Help!" he yelled out into the night, but only silence responded.

The goat spun him around to face the white stag. Argile held a hand in front of his nose, blood staining his white fur. "Cut the clothes off him," he snarled, "and bring him up to my bedroom."

Well, Danilo thought, his heart pounding, his groin aching again, at least I took his attention off of Luc.

The Archbishop turned and stomped out the door, into the next room. The goat pushed Danilo down to his knees, and then the hiss of steel on leather made the tiger's ears fold back. He had run out of options and ideas. So here was where his adventure would end.

Eyes shut, his mind curiously empty and at peace, he waited for the touch of steel on his body for the third time in a week, but what he heard was Dornier's, "Uhh?" cut off in mid-exhalation, and then a clatter of metal on stone. He turned, and gaped.

The goat writhed with back arched, both hands scrabbling at the fur of his throat. His eyes bugged out and his body twisted, but behind him, the slight figure of Théodore remained grimly motionless. It took Danilo a moment to realize that the mouse was holding something to the goat's throat, a moment longer to realize that the soldier was being strangled.

And then Théodore dropped one paw to his waist, brought it back up in a smooth motion to the goat's neck. When he withdrew it, the hilt of a blade protruded from the brownish fur.

Blood bubbled out around the blade. Dornier dropped to his knees, making one horrible wheeze before Théodore reached around the large head to clamp both paws around the long mouth. "Quiet," the mouse muttered.

That word broke Danilo's fascinated paralysis. "How did you… where did you come from?"

Théodore turned, holding the dying goat's mouth shut as his struggles weakened. "Shhh. I followed you, of course. I thought you might try something ridiculously stupid and I wanted to bear witness to it, if I couldn't help. I must say I did not expect to be killing the Archbishop's bodyguard in His Excellency's study." His eyes flicked to the doorway the Archbishop had disappeared through.

"Thank you." Danilo's throat felt tight.

The goat—Dornier—made more noises in his throat, but not loudly. His eyes glazed over and his body slumped. Théodore let go of the long muzzle and pulled his knife out in a bubbling fountain of blood that quickly subsided under Danilo's horrified, fascinated eyes. The mouse walked over to Danilo, behind him, and a moment later, Danilo's paws were free.

He rubbed them together as pins and needles burned through his arms, but he couldn't take his eyes from Dornier's twitching body. "Come on," the mouse said. "Help me get him to the front door."

"What?"

Théodore picked up the goat's shoulders, handling the bloody cloth unflinchingly. "That way it looks like he went back to his post and someone stabbed him in the night. Maybe broke in; we'll leave the door open. It won't necessarily be connected to you."

"The Archbishop will know." Danilo gripped the bodyguard's ankles.

"Won't matter." They lifted him. The smell of piss rose to Danilo's nostrils. If the mouse smelled it, though, it didn't bother him any more than the blood seeping around his paws. "And we can get out of here, be far away before they raise the alarm."

They carried him to the front door and laid him down. Théodore opened the door and then gestured to Danilo. "Come on." He spoke a little more loudly here, where there was less chance of being overheard.

Danilo bit his lip. "What about Luc?"

The mouse's expression darkened. "You haven't seen with your own eyes that there is nothing you can do?"

"The study." The tiger gestured back. "I can write a letter, get his seal on it…we can have him released!"

"It's impossible." But Théodore paused, looking at the study.

The same anger that had propelled his head into the Archbishop's nose swept through him. "You told me—a letter from the Archbishop with his seal—I can write it, if you can show me how to seal a letter—"

The mouse's ears settled back, and for the first time since Danilo'd met him on the bank of the Saône, he looked uncertain. "That's a crime," he said.

Danilo stared pointedly down at the dead goat. Théodore scowled. "That is no crime. That is just fighting. Fellow attacked one of mine, I get to attack him."

"The Archbishop attacked Luc, you know." Danilo didn't bother to keep his voice low. "Raped him."

The mouse stared at him. "I heard something of it. I also heard that he means to do the same to you, so what say we take the start this fellow's death bought us? We can be at the edge of the city before he manages to rouse a guard."

"You don't want revenge on him?"

The mouse shook his head impatiently. "Want? Aye. But as my mother said, shit in one paw and wish in the other and see which fills up first. What can the likes of us do to him?"

Again, Danilo looked at the goat, at Théodore's bloody paw. The mouse recoiled. "Kill a priest? Do you not fear for your soul?"

"My soul is my business. And how can you think he's holy? You know what he does."

Théodore sat back. "He speaks with the Pope, who has God's ear. His actions may appear horrible, but if that is how he has been instructed to punish demons…"

Danilo's fur prickled. He curled his tail tightly around himself in the silent dimness of the house. "Do you think you're possessed by a demon?"

"We don't talk of such things," Théodore snapped, but he wasn't looking at Danilo.

"Okay, then…" The tiger groped for words. "Do, uh. Do you think the Church's punishment of people like…like us…is just?"

The mouse reached out to the door. "This is not the time to be discussing this."

"Just answer the question," Danilo said. "Yes or no?"

Théodore let his paw fall. "It is not so easy to answer," he said. "Part of me thinks that yes, my behavior is deviant and perhaps demonic. The danger in which I put my wife simply by sating my desires—how can that be God's way? And yet," he patted his chest, "I do not feel possessed. I feel…"

"Love?"

"Something similar, if not that which is blessed by God." His mouth twisted into a wry smile.

"Théodore," Danilo said. "Where I come from, those such as us are not seen to be demons."

"Do the priests in your land favor us, then?"

"Well…" He hesitated. "No. But we are not tortured, mutilated, burned." Except in some parts of the world, he remembered, but he didn't need to go into all that. "And acceptance is growing. A cousin of mine is…working hard for that."

"It sounds lovely." The mouse's smile turned grim. "But barring another witch's curse, I do not hold out much hope that we can escape to your land. And while this goat matters little, if we…kill the Archbishop, we will be hunted across the land as heretics, our land forfeit to the Church, our families ruined."

"Not both of us," Danilo said.

Théodore measured him with his eyes. "So you do not think you were seen by any person in the street tonight? On the way here? Because the death of a Church official will bring the royal guard, and the presence of such a distinctive foreigner will not go unnoticed."

"I can handle—"

"And once you are identified, questions will be asked of all those who have been seen with you. Not only me, but *anyone* you have spoken with in Tigue. And if by some miracle you have managed to save Luc, neither of you will have any sort of life remaining to you."

Danilo bit his lip. Théodore went on. "But if we leave Tigue now then we will not be pursued, which is why," he grabbed Danilo's wrist, fortunately with the paw that was not bloody, "I am telling you for the last time—"

Danilo yanked his paw away. "So you'd let Luc burn." Théodore didn't answer. "Fine. I'll do it without you, then. I'll figure out the seal, I'll go to the guard, and somehow I'll get Luc free, and we'll head north, get out of Tigue."

He turned and started to walk back to the study. At the door, Théodore's voice stopped him, just a couple feet behind. "You can't go to the guards with a letter in the middle of the night."

Danilo jumped; the mouse had followed him silently back. Behind them, the front door was closed, Dornier's corpse just inside. "When, then?"

"Sunrise. Four, five hours from now."

The tiger put a paw to the door frame and stared at the desk, the quills and ink and candles, now burned down to half their height. "Four hours? We can't wait that long. He thinks I'm coming upstairs."

"Aye." Théodore folded his arms. "You'd best get to writing then."

The smell of blood still hung in the air, though he couldn't see any stains on the dark carpeted floor. But there were the leather straps that had bound him, lying curled and askew. Danilo rubbed his wrists. "I'm going to have to go up to him." He looked back to Théodore for confirmation, and the mouse just looked back with steady, sad eyes. "He might fall asleep, but...I have to go up. I can keep him there for a while. And then I can sneak out, if—if you can take the letter over?"

Slowly, the mouse shook his head. "You've been seen with the Bishop. It'll have to be you. And," he added, "you'll have to write the letter, too. I can't write."

"Can you tell me what it should say?"

Théodore rubbed his whiskers. "Heard a few military orders. I suppose it wouldn't be so different. Anyway, guards likely can't read either. They'll recognize the seal well enough, though."

It took precious seconds to find paper, even longer for Danilo to figure out how to get the quill to write on it. Théodore dictated the note, a simple "By order of His Excellency the Archbishop, the prisoner Luc de Fleuve will be transferred to the prison at Lutèce. Please release him immediately to the custody of the tiger Danilo Mitini."

As Danilo wrote the words, they became old Gallic, and though they looked foreign, he understood them and even noticed when he made a mistake. "How do I sign it?" he asked when he'd finished.

"Archbishop Argile." The mouse shrugged. "Perhaps he has some holy title he adds, but again...the seal is the thing."

"Right." Danilo signed the paper and then stood. "Can you seal it?"

Théodore nodded. "I will take the letter and meet you behind that empty house at sunrise."

"Take these as well." Danilo pulled Luc's tunic off him for the first time since—since he'd washed with Maria? It smelled like him now more than Luc, but it would still fit the otter. He hesitated, and then slid his pants down as well. "He's expecting me to be naked anyway, and Luc will need clothes to wear—I mean, that aren't dirty from—from prison."

The mouse didn't stare at Danilo's body, even when Danilo took off the bandage and exposed his scar; of course he'd already seen Danilo's privates. He simply nodded and took the clothes. "If you do not come to the house before the sun is fully over the horizon, I will assume you have been taken."

Théodore's acceptance of his nakedness let Danilo relax. A cool breeze from the open window caressed his sheath and balls, and he reached down to brush a finger along the stitches. The wound below them felt drier, less sore, which he hoped was a good sign.

"You are healing well, I told you. That polecat does good work." Théodore draped the clothes over his arm and picked up a heavy metal piece as long as his paw. "Go. I will find the wax and make the seal, and see you in four hours, God willing."

"God keep you," Danilo said, and turned his eyes to the portrait of the Stag Jesus before walking out the other door.

"Danilo."

He turned to see the mouse framed in the door, a hard smile on his muzzle. "I am serious. Don't kill him."

"I'm not sure I could," Danilo said.

Théodore appraised him. "You might be surprised," he said with a raised paw. Danilo curled his tail around his legs and walked on out of the room.

Chapter Seventeen

Just as he found the stairs up, the Archbishop's voice came stridently down. "Dornier, what takes so long?"

Danilo almost answered himself, but had the presence of mind to imitate the goat's "Uhhh" in response, which brought only silence from above.

Danilo had roamed his own house naked on a couple occasions and had always found it titillating, but here his thoughts were far from enjoyable. As he had searched for the stairs, he played out in his head how he would handle the Archbishop's certain demands, and trying to focus more on how he would make sure Argile (don't think of him as Cobb) would fall asleep afterwards and remain asleep at least until sunrise.

That part he didn't think would be difficult. Though he himself was keyed up, he was aware that his body dragged as he walked, that lifting his arms felt heavier than normal, that if he paused, his eyelids drifted downward. Argile would be just as tired here on the far side of midnight, and if Danilo let him do those things that he was trying not to picture too much, certainly, surely, the older Archbishop would fall asleep soon after.

When he put his foot on the stairs, his resolve failed him. He seemed to see the shadows from the prison wall again on the stair in the flickering lamplight, grown to cackling grotesque puppets. His memory of the Archbishop's form grew larger and larger, and even though he had stood and looked the stag right in the eyes not half an hour before, he imagined Argile as large as Cobb, half a foot taller and forty kilos heavier. He imagined the stag's cock the size of the cucumber he'd tried to play with once, the no-fucking-way one, forced inside him.

What was more, his lightened sac hung below his sheath, reminding him what had been taken from him. Though he knew

it was ridiculous, knew it had no bearing on his fitness, having his "halfie" nature exposed made his tail curl down below him, made his shoulders hunch and one paw drop low to hide the scar and the emptiness behind it from the shadows of the stair.

"Dornier! Send him up at once!" Argile's voice commanded.

A beam of light fell directly on a painting halfway up the stair, and with a gasp, Danilo saw Luc's features staring up, paws held out catching a small amount of the halo around his head. He remembered the burning otter, the noble sacrifice Luc had made, the sounds coming from the cell as the Archbishop had raped him. He set his jaw. Whatever Luc had endured, he could also endure, and would endure, to set his friend free.

He made the indistinct noise of the goat soldier again, and stepped up onto the stair, his eyes on the painting. Three steps up, the reflections of the light caught the otter's eyes and they glowed as if lit from within.

It wasn't Luc in the painting. That had been an illusion, or he hadn't been seeing it properly. This otter had silver fur along his muzzle and a leaner build, darker brown fur. Up close, Danilo could see the shadowy shapes around his legs, black featureless jaws that tore at his white robe, and yet the otter smiled upward.

At the top of the stairs, Archbishop Argile stood in a doorway holding a lantern in one thick hand. The light played over his naked body, every inch of it pale white except for the bright pink of his erection hanging between his legs. He was still only Danilo's height, still only slightly stockier than the tiger, and his shaft, which drew Danilo's eyes, was only the size of two fingers, not an entire forearm. But his expression was hungrier, his eyes narrower and his smile more savage than Danilo had ever seen on Cobb.

"Where's Dornier?" he demanded, peering down the stairs. "And why are your paws not bound?"

"I worked them free," Danilo said. "And Dornier just left. I don't know why."

It looked like Argile might lean past him, to call out again, so Danilo steeled himself and reached down to wrap a paw around the exposed erection. "I thought it would be better with my paws free," he said.

The hand that was not holding a lantern smacked his muzzle. He let go and staggered to the side, as the Archbishop's eyes burned into his. "You will not touch me until I allow you to," he said, and stepped aside, gesturing Danilo through the doorway. "Go."

The relief when Argile forgot about Dornier was worth the sting in his muzzle. Danilo walked into the bedroom, trying not to betray the pounding of his heart. He couldn't keep his tail from curling tightly against him, but the Archbishop probably preferred him afraid. Maybe he should be less confident.

"May I ask you something?" He tried to put a tremor into his voice and found it rather easy, when he tried.

"Get on the bed."

The lantern provided the only light in the large room, casting Danilo's shadow on the wall and windows beyond the large four-poster bed. Paintings hung around the room, but shadows skittered across them and Danilo couldn't pick out the images on any of them. He crawled up onto the white linen sheets that stank of stag and turned to sit on the edge of the bed.

"Don't face me." Argile closed the door behind him and then, as Danilo began to turn, said, "Wait."

He set the lantern on the side table and stood, supporting his shaft with one hand while he stared down at Danilo's body. "Ask your question," he said, and reached down to brush a finger along Danilo's wound.

The tiger gritted his teeth and tried to ignore the touch, as gentle as it was unwelcome. "The painting," he forced out, "on the stair."

"Mmm." The Archbishop's hands pushed Danilo's thighs apart. He cradled the tiger's single testicle, his rough nails snagging the stitches. "What of it?"

Danilo felt each little tug, but refused to flinch. "Who—which saint is it?"

"That?" The stag's eyes glittered down at him. "Épipode. One of Tigue's native saints. Had you continued your education here, you would have learned much about him."

"I—" Épipode was an otter? *You have stood on his remains,* Bishop Lukin had told him. It was hard to focus with the Archbishop's fingers caressing his privates, not only because his wound stung as if it knew who was touching it, but also because he had the feeling that at any moment, the stag might push his fingers past the stitches, dig in, and tear out Danilo's remaining testicle. "I still wish to—to continue my education."

The stag rubbed again at his groin and then stood, a sour smile on his face. "Roll over," he said. "Keep your paws below you."

As Danilo complied, his heart speeding up, Argile continued, as calmly as if they were both simply sitting across a desk from each other. "I have not yet decided your fate. Perhaps it will depend upon how well you please me tonight."

A nervous, inappropriate giggle burst up from Danilo's throat. He muffled it in the sheets, but fear kept him shaking. As soon as the Archbishop discovered the corpse of his bodyguard—one he trusted enough to appear naked and reveal his homosexuality to—he would be displeased no matter what Danilo did.

"But Épipode is a significant saint for you. He more than any other could be your patron."

The herbal smell of scented oil reached Danilo's nose. He didn't speak, and Argile went on. "He is the patron saint of bachelors, the betrayed, and the tortured. And you will always be a bachelor, for your inner demons have betrayed you, and you have already suffered torture." His hand crept beneath Danilo's hips to hold his testicle again. "Though it is nothing to what you will feel should you displease me."

"My inner demons," Danilo breathed, thinking *keep him talking.* "There is nothing demonic about an attraction to males. Where I come from, we are learning that people can live that way."

"That is not something you learned at the Vatican." The fingers released his testicle and returned a moment later to press something slick into him.

"No," Danilo gasped, talking faster, trying to keep his mind off the sensations. "It is something from my home. There are some who are ashamed of it still. I was ashamed to think it was part of me."

"That was the word of God speaking to you through the demon's words." The finger withdrew from him, and he knew what was coming next.

"God speaks of love," he said quickly. "Love, and this is love, how can it be wrong?"

"Quiet," Argile said. "There is nothing of love in this."

And there was not. It was rough and it was fast. The stag's weight drove him into the bed, the thick hands pressed his neck down until he had to twist his head to the side to breathe, and the stag's shaft felt twice as thick as it had looked. He squeezed his eyes shut and reminded himself that he was doing this for Luc. As he tried to picture the otter, the image that came into his mind was the glowing-eyed painting from the stair. That calmed him, quelled his urge to squirm and struggle and run away from the violation. He had worried that he might feel aroused, but his own shaft remained pulled into his sheath throughout the ordeal, through the initial pain and the numbness that followed, from the stag's first satisfied grunt to the last throes of his orgasm. At the end of it, Argile cried, "Demons! Out!" and there was a rawness to his voice that Danilo had not heard in the prison.

When the stag withdrew, the tiger bit his lip and then exhaled in relief. He lay quiet until Argile said, "Get up," and then turned and called, "Dornier!"

The name of the guard set Danilo to panicking again. He nearly fell backing himself off the bed and struggled to his feet. His rear felt sore and warm and he badly needed to use the chamberpot. But he hurried for the door. "I hope I have pleased you, Your Excellency," he said, pulling the door open.

The stag lay sprawled back on his bed, gazing up at the ceiling, his expression empty. "I told you, there is nothing in this of pleasure. I will decide your fate in the morning. Dornier!"

Danilo stepped outside the door and could think of nothing to do but make the guard's guttural vocal noise. It was desperate, but the call echoed from the stair and sounded as though it had come from below. It should not have worked, but whether the Archbishop was fooled or simply tired, it did.

"Take this tiger away," Argile said loudly. "Bind his paws and put him in the wine cellar."

Danilo acknowledged the order with another noise, and risked a look back at the stag. The Archbishop sat on the edge of his bed, his eyes drooping. He looked about as tired as Danilo felt, and the tiger hoped he would remain in his room and sleep. He closed the door.

He'd intended to go downstairs, but he was still very aware of his nakedness, and there was another door half-open down the way. The house had fallen silent; Dornier's body remained undiscovered, and the Archbishop did not stir. So Danilo kept his claws in and padded quietly along the hall to the room, pushing gently through the door.

In the moon's silver half-light, the room appeared full of ghosts. Robes hung and fluttered in the breeze from the open window, white linens with trim in various colors, scarves of office with elaborate crosses sewn into them hung over wooden racks. Three wardrobes stood to one side, one with an open door that allowed Danilo to see still white garments within.

He padded over to a large vanity and examined himself in the nearly full-length mirror, his blue eyes traveling the length of his body. He'd lost weight, that was certain. Since emerging in 1508, he couldn't recall a time when he'd not been hungry. He traced a finger down his ribs, along the stripes. How much weight could someone lose in four days and still be healthy? Aside from that, though, he looked…much the same. One paw reached down to his wound, where the stitches were coming loose. He picked at them out of habit and then covered himself with a paw and looked up, surprised at the grim determination his expression took on. He let go and turned away from the mirror.

After finding a chamber pot in the corner and availing himself of it, he sought out the plainest white robe he could find and slipped it over his head. He returned to the vanity and looked at himself, adjusting the robe. It fit better than Luc's clothes had, and it didn't smell too much like the stag, just enough to remind him of the violation he'd just undergone. He could bear to wear this and be seen in it. As for the rape—that's what it had been—it helped if he reminded himself that he'd walked into it knowing what he was in for, that he was sacrificing his body to give Luc a better chance at freedom. Then he felt more noble than soiled, more powerful than powerless.

His eyes glanced down and happened to see the robes the Archbishop had been wearing that evening, cast casually across the table. He wondered if they smelled like Luc, if he could take them and present them to the Bishop as evidence of the Archbishop's activities. And then he shifted his weight and felt the soreness and dampness under his tail. By the chamberpot was a cloth he'd used to clean himself up, and his eyes returned to it.

He'd rested one paw on the robes while thinking and now left it there, planning. Luc's safety came first, of course, but once the otter had been freed, could he go to the Bishop? Lukin had hesitated at the Archbishop's condemnation of Luc, hadn't he? He'd said Danilo hadn't disappointed him. But still—it was Georg. He had stared so avidly at the burning otter, had been so eager for Danilo to watch Luc's castration, that those images still burned in Danilo's mind. And yet, once Luc's crime had been wiped away by Danilo's sacrifice, the Bishop had not wanted to see him suffer further. Had he? Danilo tried to recall through the haze of remembered pain and shock, his remaining testicle throbbing as he did.

If the Bishop truly wished only to punish the guilty, then Danilo could turn that against the Archbishop. But that was an "if" the size of the Cathédrale, and Danilo would have to be certain that his intuition was correct. He tried to recall all the conversations he'd had with the black wolf since then. Did Lukin respect him now for his sacrifice, even though he'd argued against it? The Archbishop had approved it; Argile had wanted to see Danilo mutilated, knowing that he would get to rape Luc and see him burn. Bishop Lukin had wanted Luc to suffer what he thought was a just punishment. So he would feel the same about the Archbishop, right?

Right, because no Church official ever had a double standard when it came to protecting his own. Even Théodore could view the Archbishop as hateful and yet still holy. Danilo sighed.

Still debating, he spied the plain brown robe the stag had worn earlier, and in a pocket, found the key that opened the door of the empty house beside the prison. His fingers moved to undo the silk cord that bound the key even as he formed the idea that that would be a good place to wait out the rest of the night, if not the most comfortable.

He could ask Théodore's opinion then, when they went to rescue Luc. He would extract the otter from the prison and leave him in Théodore's care, and he could go report the Archbishop to whatever authorities there were, or else he would go with Théodore and Luc. He suspected the mouse would tell him to come with them, to flee this city and not put himself at any more risk from the Church, and part of him—the exhausted part that would have traded almost anything, if he had anything to trade, for a Red Bull or a Pro

241

Plus—wanted to go. But the part of him that still ached from the stag's weight atop him, that still felt the violation he had endured, that still saw the shadow puppets enacting Luc's rape—that part wanted the Archbishop brought to justice, his hypocrisy exposed.

Théodore's last words came back to him. Could he kill the Archbishop while he slept? At least then the stag would be punished for sure. Danilo could hurry downstairs, find Dornier's sword, and come back up and do it quickly.

He looked up again at his reflection in the mirror, and his paws flexed. He remembered again Seline telling him to leave punishment to God, and Bertrand yelling at him from the cell. How many worse things could happen if he killed the Archbishop? The Church would pursue him and Théodore; their scents were all over the downstairs. None of them would ever know peace.

His reflection tried to smile. He had to do something, though. So he gathered up the cloth, stained with the Archbishop's unmistakable scent, and slipped it into the pocket of his robe beside the key. Then he left the room and padded down the short hallway.

Halfway down the stairs, he looked again at the portrait of St. Épipode. The otter continued to stare upwards, and again Danilo was struck by the resemblance to Luc. But no, that was fanciful. He hadn't actually seen Luc face-on in a day or two. This otter was older, different.

The Archbishop had been wrong. Épipode wasn't Danilo's patron saint; he was Luc's. Luc had been tortured, Luc was a bachelor, and Luc had been betrayed, first by his own nature, then by Danilo and Bertrand, and finally by the church he revered. But it was no use waiting around for this saint to perform a miracle to save Luc. Danilo was going to have to do it.

He walked down one more step and then stopped. What if St. Épipode had already performed a miracle? What if he were the one who'd brought Danilo here? He was an otter; he would work through water, would he not? Danilo studied the expression of the otter, the shadowy mouths that tore at him, but the painting revealed nothing new to him.

Was it you? he asked silently. The painting made no answer, and after a moment Danilo realized that his eyes were drooping and he was falling asleep on the stair.

He shook himself awake and walked slowly on down the stairs, keeping his tread as light as possible. In the lower floor, nothing stirred; the body of Dornier still lay where they had left it, an indistinct lump in the shadows of the front room, a smell of blood and urine that curled through the air and wrinkled his nose.

Rather than walk past him, Danilo began to climb out the window despite the soreness in his groin. He let himself down to the ground below and braced himself against the side of the house. The stone against his paw gave no indication of the horrors that lay within this house, that spread from it out into the city of Tigue. It wasn't a bad place, even here without cell phones and caffeine pills. Most of the people he'd met were trying hard to have a good life. You could argue that the twenty-first century was no less subject to corrupt people hiding behind institutions; he'd read all the stories of greedy bankers and self-serving politicians whose actions had destroyed lives, of priests who had abused children—that made him wonder what Archbishop Argile had done as a young priest—but there were so many people and so many institutions that few of them touched everyone's life. Here, everyone looked to the church, and to find this evil at its heart felt more pervasive to him than anything he had encountered in 2008.

The night air chilled his whiskers and ears and lungs. He drew in a breath and hurried around the back of the house, out to the street, and back to the prison.

Without the tension of danger, he found it more and more difficult to keep his eyes open. Twice he woke to find himself leaning against a wall; the second time, he thought there were shadows moving in front of him. He snapped awake and stared around him, and the street faded back to stillness.

On the Rue St. Bartholème, two mice sauntered about on errands. Danilo greeted them with exhausted nods, making his way to the empty house. When the street was clear, he took out the key, fumbled at the lock, and let himself in.

He tried to lock the door behind him and succeeded on the third try. Then he stumbled to the far back of the house, facing a window to the east so the sun would wake him, and collapsed to the ground.

It seemed that as he fell, he kept falling, that the dirt was liquid but allowed him to breathe. He looked around and saw shadowy creatures circling him, their teeth gleaming in the moonlight. Then one approached and it was not the teeth that gleamed; it was the knife in the paw of the savage weasel. Danilo swiped at the knife, but his paw passed through it and the knife stabbed him in the groin. Pain flared dully, and when he looked down again it was the blanched stag removing his antlers from Danilo's wounded sac, with a grim smile and empty black eyes. He opened his mouth, put it around Danilo's sheath, and pulled his lips back to show his flat white teeth. They bit around his base, pressure becoming gentle pain. No, Danilo moaned, and kicked out, but his ankles were in the jaws of a pair of wolves, black and white. He reached down and grabbed the white stag's antlers, and the head came away, the mouth sliding harmlessly off his sheath, and he was holding a skull by the antlers. It stared at him with those same black eyes and then the mouth opened and it laughed. "Foolish tiger," it said, "do you think you can cheat death?" The white fur of his paw was bone, his skin and flesh gone, and he was nothing but a skeleton hanging in darkness. No; not complete darkness. Two points of light floated in front of him, a little way away. When he focused on them, warmth blossomed around him and his body was made flesh again. He kept his eyes on them, and the wolves and the dead stag melted away. Words struggled through the thick liquid toward him, indistinct and muffled. What? He swam toward the lights. What are you saying? The lights were eyes for a moment and then they blazed into twin suns, and he brought a paw to his eyes to shield them.

Chapter Eighteen

D anilo woke to a red haze, sun forcing its way through his eyelids. He yawned, feeling every bit as tired as he had the night before. He turned away from the sun, keeping his eyes shut, and his sluggish mind revisited the dream. He was floating, and someone had a message for him. Well, he had until the sun was over the horizon—

With a burst of fear, he jerked awake. If the sun was already up, if he'd overslept—

Even as he hurried to the shutters, he heard voices outside. "Another ten minutes, I reckon, if you are not convinced he is a liar."

That was Armand, the weasel. The voice that replied was Théodore's. "Even if he is not, he might simply have been caught."

"You give him entirely too much credit."

"I made sure he was one of us, and besides, he has earned my respect. At least enough to wait until the time I told him I would."

"I'm here!" Danilo hissed.

Both voices fell silent. Then movement, and a shadow across the window. "Danilo? You are inside?"

"Yes! I took the key—I was asleep in here. I'm sorry. I was very tired."

"No matter. I will come around to the door." Théodore sounded amused. "You see, Armand? Wait here and do not forget what I told you."

"I will be watching," the weasel said, with a bit of menace to his tone, Danilo thought.

Danilo padded through the house to the door. When he unlocked it, Théodore pushed it open and hurried through, closing it behind him. The mouse looked around and wrinkled his nose. "This doesn't resemble my idea of a secret church office. Does he have the prisoners brought here?"

"There's a passage that leads to the prison." Danilo pointed to the back corner of the house. "It comes out in the basement."

"Ah-ha." Théodore nodded. "I believe the prison was an old monastery. All the monasteries I know have ways for the monks to sneak out."

"I thought I could sneak Luc out this way." The decrepit house looked much more ordinary in the daylight, sad and broken.

The mouse produced the letter. "This way will work," he said confidently. "When they turn Luc over to you, walk past this house and Armand and I will accompany you to the Saône. I have a captain waiting there to take us downriver to my farm. He's an otter. He will hide Luc if need be."

Danilo took a breath. "I can't go with you right away."

The mouse's whiskers lowered. "The longer you stay—when that goat is discovered, your life won't be worth a piece of river garbage."

"I have—I have evidence that the Archbishop is one of us." He pulled the cloth partly from his robe.

Théodore's eyes traveled down Danilo's body to his waist and tail. "You think you can get someone to pay attention?"

The tiger's ears drooped. "I'm waiting for you to talk me out of it. I know it's crazy."

The old house fell silent enough that Danilo could hear murmurs of conversation from people passing in the street outside. Théodore's eyes were fixed on his, the mouse's expression curiously blank. At length, he said, "It is madness. To submit yourself to the police, to confess to this crime in the hope of implicating the most powerful figure in the Church…it has no chance of succeeding. I am as certain of that as I am of the rise of the sun in the east."

Danilo nodded, and opened his mouth, but Théodore held up the paw containing the Archbishop's falsified letter. "And yet," he went on, speaking fast and low, "I would have said the same about the chances of rescuing anyone from prison. Had you listened to me, we would be well on our way to my farm, and Luc would be awaiting immolation. Instead…" The mouse held Danilo's eyes. "You have shown me what it means to believe, have restored a faith I had thought lost. When I fought with the army, I felt part of a whole, part of a country and a church that would in turn welcome me back. I returned to find myself even more outcast. I looked down on people like Coumier and Luc, because they could not be practical, could not understand that you can hide yourself and still satisfy the urges inside you." He held the paper out to Danilo. "You proved me wrong. You showed me that we can love each other and that our actions, no matter how 'crazy' they might seem, are not wasted. So... go to the police. If you believe you can make them listen, then I will not gainsay you."

The tiger's fingers closed around the thick paper, his mouth slightly open. Théodore released the paper and reached up with two fingers to lift the tiger's jaw shut, his lips creasing into a smile. "Is it so unusual, what I have said? No more unusual than you yourself, blessed Danilo. I was a romantic too, once, before the war." He stood on the tips of his toes and kissed Danilo quickly on the lips, then stepped back, rubbing his whiskers and looking off to one side. "I will hold the barge as long as I may. If we are not pursued, I may persuade the captain to remain until noon. If you cannot join us then, come downriver when you can and when you have sailed half a day, make landing at the Pas-de-Reynard dock and ask after the Belle Soleil farm. There you will find me and, God willing, Luc."

"Pas-de-Reynard," Danilo repeated. "Belle Soleil." His fingers closed around the paper. "Do you really think I can do it?"

"If anyone can." Théodore laughed softly. "Only—do not go to LeSevre. But I believe you knew that already. Certainly some power guided us to the dock that day to pull you from the river. I suppose your witch's curse proved a blessing for us."

"Théodore," Danilo said quietly. "I have not been...entirely truthful with you."

The mouse fell silent, his smile faltering. "Only in the story of the witch's curse," Danilo said. "Only there. The truth is...I do not know how I came to this place. But I came from a very different land. I speak your language through some kind of power I do not understand, and I do not know how I came to be here. But truthfully..." He tried to say that he'd come from the future, and still could not quite form the words, "...in my land, people such as you and I are not treated viciously. We are scorned sometimes, and lives are more difficult, but...but we are not tortured, mutilated, put to death."

Théodore released a breath. "I had thought you were going to confess to being a servant of the Church. So you were brought here by some magic."

"I think it might have been a miracle." Danilo curled his tail around his leg and turned toward the back of the house, where the sun shone brightly on the closed shutters.

"In that case, I am doubly pleased to have borne witness to it and to have met you." Théodore patted Danilo's paw. "If you discover which saint effected the miracle, tell me and I will include him in my prayers."

"Épipode." Danilo recalled the otter's portrait, and his dream. "I think."

The mouse tapped his head. "Tigue's own saint. I will remember him. Now…let us hope he is watching over us still. Remember: you are taking him to Lutèce. Do not mention the boat; he would be transported by carriage. But Armand and I will take him here, and we may walk with you as far as the Cathédrale. You should be able to find the police there, or in the Bishop's offices."

He moved toward the door, but Danilo reached out and hugged him, and Théodore made a startled noise and then hugged back. "Thank you," Danilo said. "I couldn't have done this without you."

"Then go." Théodore's paws held Danilo tightly against him. "And know that I am still with you."

They emerged from the dark house into a sunlit morning. The Rue St. Bartholème bustled with activity now, but to the right, Danilo could see larger crowds in the direction of the Cathédrale. He took a breath, gripped the paper in his paw, and walked toward the prison. The Archbishop's robe moved lightly over his fur in the breeze, shielding him from very little of the wind. Possibly it was just an indoor robe, or was meant to be worn beneath something— but no, Théodore would have told him. Stop second-guessing your-self, he said sternly, and marched along the street with his head up, breathing in the smoky, filthy scent of the prison.

An unfamiliar guard met him at the door, a bored-looking hare. "No visitors," he said before glancing down at the paper Danilo held.

"I have orders to move one of the prisoners."

"Move?" The hare snapped his head up, and his ears came for-ward. "Move to where?"

"To Lutèce." Danilo kept his paws steady as he presented the paper. "The Archbishop has sealed the orders himself."

The hare stared at the paper without touching it, but his eyes did not move across the words. "One moment," he said, and then called back into the prison, "Captain!"

Danilo's fur prickled under his robe. A wolf's shadow appeared in the doorway, and Danilo saw LeSevre's wicked smile and piercing eyes. But when the wolf stepped into the diffuse morning light, he was smaller, with browner fur and less intensity to his stare, his eyes partly-lidded as though he'd been napping. "What is it?" His eyes opened wider when he saw Danilo, and he looked up at the sun. "No visits to prisoners until after noon."

"The execution is moved to Lutèce." The hare gestured to the paper.

The wolf took his eyes from Danilo and leaned forward to the paper. "That's the Archbishop's seal," he said slowly. "Most unusual. Why Lutèce?"

Stories to explain the move flitted through Danilo's mind, but he remembered to keep his story simple. He shook his head. "I was not told."

"Huh." The wolf examined the paper again. "The otter, isn't it?"

"Luc de Fleuve." Danilo cleared his throat.

"Perhaps the Archbishop wishes to provide some entertainment for the people of Lutèce, since we have had so many here, what?" The hare smiled, and Danilo wanted to punch his buckteeth in.

"Perhaps." At least the wolf didn't seem amused. He looked up at Danilo and scratched behind his ear. "I've not seen you before."

Danilo swallowed. "I'm newly arrived in Tigue," he said.

"Aye." The hare elbowed the wolf. "You've not heard of the white tiger? Attended the last burning with the Bishop himself. LeSevre says he's a degenerate."

The brown wolf's expression tightened. "LeSevre doesn't like him? Good enough for me. Fetch the otter. Second floor."

"Right." The hare turned and ambled back into the prison. Danilo heard the clink of keys, and then the wolf started talking to him, asking where he'd come in from, what he thought of Tigue, how it compared to other places he'd been.

Danilo tried to answer, as it was clear that the wolf was proud of his city, but his responses were short, and a moment later, he didn't remember any of what had been said, because the hare reappeared leading a figure behind him that resolved into Luc.

The otter wore only a rope around his neck and filthy pants that had been ripped in several spots. They had not been in such bad shape the night he'd been arrested, Danilo was sure, but the same could also be said for Luc himself. Dried blood clung to the fur of his muzzle and in patches on his chest and arms, and he favored one leg. When the hare pulled him to a stop, he squinted up at the tiger. "Danilo?" he whispered.

"I'm here to transport you to Lutèce." Danilo tried to make his voice sound harsh. He remembered Luc insisting to LeSevre that Danilo didn't matter, and squared his shoulders, looking up at the hare. "Is he well bound?"

"Aye." The hare handed Danilo the end of the rope that was tied around Luc's neck. "Paws are behind his back. Just yank on this if he falls or fights. I don't expect he will. He's been quiet. Haven't you?"

He prodded Luc in the ribs, and Luc winced. "Aye, sir," he said in a low raspy voice.

"Cheer up," the hare said. "You're to have a much larger audience in Lutèce."

"Thank you," Danilo said, and began to walk away. Beside the empty house, he saw Théodore's shadow, only twenty feet away.

"Ah, sir?" The wolf called after him.

Panic gripped his chest. The wolf had been watching him. He'd given himself away. He'd forgotten something important. Danilo breathed in, and turned around as carelessly as he could. "Aye?"

"The orders?"

He stared, and the wolf held out a paw. "You're to leave the orders, so we can account for the prisoner."

Luc didn't move, and neither did the hare or wolf. Was this a test? Did the wolf suspect him? What if he offered to leave the orders and that wasn't the way things were done?

Stop, he told himself, and carelessly handed the paper over to the wolf. "Thank you for your attention to detail, Captain."

"Aye. God keep you."

"God keep you." He turned again, and this time nobody stopped him.

He walked toward the empty house and the mouse's shadow, holding the rope, though he took care not to pull on it. Luc stumbled after him, remaining silent until they rounded the corner into the sheltered alley and came face to face with the mouse and weasel, both dressed in a blue uniform upon which a red, white, and blue rosette shone proudly. Then Luc stared and stopped. "Théodore?" he whispered. "Armand?"

"Old army uniforms still fit, aye?" Théodore clapped Luc on the shoulder. "Apologies, *ami*, but you must remain tied until we reach the barge."

"How..." Luc turned his head from one to the other, and up to Danilo. "How is this happening?"

"It's Danilo," the mouse said, and even the weasel's face bore grudging appreciation, though he sulked and stared out at the city. "He would not listen to me, but broke into the Archbishop's house, wrote a letter, and procured your release."

"The Archbishop." Luc winced, a reaction Danilo suppressed in himself.

"Could you..." Danilo waved to the mouse and weasel. "Give us a moment alone?"

"Aye." Théodore backed up, taking the weasel with him. They watched from a distance.

Luc looked up. "You did this for me?"

Danilo leaned down and breathed the words softly. "I know what the Archbishop did to you." Luc's eyes widened, but before he could ask how, Danilo added, "He did the same to me. I hope to provide evidence to the Church."

The otter shook his head. "Oh, Danilo, no. It is too dangerous. They will not let you..."

"If it doesn't go well, I will escape and come join you. Théodore has told me the way. But I wanted to get you to safety first."

Luc struggled to free his paws. "No. Come with us. I have put you in this position, and caused you to be harmed. I will not suffer any more danger."

Gently, Danilo laid a paw on Luc's shoulder. "You've suffered most of the danger so far."

"You have made sacrifices—more than anyone should ask—"

"And I have a chance to right a wrong. Two wrongs. Well, several. Who knows how many? At least I will see him punished for what he did to us."

Luc's eyes rested on Danilo's, and then the otter smiled. "I care little for his fate. I only want to see you alive again."

"You will," Danilo promised. "Go with Théodore and live a happy life."

Luc stepped forward to press against him, but only briefly, and before Danilo could return the embrace, the otter had stepped back again. Danilo waved Théodore and Armand forward, and handed the rope to the mouse. "Take care of him," he said.

"I will." The mouse's eyes sparkled even in the dim alley light. "And take care of yourself."

They walked together in silence out into the street, leading Luc behind them. Armand brought up the rear, with one paw on the knife at his belt. At least, that's where the paw was whenever Danilo turned to check on Luc, which he did often enough that as they walked through the narrow arcade of houses, Théodore hissed at him to keep his eyes forward. They passed beneath the brick archway onto the main street that led to the Cathédrale, and here the crowds parted around them, murmuring at the uniformed guards, the tall white tiger in holy robes, the limping prisoner led by a rope.

At the bridge, Théodore turned to Danilo and saluted smartly. "We will take charge of the prisoner from here, sir," he said. A small crowd paused to watch the transfer.

"Very good," Danilo said, and then, glimpsing the spires of the cathedral ahead of him and remembering that he was dressed in holy robes, said, "May God guide your steps."

He met Luc's eyes as they guided the otter around the corner, to the bridge, to the barge and away to freedom. Neither of them risked a word, but Danilo hoped to say as much with his eyes as Luc said with his.

And then Théodore and Luc and Armand were but tails in a busy street, and then the crowd surrounded them and they were no longer even that. Danilo spent another moment staring after them, said a quick prayer for their safety, and set his eyes on the spires ahead of him.

Chapter Nineteen

Of course, Lauds was in progress at the Cathédrale. Danilo had heard the bells, but did not realize he had until he found the Bishop's offices locked and heard the murmurs of prayer from the immense building behind him. He made his way to the side door and tried to remember how long it had been since he'd heard the bells, how much longer he would have to wait. The Archbishop had to have discovered his dead servant by now.

People still stared as they passed him, but now he met their eyes and inclined his head. If they were close, he said, "God keep you," and sometimes they replied in kind. The gesture had become second nature to him, and as he spoke the words and nodded his head, he thought about the power that had called him here. He had been called for a purpose, he now believed, but when (if) that purpose had been fulfilled, would he be sent back to his own time? He thought about what his life would be like here in 1508. The Archbishop would be after him, and perhaps Théodore's farm would be remote enough for a white tiger to hide in, and perhaps it would not. He could cover himself in dirt, or find dyes to rub into his fur, but he could not hide his stature, and even orange tigers were unusual enough around Tigue to be remarked upon.

And if he were spotted, he would lead the church directly to Luc. Danilo turned his eyes toward the river, invisible behind the red clay roofs and wooden beams, and imagined Luc and Théodore boarding the barge, waiting for him until the sun had reached its zenith. Whatever happened with the Bishop, it would likely be better if Danilo never boarded the barge, if he could slip away. He could travel to Lutèce, or perhaps even Londinium, larger cities where a tiger might not be so remarkable; or he could ride south to Etrusca where he might find others of his kind.

None of those options appealed to him as much as returning to Théodore's farm. Maybe he could stay for a couple days, figure out a way they could hide him. He didn't need to live in a city, not after he'd gone from the modern conveniences of 2008 to this primitive world. He scratched at flea bites on his hip and then, to stop his paw moving to the sore, itchy wound below his sheath, he lifted his fingers to the cathedral wall.

The limestone chilled his fingertips here in the morning breeze and shadow. Above him, the building loomed, but he no longer saw death in it, nor God. It was a magnificent achievement of people, and he felt privileged for the chance to have seen it, to have walked in it when it was but a generation old. He would want to see more of the buildings, the Duomo in Firenza, the Nôtre Dame in Lutèce, more of da Vinci's paintings—if he traveled to Firenza, could he meet the old rabbit himself?—and the art and buildings that were flowering in the Renaissance. If he could not get home, at least exploring this world would be better than an existence in a small farmhouse, with the danger of discovery always hovering over him.

If his interview with the Bishop went well, then perhaps he would be exonerated from some of his crimes and be afforded more freedom. Tigue itself would be a lovely city to explore, though he would want to get out before the religious wars started in the later half of this century. If he lived that long, he thought; he was still not used to viewing history on a personal scale. For the next forty years or so, at least, the city would be prosperous and relatively peaceful, and he could still be part of it. He held to this faint hope as motion built inside the cathedral and people began to spill out of it.

Another ten minutes passed before the side door opened. The heavy boar emerged first and stared at Danilo, then turned and said, "That tiger's back," to the person behind him.

Bishop Lukin peered around the boar's frame. His ears came up, though he did not smile. "Danilo," he said, stepping forward. "What a pleasant surprise. I approve of your clothing, although..." He reached out to take Danilo's robe in his fingers, and frowned.

"I can explain," Danilo said quickly. "Please, Your Excellency, I must speak with you in private."

The wolf let the robe drop. "I have duties to attend to, and you have lessons. Next week, perhaps we can resume your private instruction. After today's ceremony, of course."

Once Danilo might have trembled before that statement. Now, he saw no threat in it. "It cannot wait." The tiger kept his eyes on the Bishop's yellow-green ones. "Please."

"Very well." Lukin spoke slowly.

"And if you could summon…Perchet? The fox from LeSevre's group?"

Now the black wolf's ears flattened. "What is this about, Danilo?"

The boar stood nearby, listening. Other people milled about a respectful distance away, trying not to stare at the Bishop and the white tiger, but Danilo saw the insides of a dozen ears. He quailed, but the violation burned inside him, and then he was speaking the words and it was too late, he had committed himself. "I must report a serious crime," he said. "Very serious, Your Excellency."

"And you require Perchet." The Bishop's eyes widened and dropped to Danilo's groin, then rose again to meet the tiger's eyes, and his brow lowered. "I trusted you, Danilo. Have you betrayed my trust?"

"I have not, but another has." Danilo slipped his paw into the pocket of his robe. The cloth rustled against his fingers. "I will tell you, only—in private. Your Excellency."

"Yes." The Bishop shook off his shock, but Danilo thought he already guessed what crimes would be reported, because when he turned back into the church and ordered Culliver to fetch Perchet, his voice shook, and when he set off for his offices, he did not wait for the boar to lead the way.

The guard hurried to take up his position in front of the Bishop; Danilo followed at his side. They had reached the door of the Bishop's offices when a loud voice froze all three of them. "Stop! Stop him!"

LeSevre. Danilo's heart sank. He had seconds, at most. "Your Excellency," he said, "Please forgive me."

"What—?" The Bishop's words died as Danilo pulled the cloth from his pocket.

"LeSevre is going to accuse me of a crime. I swear to—" He fumbled, remembering Seline's frosty objection to his use of God's name. "By my parents, by everything I hold sacred, that I am not guilty of it. I wanted Perchet to examine the evidence, but…"

The Bishop recoiled as Danilo held the stained cloth out, and the boar stepped between them. "How *dare* you?" he growled, and cocked an arm back, but Bishop Lukin rested a paw on the massive forearm.

"Your Excellency!" LeSevre was shouting. "He's dangerous! Be wary!"

Danilo wanted to shove his evidence under the wolf's nose. Lukin's pink tongue flicked at his lips, and his ears had flattened all the way back, but he did not appear able to bring himself to lean forward to smell.

It was possible he could already smell, with his keen nose. Danilo spoke quickly. "Archbishop Argile," he said, "performs unnatural acts." The boar guard growled an imprecation, but the Bishop held up a paw, his eyes fixed on Danilo's, and the tiger went on. "Not just on me, against my will. On Luc, this very night. On other prisoners awaiting execution. He visits the prisons and—"

Running footsteps click-clicked staccato urgency behind his words, and he did not finish his sentence before they overtook him. LeSevre's body slammed Danilo against the wall of the alcove, and a deadly pinprick with a knife's weight of pressure behind it threatened the base of his skull. "This vermin has stolen away the otter meant for execution," the wolf growled. "Where is he?"

Bishop Lukin sounded old and uncertain. "What other evidence have you?"

LeSevre answered, "The guards at the prison identified him!" but Danilo knew the question was for him, and he spoke over the wolf, loudly.

"My own evidence," he said. "The guards are sent away but the priest is a mute, the Archbishop comes in through the passageway to the basement from the empty hou—nggh!"

The captain had put his weight behind Danilo, shoving his chest against the stone. "Where is the prisoner?" he shouted.

Danilo kept his ears back, listening for the Bishop's response. The wolf exhaled and said, "Where is the otter?"

"Your Excellency," Danilo pleaded.

"I have heard your evidence." Lukin's voice had gained confidence and strength. "Rest assured it will not go for naught. But the prisoner must still answer for his crimes. Where is he?"

"I don't know." Wildly he wondered if the Bishop would let Luc go if he offered to forget about the Archbishop. Danilo would make that trade. But Lukin, he suspected, would not.

A crowd had gathered in the street, and now a high voice piped up. "They went to the river. I saw 'em."

"River, eh." LeSevre growled. The pressure on Danilo's neck eased slightly. "Won't get far, then."

Everything was coming undone. If Luc were recaptured, if Danilo still had to watch his friend burn, then none of this was worthwhile. He closed his eyes and said in his head, *St. Épipode, I know you lie nearby. If you can, I need your help one last time.*

He felt the weight of the Cathédrale, the pressure of the wolf behind him, and the cold of the stone against his paws. His paws—no, only one paw. The other was not touching the stone directly, but insulated from it by…

The wolf's muzzle was just over his shoulder. He turned the paw with the filthy cloth in it and pushed it back at LeSevre's nose. "Smell this," he said, twisting his neck at the same time.

With a cry, LeSevre jerked back and reflexively pushed the knife forward, but it skimmed through Danilo's neck fur and did not even graze the skin. Danilo dropped the cloth and leapt from the alcove, knifing through the crowd, his long legs carrying him down the street toward the bridge, his only thought to come within sight of the barge so he could tell them to cast off while he fended off LeSevre.

People attempted to block his way, but he dodged them easily enough; one mouse he knocked over when the mouse anticipated his dodge. Behind him, LeSevre cried, "Stop him!" But the people of Tigue appeared more interested in a show than in apprehending a fugitive, and Danilo heard a soft cheer as he passed the corner.

There was the bridge; there, beyond it, the barge. He sprinted for the bridge, leaned over the balustrade, and waved at the figures on the barge. "Cast off! Cast off!"

Théodore and Luc turned and saw him at the same time. He only had time to see the captain and Théodore both spring for the rope tying the barge to the shore before LeSevre's paw seized his shoulder and spun him around, and the wolf's weight knocked him hard to the stone. Pain flared through him: his groin, his shoulder, his side.

The wolf's breath came hot across his muzzle. "On the barge, eh? No matter. My men can ride alongside as easy as sail behind." His weight shifted atop Danilo, and the tiger was reminded of the stag who'd lain atop him. "You'll see your friends in that prison soon enough."

"Didn't you..." Danilo coughed, struggling for leverage. "Smell? What your Archbishop does?" He managed to get LeSevre partly off him, before the wolf re-settled himself. He wore only a padded shirt, not his uniform, and even that rode askew on him, as though it had been donned in haste.

"Whatever you might have tricked him into, you mean." The wolf paused and then the click of a knife drawn from its sheath punctuated his words. "His Excellency is not under my jurisdiction. You are, halfie, and you've just admitted to enough crimes to merit execution."

There were people all around. Couldn't anyone intervene? Danilo called, "Help!" once before the wolf's paw smacked his muzzle into the stone.

"There's no help for you. I'll cheat the people of a show, but they'll get one when we retrieve your friend." Cold steel came to Danilo's throat.

He closed his eyes. What would happen if he died in 1508? Would he simply vanish from 2008? Would his bones appear there in some forgotten grave?

"Get off him!" The cry came from behind them, enough to make the knife hesitate as LeSevre looked around.

"Too late," he said, but Danilo twisted, and once again his neck spun out of the way of the knife as it slammed down. This time it sliced through his skin, leaving a painful weal but no other damage. One of his shoulders slid free of LeSevre's weight, and he punched upward with the free arm, striking with less force than the movie-hero punch he'd hoped to land.

LeSevre shifted anyway, sliding off him, but as Danilo rolled to his feet, pressing a paw to his throat, he saw that it was not because of his punch. Rather, the wolf crouched facing Théodore, who held his long, narrow knife at the ready.

"Been waiting to get my paws on you," LeSevre said. The wolf's tail wagged, and though his back was to Danilo, his smile purred through his voice. "You're a slippery one. Missed you at the river. Thought we'd get you at the Repos."

"You've done enough," the mouse said, keeping his eyes on the larger wolf. "Danilo, go."

Danilo's fingers were sticky with blood from the cut on his neck. He risked a glance at the river. The barge had sailed down the Saône toward the junction with the Rhône. In maybe ten or fifteen minutes it would be out of sight. But LeSevre wouldn't let it go. He'd tell his guard, they would ride along the bank, and then not only Luc but Théodore as well would be captured, all because Danilo hadn't simply followed their plan and gotten onto the barge. He'd had to try to punish the Archbishop, and now not only had that gone wrong, but it had ruined everything else.

He stepped toward LeSevre, but the wolf's ears flicked back immediately and he half-turned, brandishing his sword at Théodore while pointing the knife in his off hand directly at Danilo's chest. "No, my boy, you won't get me so easily," he said. "I took on five Iberian wolves at once and ended with three notches on my belt. The other two ran before I could dispatch them."

"I fought the Iberians too," Théodore said. "But I don't see the need to inflate my accomplishments with incredible stories."

LeSevre didn't respond to this, but turned on Danilo, spinning and lunging with the sword. Danilo barely twisted aside, losing his balance, but before he fell to the stone, LeSevre had spun back to engage the mouse. Théodore leapt forward and scored a hit along the wolf's knife arm, but the wolf slashed down with his sword.

The mouse cried out in pain; his knife clattered to the stone. Danilo watched as LeSevre jabbed at Théodore with the tip of his sword, adroitly heading off every attempt the mouse made to get close to his knife again. "What is it?" he asked, to the chuckles of the onlookers ringing the fight. "Want your knife? Go get it. Go on. Ah-hah." His swordpoint sank into the mouse's upper arm as Théodore got too close to the knife; the mouse jumped back, holding his arm and cursing. "Have to be quicker."

If he thought about it…

Danilo didn't think. He unsheathed his claws and scrambled to his feet, launching himself in a clumsy charge at LeSevre. The wolf had time to turn halfway and then Danilo was upon him, claws digging into the off arm, teeth sinking into the padded shirt and through it to the fur and flesh of the shoulder.

The wolf howled indignant fury and brought his sword around, smacking Danilo with the flat of it, first in the side, then in the head. Danilo pulled with his jaws, the shirt and flesh alike rending and coming away as he fell back to the ground.

"Son of a whore!" LeSevre cried, but a grey blur behind him caught his attention. Théodore had reclaimed his knife, and one of the watchers called to LeSevre to look out, giving the wolf enough warning to dodge the mouse's attack. He brought the sword around again and slashed down, and again the mouse's knife clattered to the ground as Théodore yelped and clutched his arm.

Danilo spit cloth and blood from his mouth and pushed at the ground, trying to get upright again. In front of him, LeSevre said, "Enough games," and raised his sword in both paws.

His knife lay on the ground, a foot from Danilo. He must have dropped it when Danilo attacked him.

The tiger watched the sword rise, catch the sun at its zenith. He reached out for the knife, finding its handle warm. The sword began to descend. Danilo and the knife rose.

The sword drew level with the ground. The knife drew level with LeSevre's ribs.

The sword jerked to the side.

The knife went in surprisingly easily, through a tear in the padded shirt that Danilo had made when he ripped it, through the thin undershirt, beneath the wolf's ribs and up into his lungs. Danilo held on as he and the wolf toppled toward the balustrade.

The sword clattered to the stone.

Danilo saw again the wolf's paw battering Luc's muzzle, the glee at the capture and anticipated torture of Luc, and later Théodore and Danilo himself. He saw the promise to track down Luc and Théodore gleam and fade in those sinister eyes.

Blood bubbled from the wolf's mouth. He grasped at the knife, but Danilo held it in.

Théodore stumbled to his side. "Pull it out," he said.

261

"What?"

The mouse bent and grasped Danilo's paw. With a jerk, the knife came free, and LeSevre collapsed as though that had been the only thing holding him upright. His breathing became a horrible, gruesome wheeze. More blood sprayed across the stone.

"There." Théodore pulled Danilo upright. "I told you you could do it."

"It was because he threatened you," Danilo said.

The mouse favored him with a warm smile, then turned and glared out at the crowd. "He tried to kill us," he said. "You bear witness."

They murmured, not entirely convinced, Danilo thought. Standing to his full height, he saw over them to the street leading from the Cathédrale, where more uniforms were making their way down. "More of them come," he said.

"Right." Théodore grasped his paw and pulled. "Can you run?"

Danilo ached all over, no longer able to distinguish between old wounds and new. "For a bit," he said. He turned to look at LeSevre, whose choking breaths were fainter. The wolf's glazed eyes barely saw them.

Without another word, the mouse sprang to the top of the balustrade and ran along it to the end. Danilo muscled his way through the crowd, following as best he could to the stair and down to the river bank. A few of the onlookers followed them, but when one tried to pull Danilo back, the tiger shrugged him off easily, and none interfered with him after that.

Twenty feet ahead of him, Théodore ran down the bank of the river. The barge was not quite out of sight, and they were running barely faster than it was drifting, but Danilo remembered that the Rhône flowed faster than the Saône, and when the barge reached the junction, there would be no more question of catching it.

"We can...catch up to it later..." He gasped out the words, but Théodore heard him and called back.

"Soldiers...after us...safest is to...get on board..."

It looked as though the barge were holding up to try to give them a chance to reach them. Luc and the captain held ropes, and as Théodore pulled ahead of Danilo, they threw a rope into the water for him. The mouse ran another minute, two minutes, three, and then pulled slightly ahead of the rope and dove into the water.

He struggled, but surfaced holding the rope and swarmed up it as Luc and the captain pulled. Luc's voice floated across the water. "Now to you, Danilo!"

Danilo had a terrible stitch in his side, not to mention his ringing head and the increasing pain in his groin with every jarring step. He forced himself to go on and on. The rope splashed into the water, yards ahead of him. He would never catch up. Footsteps had not died away behind him, shouts still followed him. People would tell the soldiers about the boat and then they would ride after it and what was the point? He might as well stop here and let himself be caught, and then he could at least rest.

But Luc's face and now Théodore's bobbed before him, shouting, encouraging, and he put on one last burst of speed. There was the rope, in the water, there in front of him, beside him, slightly behind him…he veered to the left and leapt.

Cold water engulfed him. He tasted dirt and garbage and algae, and kept his eyes squeezed tightly shut. His paws flailed in the water, struck the rope, lost it, found it again. But his muscles seized up and the claw he'd wrenched snagged on the fibrous rope, and then some obstacle struck him in the groin. In the burst of pain, the rope slid past his pads and through.

He cast out, desperately groping for it, and his eyes flew open to a sea of white; the filmy robe had bunched up and clung to his face. He ripped it from him, staring through the water for any sign of the rope, but nothing showed in the faint glow of the sun breaking through the brown, filthy water. And then the sun split into two, and seemed to be looking down at him, and Danilo stopped struggling, and the twin suns faded away.

Chapter Twenty

The sun shone down on Danilo. He lay on cold stone, but the Archbishop's robe covered his nakedness. He'd awakened with an urgent pressure in his stomach, and now he gave in to it, turning to one side and vomiting water onto the stone.

"Thank God," Luc's voice said.

Danilo turned, his eyes still blurry from the river water, and there was the otter, kneeling next to him. "I thought you might be dead," he said, and his voice fluttered with panic. "You weren't breathing, and I got some water out of you, but there was more and more…"

He leaned over and buried Danilo in a tight hug, which Danilo tried feebly to raise his arms to return. "Ow," he said.

"Saints, I'm sorry." Luc pulled back and looked down. "Where does it hurt?"

"Everywhere." And then it filtered in to him. "You jumped in after me."

"Well, yes. You'd have drowned otherwise."

Danilo groaned and closed his eyes. "Fool," he said. "They'll be here any minute. We tried so hard to save you…"

"They?" Luc's worried tone got sharper. "Cobb and Georg? And why were you trying to save me?"

With enormous effort, Danilo reached up to rub his eyes. "The Church," he said. "They're coming…"

"Church?" Luc laughed. "I thought you were running from Cobb and Georg. No, the only people coming are the SAMU. I called 112, they should be here soon. Just relax."

112, the emergency number? Cobb? Georg? Danilo's paws fell away, and he looked beyond Luc for the first time.

There above the river bank rose buildings of bright colors and sandy-blond stone, and atop Fourvière Hill, the basilica sat serenely next to the Metal Tower. In the other direction, bridges lay across the river like shackles, five hundred years of stone and metal and bone and life dropped on top of Tigue in a heartbeat. "Oh, God," he breathed. "Oh, God."

"Hey," Luc said as Danilo started to sob, his whole body shaking. "Hey, you're going to be okay. There's only a little blood, you're fine. Danilo, come on, what's the matter?"

Luc and Théodore had slipped away, the church still chasing them. The Archbishop lay in his bed, perhaps never to answer for his crimes. The Bishop weighed Danilo's evidence. Seline and Marie cleaned up at the inn; Bertrand perhaps sat in prison; Anita cleaned St. Nizier's after Lauds and tended to its people. No; they had been dust for almost five hundred years. Had they ever truly existed? The glass and brick, the airplane that crawled across the sky overhead, those were real, those were solid, those were part of Danilo's world. And yet his wounds ached, the urgency of his flight still pounded in his blood, the underlying ghost of 1508 Tigue would not be banished. "I'm back." Danilo spoke English, without magic, without the words being translated by some other entity. Of course, that couldn't happen, could it? Not really? Longing and relief battled in his chest, wracked him, brought his paws to his face again. "I'm home. I…"

He'd stopped hoping for it, had almost forgotten that he'd lived in another time. He'd watched people die, had killed one himself, and now he was lying on the bank of the Saône in 2008 and the sun stroked his fur and the breeze ruffled his ears, and now he could smell the sweet scent of automobile exhaust, the ground damp with recently-passed rain, the blanket covering him (not the Archbishop's robe) smelling of some unwashed unfamiliar scent, the otter above him—

"Wait. Who are you?"

The otter laughed, full of relief and affection. "Me? You knew my name a minute ago. Just settle down. The ambulance is coming—listen, you can hear the siren already."

And he could, along with the traffic noise and the murmurs of millions, not thousands, of people, the buzzing background noise of the world, his world. He shook his head and focused on the otter. "You're Luc."

"That's right." The otter smiled.

"How—" His mind was blank. "How did you *get* here?"

"Well. Anita told me you'd had some trouble, and when you didn't show up to class, I skipped out to go looking for you. Taye would've come, but he had a test and he couldn't skip out, and, well," the otter shrugged. "My classes can fuck themselves. Good thing I did. I thought you might go down to the river, and I saw you jump in. Then some asshole with a skidoo came along…even in the rain, those *putains de merde*…"

"But…"

Luc glanced down Danilo's body. "It beat you up pretty bad. Must've torn off your boxers, I guess, but I found this smelly blanket…"

He lifted his head, or tried to, and Luc pushed it back down. "But how do you know me?"

The otter frowned. "We met a few weeks ago. When you came to see Taye?" When Danilo didn't respond, Luc said, "The fellow on the other bed? We went to dinner, to that Moroccan place, and I laughed at you for burning your fingers?"

"Right," Danilo said. "You…live with Taye?"

"Second year."

"Are you and he…?"

Luc frowned. "Why don't you rest?" he said. "There's the medics."

Danilo gripped his arm. "You're not, though…are you?"

Luc's laugh sounded forced. "No, dear. Taye and I fooled around last year, but we're better roommates than boyfriends. I think you two work well together, though. Or would, if you'd give it a chance."

And then a pair of foxes in red-crossed uniforms were bending over him, lifting the cloth from his body and talking to each other in rapid Gallic. Danilo caught "testicle" and "poor bastard," and then Luc gripped his paw. "I'll ride with you to hospital," he said. "I'm not going to leave you."

I was afraid I'd left you, Danilo wanted to say, but all he could do was squeeze the otter's paw as the medics loaded him onto a stretcher.

***

The thing of it was, he was sure Taye didn't have a roommate. Positive. He'd been in the mouse's room, which had only one bed; he'd met Taye's close friends, and none of them was an otter. Danilo's roommate Orwin was an otter, but he hadn't figured into Danilo's… adventure…at all.

And what had that adventure meant? Danilo had the scar on his side, the fresh wound on his throat, and of course, his missing testicle to testify to the reality of it. But had that all happened while he was in the water? Had he gotten the scar in his side without noticing it a couple days ago? If he didn't remember burning his fingers on Moroccan food with an otter, what else had he forgotten about his recent past? Had his subconscious mind manufactured the fantasy to account for his injuries?

If it had, that would mean that it had also suppressed his memories of Luc in 2008. But why? There was no reason to add that dimension to a dream, except perhaps to make him doubt that it was a dream. Everyone else remembered Luc—Orwin said they had gone to some otter thing together and Anita reminded Danilo that Luc had helped him with his homework, and Taye, once he'd properly hugged Danilo, said that of course, he'd known Luc forever it seemed like, and perhaps Danilo had bumped his head.

He had, undeniably. Taye stayed with him overnight at the hospital, while the doctors checked him for concussion and other neurological damage. Danilo hoped, perversely, that they would find something, a lump or a mark that would have the doctors asking, *Did you have any hallucinations? Imagine you went back in time perhaps? Ah, yes, with this kind of injury that is quite common.* But the scan came back clean, and they held him the next day only long enough to make sure that his orchiectomy (the removal of a testicle) was not infected.

"You had this done before the incident, yes?" the doctor said. "Is this your Anglian medical care?"

"It happened in the water," Danilo said. The stitches had been ripped out or fallen out or something, and the wound had been open by the time he got to the hospital.

"Hm. People throw all manner of things into the river. Well, it is a most unfortunate accident, but you will not suffer much from it. Many people live healthy lives with one testicle. You will be able to father cubs and your sex life should be unaffected." The doctor paused, looking again at the area, which felt mostly sore to Danilo. Exposed to a doctor in the hospital was much different from being exposed to a surgeon on a bloody operating table in the basement of a prison, and this doctor, a ram, had gentle, skilled fingers. "I will close it up properly. It appears you have no infection, a lucky thing after a fall in the Saône."

The memory of the prison basement remained as clear in his mind as the doctor's stitches, and despite the loss of the original stitches, he thought as he left the hospital, the absence of a testicle proved his adventure had been real.

And yet, by the time he arrived at his dorm, he was thrown back into doubt. If his mind had forgotten Luc, maybe it had forgotten the trauma of having a ball ripped away. Certainly stranger things had happened. In fact, he theorized as he opened the door to the dorm, perhaps Luc had been involved somehow, and his memory had blocked it all out, and this fall in the water had given him an elaborate scenario by which it could all have happened.

Because what was the alternative? That he had been yanked back into the past by a saint, that he had saved Luc—a gay otter—and somehow ensured the future existence of a descendant of his? The improbability of a trick of memory paled in comparison.

He did not want it to be simply a trick of memory. He had been brave in 1508, he had stood up for friends and found friends who stood up for him. As much as he loved being back in his own time, part of his heart ached for Luc and Théodore, for the friend-ships they'd formed under the pressure of the church's tyranny. He could understand a little better why Luc would have risked his life to continue sleeping with the males he encountered. He'd known Taye a few weeks longer than Théodore, but with Théodore he had been through more in 1508 than he was likely to share with anyone in this time for the rest of his life, unless he was drafted in a war perhaps.

Then again, he thought, settling back into his own bed, looking around at his computer and books, reaching down to feel the mod-ern medical bandages on his wounds, 2008 had a lot to offer. He no longer itched with fleas, his fur felt clean for the first time in a week, and he was sleeping on comfortable fabric and a mattress that anyone five hundred years ago would have killed for—perhaps literally—and which here was the subject of grousing in the hallways, demands that the school buy new mattresses because of students' back issues. He almost laughed—back issues!

No, given the choice, he would stay in 2008 in a heartbeat. But he wished he could bring his friends here as well.

Chapter Twenty-One

He worked on his classes, made up the reading and assignments for the days he'd missed, and tried to throw himself into his schoolwork. But he found his attention wandering during lectures, writing down the names of Seline and Marie, Bertrand and Culliver, or drawing the kitchen he'd worked in or the seminary, or practicing an illustrated letter the way he'd spent a single afternoon learning. The words and drawings lurked in the margins of his notes, on scraps of paper he saved in a growing pile in his messenger bag without really understanding why. In case he forgot? But how could he forget? The reminders were etched as deeply into his mind as into his body.

But it had been a dream, a hallucination.

Or it had been real and a miracle.

He searched for Archbishop Argile and found nothing but a name on the web. In his school's library, after days of research, he found little more. There had been an Archbishop of Tigue named Argile who had died in 1509. He had been represented by a stag, but personages high in the Church, Archbishops and Popes, were represented by an aspect of Jesus, not their actual species. This particular Archbishop had not been of a noble Gallic house and so little had been written about him; the cause of his death was not described anywhere, nor were his views on homosexuality. What little Danilo found about the practices of the Catholic Church at that time jibed with what he'd experienced, but they were not attributed to any one person. About a "Bishop Lukin," he found nothing save for one wolf in 1800s Moskva.

Taye, and sometimes Luc, tried their best to spend time with him, but Taye shared no classes with him and Luc only one. Anita fussed over him and helped him catch up with his schoolwork. A week ago he would have basked in her attentions; now he found resentment creeping in when she stayed too long and prevented him from remembering his adventure. Paradoxically, when he was alone, the memories overwhelmed him, the need to know what had happened and whether it mattered, whether any of it was real, and he sought out company or plugged in his music player when the questions became too much. In the shower, he lathered his groin, feeling the space in his scrotum where his testicle had been, and wondered where it was now. At the bottom of the Saône? In a medical waste bin somewhere in Anglia or Gallia? Consumed by five hundred years of decay?

Much as it had in 1508, it took a few days for the strange dichotomy of worlds to fade. With Taye and Luc, it remained the strongest, which became a problem. They were the ones who understood him best, but their presence brought all his worries to the forefront. Orwin, his roommate, proved the perfect companion in these few days, because he didn't talk much, and Danilo had not met any 1508 version of him.

And then, of course, there were Cobb and Georg.

The school announced a seminar on bullying to take place in a month, and though Danilo's name was not used, everyone knew it was about the white tiger who'd been harassed and then jumped in the river. On some of the Internet message boards, Danilo saw comments that white tigers often did crazy shit and why did the whole school have to suffer through this seminar because of one incident? He hadn't asked for the seminar and didn't want to go to it, but he didn't think saying so would be of any use. There were also messages of support, Christian messages of mercy and understanding, but he stopped reading the boards anyway. He didn't want to be an object of pity any more than an object of scorn.

Cobb, if anything, seemed to take pride in having inspired the seminar. On the bulletin board next to the announcement, he tacked up the newspaper with the picture of Danilo's gay cousin. Orwin urged Danilo to take it down, but the tiger just shrugged. "It's news," he said, "and I'm proud of him." He had asked his sister to relay that sentiment to Devlin's parents; the football star himself was swamped with the media attention over his coming-out.

Still, Cobb left Danilo alone for the first day or two after his adventure. For Danilo, Cobb's bullying in the student hall was so remote as to be nearly forgotten; the first few times he saw the elk, he remembered more clearly the large bed and silk white sheets from 1508, the stag's cruel smile as he'd condemned Luc to death. He'd avoided Cobb as much as Cobb had avoided him. So when the big elk happened to pass him in the hallway and bumped his shoulder hard, Danilo did not connect it at first to that incident. He had been lost in thought and Cobb's presence and antlers reminded him much more of the Archbishop, which is what had been in his mind when the elk's shoulder slammed into his.

"Sorry," Cobb said, and laughed.

Danilo almost kept walking and then paused. One of the many things weighing on his mind was the fate of the Archbishop, whether he'd been made to answer for his crimes. The insulting bump on the shoulder was petty and small, but added to his worries, it sparked a fire in his chest. Here, among their fellow students, Cobb was still carrying on the bullying of his spiritual predecessor? Danilo turned as Cobb continued down the hall. "Hey," he said.

Cobb turned, nostrils flared. He narrowed his eyes. "What?"

"I never answered your question." People in the hall paused, not wanting to get between them.

"What question?" The elk balled his hands into fists.

"Well," Danilo said, "You asked if I wanted to suck your dick. I didn't answer the question."

"Hey," Cobb started, and lifted a hand to point at Danilo. "Look, I—"

"The answer is no." What did this bully think he could do to Danilo? He wasn't the white stag. He had no real power. Danilo's rage ebbed as soon as it had come, almost giving way to pity. Almost. "I don't want to suck your dick. You'll have to find some other guy to do that."

The hallway fell silent. Cobb's ears went back as though slammed by a violent wind, and he took a step forward, then looked at all the people watching. "Your cousin sure wants to," he said.

"That's between you and him. If I ever do want to suck someone's dick," he said, waving as he turned, "It sure as hell won't be yours."

The people around them muttered as he walked away. It was ill-advised to say in public, and in fact, he was rebuked for his language later (though the fossa in charge of his dorm floor, who had heard the complaint, made the rebuke gentle, starting with, "I know you have been through a great crisis"). But Cobb stayed away from him after that, and the newspaper disappeared from the bulletin board that night.

Georg was more problematic. He was with Cobb much of the time Danilo saw him, and followed the elk's lead in leaving Danilo alone. But as with Cobb, Danilo saw over Georg the shadow of Bishop Lukin, who had forced Danilo to watch a person burn to death. Who had helped arrest Luc. Who had sympathized with Danilo after his mutilation, who had listened to him and believed him—maybe—when he reported the Archbishop's crimes. In all of his obsessive replaying of his adventure in the days after his return, he came to believe that the Bishop was a harsh, misguided person who truly wanted to cleanse the world of evil. And he thought that perhaps, in this modern day, he might convince Georg that evil was not what he had assumed it was.

He might have been wrong. But when he looked at Georg in that light, he saw someone who'd come under the sway of Cobb's powerful personality, who found it easy to go along with a forceful personality. So when he happened upon Georg alone in the lounge on his floor, ears down and grimacing at the math textbook in his lap, Danilo sat near him and cleared his throat.

The wolf flicked an ear, but didn't look over. Danilo tried a Siberian greeting. "*Kak dela?*"

Without looking up, Georg rattled off a sentence in fluid, sharp barks that Danilo recognized as Siberian but did not understand at all. "I'm sorry," he said. "I want to learn Siberian but I only know how to say 'Are you feeling well' and 'Thank you.' My grandmother taught me a bit."

"I said, I am not to be talking to you."

"Really? Who told you that?"

The wolf shrugged. "Is up on bulletin board."

Danilo exhaled and leaned back. "As long as you don't ask me for sexual favors like Cobb did, I think you can talk to me."

He'd hoped that humor would work, but Georg just flicked his ears forward and turned the page of his math book. The tiger cleared his throat and tried again. "You played great in the football game."

"I know," Georg said, still without looking up.

This wasn't Bishop Lukin. This was Georg Lukin, Siberian student who had come to Tigue to study science and history, and who played footie with the foreign student team. Danilo leaned back. "My roommate's good at math, if you want some help."

Georg looked up then, fixing Danilo with his eyes. "I do not need help," he said, then closed his math book, stood, and walked away.

Chapter Twenty-Two

Two weeks after his fall into the Saône—or, rather, two weeks after he'd re-emerged from it—Danilo failed a history test. He had been doing well in the class, and his teacher, a middle-aged wolf, asked to see him during office hours.

Father Lafontaine's office, on the second floor of the history building, reminded Danilo of his seminary room. On the wall beside the window hung a picture of Jesus in his Dog incarnation, here looking very wolfish, below a simple wooden cross. The teacher himself had a short grey muzzle and had always been very serious in class; when he greeted Danilo and asked him to be seated, Danilo was reminded of the priest at the seminary in 1508.

"I understand the material," Danilo said, in response to the teacher's initial question. "I'm just having trouble studying. I had a…a thing a couple weeks ago."

"When you missed class."

"Yes." Danilo extended and retracted his claws.

"This…thing, it is preventing you from studying?"

"I can't stop thinking about it." Because it was unseemly to rub his groin in public, he had taken to tracing the scar on his side. His paw drifted there now.

The wolf leaned forward on his desk. "There are counseling resources available at the university."

His eyes, wise and steady, calmed Danilo. "I know. But I don't know if they can help me."

Father Lafontaine nodded. "So say many troubled young people. I would counter that there is no harm in trying, no?"

"It's not really a question of being troubled. I mean, it is, but it's not…it's not about me. It's about how the world works."

"Ah." The wolf smiled. "A question of faith. I believe there may be a few qualified people here to discuss that with you."

"Actually," Danilo cleared his throat. "It's kind of a question of history."

Father Lafontaine's eyebrows shot up, and his ears perked. "Well," he said. "I must say it is not often I hear a student consumed by a problem of history. I must assume that it is a period other than the expansion of the Roman Empire."

Danilo relaxed still further. "Father," he said, "what do you know about miracles?"

***

He talked to Father Lafontaine for the better part of an hour, and though he hadn't gone so far as to reveal his entire adventure, he had confessed to having a hallucination, or a vision, while he'd been in the water of the Saône. Father Lafontaine repeated very nearly the same thing Bishop Lukin had told him about miracles, and when Danilo asked for evidence of miracles in the present day, the wolf laughed. "We live in an age where people want desperately to see miracles, and so they manufacture them out of the slightest evidence. The face of our Saviour appearing in bread, a rock face that resembles the Blessed Virgin and weeps tears…these may be miracles indeed. Who can say?"

"But what is the purpose of the miracles?" Danilo felt he was participating in the conversation as an equal, and that the teacher understood him without judging him crazy. "Why a face in a piece of toast?"

"To bolster faith?" Father Lafontaine spread his paws. "Perhaps there are other motives it is not given to us to know."

"But they're definitely miracles."

"To the people who witnessed them, they are."

Danilo scrunched his eyebrows. "Wait. If it's a miracle, it's a miracle, right? I mean, if I get healed or something, then everyone can see that. That means it's a real miracle."

"A 'real' miracle." The wolf shook his head. "I feel we should call Father Bolle to join this conversation. Danilo, the validity of miracles is something discussed and debated within the Church for years, decades. Miracles are declared after the fact, revoked after years of perusal. But." He held up a paw as Danilo began to respond. "You are asking me, and I will give you my answer, which is also

275

the product of years of thought. There have been many miracles throughout history, far too numerous to count, from the grandiose and well-documented to the nearly unknown. The only thing they have in common is this: the person witnessing each one believed it to be a miracle. And so I believe that anything you choose to see as a miracle is one. God does not make His plan known to all; perhaps He wishes only to show His son's face to a certain number of people. Others who are not meant to see it will see nothing but a piece of bread."

"But to the people who see it," Danilo persisted, "what is it supposed to mean?"

"Ah, well." The wolf brushed his whiskers back. "Along with the privilege of witnessing, perhaps, a personal miracle, we must assume the duty of deciding what the meaning is. If God is speaking to us and us alone, as He has been known to do, then we must assume that the message has been sent in a way we can understand, and do our best to find meaning in it." He smiled and reached forward to pat Danilo's paw, which lay on his desk. "God is not going to send you an e-mail telling you the meaning of your vision, or your life. It may require years of study, both of the world and of yourself."

Years. Danilo groaned inwardly. "I worry I'll keep failing tests."

"To my mind," Father Lafontaine said, "if the vision works upon your mind with such strength, it must have some kind of personal significance to you, and is therefore well worth the effort to study."

"But I don't know how to start studying it!" Danilo snapped his mouth shut. "I mean—do you know anyone who might be able to help?"

"If I might make a suggestion: you could take an independent study class in history. If your vision has piqued your interest in— when was it, about fifteen-hundred?" Danilo nodded, and Father Lafontaine went on. "That was quite an interesting time. The merchant class was rising, and it was the last great era of the Church before the Reformation. The Cathédrale Saint-Jean had recently been completed."

"I know," Danilo said. "On the site where Saint Épipode was buried."

"Ah, you've already begun your research. Yes, one of Tigue's more venerable saints."

"He was an otter."

The wolf frowned. "That is one favored theory, but sadly, no images of him have survived."

Danilo saw again the painting in the stairwell, and remained silent. After a moment, Father Lafontaine continued. "In any case, it is a time well worth studying. It is the last century of Tigue's status as a truly great city; in fact, around that time there was great correspondence with Etrusca and many political figures and works of art traveled back and forth."

"Da Vinci," Danilo murmured.

Father Lafontaine stopped, his eyes piercing Danilo's. "Yes, some of his works, although again, none that survive to the present. Not in Tigue, at any rate."

The image of Saint Jean de Baptiste Danilo had seen in the Bishop's office was documented online, but no records existed of it being sent to Tigue. So it was best not to mention it. He smiled and nodded. "I would be happy to do an independent study," he said.

"Good." Father Lafontaine beamed. "Now, you'll have to select a topic. You can't just study 'Tigue in 1500.' It could be about the decline in political power here, or the role of the Church in politics, the effect of the distance of the King, or the imminent Reformation and why conditions were right for the Hugenots to gather…"

"I want to study the Church's treatment of homosexuals," Danilo said.

The wolf's good humor evaporated; his smile disappeared and the eyes fixed on Danilo's grew serious. "This is not a confessional," he said evenly.

Silence settled over the office while Danilo absorbed the impact of those words. "I am not confessing to anything," he said, finally. "But I can understand why you would think my choice of subject has something to do with my preoccupation. And you are correct," he said, meeting the priest's gaze.

He watched for any change in expression, but the wolf remained neutral. "Making this known will make your career here harder," he said. "I expect you will encounter serious pressure to explore another topic."

"If you will not do the study with me, then I will find someone who will." What would they do to him? Burn him? Take his other testicle? The worst that would happen would be expulsion, and he found that he was not afraid of that, not enough to hide his nature.

One of the wolf's ears twitched. "I will do the study with you. I wanted only to warn you. You have two months before you will need to declare a topic."

Danilo sat up straighter in the chair. "Father, I have made my choice. I will bear the consequences."

Father Lafontaine inclined his head. "We may continue to meet. In the meantime, please do spare at least a little time for the Roman Empire. Otherwise you will have to take this class again next term instead of an independent study."

If he'd been going to plan to out himself to anyone, Danilo thought as his feet trod the neatly-manicured grass, he would have chosen his Psychology professor, a vixen with a sharp sense of humor who reminded him a little of Anita. But Father Lafontaine had been accepting, if not approving, and in this Catholic university, that was perhaps the best he could hope for. Others would make their feelings known, he was certain.

He rounded a corner of the History building into the sun and stood for a moment, placing his white paw on the warm red brick and closing his eyes.

"Deep in thought?" Taye's voice came to him out of the haze of sun and memory. Danilo blinked, but the vision of Théodore lasted only a fraction of a second.

"I had a meeting with Lafontaine," Danilo said. "About my test. It went fine."

Taye nodded. "You look very—artistic? White fur against the red brick. I saw you all the way across the lawn."

Danilo smiled and stretched. "The sun feels good." He reached out and held Taye's shoulders, pulling the mouse against his sun-warm clothes.

"Careful." Taye allowed the hug and then pulled back, looking around.

"Let them see." Danilo laughed and joined the mouse in a slow stroll along the grassy path. The air here in the enclave of the university's buildings was sweet and clear, almost free of automobile exhaust. If he pretended, he could tell himself that it was the smoke of fires rather than exhaust, but whatever he thought, it was the smell of people, of life going on. "What are they going to do? Talk about us?"

Taye shook his head. "Perhaps worse."

"Let them. Father Lafontaine doesn't think I'll be expelled."

"Expelled?" Taye's grey muzzle wrinkled, and then his eyes widened in alarm. "Danilo, you didn't—?"

"I rather almost did." He told Taye about their conversation, and the mouse remained silent throughout. "He's a nice chap. I'd never talked to him."

"It's dangerous," Taye said.

"No more so than for my cousin." Danilo and Taye passed a group of rugby players, but Cobb and Georg were not among them. "Maybe I'll call him."

They walked back to Danilo's dorm, and as they entered, Taye said, "This vision you mentioned, it must have been quite remarkable."

"It was." Danilo followed Taye up the stairs. "I'm still trying to figure it out, but at least I have someplace to start now."

"I would like to hear about it sometime."

"Sometime."

And when they came into the open lounge on his floor, they saw an otter and black wolf sitting together. Danilo recognized Orwin immediately, but even though there were no other large, muscular black wolves in their class, it wasn't until Georg raised his head and fixed Danilo with yellow-green eyes that recognition dawned. "*Dobryj dyen*," the wolf said.

"Good afternoon," Danilo replied.

"Oh, hi," Orwin said, looking up. "Just working on some math."

Danilo met Georg's eyes and smiled. The wolf's ears flicked, and briefly his lips curved upwards in response. Then he bent back to his math homework.

Chapter Twenty-Three

The conversation with Father Lafontaine did not ease Danilo's stress, but it helped. He applied himself to history and to his other classes, and kept his worrying about the adventure (as he had fallen into the habit of calling it) to his spare time—mostly. He collected notes and drawings in a folder and scanned them on the scanner in the school lab, and during evenings when he wasn't studying, sometimes he would take them out and flip through them.

The memories of his adventure never faded the way a dream would; they stayed solidly in his consciousness, slowly being covered by other memories, but still visible in daydreams and bursts of recollection. Danilo took to seeking out these recollections, wandering around Tigue on weekends, sometimes with Taye, sometimes with Luc, sometimes alone. On the site of the Repos du Saint (as best he could figure it), an office building stood, the back yard and well covered by a receptionist's lobby and restroom. Danilo washed his paws, watching the water flow through his fur for several seconds, turned on and off by the simple twist of a faucet.

The site of the seminary was harder to locate; the roads must have been rearranged at some point in the intervening years. But then he found a historical marker commemorating one of the first educational institutions in Tigue two blocks away, and he supposed he was in the right place, or the marker was not.

The Cathédrale Saint-Jean was familiar, of course, although diminished amid the larger, modern buildings. The interior had changed little below the decorations: wires and lights ran discreetly inside, carpet covered the cold stone, signs warned tourists to refrain from using their mobile phones. The altar area where he'd stood with the Bishop, below which St. Épipode supposedly rested, was roped off. Velvet ropes surrounded the astronomical clock, too, enforcing the respect that alone in 1508 had kept people from touching it.

He stood with Taye on a cool Saturday afternoon with the cloud-filtered sunlight brightening the windows and watched the clock strike two. It seemed as much a marvel to him now as it had then, perhaps even more so because the people around him did not grasp how extraordinary the clockwork creation had been to the people of the 1500s, starved for miracles in their world. The people of 2008 snapped pictures, talked to each other while the clock was striking and all the marvelous clockwork spun and danced and played hymns just as it had five hundred years prior. Danilo felt very much alone in the crowd and had to hurry to an alcove rubbing at his eyes, overwhelmed and unable to explain to Taye the flash of wonder, the sense of the permanence of the world that the clock had inspired in him, as if it and he alone had traveled safely to this land, as if the hymns were a song that had followed him from the past, had survived five hundred years to bring him a message, and yet he still could not tell what that message was.

Services were still held at the cathedral, but Danilo did not stay for them. He and Taye passed the building that had housed the Bishop's offices, now an ecclesiastical museum off limits to the public (though the doorway where Danilo remembered standing while LeSevre threatened him was still there, and he put his paws to the wall and closed his eyes). Taye held his paw as they walked along the Rue St. Barthólème, where to his relief, he found the prison gone. The small cemetery remained, although it had been repurposed as a military graveyard for the dead from two world wars. The haphazard-seeming stone markers were gone, replaced by clean crosses of stone and traditional rectangular gravestones. None of the graves dated from the fifteen-hundreds.

"What are you looking for, Tiguey?" Taye asked him.

Danilo shook his head and squinted up at the brightest part of the sky, where the sun was pressing to break through the cloud cover. "I don't know," he said. "But I don't think it's here."

Without Taye, two weekends later, he walked down to St. Nizier's, which, unlike the Cathédrale, had changed significantly. It had gained a high steeple that he didn't remember, and the Lion Christ over the entrance was gone; in fact, the whole front of the church was more elaborate. The corners and lines of the building had softened with age and wear, but its weight remained unchanged.

As in 1508, a small plaza opened up in front of the church, but now it housed only flowers, though one small store to the right of the church sold fruit out on the sidewalk. The chatter of the marketplace had given way to the crunching of fallen leaves, the murmurs of phone conversations, hundreds of people barely glancing at the church or the trees or the buildings. Perhaps because it was smaller in scale, St. Nizier's retained more dignity and elegance in her age than the Cathédrale had.

Inside, Danilo recognized the layout, but the windows had been replaced, the pews were fresh, polished wood, and new paintings and gold artifacts lined the walls. It was the same, and yet not the same, and again he felt familiarity without understanding his place in it. An old fox in a priest's robe took his donation and thanked him, and allowed him to walk up and down the church, breathing in the scent. As at the cathedral, the air felt different here, but not so different that Danilo couldn't close his eyes and stand before what had been Anita's office, feel the solemn stone rising around him, and imagine that Sister Colquez herself might touch his shoulder and ask how she could help.

And then he opened his eyes and the reliefs were covered in plastic, the shrines roped off, the floor worn and polished by five more centuries of feet. But here more so than the cathedral, he felt comfortable. Fewer tourists crowded the space, for one thing, and for another, it had been here that he'd rested and prayed, here that aid had come to him.

He wanted to pray to St. Épipode, but here there was only a modern crucifix bearing the Lion Jesus looking upward, arms and legs covered in blood, His head shaven of its mane and bleeding as well. The golden halo stood in for a mane, brighter than the golden fur beneath the white robes. This crucifix was more elaborate than any he'd seen on the campus of the university, the robes and fur intricately detailed, so realistic that Danilo found his gaze wandering down to the Lion's midriff, wondering if the Romans had taken one of His testicles as well.

That was probably blasphemous or heretical or whatever. He dropped his eyes and crossed himself, and walked out.

In front of the church, he waited for a city bus to pass, glancing idly at the destination on the front marquee: "Padrenard." The bus chugged past him; he frowned and stood on the street while people shouldered past him, reading the name over in his head.

Across the plaza, he spotted a small bookstore, and there in the front they had a map of Tigue. He hurried into the shop, grabbed the map, and scanned it. One claw followed the Rhône south from its junction with the Saône, and there it was, about fifteen km south of the city. Padrenard. *Pas de Renard.*

***

Nobody he knew had a car, so it would be the bus: an hour to the end of the line, time to look at whatever Danilo wanted, and an hour back. He talked Luc into going with him. Taye was studying for a test, and didn't have time to spare for a long trip. Anyway, truth be told, Danilo preferred Luc for this trip.

Not that he liked Luc better than Taye. He'd worried about that, soon after his return, when Taye and Luc had both been friendly, but Luc was carefully deferential to their relationship. Danilo had preferred Luc to Théodore in 1508, but the mouse had grown on him those last few days, and their fight against LeSevre was something he wished he could relive with someone. As horrible as plunging the knife into the wolf had been—even Cobb was not someone Danilo wanted to kill—he had felt a glorious sense of triumph while fleeing along the river. At the time, it had been overwhelmed by the need to get to the barge and the fear of the people pursuing them. In retrospect, he and Théodore had overwhelmed a superior opponent, and having Taye nearby had made Danilo want to say, "Hey, that time we fought LeSevre together was brilliant," on more than one occasion. And Luc, though friendly, never became as affectionate as his five-hundred-year-ago counterpart had. So in the end, Danilo was comfortable exploring his relationship with Taye, and having Luc as a friend.

For this trip, the level of their relationship had nothing to do with it. Taye was Romany, and though his ancestors might have lived in Gallia, he was unlikely to know their names or where they were buried. Luc, though, was Gallic, and Danilo thought that maybe he would have relatives in Tigue somewhere.

"No," Luc said when Danilo asked, as the bus pulled away from the station in Presqu'ile. "My family is from Lutèce. Many generations of otters, on the Seine upstream of the city."

"How many generations?"

"Oh." Luc waved a paw. "Who can count? My grandmother said her grandmother was a cub on the Seine and she remembered the great Exhibition Universelle and the unveiling of the Tour Koechlin."

That had been in 1889, nearly four hundred years later than Danilo was interested in. He stared morosely out the window at the cityscape passing by. Most of the buildings, even the oldest, were different than he remembered, with the obvious exceptions of the churches. There was little chance that he would stumble across something he had visited enough for the memory to be solid. He was wasting his time and Luc's.

But halfway through the ride, the otter's genial manner broke through Danilo's moodiness. Luc pointed out an otter housing block on the river, like a great stone behemoth that had half-fallen into the river and remained there. "Must be outside the city limits," he said, leaning across Danilo with a whiskered grin. "I should pay them a visit sometime."

Luc in 1508 had been estranged from his family, had never talked about going down to the otter-house Danilo had seen on the Saône. "Can you just walk in like that?"

"For sure. Otters, we are all like a family. Until we get to know each other and start fighting." Luc grinned at him. "That's why I stay with Taye. With a mouse, there is no trouble."

"Otter and mouse," Danilo said softly.

"*Ouais.* It worked well last year."

This otter leaning across him to look out, his brown fur and white whiskers like narrow sunbeams, this was a miracle, a tangible, solid miracle, and it killed Danilo that everyone saw it and nobody understood how miraculous it was. Or else it was not a miracle and nobody else appreciated Luc because he was normal, just like Danilo himself, and Danilo was driving himself crazy, wasting time digging through layers of Tigue in the hope of finding one thing that would speak to him and tell him whether his experience had been real, what it had meant.

If it had been real, then he had been sent back for a reason. But in all the time-travel stories he'd read summaries of on the Internet in the past few weeks—the fictional ones—the hero had been sent back after his mission had been completely resolved, not dragged back in the middle of a chase. Had he accomplished his goal? Or had he been dragged back simply because he'd fallen into the water at that moment? If he'd jumped off the bridge any of the times he'd thought about it, would he have emerged back in 2008? Could it really have been that easy?

The surface of the river sparkled, hiding whatever lay beneath. Danilo watched the patterns caper and dance, and remembered the water closing over him. If he dove in again, would he wake up in 1508? Or maybe 1008? That would probably be less fun: in the middle of the actual Dark Ages, Tigue would be unrecognizable, a collection of moldering Roman buildings and wood, brick, and stone houses. Maybe he'd come up in 2508, and all the sleek blue-glass civilization would be just another layer beneath another five hundred years, and there would be jet cars and floating cities and space shuttles and white tigers would be as common as mice and otters.

He smiled at that, and asked Luc what it was like in an otter house, and they conversed the rest of the way down to Padrenard.

The bus let them out at a small bus stop on a square. As they stood blinking in the sunlight, the bus rumbled forward, around the square, and back the way it had come. "Well," Luc said, "here we are. What did you want to see?"

"I don't know. The Old Town maybe. Is there one?"

"I'll ask." He checked signs first, then asked a passing rat, who pointed him down one of the streets. Danilo followed him in that direction, looking around as they walked. Padrenard was a suburb like many others, like all the ones the bus had taken them through: neighborhoods of small houses as alike and different as the people who lived in them, blocks of apartments with grids of balconies, commercial sectors of faded awnings and cheerful crowds. From the balconies of taller buildings, Danilo spotted a bat hanging laundry over the railing and a squirrel smoking as he watched the city go by below him. At a small boulangerie, he bought a baguette and shared it with Luc, and as they were tearing apart the warm, crunchy bread (*just like in 1508*), they turned a corner and found themselves facing a church.

His pulse quickened. It had been the churches that connected him most closely to the past, and here was a steeple and a cross. But he knew directly that this was not a church that was going to help. The steeple gleamed, the sides shone, and the style screamed nineteenth century. Most likely it dated from when Padrenard had made the transition from farming community to suburb of Tigue.

They entered the church anyway, a lovely small affair that was definitely no more than two hundred years old, if that. Danilo sniffed at the wood reliefs on the walls, examined the fresh-looking stained glass, and walked outside again after one circuit through the church.

Luc emerged some five minutes later with an excited priest in tow. The priest, a squirrel, was jabbering in Gallic, and his eyes lit up when he saw Danilo. "He says," Luc told Danilo as the squirrel nodded vigorously, "that we should go see an old church called 'Lamerci'?"

"*Oui, oui! Lamerci!*" The squirrel pointed at Danilo and rattled off more Gallic.

"He says it's really old, and that it must be what you've come here to see? He won't say why, though, just that we should go and we'll see." Luc thanked the priest, and Danilo did as well. The old squirrel beamed and waited, watching them. "It's about two kilometers that way. Well? You game?"

"Sure." Something really old; that was promising. The priest walked with them for the first block and then pointed up the street and chittered some more directions. Luc assured him they understood, and they walked on.

The houses did get older as they walked up the hill, but nothing like as old as Danilo was hoping for. Sprinkled among the nineteenth and twentieth century houses were some old stone farmhouses, and though he scanned every wall for the words "Belle Soleil" or a sunburst, he saw nothing that connected to his adventure.

And then they followed a sign that read 'Eglise,' turned a corner and Danilo's heart quickened. Facing them on a small square, a weathered stone church sat with quiet dignity amid the houses and shops. It rose only one story and the cross atop its slightly gabled roof was simple stone. Below that, a large, welcoming arch framed two wooden doors, one of which was open.

"Impressive," Luc said.

"It's called 'Lamerci'?" Danilo's eyes fixed on a robed figure standing above the arch. Its curves had been smoothed by hundreds of years of wind and rain and its head was missing—in the Religious Wars, many saints had been disfigured—but the thick tail looked like an otter's. It could have been a fox's, or a wolf's, or even a weasel's, but Danilo didn't think it was any of those. "Is that 'merci' like 'thank you'?"

"In churches, it usually means 'mercy,'" Luc said. He, too, studied the church. "Otter, you think?"

"Yeah." Danilo smiled, though his heart beat faster than ever. "Saint Épipode, I bet."

Luc gave him a strange look. "Did you hear the priest say that?"

"No. Did he?"

"He said Épipode is rumored to have performed a miracle at this church. But I thought you were outside when he said that."

"I was close to the door." Danilo forced a smile. "My Gallic must be getting better."

"Uh-huh. Well, good." Luc's expression cleared; he never stayed troubled for long. "Let's see what's inside."

Inside was the closest thing Danilo had found to a church from 1508. No velvet ropes, no plastic shielding, not even a sign asking that cell phones be turned off. There were only pews, dark and pitted with age, hymnals brown and worn, and a simple altar above which hung a white crucifix of the Lion Jesus, softly gleaming in the afternoon light.

Danilo stepped forward slowly, taking in the smell of old stone and wood, of thousands of knees, scents laid down atop one another for hundreds of years until they blended into a community, a family of people passing through this church. He rested a paw on one of the pews. The crucifix drew his attention; though there were designs on and around the windows, this had been placed to catch the light, so striking against the grey stone that it seemed a miraculous vision. Danilo could almost believe that it had simply appeared, pure and unadorned, and the church been built around it.

Behind him, he heard paper rustling, crinkling in Luc's paw. "There's a flyer," the otter said, and then padded after Danilo.

The crucifix, so simple, was not pure white, Danilo could see now; veins of natural black ran through the marble. The head of the Lion looked downward at the congregation, rather than beseechingly upward, and a plain circle in the marble denoted the halo behind it, free of gold leaf.

Danilo took another step closer, and then heard Luc chuckle behind him. "Ah, mystery solved. Here is why the priest wanted us to come up. Listen: 'The Marble Lion Christ of Lamerci is a unique artifact. Most Christ figures in marble are pure white, but the Christ of Lamerci bears black veins throughout it, which some say resemble the *stripes of a tiger.*' Hah, you see?" He went on: "'This has never been explained. Perhaps lower-quality marble was all this community could afford, but the detail on the Christ is beautiful and appears to be the work of a well-regarded sculptor. Most sculptors in the Renaissance would not work with veined marble when the pure variant was so readily available.'" Luc drew level with Danilo and put an arm around his side. "To me, it's beautiful. The marble might be considered 'lower quality,' but look what this sculptor did with it. He created the one and only White Tiger Christ."

A curious sensation made its way from Danilo's chest outward, expanding with each breath, with each beat of his heart, like the feeling he'd had watching the clock strike, like the feeling he'd had emerging from the Saône in the twentieth century. Here, too, was another traveler from the sixteenth century; here was his nearly-abandoned hope fulfilled. For unlike the clock, the Christ of Lamerci had a message for him: Théodore and Luc had lived on here, had prospered long enough to commission this statue in his memory. He could hear the mouse's sharp tone saying, *yes, you heard correctly, we want the marble with black veins.* His adventure, his friends, had at the very least been that real.

The church and the bright crucifix blurred; he reached up a paw to rub his eyes clear. Luc stood by his side; for a moment, breathing in the scent of the otter unsullied by modernity, he imagined himself in the early 1500s, walking through the church with the Luc of that time, Théodore close behind them. He saw their smiles and felt the peace of their existence thrum through him like morning breaking over a still lake. The feeling was so overwhelming that when he did open his eyes, he thought for a moment that he was back in time again. Then he took in Luc's collared shirt, the piece of paper with printed information on it, the age and wear on the stones.

He had been so obsessed with finding evidence for his adventure that he'd forgotten how real it had been when he'd lived it. Its scars had shaped him into a different person from the one who'd fallen into the Saône, one who wanted more than to fade into the background. He could sit before a priest and calmly confess his sexuality; he would not tolerate Cobb and Georg; he could encourage Taye to be more open as the mouse had once encouraged him. The crucifix before him at once proved his adventure real and made its reality irrelevant. Already the back corners of his mind worked at a rationalization: perhaps he'd seen an article about the White Tiger Jesus in Padrenard and incorporated that into his fantasy. But the *feeling*, the peace and friendship he felt from Luc and Théodore, that was as real as anything he'd felt, no matter what material that feeling was sculpted from.

Who was to say that this church was any more or less real than the St. Nizier's of 1508? When he returned to Tigue proper, it would be just as much a memory. He shared its reality because he stood here now, and when he and Luc walked out, it would remain real because he would remember it.

"Lamerci," indeed. "La Merci de St. Épipode," he thought it might have originally been called. To him, the name held a dual meaning; it could mean that the church had been erected in honor of the mercy of St. Épipode, a thank-you from those whose lives he had helped. And it could mean "the *thanks* of St. Épipode," the church a thank-you from the saint to those who had followed his guidance. To Théodore and Luc. To Danilo.

He took Luc's paw in his own. The otter's fingers gripped his, solid, warm, and real in that moment, and gratitude filled him. "*Merci*," Danilo whispered, bowed his head, and smiled.

Acknowledgments

A number of people and sources have contributed to this manuscript over the last four years, and if I omit any here, I apologize for my poor memory. First of all, I have to thank the British furry convention Confuzzled, because it was while serving as a guest of honour at their event in 2013 that I had the idea for the beginning of this novel. Had Confuzzled never extended that invitation to me, this novel probably would look very different, if indeed it existed at all.

The city of Lyon, the real-world inspiration for Tigue, was as lovely in person as on the Internet. I chose it with a small amount of research and it proved perfect for the story I wanted to tell. You can go there and walk into Saint-Nizier, you can visit Saint Jean le Baptiste and see the marvelous clock, you can walk under a bridge by the Saône and up to the Roman amphitheaters atop Fourvière hill. I also consulted a few texts, most notably "Vivre à Lyon au XVIe siècle" by Jacqueline Boucher (Editions Lyonnaises d'Art et d'Histoire) and "The Martyrs of Lyons in 177" by the Archbishopry of Lyon, Oeuvres Pontificales Missionaires. The former provided a wonderful picture of the forces shaping people's lives in Lyon around 1500 and forward; the latter is where most of the information about the saints came from (except for their species, obviously).

Many thanks are due to all my fans who followed the first draft through its online incarnation and kept me motivated to finish it. I enjoyed writing in the spotlight and that experience gave me the confidence to launch a Patreon in which I would do the same thing (for five years and counting now).

Of course, many of the usual people helped make this book the final product you have just read: Ryan Campbell, David Cowan, and Watts Martin of our writing group The Unreliable Narrators chief among them. Malcolm "foozzzball" Cross provided insight, my husband Kit contributed advice and thoughts, and Rukis, who drew the lovely illustrations, also chimed in on story points.

Thanks especially to Teiran from FurPlanet, who pestered me about publishing the book, and his partner Fuzz, who worked with me to get it into shape.

And of course, thanks as always to my family of Kit, Jack, and Kobalt for their love and support day in and day out.

About the Author

Kyell Gold has won twelve Ursa Major awards for his stories and novels, and his acclaimed novel "Out of Position" co-won the Rainbow Award for Best Gay Novel of 2009. His novel "Green Fairy" was nominated for inclusion in the ALA's "Over the Rainbow" list for 2012. He helped create RAWR, the first residential furry writing workshop, and has instructed at each of its sessions through 2017.

He lives in California, loves to travel and dine out with his partners, and can be seen at furry conventions around the world. More information about him and his books is available at

http://www.kyellgold.com

About the Artist

Rukis is a freelance illustrator and writer who grew up in the Appalachian region, working with animals and on farms from a young age. After earning a Bachelors in Traditional Animation, she started a career in freelance art, writing and illustrating a small collection of comics and novels in the Anthropomorphic fandom. You can see more of her work at http://www.furaffinity.net/rukis

Other Books by Kyell Gold

For more information about Kyell Gold's books, please visit his web-site: http://www.kyellgold.com/books.html. If you would like to get monthly updates on upcoming publications, excerpts of works in progress, and writing tips, sign up for his mailing list (your e-mail address will not be sold or used for anything else).

Love Match
Love Match (vol. 1, 2008-2010) — Rocky arrives in the States from Africa and navigates the treacherous worlds of professional ten-nis and high school.

Out of Position (Dev and Lee)
Out of Position – Dev the football player and Lee the gay activist discover how to navigate their relationship.

Isolation Play – The continuing story of Dev and Lee, as they contend with family and friends in their search for acceptance.

Divisions – As Dev's team fights to make the playoffs, Lee fights to keep his sense of self.

Uncovered – The playoffs are here, and Dev needs his focus more than ever. So when Lee becomes too distracting, something has to give.

Over Time – Dev and Lee try to plan their future while dealing with crises all around them.

Dangerous Spirits
Green Fairy – A gay high school senior struggling through his final year finds a strange old book that changes his dreams and his life.

Red Devil – A gay fox who fled his abusive family in Siberia seeks help from a ghost who demands he give up his gay lifestyle.

Black Angel – A young otter struggles to understand her sexu-ality as her friends prepare for post-high school life and dreams of women in other times plague her.

Argaea

Volle – The story of how Volle came to Tephos, a spy masquerading as a noble, and the first adventure he had there.

The Prisoner's Release and Other Stories – The story of how Volle escaped from prison, and the story of what happened after, plus two other stories following characters from "Volle."

Pendant of Fortune – Volle returns to Tephos to defend his honor, but soon finds himself fighting for much more.

Shadow of the Father – Volle's son, Yilon, must travel to the far-off land he is meant to rule, but he will have to fight treachery to take the lordship.

Weasel Presents – Five short stories from the land of Argaea, including "Helfer's Busy Day" and "Yilon's Journal."

Forester Universe

Waterways – The full story of Kory's journey to understand himself and what it means to be gay.

Bridges – Hayward seems content to set up pairs of his friends. But what does he really need for himself?

Science Friction – Vaxy never took sex seriously, until he found out the professor he was sleeping with was married…

Winter Games – Sierra Snowpaw was an unsure high school student when someone he thought was a friend changed his life. Now he's fifteen years older and still looking for answers.

The Mysterious Affair of Giles – A servant in a British manor house tries to solve a murder.

Dude, Where's My Fox? – Lonnie chases down a fox he hooked up with at a party as a way to get over his breakup.

Losing My Religion – On tour with his R.E.M. cover band, Jackson mentors the new guy in the band as his own life falls apart.

Other Books

The Silver Circle – Valerie thought the old hunter was crazy when he warned her about werewolves—until she met one.

In the Doghouse of Justice – Seven stories of superheroes and their not-so-super relationships.